BY THE SAME AUTHOR:

Fiction
The Kicking Tree

Non-fiction
*WYSIWYG Christianity: Young People and
Faith in the Twenty-First Century*

ULTIMATE JUSTICE

JUSTICE

TREVOR STUBBS

Matador
9 Priory Business Park
Kibworth Beauchamp
Leicestershire LE8 0RX, UK
Tel: (+44) 116 279 2299
Fax: (+44) 116 279 2277
Email: books@troubador.co.uk
Web: www.troubador.co.uk/matador

ISBN 978 1784622 121

British Library Cataloguing in Publication Data.
A catalogue record for this book is available from the British Library.

Printed and bound by CPI Group (UK) Ltd, Croydon, CR0 4YY
Typeset in Aldine by Troubador Publishing Ltd

Matador is an imprint of Troubador Publishing Ltd

This book is dedicated to those for whom there is no justice: those who are trampled on, exploited, abused, deprived of freedom and opportunity, never consulted, or simply ignored…

"When a country decides to invest in arms, rather than in education, housing, the environment, and health services for its people, it is depriving a whole generation of its right to prosperity and happiness. We have produced one firearm for every ten inhabitants of this planet, and yet we have not bothered to end hunger when such a feat is well within our reach. Our international regulations allow almost three-quarters of all global arms sales to pour into the developing world with no binding international guidelines whatsoever. Our regulations do not hold countries accountable for what is done with the weapons they sell, even when the probable use of such weapons is obvious."

Oscar Arias Sanchez,
Former President of Costa Rica

1

"Sis! What're you looking at?"

Kakko Smith was standing perfectly still, her feet firmly planted on the hard sand, hands on hips, her hair blowing gently in the warm sea breeze. She appeared to be staring intently at something so far away that the slightest movement might make it vanish from her sight. Her brother Shaun, two years her junior, followed her gaze but could see nothing. When she did not reply he shouted louder so that even his parents, Jalli and Jack, and his grandmother, Matilda, sitting in the shade of the palms further up the beach, could hear him.

"Kakko are you playing?"

Still she did not move. Her mind was closed to all but what she was studying. Shaun gave up and continued to juggle his football by himself. He had been selected to play in the local reserve team the following week. He was happy but wanted some practice. Kakko was a natural footballer. Their mother and grandmother watched them.

"Kakko needs an adventure," said Jalli. "Look at her."

"What's she staring at?" asked Matilda.

"The horizon, she's longing to look beyond it."

Jack couldn't see his daughter (he had never seen her because he had been blind since before she was born) but knew that his wife was right. "I've felt it coming on for a month or two," he agreed.

"What do you mean?" asked Matilda, balancing her folding chair as it settled a little in the hot dry sand.

"The things she says, but especially the little noises she makes as she moves around. The way she sits down and stands up, and the slight change in her voice… "

"I know," said Jalli. "I've noticed that too. But what are we going to do with her?"

"Nothing," said Jack. "She is eighteen. It is right that she should seek to leave the nest and test her wings. If she stares at the horizon long enough, one day she's bound to set out for it."

"You're right, but…"

"*You* were only seventeen, Jalli, when you started your adventures," reminded Matilda.

"That was a kind of accident. I mean, intended by the Creator but not necessarily by me. The Creator wanted it that way, arranged it like that," said her daughter-in-law.

"And I whisked you off your feet before you knew what was happening!" added Jack.

"Quite so, before either of us knew it. And you were my 'kind sir' and I couldn't resist you!" Jalli jabbed Jack playfully in the side.

"Now how could I have helped being anything other than that? I was just so utterly perfect…! Or not," he added quickly as he heard Jalli prepare to cuff him.

Matilda was still thinking about Kakko. "What about her boyfriend? He seems very keen on her and she has been dating him for years."

"Tam? He's too safe," said Jalli.

"Safe!" exclaimed her mother-in-law. "He drags her up mountains and dangles her on the end of a rope!"

"No, not mountains," said Jack. "It's only a climbing wall in the gym, and she drags him there, and, sadly for him, it is she who is dangling him – on a metaphorical rope as well as an actual one. He follows her everywhere and will do anything to please her, but I doubt he can give her the adventures she craves. She's never been serious about him."

"But he's such a nice boy. Why can't she see how lucky she is and just settle down?"

"Like her parents?" smiled Jack. "We settled, but only after we had zoomed across the universe and back. She needs to fly, and I'm sure the Creator will give her the opportunity some day."

Kakko had ceased to stare out to sea and had begun playing football again with her brother. He might have been selected for the reserve team, but his sister was every bit his equal. She was as tall as him, sturdily built and strong for a young woman. She was quite unlike her mother who was a slight woman, slight enough for Jack to have "'swept her up'" when he was eighteen. But Kakko was going to have to find someone much bigger than her father if she was to be swept up in someone's arms. Yet that wasn't anything that appealed to her; she wasn't a romantic at heart. She was as agile as a monkey and would climb up the outside of the house to her bedroom instead of using the front door (the windowsills and lintels made excellent holds). When she wasn't climbing or playing football she was driving tractors and harvesters, and anything she could get her hands on. As a child she had delighted in the farm machinery that operated in the fields beside their house and was now training as an agricultural engineer at the agricultural college; yet her heart was set for adventure and she was just beginning to realise it.

Kakko was physically strong, but she was also attractive. She didn't lack confidence – at least outwardly – and that had made her popular among both sexes. The problem was that the Smith family lived on Planet Joh with its beauty and order and with none of the hardships that both Jack and Jalli had had to contend with in the years before they met as teenagers. The people of Planet Joh would have to leave their home for dramatic adventures, and unless they were part of a crew on an interplanetary spaceship (which was not so much of an adventure as an endurance) it depended on whether they were privileged to be called through the very occasional portals that the Creator provided. Planet Joh was light years away (literally) from any other civilization.

Jalli and Jack, together with Matilda and Jalli's grandmother, Momori, had been led to Joh through a white gate, a portal from their own worlds. Jack and Matilda were from Britain on Earth One, while Jalli and Momori were natives of Wanulka, a country on Planet Raika in the Elbib galaxy (or Andromeda to give it its Earth One name). All three planets (Joh, Earth One and Raika) were different from each other, but bore many similarities. They were all populated by human beings with a common DNA and were within comparable cultural development periods. Some of the other inhabitants of Joh had found their way through a similar system of portals. Both Jack and Jalli hoped and prayed that this was the way Kakko was going to travel one day too. They knew she would not be truly fulfilled unless she went beyond the horizon, beyond the limitations of a peaceful planet with a small, mostly rural, population. So far, though, nothing had occurred. Kakko was doing all she could to find adventure at home by learning to climb, swim and play football in the women's team where she was quite a star as a forward.

Shaun, at sixteen, might have been a footballer too, but was otherwise rather different from his sister. Unlike Kakko he was not so practical. He hoped to specialise in language and communication and was earnestly hoping to go to the university on Joh.

The youngest sibling, Bandi, aged fourteen, loved computing and reading. He was rather reserved and didn't care for a lot of fuss and wished his sister was a little less 'visible'. Even now, as he sat under a tree behind the beach with a book, he was conscious of the way Kakko was the centre of everyone's attention.

All three of Jack and Jalli's children, in their different ways, took life seriously. None of them were laid back. Their grandparents, Matilda and Momori, put it down to being born to naturally reflective parents – a trait which they traced back to their own, rather tough, childhoods.

Just then, Jack's phone rang in his pocket. In all the years since arriving on Joh he had changed his phone a number of times but never the ring tone, which was still the tune of *Be Not Afraid* that he had had soon after arriving. He pulled it out and put it to his ear.

"It's Grandma," he said, "she wants to know what time we think we'll be home so she can put some beans on to cook."

Jalli took the phone. "Don't worry Grandma, you don't have to go to the trouble of doing any cooking." Momori had not come with them because she hadn't felt well. "Oh, all right then," continued Jalli, "but don't do more than you feel like… yes, put the dried ones on now, they'll take a couple of hours."

"I'm worried about her," said Jalli after she had hung up. "She isn't well. She's not herself. Let's not be too late back."

"Agreed," said Jack.

Matilda echoed Jalli's concern. "I think there's something she's not telling us. Something's wrong."

"We can give them another half hour and then we must be off," said Jack. Their home, White Gates Cottage, was in Woodglade, a tiny group of houses in the countryside several kilometres out of Joh City, the primary centre of population on the planet. There was a bus every hour which would take them the whole way.

Bandi was trying to ignore his siblings who kept 'accidentally' kicking the ball in his direction. He was determined not to join in and pretended to read his book, but it had become rather impossible. When finally the ball landed fairly and squarely in his lap scattering book, glasses and his dignity, he kicked the ball back so hard that it flew over his sister's head where it landed in the surf. In an instant, she had plunged in after it, clothes and all, to rescue it before the current took it. If it had been Shaun, Jalli would have been worried that he might have been taken by the current too, but Kakko was fast and seemingly unimpeded by her shorts and T-shirt. The ball was rescued and Kakko shouted a rather unsavoury remark in the direction of her little brother. "Kakko!" exclaimed Jalli, who had walked down the beach to the water's edge. "That'll do!" While this girl remained at home, Jalli resolved, she was going to have to curb her exuberance.

★★★

When they got home, Kakko was in her swim-suit covered in a towel because her clothes were still wet. Jack would not hear of staying until they dried out because they had been anxious about Momori. However, they were relieved to find her much better than when they had left that morning.

2

Momori's beans were a treat. It was a Wanulkan recipe that she had perfected over the years. No-one could make a bean dish like Grandma. That night they all slept well and the following day was a public holiday so they woke late.

The morning had begun with a thick mist but, by the time Jalli drew back the curtains of their cottage bedroom, the fog was clearing a little. Through the gentle whiteness her attention was drawn to a glow low down behind the tree in the middle of the front garden. She dismissed it with a shrug and turned away and headed for the little upstairs bathroom. As she washed her hands she pondered what she had seen and began to wonder. At first she had assumed that it was just a trick of sunlight on the fog, but hadn't it had a familiar feel? *Of course*, how could she have missed it? It was a white gate, *a white gate* of the sort that had brought them to Joh more than twenty years before – a portal between planets, galaxies and perhaps universes. She had given up all thought of seeing one again!

Jalli dried her face and quickly returned to the bedroom window. The mist was now lifting properly and the sun was breaking through. There it was, clear as any special white gate had ever been, in a part of the hedge that had not ever had a gate in it! Jalli roused Jack who was still enjoying not having to get up at the crack of dawn.

"Jack. Jack! I think I can… I *know* I can see a *white gate*… in the hedge behind the tree."

"A… what?" exclaimed Jack, pulling himself up.

"You heard – *a white gate*."

"A white gate? You're kidding."

"Do I sound like I am kidding you?"

"No. Where?"

"Behind the tree."

"We've never had a gate there – of any sort."

"Precisely. It is completely new."

"Take me to it," ordered Jack.

"The grass is damp. Get your shoes on." Jalli found her dressing-gown and her own shoes and they descended the stairs. Jalli led her husband across the lawn and around the tree. The gate was new, clean and bright. Jalli touched it and the feel of its shiny surface sent a powerful sense of nostalgia through her brain. Memories of the time before the children were born swept though her – the joys *and* the pain.

Jack stood waiting. He could neither see nor sense anything but the crisp scent of the hedge in front of him. Jalli took his hand and placed it on the top of the gate, but just like the last time when he was not called, his hand passed straight through it. All he felt was hedge.

"Are you sure you can see it?" he asked meekly.

"Sharp and solid, with a two-metre-long pathway that leads into some kind of building."

"Any shed or clothes and things?" In the past there had often been 'supplies' for the adventure – clothes, equipment, even bank notes laid out for them.

"There's a box here. Let me see… two pairs of blue overalls and caps to match."

"Is that it?"

"Yes."

Jalli held up the overalls. The larger of the two, however, was never going to fit Jack.

"This is definitely not for you!"

Jack held out his hand to feel the overalls.

"Then who?"

"That we are going to have to find out. But first let us get dressed and get some breakfast. I am not going anywhere without my Jack unless I have had at least a cup of hot, sweet tea."

"I will put the kettle on and call the others."

"When they have all eaten, we'll bring everyone out here and see who can see the gate. If we tell them what I can see before breakfast they'll never eat."

"Especially Kakko. She has reactions faster than lightning."

"I wish she would stop and think sometimes."

"She will… one day."

"When she is seventy-five – if she's lucky!"

There was a lot of grumbling when Jack and Jalli called everyone to the kitchen. Wasn't this supposed to be a holiday? But Jack told them that they had a surprise for them after they had finished their breakfast.

"What surprise?" said Kakko languidly.

"Just wait and see," said her mother.

"Wait! Wait! It's always wait. 'Kakko wait.' 'Kakko take it slowly.' 'Steady down Kakko!'"

"Well, if it's *always* 'wait' then it might be that I have a point."

"But everyone's just so slow," she grumbled.

"Who's slow?" asked Shaun. "I'm not. Dad said the surprise comes after breakfast and who's eating his breakfast instead of complaining?"

As usual, Bandi said nothing.

"Does this include us?" asked Matilda putting her head round the door. "Momori is not feeling so good."

"I think you do need to come," said Jalli.

"Right you are. Tell us when you are ready."

Kakko slurped the last of her cereal and declared, "Finished!"

"Wait until your brothers have finished theirs," said her mother. "Go and call Nan and Grandma."

"Wait. Wwaa-ii-tt! It's always 'wait'… Oh, come on you two." She went and called her grandparents who followed her back into the dining room.

Bandi sat up ready. Shaun took up his glass of juice very deliberately and slowly to annoy his sister. But Jalli ignored this and began.

"OK. This morning I have noticed a new white gate in the garden."

"So …?" began Kakko. And then the penny dropped. "A *white gate*! Like the ones you had when you were having your adventures?"

"Precisely."

"Cool. Will we all be able to see it?"

"That is the thing," replied Jack. "There are only clothes for two. We were always given the things we needed for our visits. It is therefore likely that only two are invited."

"So you're going on an adventure!" blurted Kakko.

"*I'm* not," stated Jack. "The gate is not there for me. For your mother, but not for me."

"So who is the other person?" quizzed Kakko.

"That is what we are now going to find out," said Jalli. "Follow me."

Kakko didn't wait to follow but rushed out of the front door and headed for the main gate. Jalli took no notice of her and led the others behind the tree.

"Where?" asked Matilda.

Jalli stepped forward towards the gate and turned round. There was a look of puzzlement on the faces of everyone. Kakko had, by this time, realised she had headed in the wrong direction and came bounding over and, sure enough, there it was, the white gate. A new, shiny white gate was in a part of the hedge that had never had a gate. Beyond the hedge was an open field which sometimes had animals in it but now the hedge seemed much thicker and there was no sign of the field beyond it. The odd thing was that the world seemed to kind of fold in on itself above the gate. It was so strange. Kakko stood stunned for several seconds.

One by one everyone turned to look at Kakko – her silence was so unusual that it drew attention to her. All she could say was, "Cool!"

"So it's you, Kakko," said her father. "It seems, then, that you are the one chosen to look after your mother."

"Wherever this leads," said Jalli, "it appears that the Creator has a job for Kakko."

The larger set of overalls fitted Kakko perfectly. They put them on, together with the tight fitting caps. They looked so out of place that even Bandi couldn't stop giggling. Jalli took hold of the gate to unlatch it, but it refused to move.

"It's stuck," announced Jalli.

"Let me, Mum!" said Kakko exasperated, pushing her mother roughly to one side.

"Kakko!" hissed Jalli. Jalli was becoming alarmed at taking this headstrong girl with her into what was going to be a strange and different world. "When you go between planets you need to do it sensitively. Think about the people on the other side!"

But she need not have worried just then. The gate remained tightly shut. Jack was listening carefully, analysing the situation.

"You have a white gate and you have the appropriate clothes. Have you put them all on? Have you missed anything?" he asked.

"There are only two items each," said Jalli as she checked the grass for anything smaller they'd missed. "I can't see anything else."

"Overalls and caps. Could be a factory. Let me feel them." Jack ran his hands over Jalli. "Ah. I think I know. This cap is meant to contain all your hair. There could be machinery or something."

"Of course," said Kakko. "I should have thought of that. We do that in the college workshop."

"Right," said Jalli. "Kakko, if you know about these things, stop and think please."

"OK. OK," Kakko sighed.

They took off the caps and Momori and Matilda helped them gather their hair and enclose it inside them.

"Now you look the part!" declared Matilda.

Jalli tried the gate. The latch was free and the gate opened. She turned and reached for Jack.

"I'll miss you."

"You'll be too busy to worry about me. Now you had better go. Kakko come here!"

Jack gathered Kakko in his arms and cuddled her to him. "You look after your mum. Look after her like I would!"

"Yeah, Dad. I'll try…"

They all gave the departing couple appropriate cuddles. Momori lingered over Jalli. She looked tired.

"I wish you weren't going," she said, and added, "but then I never did want you to go anywhere for myself, so don't mind an old fool like me. You have your adventure girl. Have fun!"

"Yay, *fun!*" laughed Kakko.

"Come on, let's go," breathed Jalli. "Before I change my mind."

Jalli and Kakko found themselves inside a large storeroom of some kind. It had a high corrugated iron roof with a skylight. It was piled up with wooden crates on pallets. There was a forklift truck parked in one corner. It looked like a loading bay because all down one side were roller shutters right to the ground and, on the other, some large, plastic swing doors. Inside the room it was quiet but there was a steady hum from another area somewhere beyond, and the sound of traffic outside. There was not, however, any sign of people.

Kakko examined the crates. She tried to lift one of them but, although it measured no more than sixty centimetres in width and length, and thirty centimetres deep, it was far too heavy for her. Jalli studied the crates which bore what looked like a danger symbol and a picture of the contents. She had seen something similar before. Where? Then it flooded back to her. She recalled Mr. Somaf showing her a land mine in Tolfanland. That one had been disarmed but he had shown her it to warn her what lay all around his house. It had been one such devise that had killed four soldiers while she and Jack had been there. (Although she had not seen the dead bodies herself, Jack had given her a graphic description.) Whatever you thought of the necessity of war, these weapons were unethical, Jalli had declared. But Jalli had long since concluded that war did not solve anything in the long term anyway, there were far more effective ways of tackling arguments and misunderstandings. The histories of both her planet and that of Earth One were testimony to that.

"Be careful," said Jalli in horror. "I know what these are. They are land mines. This room is full of high explosive weapons, enough to blow up a small town I should guess."

"What are we supposed to do?" asked Kakko.

"Proceed with caution. Let's go through those doors. It'll become clear what our task is when we find someone."

The two women pushed carefully though the plastic doors. Immediately outside was a little glass cubicle with a man in blue overalls, like theirs, seated on a swivel chair, reading a newspaper.

"What? Have you just come through from the loading bay?"

"Er... yes," croaked Jalli.

"How did you get in there?"

"Er... it's our first day in this department. We were looking for the er... ladies."

"The toilets? In there?"

"Yes – but it's the wrong door."

"You don't say! Can't you read? It says quite clearly, 'No unauthorised entry'. Are you authorised?"

"No."

"No, you're not. How you got by me, I don't know. The toilets, ladies, are over the far side… by the canteen."

"Thanks," muttered Jalli.

"Sorry," said Kakko. She was used to saying sorry.

The man shrugged and they walked across a large workshop with benches upon benches with men and women (mostly women) assembling what looked like bombs and armoured shells.

"A munitions factory for sure," observed Jalli.

They made their way towards a sign which said, 'Canteen' in case the man was watching them, but he had long since reverted to his newspaper. A woman in front them pushed a door into the ladies' toilets. Jalli looked at Kakko and followed her. "Listen," whispered Jalli, "and learn." They each took a cubicle and listened to the conversation between the women at the wash basins.

"That sod of a section boss has got really stroppy since last week. He's really down on anyone who supported the union."

"I didn't go along with anything. Not any of the protests myself, but he's just so cocky now. Reckons he's a special friend of Big Plo."

"All we asked for was proper safety procedures."

"Yeah, but that evacuation drill occupied most of the morning. It's rumoured that Big Plo has ordered that we all work an extra shift to make up for lost production."

"And whatever he says, goes. The company has us all trapped. Me and my hubby, we tried to find somewhere of our own but with what they pay us we will have to live in a company flat for ever… Going to eat?" she asked as they stood at the drier.

"Yes. Company food. Can't afford anything else."

"Modern day slavery, that's what I call it!"

"It *is*, Yknan, they *own* us!"

Kakko and Jalli washed their own hands and decided to follow the women into the canteen.

They stepped inside the door and Kakko saw them making their way to the hot foods section.

"They are the women we've just overheard," said Kakko.

"How can you be sure? You didn't see them; you were inside a cubicle."

"Oh. I did see them. I popped my head over the top."

"Kakko!"

"Oh. It's safe. People don't look up. Anyway, they had their backs to the cubicles."

"Looking into the mirrors! And how ever did you manage to see over the door?"

"I stood with my feet on the edge of the pan."

"You should be careful you don't fall in!"

"Never have – I'm safe."

"*Never* have! How often do you stand on the rim of a toilet pan to look over the door?"

"We used to do that all the time at school. You stand on the pan and drop bits of wet loo paper on the heads of the people in the next one. That was always good for a laugh."

Her mother just stood and gaped. "You didn't learn that from me!"

"Oh, Mum. Don't be so stuffy!"

They caught up with the women at the hot food counter. Jalli had no idea what the convention was here but she guessed she did not need to pay for this. She copied what the women did and she and Kakko both took a tray. When it was their turn to order, Jalli simply said, "Same please."

"And me," said Kakko, "and can I have some of that too?"

The woman behind the counter just tipped a reddish looking splodge beside the yellow one she already had.

"I hope you're going to eat all that," said her mother.

"Mum!"

"Oh. OK. I'll stop nagging."

"Promise…"

"That depends… oh, alright but just behave yourself."

They traced their way across the canteen. The women in front of them had chosen a free table at the far end beside a large window. Jalli followed.

"Excuse me," she said, "do you mind if we join you? This is our first day here and we're a bit lost."

"Sure. Sit down," said a buxom woman with a toothy smile. "Your first day. Where have you been?"

"Er… we don't live close. I… we… this is my daughter, Kakko…"

"Pleased to meet ya… Estap. Name's Estap. And this here is my friend Yknan."

Jalli held out her hand. To her surprise Estap took it with her left, and so did Yknan. Kakko extended a left hand. *Good,* thought her mother, *she's watching.*

3

Estap and Yknan led Kakko and Jalli to a large bench in the centre of the workshop. In the centre of the bench was a wide gap along which ran large, upturned, round-ended buckets. Several women were loading them with various components.

"You begin with your shell-casing," explained Estap, showing them a low trolley stacked with the round-bottomed bucket things. It takes two of you to lift it on the rails… watch." She and Yknan stood either side of a shell-casing and lifted it up so the top slid into two parallel rails that ran along the inside edges of the gap in the bench. Then she dragged it to the first station ready for the first operation.

"Again this takes two," said Estap. They lifted a sealed box shaped to fit into the bottom of the shell-casing by two ribbons attached to it and dropped it carefully into the rounded end of the shell.

"This is the nose section. You have to be real careful of course because all the components are delicate – they contain explosives. They should be safe, but you don't want to go dropping them!

"The most dangerous thing is Charlie over there. (Him with the supercilious grin.) He's the section supervisor," Yknan nodded slightly towards a man standing upright with his arms crossed, surveying the scene. "He's a tyrant for sure. If you step out of line, he'll have you for breakfast…"

19

"OK. When your nose assembly is in place, you take a plate and clip it in like this… then you begin with the MEMs – Medium Effect Munitions. Those are the ones that go off within ten metres from the site impact. You put in twenty of these… no, not that one. *These* little bomblet things with the red tip. Then pour in ball bearings from this pipe until you've covered all the MEMs." They slid the shell further along the rails opposite another group of boxes containing small balls with wings. "Next you put in forty of these real small bomblets. They're called 'squids'. They get blown over five hundred metres and go off over several hours depending on their timing. They have four colours… you put in ten of each."

"What are they for?" asked Jalli, horrified at what she was hearing.

"The squids? The idea is that they stop anyone getting near the target afterwards because you never know when they are going to go off. Last thing: fill it up with more bearings… pack it all tight with this foam… clip on this plate making sure there is no space underneath, and then it goes on to the next machine that seals it all up. But we don't handle that. We say good-bye to it at this point."

"How many of these have you assembled since you started?" asked Jalli.

"Me? Oh hundreds and hundreds. I've been at this bench for over a year."

"Do you ever think what happens to them when they've left the factory?" asked Kakko.

"No idea. But Big Plo has a good sale for them. We can

never make enough of them. His design team are coming up with even more clever things all the time."

"Do you ever think of the people that they're dropped on?" persisted Kakko.

Estap stopped and looked her in the eye. "Do you and your mum want to live? Do you want to have food in your belly and a roof over your heads? If you had little kids you wouldn't think like that. You can't afford to."

"Now your turn," said Yknan. "Grab hold of a shell-casing… that's right. Slide it on the rails. Now begin with the nose assembly."

"I'm not doing this!" hissed Kakko.

"Kakko. Just wait. Let's go with the flow for a bit and see what the Creator wants of us."

"No! No way! I am NOT going to make a bomb with bits that kill loads of people for hours. I'm going home!" and she strode towards the plastic doors of the loading bay.

"Kakko!" called Jalli and she rushed after her, catching up with her just after she had passed the man with the newspaper. Kakko ignored his shouts and pushed open the plastic doors. Jalli followed.

Kakko looked to where the white gate had been but it was now behind a huge tower of crates.

"Damn!" she swore.

The man rushed in behind them. "What the hell do you think–" he began as he looked in the same direction as the women. "What in hell's name has been going on in here? Who's been moving this stuff around?"

Then Jalli noticed the wires. There were two red wires and two black ones emanating from underneath the pallet and leading towards the wall in which the white gate had stood.

"What are they?" demanded Jalli.

The man lay down on his stomach and looked under the pallet. "Bloody hell! They're wired to a detonator. Get the hell out of here! I've got to sound the alarm!"

They all three rushed back onto the shop floor. The man picked up a small phone-like contraption and yelled, "Sound the alarm. Get everyone out of here. There's a bloody bomb... I *know the place is full of bombs* – but not wired up to ruddy detonators! There's a detonator in Loading Bay One... How do I know? I've seen it! Just sound the bloody alarm! Let's get out of here!" he shouted to Jalli and Kakko who ran behind him to the exit he was clearly headed for. As they went they all screamed, "Get out! Get out! Now!"

"This is for real!" he yelled as he made for the door, but people were reluctant to move. They had been so intimidated after the last drill. Kakko turned and ran back to the women on the PSW bench. "This is NOT a drill. There's a detonator wired up in there," she said pointing to the loading bay.

"Come on, Yknan," shouted Estap, "let's go!" They dropped the bomblets they were counting out back in the box and ran. Then people began to react.

"Follow the drill!" yelled a man who turned out to be a union steward. "Follow the drill! You know what to do! Do NOT panic!" It worked. People began exiting the building through the allocated doors and channels.

Bang! A door burst open behind Jalli. It was Big Plo and the senior management come down from the offices above.

"A detonator," shouted Jalli, "in Loading Bay Number One."

"Rubbish," replied Big Plo. "Get back to work."

"I strongly suggest," said Jalli, "that you follow the evacuation procedures. This is NOT a drill."

"Who the hell do you think you are?"

"The question is, 'Who do you think *you* are, being so stupid?' Now get out!" barked Jalli. "Now!"

Kakko turned to see Big Plo doing as he was told. He had not come across such a confident order from a diminutive woman before – certainly not on his own factory floor.

Ten minutes later everyone was outside the building in their muster stations and the allocated people were checking off their names.

"OK. Now you've had your fun!" said Big Plo, seeing Jalli with Yknan and Estap. "I want to know who you are and what you think you are playing at." He called to one of his henchmen. "See that this woman doesn't go anywhere but my office… now how about everyone getting…" but Plokr Spraken III never got to finish his sentence.

Suddenly there was a huge explosion at the back of the building as Loading Bay One went up. Bits of shrapnel, building materials, dust and crate shot into the air amid the painful flash that transfixed the retinas of those who were unfortunate enough to be looking in that direction. Clouds of black and white smoke and a wide variety of debris billowed high above them and then began to fall on the rest of the building, the car park and the people. A piece of roofing smacked into the branches of a tree behind Kakko and Jalli.

"Open the gates!" shouted the union steward. The guards on the gates activated the electric pulley and the gates slid back. Everyone moved to push through. Jalli deliberately held onto her daughter, who, for some uncanny reason waited and didn't join the crush. Kakko was quick to move but she was also quick to sense danger. The fence around the gate and gatehouse began to bulge and then gave way. People left by whatever passage opened up and Jalli and Kakko were then borne up on a tide of people and deposited across the road outside the plant. They made for an area of wasteland with everyone else, just as another huge explosion ripped through the building – only this was five times the size of the first.

★★★

Back on Planet Joh, Matilda and Momori were helping each other hang out the washing. They had decided that now was a good time to muck out Kakko's room and had all her bedding washed. Matilda found it easier to lift the sheets with Momori's help. The day was beautiful, the soft breeze blew the sound of the birdsong from the woodland out the back of their cottage onto the peaceful garden. The men were all out about their business and Jalli and Kakko on another planet somewhere.

"I wonder what they are up to?" wondered Momori.

"Women's work for sure. No need for the men it seems." Then Matilda stood still. "Momori. I… I can see a white gate!" she said with some alarm.

"Where?"

"In the same place where Jalli and Kakko left. Can *you* see it?"

"I can't say I can. Are you sure you're not imagining it?"

Matilda strode across the lawn, touched the gate and called. "There is no doubt about it."

Momori joined her. "Not for me," she stated.

"Do you think they need rescuing?"

"No point speculating. You'd better go."

Matilda stepped through the gate just as the second explosion ripped through the factory. She was at least a kilometre away from it but she felt the blast hit her with a wall of air. People were running towards her. Matilda gasped and held on to her gate. People were rushing by her now. They were clearly anxious to get away. They suspected, rightly, that more explosions were on their way.

Then Matilda spotted Jalli and Kakko running hand-in-hand together over to her right.

"Jalli!" she called. Then, summoning up all her strength, surprised herself at the volume she managed, "Kaa-kkoo!"

Kakko thought she heard her name and looked across the waste-ground to her left. She saw the gate first and then her nan.

"Nan!" she yelled, pulling her mum round.

"Brilliant!" exclaimed Jalli and they both made a bee-line for Matilda and the gate. Jalli reached her mother-in-law. "I've never been so pleased to see you!"

"Come on! Get through!" But just as she said it, a third huge blast rocked the ground. They were out of reach of anything but hot air now though. The people around them continued to rush past. Kakko saw Yknan with Estap wobbling along behind her.

Jalli turned. "Yknan, Estap. Are you alright?"

"Never been better," breathed Estap heavily. "We're safe here."

"You've worked there years. What are you going to do?" asked Jalli.

"Now? Don't know. But we're free! I don't care what bloody Big Plo thinks. He don't own us no more. Something will turn up."

"We should stop calling him Big Plo," put in Yknan. "He's not big any more!"

They laughed like children. "What a smashing great, big bang!"

Then Estap stopped, "But we have to thank YOU! If you hadn't have come and got us to leave we'd have still been in there. You saved the whole ruddy lot of us."

"How did you know it was going to blow? You're activists I bet!"

"No. Not us," said Kakko. "We might have *wanted* to blow it all up but not with anyone in it! I just ran into the store room and… we saw the wires."

"You were definitely in the right place at the right time. If you had waited another five minutes it would have been too late," said Estap.

"Say that again!" said Kakko. "If I had *waited*…"

"…it would have been too late," concluded Estap.

"Thanks," said Kakko. "You mean we've saved hundreds of people!"

"Thousands!" exclaimed Yknan.

"Thank you," said Jalli quickly. "Thank you for making us so welcome. We do pray that you will soon find something else to do though, some alternative employment."

"I've already decided," said Estap. "Me and my husband, we'll go down south. After this there'll be nothing here."

"What about *you* and your blind husband?" asked Yknan.

"Oh, we'll manage back home. This is my mother-in-law who has come over to fetch us. She's got something lined up for us."

"Great! Better be off. I want to get to a phone to call my family before they worry."

"Good idea. Good luck! Bye."

"Bye! And thanks again!" They walked on together through the drifting smoke.

"Let's get home!" said Jalli.

"And put the kettle on!" laughed Kakko.

★★★

Kakko was insufferable for a week. Apparently her impetuous defiance had saved millions (the number grew day by day). Jalli had to acknowledge that had she been more patient and heeded her mother they, and many others, would probably have died. But Momori quietly pointed out that if it had been Kakko's brusqueness that had saved the day, it had been Creator who had called her to be there. Without the white gate nothing would have happened to mitigate the situation. Credit should be given where credit was due. Kakko would have more friends if she had just a little humility. Bandi just listened to all this, and quietly learnt.

In the privacy of their own room Jack said they should be proud of their daughter. She might not be perfect but her heart was definitely in the right place. You had to admire her for taking a stand and not going along with something she didn't hold with. That takes a lot of guts. She put her

principles before her personal safety and not many people would do that. And she was no fool either. The rest would follow, he felt, with a bit of maturity; she'd get over the inflated sense of herself. That might, he suggested, come from a degree of teenage insecurity. When she grew in confidence, her apparent lack of humility would decline.

"You mean the outward arrogance is a sign of self-doubt?" echoed Jalli.

"Yes. What she did got you into the right place at the right time, but which one of you noticed the detonator?"

"I did. I saw the wires."

"Who took charge of the situation then – you or Kakko?"

"Me," said Jalli. "After I saw the wires she just did as she was told."

"One day," said Jack, "she'll acknowledge that."

"But not yet?"

"Not yet. But one day. At the moment she may be doubting herself too much… now, though, I am very, very proud of *you*. You haven't lost your ability to act in an adventure one little bit! And I could never see my wonderful Jalli getting the slightest bit of a big head!"

"Not, even the teeny-weeniest bit?"

"Well, perhaps a teeny-weeny bit. Just enough to give her confidence to stand up to her headstrong daughter!"

★★★

Some days later, Kakko and Bandi were in the garden having a go at trimming the hedge.

"It's really not on that someone should be allowed to make

guns and bombs to sell to others so they can blow each other up!" said Kakko. "I mean, that Big Plo was making money hand over fist. I would say that makes him as bad as the people who use his weapons. Only it's worse because he doesn't even have a cause that he's fighting for. All he cares is that he makes a profit and is a big man in his town. He should be charged as a murderer."

"No. It isn't right," agreed Bandi. "There is something evil about that. I can't say, though, that I am against making weapons to defend yourself with. I mean if someone wanted to invade us."

"I'm not sure that is right either. If you have weapons then people are far more likely to use theirs on you. I mean, could we really defend ourselves against an invasion here on Joh without it resulting in the complete destruction of all of us? Actually, I think I would rather be killed than kill someone – even if they were evil."

"But what if they were going to kill someone else, someone you love?"

"Oh. Bandi, you make things so complicated!"

"Sorry. But the thing is, that the more you think about things the less black and white they become. But I do agree with you about your Big – what's his name – Plo and his factory. I expect you're glad it is all blown up."

"Yeah. But I keep wondering who it was that did it. It wasn't someone who was against killing people – they would have killed thousands."

"You mean millions!"

"Well, perhaps that's exaggerating it a bit… Bandi, are you laughing at me?"

"Who, me?"

"Stop teasing me! This is serious."

"Agreed. They have an enemy that doesn't mind using their own weapons against them… you know you mustn't ever go back there. You and Mum will be prime suspects, you know."

"Yeah, I've thought about that. I doubt we'll have a gate there again. But if we do, we'll have a reason for going. And you can count on me being very careful to watch my back."

"Good," said Bandi.

4

Things were just settling back into some kind of routine when one day, as Jack got up to make his wife a drink, he became aware of something unusual through the kitchen window. His brain was registering a sensation in the visual cortex. It was rather frightening after so long as his brain had got used to not receiving signals from his damaged eyes. It appeared to be something beyond the kitchen window and he thought he knew what it was – another white gate. It was many years since he himself had last experienced one. Yet for Jack, blind though he had become, the 'sight' of a white gate could still be made out even though he couldn't see anything else.

Jack was not given to panic and he had become even more stoic as he had matured, so he made the tea and took it up to Jalli. She sat up to take the mug from him and saw concern on his face.

"What is it?" she asked.

"Jalli, I am aware of something outside. It feels peculiar inside my head. I... I think it is a white gate... Will you look out the window and check in the hedge?"

Jalli got out of bed, padded down the stairs into the kitchen and looked across the back lawn. Sure enough there was a special white gate and beside it a small wooden shed, the kind that was used to contain stuff for the world on the other side. Jalli quietly remounted the stairs.

"I do see it. There *is* a white gate… with a shed too… Jack you realise what this means! We've *both* been invited to visit another world. Do we *have* to go?"

"It's been more than twenty years for me!" sighed Jack. "And it was a bit of a shock 'seeing' something again after all that time. It feels quite… well, quite peculiar. Rather disorientating. But I knew what it was."

"You know what we say. If we see a white gate, then we are meant to go through it. We have a job to do."

"Yes, I know. When should we…"

Jack never managed to finish his question because there was a sudden burst of excitement from Kakko's room. Bandi had seen a white gate that had matched his parents' description in all their adventure stories. He had been gazing absent-mindedly out of the downstairs bathroom window as he washed his face at the basin. He had looked up and seen a white gate in the hedge. He had wiped his eyes and looked again. There was definitely a new gate! Ignoring her indignant protests regarding her privacy, Bandi stole into his sister's bedroom which looked out in the same direction.

"Look sis, outside," he said. "Can you see a white gate?"

"Sure. There's a white gate. That's why this cottage is called 'White Gates Cottage' wouldn't you believe?" she said in mocking tone.

"No. I mean… there is *another* white gate."

"What's all the fuss about?" called Shaun, thumping down the stairs and staggering barefoot through the open door to his sister's room. He was still dressed in the T-shirt and shorts he wore to sleep in.

"A white gate, an extra white gate," declared his brother.

Kakko pushed her way to her window which overlooked the back lawn and stared. Then she yelled, "I see it! I see it!"

"Let me look!" said Shaun. "Yeah, I see it too. What does it mean?"

"What does it mean? It means adventure!" yelled Kakko, bouncing up and shouldering Shaun under the chin who staggered backwards onto the floor at the feet of his parents who had just arrived at the doorway.

"A white gate," said Jalli calmly. "So I gather you can all see it?"

"Yes, I spotted it first," said Bandi.

"Actually," said his father, "*I* spotted it first." Jalli nodded her confirmation.

"How?"

"Magic," explained his father with a grin. "The whole business is, of course, magic."

"But real magic?" uttered Shaun, troubled. "I mean, it's not pretend magic, an illusion, with some logical explanation?"

"Well it does have a logical explanation…" began Jack.

"I mean, not a regular scientific explanation."

"There will have to be some science…"

Jalli took Jack's arm, "We know what you mean, Shaun. It's *not* an illusion, it's real. This time we've *all* been invited somewhere else in the universe for some purpose we won't know until we get there."

"I suppose 'magic' is probably not the best word. I take it back," considered Jack. "'Miraculous' would be a better word. It is given by the One who holds us all in 'being'."

"Yeah! We're going through the gate – *all* of us this time! Yippee!" yelled Kakko

"What on Planet Joh is going on here?" They all turned and saw Momori and Matilda standing outside the door.

"A white gate! Come in and see!" bubbled Kakko. (Kakko's room was now very crowded.)

"Well then," sighed Momori, "we had better be ready for another disturbance in our routine. If you can allow a couple of less active people to come and look too…" The three young people, Jack and Jalli moved away from the window and allowed the ladies passage.

"I can't see a new gate," stated Matilda.

"And I can't say I can see anything out of the ordinary either," agreed Momori.

"But it's definitely there!" exclaimed her great-granddaughter.

"I don't doubt it. But not, thank God, for me," breathed Momori with audible relief.

"Or me," said Matilda. "It looks as if we're going to have the house to ourselves for a bit… but what are you all going to do about your work, and school?"

"You can tell them all we're off on an unplanned holiday?" suggested Kakko.

"No, Kakko. That won't do," said her mother. "We shall all write and explain. Tell the truth."

"But… there isn't time!" said Kakko with impatience. "You remember last time. If I had waited…"

"There is always time to do what is right," said her nan.

"So, first things first," ordered Jalli. "Let's go and see what's in the little shed."

"Exciting or what!" said Kakko, leaping to her feet. The young people didn't need a second invitation. They charged out into the garden in their pyjamas.

In the shed they found two cases and five small piles of clothes. There was also a packet with money in it. Jalli picked it up and looked at the notes.

"I think I know these. I've seen some like this before. I recognise the sort of script. I think this is the place with the Fellowship Group. You know, with Tod and Kakko – the 'Kakko' you were named after, Kakko."

"Wow! You mean I'm going to see the person whose name I share?"

"Maybe. If she's still around… and this is the place I think it is."

"I bet it's by the sea!" exclaimed Shaun. "There's beach shorts here."

"And another pair," declared Bandi, "and a cool T-shirt."

"Very summery," said Jalli. "There are women's shorts too! And a gorgeous top. And this pile is… definitely for you, Kakko."

"Let me guess, Kakko, there are swimming things," said Jack.

"How'd you know, Dad?"

"The briefest thing you will ever have worn in public. Am I right? At least you don't have a massive bruise to show off."

"Dad?"

"It's alright Kakko. Dad's reminiscing. I had a bruise when we first went to this place (if it's where we think it is) and I wore my first bikini there."

"Oh, right…" said Kakko a bit confused.

"Well let's get on with changing then," said Jalli, "then we will all write letters to whoever is expecting us tomorrow to say we've been summoned unexpectedly to somewhere else through a portal and we don't know how long we'll be away. And we're very sorry to let people down. OK? Off you go!"

"Much more organised than we were when we found our first white gate," observed Jack quietly. "We had had our first adventure, and our first kiss before we told anybody else about the gates."

"Second," said Jalli. Jack looked bemused.

"Second kiss," explained Jalli. "We kissed twice in the garden before you saw me onto the bus in Wanulka. Do you remember?"

"Second kiss," smiled Jack. "You were counting? How many is it to date?"

"One more than it was a moment ago," said Jalli engaging him in lover's kiss.

"Oh, sor-ry!" exclaimed Kakko reappearing at the door, "…but if you do choose to snog in the garden."

"I don't care where," said her mother. "And, besides, it's not snogging!"

"Sure looked like it to me!"

"OK," laughed Jack. "We're off to get ready!"

"That girl!" sighed Jalli. "That girl is quite…"

Jack took hold of his wife and declared, "I can't concentrate. Come here." And he collected Jalli into his gentle arms and kissed her again. "God bless our venture," he murmured.

Twenty minutes later they were all dressed in their various clothes and were sitting at the table eating breakfast together. Matilda collected the various notes and surveyed the addresses. "OK, I'll take the bus and get these to all the right people before the morning is out."

"Let *me* go over to the college. I can manage that far," said Momori.

"Sure?" asked Matilda.

"Quite sure. I can take it very steady."

"Thanks Grandma," said Jalli, and she put her arms around her. "I'll miss you."

"How long are you going for?"

"There's no saying," said Jack, "but I hope it's not too long."

"Will we be walking into a war or anything?" asked Shaun.

"Hope not!" replied his mother.

"You never know, do you?" wondered Bandi.

As well as the day-time clothes and the stuff for the beach, the cases contained formal evening wear – not too dressed up but still enough to impress Kakko who discovered a fetching dress.

"It looks like we're going to a party rather than war," she said somewhat allayed.

Soon they were all ready and they took their leave of the two ladies who watched as one by one the family melted through the hedge and were gone. Suddenly it was very quiet.

"That was an exciting hour," said Matilda.

"Well, I don't know about you but I'm ready to sit down to a cup of tea! And then I'll wander off to the college. You know about fifty percent of the energy comes from Kakko. Bandi hardly says anything."

"That bikini quietened her down a bit," commented Matilda.

"For about twenty seconds. I've seen one like it before. Jalli brought one back with her from this place they're talking about – nothing she ever wanted to wear in Wanulka. That was their first adventure to somewhere other than this garden you know."

"You mean the place they decided they had better tell us what was going on."

"Exactly. I wonder what they have to do as a family this time?"

5

As soon as they emerged into the new world, Jalli knew where she was. "Jack it *is* the place we were thinking of."

"I know, it smells familiar."

"And we've come out by the toilets again."

"Yuk!" declared Kakko. "Wow, look at that ocean!"

"Glad we've got this stuff on," said Shaun, "or we'd stand out like anything."

"There, over there," indicated Jalli, "it's Pero's restaurant. Gosh it's changed. It's still called 'Pero's Family Restaurant' on the front, but beside it and above it is a massive hotel!"

In small letters at the top it bore a logo saying "Comfort Hotels" and underneath it, down the side of the twelve storey building large blue letters, designed to light up in the dark, spelled, "PERO'S FAMILY HOTEL".

"Jack," said Jalli, "Mr Pero must have turned his restaurant into a multi-storey hotel."

"Cool," said Bandi. "You know the owner of this hotel?"

"Yes, if he's still around," said his father.

"Can we go in?" asked Kakko. Jalli took Jack's arm and they led their family past some outside tables into the restaurant. They took one of the larger tables and put their cases against the wall. The young people started looking at the menu while Jack and Jalli took in the surroundings. Inside the restaurant, things seemed to have changed little – only now there was a large glass door on the right that led into the lobby of the hotel.

"Wow, look at what they have!" exclaimed Bandi.

"You have just finished breakfast," said his mother, "you can have a drink but leave the rest until lunchtime."

"How come I can read this?" asked Bandi. "Do they use the same language as we do?"

"There's some sort of translating going on," explained his mother. "What we see and hear is what it all means, we don't experience exactly what the locals see and hear."

"You mean, like animals see the same thing but perceive it differently."

"A bit like that, but not quite. These people are human. Like us they all owe their origins somewhere in the past to Earth One," explained Jack.

A couple in their early forties sitting opposite started to stare in their direction and Jalli lowered her eyes.

Then, "Jalli, Jack?" called the woman. "Is it Jalli?"

Jalli looked up. "Kakko!" she exclaimed, pushing her chair back as Kakko came across the room. "And Tod! Whoa. It's wonderful to see you."

"What brings you here?"

"Same as last time," said Jack reaching out and finding Tod's arm. "It just seems to happen that way."

"Have you come for Pero's retirement party tomorrow?" asked Kakko.

"I g… guess so," stammered Jack.

"What's happening tomorrow exactly?" asked Jalli.

"There's a reception in the hotel tomorrow afternoon, but Mr. Pero doesn't know about it. It's a surprise. He thinks the suite is booked for a wedding anniversary. So mum's the word..."

"Sure thing," said Jack, "shan't say a word," and, turning towards the young people, said meaningfully, "will we guys..."

Jack and Jalli introduced their children. Jalli's friend was really delighted to discover they had named their eldest child after her. "You named her after me! That's terrific. I'm so pleased to meet you, Kakko. Is she like me?" she asked Jalli.

"In some ways – " Jalli began.

"No. I expect not," broke in Kakko Smith. "I'm me. But I'm pleased to meet you." She held out her hand and Kakko took it. Shaun and Bandi got to their feet and took Kakko's and then Tod's hands.

"So what's with this?" Tod asked Jack. "This not being able to see. Is it temporary?"

"Oh. No," replied Jack. "I've been blind for... well since about six months after we were last here. More than half my life now."

"What happened? If you don't mind me asking. Sorry, I shouldn't pry..."

"No, no!" insisted Jack. "No. Just happened during one adventure. Bit of a shock at the time. It was a salutary reminder that I'm not indestructible. And anyway I am surrounded by a wonderful family so I don't need to see."

"He can read our thoughts," contributed the younger Kakko. "You only have to think of doing something you shouldn't – well, shouldn't according to Mum and Dad – and he knows. And he's got ears that can hear anything!"

"Yeah," agreed Shaun. "He can hear round corners!"

"And smell," sighed Kakko.

Jack laughed. "I don't know what they actually look like these wonderful children of mine but I know if they haven't washed! Anyway they're getting rather grown up now."

"They are about the age you were when you were last here."

"That is true, eighteen, sixteen and fourteen." Kakko screwed up her nose. What secrets would her parents reveal next? They all crowded around the large table and ordered coffee and croissants.

"OK, Kakko. I'm not going to say anything else. I'll leave all the rest of your exploits up to you to tell," said her father.

The older Kakko exclaimed, "You really do know what they're thinking! Impressive. I wish we had children," she sighed, "but it just didn't happen. Still I'm really happy for you guys."

"When did you marry?" asked Jalli.

"A couple of years after we met you. How about you?"

"About the same time. Jack and I were not actually together as boy and girl friend when we came here. We were just friends then. We had, kind of, just bumped into each other."

"But it was kind of obvious you were… an item," said the older Kakko.

"No. We weren't at the time. We hadn't known each other very long at all."

"You could have fooled us!" said Tod. "You were clearly in love. We always thought of you as more than friends."

"It was obvious," concurred Kakko. "You were clearly meant to be together."

"We hadn't even shared a kiss when we were last here," giggled Jalli.

"Your lips might not have, but your hearts had," said Kakko. "I bet you kissed for the first time very soon after you left here."

"Same day… er… twice, I'm told," grinned Jack.

"There you go," enthused Kakko, "and not long after that you were married…"

"Two years," said Jack. "It looks as if you can read hearts like I'm supposed to read minds."

"Well, I guess we could… in your case."

Just at that moment Mr Pero appeared. "Well if it isn't my friends Kakko and Tod," he said coming over to them.

"Hey, Papa, you remember our friends Jack and Jalli?"

"It was a long time ago," smiled Jalli, taking Mr Pero by the hand.

"Yes, I remember. You were here on the wonderful weekend. The weekend that started everything."

"We were here when the place got wrecked!"

"Yes. That wonderful weekend when I met so many wonderful people. I remember you both. You are very, very welcome."

The young people sat taking it all in; listening to what their parents had done twenty-plus years ago was both fascinating and amazing. They felt rather proud of their parents, something that doesn't always come naturally to teenagers.

The conversation went on over several cups of coffee – which Mr Pero refused to allow them to pay for. He explained how things had developed in the last quarter of a century. At first his restaurant had grown so much in popularity that people were booking even midday meals up to a month in advance. When the shop next door became vacant, he had been tempted to expand but felt that that would alter the atmosphere too much. But then Comfort Hotels had approached him. They had a middle-of-the-market chain of hotels around the planet but none in this resort, which was now becoming more popular with the better-off clients. They did not want to buy him out. That was not the way they worked because they believed on building on the local 'flavour', as they put it. What they wanted was to go into partnership with Pero. They had wanted to buy the land out the back, which was at that time unoccupied, and the shop next door and build the hotel onto the restaurant. Mr Pero had driven a hard bargain.

"I told them I did not need them," he explained, "which was true. If they wanted to build a hotel they could go somewhere else. I was doing OK as I was. But, if they were willing to let me buy the shop next door and the land out the back, I would go into partnership with them for thirty percent plus ground rent, so long as I had a controlling say on what happened on the ground floor. They were all too pleased to agree to that because they wanted to preserve the restaurant as it was," declared Mr Pero. "Oh, and I insisted on the name too. 'Pero's Family Hotel'!" he said jocundly.

He went on to explain that that had happened twenty years ago. Now, however, the time had come to retire. Jack guessed he must be a rich man. Thirty-percent of the income plus ground rent of that vast hotel over twenty years must have added up to quite a lot.

"Where are you going to retire to?" asked Jalli.

"Oh. Nowhere. I still have my flat over there," he indicated in the general direction behind the sea front. "It's all I ever wanted. My wife died very soon after we were married, you see…"

"I'm sorry to hear that," said Jack.

"No. Don't be. I have the best family I could ever want!" he declared. "There is Kakko and Tod here, and all the others. Some of them have grandchildren now and they all call me Papa. I have been to many weddings and blessings for their children."

"And he comes to our worship fellowship every week without fail and has met lots of people his own age too…" put in Tod.

"And they also called me Papa," Mr Pero laughed.

"So you are retiring?" said Jack.

"Tomorrow is my last day. We are catering for a wedding anniversary. When that is done I shall hand over the keys and become a 'sleeping partner'."

"Whatever will you do with yourself?" asked Jalli.

"He's going to work part-time in the street children's centre," explained Kakko. "Well, almost full-time really. So Papa'll do very little sleeping!"

6

Pero checked the Smith family into the hotel with rooms on the top floor with a magnificent view across the beach and the ocean beyond. From that height they could make out an island that was not visible from down below. Bandi began explaining about angles and how it was possible to calculate the distance of the horizon using trigonometry, and from that, come to some conclusion about the radius of the planet. Kakko wondered if there were boat trips to the island.

"But Kakko," sighed her mother, "you haven't even explored a square metre of this part of the new world yet!"

The rest of the morning was taken up with enjoying the sea and sand, and then stuffing themselves with the local shellfish and sweet iced treats sold from cabins under the palm-like trees. In the afternoon, Tod and Kakko had organised for them to meet up with some members of the fellowship. It was wonderful to meet the group again twenty-two years on with teenagers of their own. Kakko, Shaun and Bandi were quickly absorbed into the group, grateful for the clothes and swim-wear supplied beside the white gate. They explained how it worked, but the local young people found it hard to grasp.

"You mean you just appear out of nowhere. Poof!"

"No. Not out of nowhere. We just stepped through from one place to another like entering into another room. Only those who are called can do it. Only those meant to pass through can see the gates."

"So you could just come here and go whenever you liked?"

"No. Only when the gate is there."

"Could you decide to walk through, nick a million diamonds and disappear? The police wouldn't ever be able to catch you!" said a young lad.

Shaun laughed. "*You* get me the million diamonds and I'll try it!"

"It wouldn't work," said Kakko crossly. "If you tried to do that I bet the gate would just vanish and you would be stuck here to face the music."

"I was only joking, sis!" said Shaun. "Oh, my sister can take things so seriously," he laughed.

"So was I," said the lad a little troubled, "joking, I mean!"

"Of course! Who wants a million diamonds anyway when you've got lots of good friends like you have… got a ball?"

"Sure."

"Know how to play football?"

It didn't take long for Shaun and Kakko to organise all the young people into playing football. Shaun captained one side and Kakko the other.

"The only rules are that you can't touch the ball with your hands or arms or deliberately push and trip your opponent. That's a 'foul'," said Shaun. And then pushed Kakko over to demonstrate. "See, she's not happy! And *retaliation* is an even worse foul," he added as Kakko got up with a threatening face. "You'll get sent off for that!" The teenagers laughed and, just in time, Kakko pretended she was acting.

"Whoops," said Jalli watching from the top of the sand.

"What?" asked Jack.

"No… It's OK. For a moment I thought Kakko was going to attack Shaun but, thankfully, she's thought better of it."

Just then a large, flashy, open-topped car parked up and a couple of boys and a girl pulled themselves out of it. The car caught Jalli's eye. It was designed to make a statement. Its occupants couldn't have been much above eighteen and Jalli thought the car was a bit posh for young people. They wore little more than the other kids, but somehow she could tell it was expensive kit, and the girl had a bag that looked really special, probably a designer brand, that seemed rather too grand for a beach. They glided down the sand and spread large brightly coloured towels. *In Wanulka*, thought Jalli, *they would have been the type to have had a private beach somewhere.* They looked a bit out of place here. She couldn't imagine *them* joining in the football. The game, however, seemed to fascinate them, and after Shaun called for time out they sauntered over to Kakko and Shaun's friends.

Jalli was alarmed to see one of the lads talking to her daughter. Why she should feel uncomfortable she didn't really know – they weren't drunk and didn't appear to be on drugs or anything. You couldn't see them getting violent in the way the thugs had done on their last visit here twenty years before. And besides, they already had a girl in tow. But nevertheless there was something creepy about him. Why had that boy singled out Kakko?

"Something's got your attention," said Jack. It was times like this when his blindness was hardest. He was fully aware of his wife's unease but had no clue what was causing it. But Jalli understood him and was quick to speak.

"It's just some young people talking to Kakko. I don't know. They're different from the others – not part of Tod and Kakko's group. They arrived in a big, flashy, gold coloured open-topped car. Three of them: two boys and a girl. The boy talking to Kakko seems too interested in her. I don't care for him."

"Kakko's able to look after herself. Besides, nothing untoward could happen here could it? Far too public."

"You're right. But…"

"I know. We want to protect her, but there is nothing much we can do. She's eighteen and the last thing she would want is for one of us to go over there unbidden. She knows where we are if she needs us."

"They're moving off now. The game's getting back under way. I wonder what he was saying to her." The three lads and the girl walked back up the beach to their towels and sat down. They applied liberal amounts of sun-cream and then the girl lay flat while the boys continued to watch the football.

They were still there when Kakko and Shaun finished their game and came puffing up towards their parents, passing the trio on the way. The boy called out to Kakko. She stopped and stood speaking to them for a minute, nodded and then ran after her brother to collapse breathless beside Jalli.

"So what was all that about?" asked Jalli.

"What? We were just teaching everyone to play football."

"I mean the boy you were just talking to. You know what I mean."

"Oh *him*. Nothing. They just fancy themselves a bit."

"So what did they want?" asked Jack.

"They come from that villa over there. That one on the headland. Two brothers and their sister."

"That great big place with the red roofs?" asked her mother.

"Yeah."

"So what did they want?" quizzed her father a second time.

"Oh. They've got this big boat – or at least their father has. The big white one in the harbour you can see from the hotel balcony. You can't see it from here but you can down there where we were playing. And they have invited us on board for a trip tomorrow."

"What did you tell them?"

"Oh. I said we didn't know if we were going to be here tomorrow."

"You didn't say no then?"

"Of course not. I didn't know if I wanted to go or not... or if I could... they're going to the island just over the horizon. He gave me his phone number."

"That older one," said Shaun, "he fancies you."

"So what if he does. That's his lookout. And, anyway, *you* couldn't take your eyes of that sister of theirs, could you? Can't you see she was turning it on a bit strong, standing there in her bikini, like, all sexy?"

"And you weren't?"

"Course not. Sometimes I despair of you Shaun."

"Not like your lot won the game though, was it? You'd have done better getting in the mix and passing the ball on."

"Like you? But I'm a natural forward. My skill is scoring goals."

"Sure, so long as you can get the ball. Anyway we won!"

"Alright you two, no need to let your competitive natures get too out of hand," said Jalli. "So what are you going to do about this lad?"

"What do you mean?"

"I mean, are you going to ignore him or ring him and tell him you can't go."

"So we won't be here tomorrow then?"

"That's not the point, Kakko."

"Wouldn't it be cool to go on a boat like that, though? Especially as they're going to have a picnic on the island... and he said *anyone* could go. Lot's of people are going. It wasn't just me and Shaun."

"Nah," said Shaun, "but by 'anyone' I don't think he was reckoning on your old man."

"I don't think he was for one minute," said Jack.

"And he was speaking to *you*, not the group in general," said Jalli.

"Oh, Mum!"

"I suggest you just leave it. No harm done is there?" suggested Jack. Kakko let out a protracted sigh, slumped full length on the sand and buried her face in her towel. She hadn't intended to go anyway. She didn't trust this lad any more than her mother did, but she was not going to admit that. It didn't hurt to be 'fancied' by a rich kid after all, so long as you didn't let it get out of hand.

★★★

That evening they all put on their smart stuff. Bandi felt a little awkward being smart, Kakko was transformed into a poised young adult, and Shaun looked very classy in a jacket and open-neck shirt. Jalli enjoyed dressing up too.

"Wow," said Bandi, "you look cool Mum."

"Thank you kind sir!" she said. Jack felt a bit left out and became impatient to 'explore' his wife's impressive outfit as soon as they were alone. As the family admired each other he wished he could have seen his children as they impressed the world with emerging adulthood. Jalli understood this too. She put an arm around her husband's waist, squeezed him to her and kissed his cheek.

"OK, you three. You get off and meet your new friends downstairs. Jack and I are meeting Tod and Kakko." After the door had closed, Jalli took her husband into her arms and kissed him on the lips.

"Better not get dishevelled," grunted Jalli.

"Shucks," sighed Jack.

★★★

The party went well. Pero was completely unaware that everything was really for him. There were some great speeches including one from a young woman called Vadma (a recent graduate from the university) who had been one of the first street children to be taken into his care. When she was six she was living on the streets; she and her older sister had nowhere safe to go because their mother had died. Vadma had been looked after by her older sister until she was nine when they where both rescued by the centre. That was thirteen years ago. She had never looked back she said.

Pero had prepared a magnificent cake for the anniversary

couple. To their amazement Kakko and Tod called on Jalli and Jack to cut it because they had not had an opportunity to celebrate their wedding – even though it was twenty years before! The three youngsters from Joh were amazed at just how much of an impression their parents had made so many years before.

The food was sumptuous. Jalli thought she recognised the chef supervising the spread. It was none other than the young man who had come back to apologise for his drunken behaviour on that infamous night, and whom Mr Pero had accepted to do the washing up. Jalli accosted him.

"Don't I recognise you?" she asked.

"You might," he replied, "you spoke to me kindly on the morning of the clearing up… after… after I got caught up in that vandalism…"

"Yeah, I *do* recognise you! So, you are still working here?"

"I'm head chef now. Mr Pero sent me to catering college and mentored me through everything. He says he is leaving it to me now to ensure standards don't drop."

"Congratulations! You did all this?"

"Yes, our team did it. Mr Pero came and checked on us – for the last time he said. He approved."

"As well he might. Well done for this… and for what you have achieved."

"Thank you," he coloured. "It is all down to Mr Pero – and you – for accepting me on that morning."

"You came back. That took courage. An example to all of us when we make mistakes."

"Thank you. I appreciate that."

Then Bandi came up and said, "Great food, chef. Mum

do you reckon I would make a good chef one day? It must be a cool job."

The disco boomed and the dancing went on into the small hours. Jack and Jalli departed soon after midnight, leaving their youngsters to it.

7

The following day, Papa Pero joined the Smiths at the breakfast table in the hotel breakfast room. The growing light from the window illuminated brass fittings and glass tops; potted plants were tastefully placed around the walls and against the pillars. At the windows hung light, patterned drapes that reached the floor.

"This is lovely," observed Jalli. "I like the little touches, like the posy centre pieces on each table."

"We (I mean 'they'!) try to make people feel special," explained Pero.

Just then they noticed a little boy gazing through the window. He was dirty and roughly dressed and his appearance was in shocking contrast with the ambiance of the breakfast suite.

"Ah, my little man!" Pero waved at him and indicated to the attendant who took the child a pile of pastries from behind the bar. The little face glowed with a grateful smile. He raised his grubby hand and zoomed off down the hotel steps clutching his prize.

"The staff used to chase them away but I said to myself, 'Pero these children are hungry. The only difference between the people inside and the people outside is that the ones inside can pay.' So I told them to let the children come to the kitchen door. Then I thought, 'Why should they come round the back?

Let them come to the front like other people.' But the staff, they refused to allow them to come inside. They are worried they haven't washed. Pero had to concede they have a point."

"Where do they come from?" asked Kakko. "Don't they have homes to go to? Why are they dirty?"

"They have no homes. They are dirty because they live on the street where there are no showers."

"Children without adults, living wild!" exclaimed Kakko. "Why?"

"There always have been children living on the street around here," explained Pero. "I ask myself the same question, where are all these kids coming from? I went to one of the older ones who seemed to look after the others. He told us that most of them had been thrown out of their homes by the adults supposed to look after them. Many had parents who had died and their relatives were too poor to have more children to support. Some had run away from home because their guardians abused them."

"Unbelievable!" exclaimed Kakko. "How can anyone abuse a small child?"

"Those who were abused are the most damaged," Mr Pero continued, "it is easier for those who have some good memories of their parents. If you've been loved at all, there is hope. But if you've never been loved – never known love – then you can grow up hating everyone, including yourself. These children needed somewhere to go where people would love them. So I found a warehouse on an industrial estate that was up for sale and bought it."

"I bet everyone's really proud of you for doing this," said Bandi, the first thing he had said that morning.

"Maybe some. But it also makes many feel uncomfortable. They think I am telling them they should give their money away too."

"And do you?" asked Jalli.

"No. They know what I believe and… and think I sit in judgement on them. I can see how they feel."

"Bet it makes them feel really guilty," broke in Kakko.

"In a way. But it isn't as simple as that. To feel guilty you have to have a conscience and many of them have never been brought up to have one – at least not in regard to poor people. They believe that they are rich because the Creator made them that way, and each of us should be content in our own situation in life. That's what they believe…

"But I was not brought up in a rich home. A comfortable one, yes, but not wealthy. And my parents were always sharing things. So for me it is more natural to want to help these children. It is easier for me."

"I think you are being very gracious Mr Pero," said Jalli, "that is just like you. But I think, at the bottom of their hearts, they *do* know what is right and wrong."

"Maybe you are right, but there is so much stuff that has been piled on top, generations of prejudice that smothers a sense of justice in them for these children. Some of them have inherited positions of privilege that go back centuries. They fear change, not just for their own lives, but for the whole of society."

"And you are challenging that," said Jack.

"I am a subversive influence," he laughed. "Now, I must get going. We have an outing organised for twenty of the younger ones. There are some free places for helpers. Would you three youngsters like to go along?"

"Where are they going?" asked Jalli.

"Oh. They're only going up the coast a bit. It's to get them out of town. There'll be a picnic and some swimming."

"Count me in," said Shaun.

"Me too," said Bandi.

Kakko was a bit disappointed. She had reckoned on persuading her parents to let them go on the boat with the rich kids. But she realised that there was no way she was going to be allowed to go on her own. The thought of going on a picnic with a load of little kids sounded cool, though. "And me," she said.

They all piled into Mr Pero's van.

"It's not far. It's just behind the harbour," he explained.

As they drove the short distance, Pero continued his story. "I didn't tell anyone what I was planning to do. The warehouse was just surrounded by industrial units and other warehouses. I couldn't buy ordinary houses or anything because no-one would want a place for street children near them."

"Why ever not?" asked Kakko, incensed at the idea that people didn't want children around.

"All sorts of reasons, I guess," answered her father. "These children are survivors. They have to beg, and steal too, no doubt. And they will be dirty and smelly, and half-starved kids without anyone to love them are not cute. I bet they can be pretty revolting at times."

"You are right. Some people see them as no better than vermin," agreed Mr Pero. "They cannot see the potential, nor do they feel any obligation to care for them. They do not believe they have, or should have, any responsibility for them. You see my friends here today, but I have many enemies; and many others think I am mad."

Mr Pero turned off the sea-front and away from the big buildings and houses with their trees and pots filled with flowers. In a couple of streets they were alongside the harbour.

"I've always wondered why people try to ignore street children. It doesn't take much imagination to see that they are going to grow up to pose huge and expensive problems. But if you rescue these children, society will be stronger," said Jalli.

"The true strength of a community," reflected Jack, "can be seen in the way that it looks after its most disadvantaged members. That is the thinking behind my school for blind children."

"Basically, it's about love, isn't it?" said Bandi. He was thinking hard.

"Absolutely," agreed Mr Pero. "If you have love, you have everything. And the more you give love, the more you receive. Take Vadma. I claim her as my daughter and she gives me love as if I were her father. And she is only one. I have the biggest family of anyone in the city. I get love all the time. Last year I fell sick. I thought to myself, 'Pero stay in your flat until you get better'. But I had to tell people I wasn't coming into work. Then I had more nursing and tending than I could want…" He rounded a series of warehouses associated with the port. The smell of fish was strong. "But Mr Zookas up in his villa – up there on the headland…"

"The big house with the red roof?" asked Kakko.

"That's the one. He was sick too. His children and their

friends took his yacht somewhere to have fun and left him in the care of paid nurses. Not one of his supposed friends went to see him. When I was better, I thought, 'Pero, go and visit Zookas. He was sick like you and his family have left him on his own.' When I was there he said that being sick helps you find your real friends. I was the only person who had gone to see him that hadn't been paid to. 'All they want from me is my money,' he told me, 'but you, Pero, they want you!' Ever since then he has given me money for the centre."

"A convert," smiled Jalli. "You are winning!" Kakko thought about the trio she had met the previous day but didn't say anything.

"We're here," announced Mr Pero.

The Paradise Centre looked exactly like he had described. It was a warehouse surrounded by other warehouses. A couple of men outside one of them waved as Mr Pero drove his van into the space between the units.

"They keep an eye out for the children," he said.

Inside they were greeted by dozens of excited children. Their house-mother welcomed the guests and introduced them to the children and soon each of the family were engaged in doing something with one or other of the little ones with books and crayons. The house-mother spoke quietly to Mr Pero.

Mr Pero called his guests together. "Apparently the bus has broken down. The house-mother is about to call off the picnic."

"Oh! That's sad," said Shaun. "I was quite looking forward to a picnic with these kids."

"They're going to be very disappointed. This was the first

outing for weeks. They've been looking forward to it for days. This morning they all got up early and got themselves ready and the volunteers have got the picnic ready and everything."

"So sorry," said Jalli feeling the disappointment too. "Is there nowhere else you can take them… on foot?"

"Mr Pero," said Kakko. She had got an idea. "You know you were telling us about the man that owns the big villa on the headland."

"Mr Zookas, yes."

"Well yesterday we met three of his children, and the oldest one – "

"A lad of about nineteen?"

"Yeah. And another boy and a girl."

"His younger three. He has four altogether. Go on…"

"Well the nineteen-year-old, invited me and Shaun and Bandi to go on his boat today. They're going to the island out there," she said, pointing in the direction of the sea. "He said we could bring any of our friends. I saw the boat in the harbour as we passed. It's huge. There'll be more than enough room for twenty kids and their volunteers."

"And you get to go on the boat and to the island after all," said Jalli. "I don't think this is on, Kakko."

"But Mum!"

"Wait," said Pero. "It might work. The kids would love it. But Zookas' children did not have my kids in mind I expect."

"I'm sure they didn't," said Jalli.

"But let me call Zookas. He might like to hear that his children are doing something useful with their time. If he says, yes, then his children will have to agree."

"But…" said Jalli. But Pero was already on the phone.

"Hello, my friend. How're you feeling today...? Good. Look, Zookas I've a problem..." and he explained about the bus. "But I've got some young people with me who were invited yesterday by your Adnak to go on your boat to Lona Island... yes, and his brother and sister. They're with the children here and I was wondering... yes... really. Well, they have their own picnic... well, OK. Wonderful. That's more than I could ask... thank you Zookas... yes, I'd like that but I have some guests with me... You would? My dear Zookas... good! I will. Thank you. Good-bye." Pero smiled broadly.

"Mr Zookas says that not only can all the children and their helpers go on the boat, but he will lay on food for them. He's going to have a word with his children who were just about to leave. Then he'll contact his friend in the port and get him to bring more food to the boat. He says to be there in forty minutes. Can we do that?" he asked the house-mother.

"No problem. All they have to do is go to the toilet and we can walk them to the harbour."

"And we, you and I," said Mr Pero smiling at Jack and Jalli, "have been invited to the Zookas' villa."

"Cool," said Kakko. "See what knowing the right people can do for you!"

"Kakko!" thundered Jack.

"But I really am grateful to you," the house-mother said. "This young lady has saved the day!"

Kakko smiled, but rather sheepishly. She knew her father was right. She had spoken out rather too arrogantly. But Shaun ensured the humilty didn't last.

"The power of the female," he whispered in her ear, "put

on a bikini and change the world!" and then ducked as Kakko
went to whack him. The children laughed at their clowning.

★★★

Forty minutes later Kakko, Shaun and Bandi, together with
the children and their young volunteers, arrived in a crocodile
line down at the harbour. The children were so high. This
was going to be the most brilliant day of their lives! They had
never ever dreamt that one day they were going to be allowed
onto this boat, let alone go out of the harbour on it.

However, Adnak and his friends were a mixture of
confused, disapproving and scared. They were not, however,
in charge of the cruiser which boasted a captain, two crew
members and a chef, all of whom had been fully briefed. *They*
were very welcoming. Jalli got the impression that they were
pleased not to be at the beck and call of spoilt rich kids who,
they suspected, were going to get drunk and lewd.

The children were carefully conducted up the gangway.
The house-mother gave final instructions to the volunteers
and she, Pero, Jack, and Jalli watched as the engines came to
life with a throaty roar. The children waved frantically as the
boat slid out of the harbour entrance and headed for the open
sea.

"That was wonderful!" exclaimed Pero.

"I must get back to the centre," stated the house-mother.
"The others will be coming up to their mid-morning break.
Would you like to share refreshments with us?" she asked Jack
and Jalli, who were feeling rather strange watching their
children head for the horizon.

"They'll be OK," said Jack squeezing his wife's hand.

"I know," said Jalli. "It's just that they're all growing up so fast!"

They walked back to the centre and were soon caught up with the remaining children. They all sat on mats with them as the older ones came round with plates of biscuits that they had decorated with icing. They were works of art.

"Wonderful," said Jalli. "Do we have to eat them? They look too good to eat."

But the children insisted that they be eaten. For them the decorating was as much a way of piling on sugar as the artistic designs.

"This centre must have been very hard to set up," said Jack to Mr Pero. "I mean with all the original opposition."

"Yes, I suppose so. It took time. It's easier now. But at first it was very hard. They didn't even want the children in the warehouse. The council objected on the grounds that it constituted a change of use, but they didn't just want to turf us out either because some people liked the idea of getting the children off the streets. We installed a kitchen (first things first!) then I bought beds and bedding and got in carpenters to put up partitions. In the beginning I used members of the hotel staff to do the cooking. There was no problem in attracting the children when there was food around!"

"You paid the cooks?"

"Oh, yes. They were mainly in the hotel but came here on a rota basis. There weren't so many children in those days. But gradually I got people who came to volunteer. This was hard because not all of them were suitable. I used to get the police to check the names – that put off the wrong sort."

"This must have taken a lot of your time," said Jalli.

"It did. But in those days we didn't have anyone with the children overnight. After all, they had been living rough for years. But then one day some men attempted to get in. The children had bolted the doors, but they tried to get in through the windows. The children let up so much noise that eventually the men ran away. After that we had to have paid guards, and I knew we had to be much more coordinated. So, I met with the volunteers and we agreed to set up a proper organisation. We appointed governors and founded a company that employed people. We soon had house-mothers, kitchen staff, security people seven days and nights a week. We took in more children and they were properly enrolled. They had to commit to staying – they couldn't just come and go any more."

"Didn't that put them off?" asked Jalli.

"We lost some of them, but most stayed."

The house-mother told Jalli that the children were all there voluntarily. However, while they were there, there were house rules that required the children to wash and keep their clothes and rooms tidy and swept. The only other rule that was non-negotiable was that they had to be present at all meals, three times a day. If they wanted to skip school they could, so long as they were back at lunchtime and tea-time. If they missed a meal they ran the risk of exclusion from the centre.

"Do they often miss school?" asked Jalli.

"Hardly ever. The schools have their own rules – but most like learning anyway. They appreciate the opportunity."

"You've done well," said Jack.

"And now it is time for your trip," said Pero. "We should

go up to the headland and check in with Zookas. You can see the island from there."

"We are taking all your time," said Jalli. "You must have so much to do."

"I'm retired!" replied Pero. "Today, I can do what I want!"

8

As soon as the boat was beyond the harbour entrance the children had started to explore every bit of it. The crewmen came to the volunteer leaders and urged them to make sure the kids moved about safely. There was too much to trip up on and they didn't want anyone overboard. But they needn't have worried. As soon as the boat began to rise and fall in the swell the children calmed down and found seats inside and outside. This was a new experience for all of them. None of them had ever been on the sea before. Some began to look queasy and Kakko, Shaun, Bandi and the other volunteers were hard at it, reassuring and cuddling where necessary. Kakko soon found that the romance of the trip was to be enhanced for her as she dealt with a child who was sick – fortunately on the lee side of the vessel. She took note of this. Had he been leaning over the other side they would all have got some! As it was, there was not much clearing up. To her surprise as soon as the boy had finished being sick, his colour changed back to normal and within a minute he was happy and chirpy again.

At first Adnak and his friends kept themselves aloof. But one by one they resigned themselves to the fact that this was not going to be the kind of outing they had envisaged when they set out, and then got involved with the children until it was difficult to distinguish them from the volunteer leaders.

One or two held back, Adnak in particular, Kakko noticed. Some of the girls in his party normally turned on by his personal attractions – he was rich, good looking, tall, self-confident – were now succumbing to the lure of the children instead.

"Who needs men when you've got kids to amuse you!" said a tall girl about the same age as Kakko.

Kakko agreed. There was no competition. She struck up a conversation with Kloa, the volunteer leader in charge. Kloa was still getting over being on the boat herself.

"Funny to think that some of these people come from the part of society that wants to get rid of these kids for being on the street," she remarked. "Even our government would rather deny there is a problem. They have nowhere secure to take them."

"What, nothing else? Is the Paradise Centre the only place for them?" marvelled Kakko.

"There used to be an institution but it was so bad that many of the children got sick and died in it. It was such a scandal it became an election issue. When the new government came into power they closed it down, but they didn't put anything in its place. Some of us still say it was more of a cost-cutting exercise."

"What about those children who don't come to the centre? There must be others."

"Lots of them. We have two outreach workers who try to look after those on the streets," she said. "They make sure they don't starve and get them medical care when they can. Most of what they do is just protecting them from the gangs who go round abusing or killing them."

"Killing them!" Kakko almost shouted. "Killing children?"

"It doesn't happen where you come from?"

"No-way! How can you kill children and not be locked up?" exclaimed Kakko.

"Very easily," said the girl. "As long as you don't get caught doing it, it is not regarded as anything serious here. Some people see it as culling vermin, but our outreach workers are there and can call in help if they see anyone with guns."

"It sounds a dangerous job," said Shaun, coming into the conversation.

"It can be. But they are properly equipped with phone links. They are told not to confront the gangs. Last year some of the gang members were caught and the police had no choice but to charge them because public opinion is changing… slowly."

"Same thing with the centre," added a second volunteer. "At first there were petitions against it, but now it is different. When the council tried to tell us we were to move, some local businesses around us wrote up and told them they wanted us to stay. The council backed down."

The cruiser covered the distance to the island in less than half-an-hour. It wasn't a slouch. And anyway, the captain knew that the young children were not going to want the slow journey he had anticipated for the young people who sought to sun themselves in various states of undress while they supped on bottles of cold, alcoholic beverages. But now the fridges remained shut and the young people were nearly all involved with the Paradise children. On reaching the island, the captain pulled into a small narrow inlet with a long white beach on one side and trees right down to the water's edge on the other. They approached the end of the beach from which a jetty had been built.

"The island's uninhabited these days," said the girl Kakko had been chatting to. "There was an old recluse but he got sick and had to leave. Since then people only come here for fun or to study the birds."

The children were all anxious to get off the boat and explore!

"OK. Listen up," said Kloa. She waited for the noise to subside. Eventually the children realised there was no going ashore until they had heard her out.

"You can go in any direction you like. There is no-one else here on this island so you can't get into trouble, but you need to be safe. There are three rules. Remember the house up there is derelict. So the first rule is this: if you go into the house, DO NOT GO UP THE STAIRS. Why? Because you might very well fall through. I mean this. Fran, Jeno," she said looking at the more lively of the girls and boys whom she deemed the most venturesome and the more likely to disobey her, "I am putting you in charge of making sure that people DO NOT GO UP THE STAIRS. Got it?" Fran and Jeno nodded their agreement, chuffed that they had been given responsibility.

"OK. Second rule. This island is used by ground nesting birds. What does that mean Jess?" she asked one of the bright girls.

"That there might be nests with eggs in them, miss."

"Correct, nests on the ground but hidden among the grass and undergrowth. So if you leave the paths what might you do?"

"Tread on the eggs, miss," said Jess.

"So the second rule is, KEEP TO THE PATHS. OK?"

They all shouted their agreement.

"Besides," said Kloa, "there are goof-adders and you don't want to disturb them, do you?"

The children stood silent and shook their heads.

"OK?"

"What's the third rule, miss?" asked Jess, feeling bold.

"Oh. I nearly forgot. Mr Captain, can you make the boat hoot?"

"Sure," he said and gave a blast on the horn.

"When you hear that you are all to come back here, OK? It will mean there is food!" The children cheered loudly. The gangway was deployed and they filed over it... and then disappeared!

Kakko was alarmed. But the volunteers didn't seem to be fazed.

"Will they be OK?" asked Shaun.

"This peace is bliss!" said Kloa. "They'd do it wherever we take them. At least here they can't get lost or picked up."

The crew began to deploy the picnic stuff at the top of the beach.

"When would you like to eat?" asked the captain.

"Give them an hour. That's all they'll need. Most of them will be back before then anyway."

"Fine."

"Do you want any help?"

"No. We've got it covered. You go off and check on the kids."

Adnak made a suggestion to some of the others that now

71

was the time to chill out on the beach as they had planned. But no-one else seemed interested. The distinction between his 'guests' and the volunteers had virtually vanished. Before long, most had also disappeared to join the children. Adnak was left either to help the crew, which was way beneath him he thought, or join the rest. He slowly made his way up the path that led to the old house, which had become the subject of an invasion. The children were darting about it, in and out of the doors and some even climbing through the windows. When he got there, he discovered there was a board across the bottom of the stairs bearing the word 'danger' on it. He recalled that the owners of the island had been warned to protect the public. There had been an article in the local newspaper about how some person had reported the floor was rotting. That's where Kloa had probably got her information from. He looked up the stairs. There were boot prints in the dust, but nothing recent. The kids were following the rules. They zoomed past him and even played hide and seek behind him. There didn't seem to be any other leaders about.

"Sir?" said one. "What're goof-adders?"

"Dunno. Never heard of them," said Adnak.

"What do they do to you if they get you?" asked another.

"I suppose they might bite you."

"Yu-urk! I ain't never going to go off the path. They don't come onto the paths do they?"

"Never seen one."

"That's OK then."

And they were off. "Bet you can't catch Jeno?"

Adnak had nothing better to do and soon he was traipsing all over the island the same as the others.

At last there was a blast of the boat's horn, and suddenly from all ends of the island people emerged at top speed – none of them leaving the paths though.

What a spread! Zookas had not just provided a picnic but a banquet! There was exotic stuff the kids had never even seen, let alone eaten. The seafood didn't go down so well as the pastries. Even after everyone had eaten as much as they could there appeared to be just as much left over. The beer and the wine, however, remained in the fridges. It just wasn't appropriate, and, to his own amazement, not even Adnak missed it much – these kids were really entertaining, even if they never stopped talking or yelling!

9

As Mr Pero drove Jack and Jalli up the headland to Zookas' place he explained, "Our numbers grew. We were getting new kids all the time – and they weren't leaving. Eventually we got more support from the town – people like Zookas. Some of them gave generously and we were able to build a new purpose-built house for the teenagers round the corner from the warehouse. We call it 'Paradise House'. It has up-to-date facilities with two to a room and tiled bathrooms. That helps the children gain self-respect. We promise to keep them there until they find somewhere to go to as older teens."

Jalli saw the blue sea on her left and the red roofs of the villa in front of them.

"We asked the children what it should be called and they all wanted to keep the name 'Paradise', so we call it 'Paradise House' to distinguish it from the centre. Would you like to visit it?"

"Certainly," said Jack.

"We'll go there when we get back."

They topped the rise and saw Zookas' villa in front of them. Pero drove the van into the courtyard and they got out and Jalli took in the view. The town and harbour were down below them.

"That's Lona Island," said Mr Pero, pointing out a large island some distance towards the horizon.

"Pero!" exclaimed a man behind them, coming out of the house. "Welcome!" Zookas was a big man and not a shy one. He engulfed his friend in his bear-like arms and patted him on the back. Jalli was half wondering if that was going to be her fate too. But not this time. After they had been introduced, Zookas just took their hands in an enthusiastic handshake. The hugs were to be kept for the next meeting.

"Come! Come!" Zookas conducted them through the front door into a courtyard with a view of the sea. He motioned them to sit on an upholstered bench behind a metal table from which sprouted a large, brightly-coloured sunshade.

Jalli led Jack to the bench as he took stock of his new surroundings. She knew he was conjuring up a site plan in his mind, so turning in the direction of the view in a way that he could feel, said, "What a marvellous view you have. Right across to the island."

"Indeed, I have."

A servant appeared with a tray.

"What would you like to drink?"

"Oh. Something simple, and cold," said Pero.

"Local beer?"

"Good," said Pero.

"Same for me," said Jack.

"And for the lady? How about the local red wine?"

Jalli nodded and forced a smile. She wasn't sure, but Mr Pero didn't seem to think it was out of order, so she relaxed.

"Bring us a bottle of the eighth year vintage," said Zookas to the servant.

"Eighth year!" exclaimed Pero. "You still have some of that? The best vintage ever."

"I have a few bottles."

"I am honoured," said Jalli, thinking that it would probably be wasted on her.

The conversation began with the latest news of the Paradise Centre and Paradise House, which Jack and Jalli couldn't really follow. But they ascertained that Zookas was interested in the details.

Then Pero brought up the whole intriguing business of the white gates. There were the usual questions of how it worked. Interestingly, Zookas accepted without question the fact that it didn't happen for everyone. Often people asked the question why only some and not others, but this fact didn't seem to bother Zookas. Later Jack reflected that that might be because he was used to privilege. In his world, the fact that only some are permitted was not a strange concept. He followed with the question of Jack's blindness, complimenting him on how he managed and asking him how it came about. Jack gave him his stock answers, including the explanation of a mishap with a baton. Again, Zookas accepted it at face value. Perhaps baton swinging was a regular hazard in this place.

What Zookas seemed more interested in than anything else, was their children. He wanted to know all about them. After taking in a brief resume of each from Jalli, he said, "I expect you are very proud of them."

"Of course. They are good young people. I'm not saying they're perfect…"

"But their imperfections are small… I am afraid I cannot say that about my four."

"But, Zookas," said Pero kindly, "you do everything you can for them."

"Too much. They're spoilt. My eldest, all she can think about is spending money on clothes and luxuries and going about with her friends. She left me all on my own when I was ill. And the others are going the same way I'm afraid. I shouldn't have let them take the boat today. They'll most probably get drunk and cavort half naked, if not more, and it'll get all over the papers…"

Jack and Jalli were alarmed. "But they have all the children!" said Jalli with some force. "They will have to look after *them*."

"Oh. I expect they'll leave the kids to your three and the volunteer leaders and go off on the back beach or something… and then they'll be exposed to the paparazzi with their telephoto lenses!"

Mr Pero made noises of disagreement. But, secretly, he agreed. Allowing the Zookas youngsters and their friends the boat may have been a mistake. It was as if Zookas didn't seem to have the choice any more. Giving in to his children had become a habit. Jack and Jalli were relieved that at least Zookas felt their three would stay with the children. She didn't doubt that Bandi would, but to be perfectly honest, she wondered if her extrovert and impetuous daughter would find herself in deeper water than she cared to think. As for Shaun, who knows? He wouldn't look for it, but if Kakko was going he might go along for the ride. *Mind you*, she thought, *that might not be a bad thing because him being there might provide some protection for Kakko*. The thought of it all being photographed was really scary – even if it was on a planet on the other side of the universe. Once pictures had been taken you never knew…

Jalli was lost in thought and realised the conversation had

moved on. They were going to get a guided tour of the villa.

Her immediate impression of the place was to wonder how anyone could live in such a large place. Jack thought likewise. He had given up trying to map it in his mind.

"I'd never find you if we lived here," he said to Jalli.

"Oh. And I was just thinking I might like a place just like it on Joh."

Jack squeezed her hand.

"I can recommend it," Zookas was saying, taking Jalli's tease at face value. "If you would like a copy of the architect's drawings you are welcome."

"Thanks, but we don't have the resources," smiled Jack politely, "and in any case, with not seeing I have to keep things simple." Zookas took his arm.

"I understand. I completely understand. The worse thing about having wealth is that children grow up with it. If ever things change for them I worry they won't cope. There are downsides to being rich. I wanted my children to go to the local secondary school but I was warned they could be bullied because they were different – they just wouldn't fit in. So they went to the boarding school and now think those who go to the local school are beneath them."

★★★

On their way back to town, Pero said that he thought the way Zookas' children were turning out was probably one of the reasons their father was so keen on the Paradise Centre.

"When he comes to us," he said, "the children are pleased to see him. He gets more appreciation from the street children than he does from his own. He sometimes sits on the floor with them."

★★★

Paradise House was great. Every effort had gone into allowing the children to own it. You could see the young people were very proud of it. The children had decided on their own rules in addition to cleanliness and being at meals. They had an elected house council. The chief member of staff called herself 'Service Manager'. She saw herself in charge of the running of the house and the other staff members, rather than directing the children whom she called residents.

"But don't they have problems?" asked Kakko.

"All the time," she said, "but for that we have several care-workers to whom they can turn. We encourage them to talk to them, but if they don't want to they don't have to. They are here voluntarily after all."

"And do any of them choose to leave?"

"Occasionally. But in every case so far, except one, they have come back within twenty-four hours. The other children see it as their job to persuade them to come back. They know, however, they can't just come and go as they please. If they want to be here they still have to be at every meal. The thing is that all of these children have spent time at the Paradise Centre. Many of them lived there for years. We don't accept teenagers from the street here. We can't because we are overfull with our own children from the centre."

"What happens to homeless teenagers, then?"

"There are some over-night shelters. We are a small

organisation and we can't do everything, and we have to accept that. That is one of the rules we set ourselves, as care-workers we must not beat ourselves up about the things that remain undone. Nobody can do everything; there will always be children out there whose needs are not being met. What we have to do, is do as much as we can without compromising on the standard of care we give. My motto is: 'Do what you can well, and leave the rest to God'."

It was quiet in Paradise House. Most of the children were at school. They were given a short tour and then invited to stop for lunch. There they met two girls who had no school that day – their school had a day off for some staff training, they explained. It was amazing. They treated them with so much respect. Visitors were accorded the highest honour. It was hard to imagine that they were once living on the streets. Neither of them had any family apart from Paradise.

Jack thanked them for allowing them into their home.

"You are welcome," they said. "Tell us about *your* home." So they told them all about Joh, White Gates Cottage and Matilda and Momori.

"That's three generations!" said one of the girls. "Your children are so lucky."

"They are," agreed Jalli. "Actually, it's four generations because I was brought up by my grandmother. My parents both died when I was three."

"But your grandmother wanted you?"

"Absolutely. She lost everyone on the same day – her husband, her brothers and sisters and her children. Her house, her whole village disappeared. I was all she had."

"That is bad. She must hurt. But she had you. She loves you."

"She does. Sometimes it only takes one person to love and look after you. She loves me very, very well. She always wants the best for me – even if it would mean letting me go. "

"But she didn't have to. Now she has a whole house full! And you."

"Yes. And I am ever appreciative of it… even if I worry about my children sometimes."

"You worry? Why?"

"I worry that, maybe, they might find… bad friends."

"No! Your children will never make friends with bad people. You love them. They will know when people don't love well – it tastes different."

10

"We need a quiet activity for fifteen minutes," said Kloa to the volunteers. "We can't play games right on top of this feast."

"Would you like me to tell them a story?" Kakko offered.

"Doubt they will sit still for fifteen, but you can give it a try."

Kloa stood up.

"OK everyone, listen up!" But the noise was so great no-one heard. Kloa looked over to the captain who smiled and went to his little bridge and sounded the horn. It worked.

"OK. Listen up. I want you all to gather round Kakko... when *I say* Jeno – wait... Kakko's got a story from her world to tell you. But before she begins, did you all enjoy the food?" (A huge cry of, "Ye-eee-s".) "So let's say thank you to Mr. Zookas. He's not here but if you shout loud enough he might hear you. Are you ready? One, two, three..."

"THANK-YO-OU!!!" they screamed together.

"OK, go and find a space near Kakko and sit down... That's it but don't crowd her... Jeno, sit down... Right down... on your bottom." Kloa stood beside Kakko with her hand in the air. "Put your hand up like me," she called. Kakko did the same and then slowly one by one everyone followed suit, including Adnak. There was silence.

"Now, over to Kakko."

"Hi, everyone."

"Hiiii," replied the kids.

"OK. Shhh. This won't work unless you are all listening…
" She raised her hand and silence was restored. "So this story
doesn't come from my planet, but my father's. He told it to
us when we were kids and I liked it. So here goes.

"Once upon a time there were three bears. (Bears are big
furry animals that, like, live in woods). There was a daddy
bear, a mummy bear and a baby bear. Well, they had this house
in the middle of the woods. They were *bears*, but they were
kind of, like, people, because they slept in beds and sat on
chairs and ate porridge for breakfast…"

"What's porridge, miss?"

"I don't know. Never had it – we don't eat it at home. But
on Planet Earth they cook it for breakfast and it gets real hot.
So this porridge was too hot to eat. It was a nice day and they
thought they would all go out for a walk while it cooled down.
So they put their boots on and headed off into the woods.
Well, while they were gone, along came this girl with blonde
hair… a bit like Kloa's here. Her name was Goldilocks
because of her hair being yellow. Anyway, she went into the
house and smelled the porridge. She was hungry. Goldilocks
could have waited for the bears to come back and asked for
some, but she was not going to. She was not a good girl. So
she saw the big bowl, which was Daddy Bear's, and tried
some. It was still too hot. Then she looked at the medium-
sized bowl – this was Mummy Bear's – but Mummy Bear
puts salt in her porridge and Goldilocks didn't like it. So then
she tried Baby Bear's which was not too hot and had lots of
sugar… and she ate it all up. But while she was doing it she

Ultimate Justice

was sitting on Baby Bear's chair and it was too small for her and it broke, but Goldilocks didn't care. Then she saw the beds and thought she would have a lie down. There were three beds. There was a big one for Daddy Bear. She tried it but it was far too hard. Then she went on Mummy Bear's bed, but that was too soft. Finally, in the corner, she spotted Baby Bear's and got right in under the covers, and it was so comfy she went straight to sleep."

The children were all quiet and attentive, but some of them were getting sleepy, so Kakko decided not to drag the story out.

"Well, then the bears got home and there was trouble. Baby Bear's porridge had been gobbled up and his chair was broken. Daddy Bear noticed that someone had been in his bed and said, 'Who's been sleeping in my bed?'" Kakko used an appropriate deep, gruff voice. Some of the children laughed. "Then Mummy Bear noticed her bed had been slept in too." Kakko spoke in a lighter voice, "Who's been sleeping in my bed?" Then, with a high pitched squeal, she made the children jump, "'Help! There's someone in my bed!' It was Baby Bear. The bears all looked and saw Goldilocks' hair on Baby Bear's pillow. She had been fast asleep but Baby Bear's squeal had woken her up. She looked up and saw the three bears… and then she shrieked. She was no match for three bears! She leaped out of the bed and out of the door as fast as she could. But the bears ran after her and caught her!"

The children gasped. What would the bears do to her?!

"They carried her back to the house and sat her on the floor. 'Tell us where you live,' demanded Daddy Bear. 'Nowhere,' she answered." Kakko put on a wistful expression.

"'No-where?' said Mummy Bear. 'But you have to live somewhere? Where are your mother and father?' 'I don't know,' said Goldilocks truthfully. She had never known her mother or her father."

The children were all ears. Those who had been nodding off were now wide awake. What were these bears going to do with this street kid? Each of them was thinking of his or her own history.

Kakko continued, "'I haven't got a mother or a father,' said Goldilocks, 'or even a grandma, or anyone.' 'So,' said Daddy Bear, 'whose been looking after you?' 'When I was little there were these kids. But then the kind one died and the others bullied me, so I ran away, and now I eat and sleep where I can.'"

Kakko put on her soft Mummy Bear voice, "'Well, why didn't you tell us you haven't got any parents instead of coming into our house and stealing?' 'Because most people just throw things at me, and tell me to go away,' replied Goldilocks. 'Well, we aren't like that,' said Daddy Bear. 'Are you still hungry?' Goldilocks said she was, and do you know what? Daddy Bear let her eat all *his* porridge, which was now cool enough, and Mummy Bear made some more for him and Baby Bear. Then they got out another bed just for Goldilocks and she went to sleep for a long time."

The children looked happy and relieved for her.

"But do you know what the worst thing was?"

"Noo-oo," sighed the children expecting a sad ending after all.

"They made her wash! All over. She felt funny being clean. But today her yellow hair is as bright as the brightest sunflower and she's happy," said Kakko in a voice that indicated the story had come to an end.

'*Happy*', thought Adnak. *A good word to end a sentence with.* He found himself asking himself whether *he* was happy.

"What's a sunflower?" asked Jess.

"Oh. It's a flower that turns towards the star that shines on the Earth. Exactly like yours here. They call their star the 'Sun'."

"Miss," asked Jess. "Have you been to Planet Err…"

"Planet Earth? Earth One to give it its full name – there is more than one planet called Earth these days. No, I haven't. I've only been to one other planet apart from yours and Planet Joh where I live. But my parents have been to lots of places."

"Do you like going to other planets?"

"Oh, yes. I like adventures."

"How do you get here… from other planets with other stars?" asked Adnak.

"That," smiled Kakko, "is a mystery even to us. The Creator makes a special gate. We are very, very privileged."

"What's 'privileged', miss?"

"It's what we are when we meet all you here and we can have fun with you."

"But we're not special, miss," said Fran.

"Oh, but you are! You make us happy… and Adnak here and his friends too. Isn't that true?" she asked, looking Adnak in the eyes.

"Guess it is," he replied.

Then Kakko sat up straight, took a deep breath, and declared, "Adnak likes to watch us play football. Would you like to learn to play football?"

"Ye-eee-es!" went up the cry.

"Can we teach them football?" asked Kakko of Kloa.

"Of course. Teach us all!" The volunteers were delighted to have found such a talented young visitor.

Kakko called for the children's attention. "OK, listen carefully and I'll tell you how it works. It's called football because you mustn't touch the ball with your hands or arms – but you can use your body or your head. The object of the game is to get the ball between your opponent's goal posts – Bandi will you set these up now for us on the sand? That's called a 'goal'. And you're not supposed to push people – you try to get the ball off them with your feet. Like this." She and Shaun demonstrated, controlling the ball and tackling each other in turn a few times. "But you pass the ball to people on your own team." And she and Shaun passed the ball back and forth, and finally Kakko kicked the ball through one of the goals Bandi had marked out. "See? That's one goal to me!"

"OK. Let's divide into girls and boys. The ten boys go with Shaun and the ten girls come with me and we'll talk tactics. OK, go!"

The ten girls all crowded round Kakko.

"The clue to playing this game is passing the ball to someone else before you get tackled," she explained. "As soon as one of us has the ball, all the rest of you scatter into a space. If you have the ball and see someone in a space, pass it to them and keep passing it to people in spaces until you can get near the goal in front of you, then hit it as hard as you can to get it between the posts. Their goalkeeper (Shaun) will try and stop it. A goalkeeper is allowed to stop the ball with his hands. I'll be the girls' goalkeeper which means I can use my hands too. But *don't forget* none of the rest of you can use your hands… Are you ready Shaun?"

"Sure. We're ready."

At first the game was a real mess and Kakko and Shaun kept stopping the game to explain, but soon they got the idea and talent started to emerge. Some of the children managed to keep the ball long enough to do something with it. Shaun and Kakko were very generous in letting the ball through nearly every time it was on target to encourage them. The kids ran and ran – much more than they need to have done. It was excellent exercise but they were soon tired out.

"OK," said Kakko. "That's a draw. Four goals each. Now, how about the leaders? Come on, seven-a-side – girls versus boys."

"Count me out," said Adnak.

"No. That won't work," said Shaun. "We need you. Look even Bandi's playing. We can't beat them with only six players. You can't let the boys down."

"But I can't run!"

"OK. You're goalkeeper. You won't have to run."

Since the seven girls – volunteers *and* guests – were all around Kakko getting instructions, Adnak realised he had no choice. He'd be the only one sitting out with the children.

Kakko gave the same advice about running into space but she was to be up front while another took the role of goalkeeper. Three were to stay back a bit and pass the ball to the three in front of them.

The game kicked off and it was frenetic from the start. The gender rivalry was intense. When a boy tripped a girl up, the girl children all started yelling. "Unfair! Unfair!" Shaun did the gentlemanly thing and stopped the game giving the girls a free kick. After that they were more careful about fouling. The children were all shouting. The boys scored and their supporters all danced up and down while the girls jeered. They were certainly getting into the spirit of it. Then the girls scored and the roles were reversed. After ten more minutes they were level, two all. But Kakko, herself, hadn't scored.

"OK," said Shaun. "Next goal wins!"

Soon the ball was passed to Kakko in just the right place and she hit it sweetly and powerfully just inside the right-hand post! She was getting ready to celebrate when she saw Adnak leaping to his left and getting his hand to it. The boys cheered and whooped and began chanting his name. It was a close thing. The game continued for several more minutes before eventually the boys managed to score. The boys were all delighted.

"Well done!" shouted Kakko and shook her brother's hand and got all the other players to do the same.

"Victors can get us all a drink!" she said, bending forward with her hands on her knees.

Shaun and the boy leaders went over to the boat.

"That was fun," said one. "That's a great game. We've got team games here but not quite like this."

"Adnak," said Shaun, "you were brilliant. How you got across to stop that shot from Kakko was top drawer. She hit that so sweetly. You read it."

"Read it?"

"Realised where it was going to go before she hit it."

"Well. Yes. She is good is your sister. I watched her

89

yesterday. She doesn't just hit the ball anywhere, she puts it where you don't think you can reach it. I knew where she would aim so I suppose I was already moving."

"Great stuff, Adnak," said his brother who wasn't noted for complimenting him. "Did you hear the kids chanting your name?"

"Glad you played?" smiled Shaun. "You're a natural in goal."

"Thanks," said Adnak.

When everyone had finished drinking it was time for more activities.

"Who here can swim?" asked Kloa.

Not one of the children raised their hands, only the leaders.

"Well it's about time you learnt," said Kloa. "Each of you children… when I say… Fran you don't know what you're doing yet… wait. When I say… find a leader to teach you… wait for it… if there are more than two of you, find someone else. Wait… Go!"

Adnak and Shaun were rushed at by the boys. They all wanted them. But it soon worked out. They all took off their T-shirts and shorts. It was now mid-afternoon and this was the first time anyone had glimpsed a swim-suit. The children, on the other hand, had no swimming things, but they did not hesitate before ripping off all of their clothes and trotting down the beach naked. The waves were gentle in this part of the inlet and the beach shelving, ideal for safe swimming. Kakko wondered what it must be like to own an island. Beautiful view, lovely sand, blue sea – but lonely. (She needed her friends and family around her on a beach.) Without anyone to share it with, you could be very sad. It wasn't surprising that the island was uninhabited.

Soon the leaders were demonstrating and then holding the children while they tried the strokes. It was interesting for Kakko, Shaun and Bandi to watch because in this place it appeared they all began learning on their backs.

The kids were definitely nervous, but all of them brave. Some of them were noisy, some quiet, some out-going, some shy – but they were all brave. *I guess they have to be to survive without parents,* thought Kakko. Her mother had taken her to the swimming baths for as long as she could remember. She couldn't really recall learning to swim any more than she could remember learning to walk. But this was probably the first time these children had even tried it. They made good progress for a first lesson and Kloa congratulated them all.

Then she led them all off to the shade of some trees that overhung the beach. They dressed and put large quantities of sun-oil on their faces and exposed skin. This was a game in itself.

The day concluded with a nature tour of the island with Kloa and the others finding interesting shells, leaves and flowers. They even saw the nest of a ground-nesting bird with little chicks in it. They left it carefully covered up. Needless to say, they didn't see any goof-adders.

"Time to go, I think," called Kloa eventually.

"Oh. My binoculars! I left them in the house," said Adnak. "I meant to go back there but I never got a chance. I'll go and get them."

He charged up towards the house while the kids filed onto the boat. Within minutes he was back.

"I need help," he yelled to the crewmen. "There's a man in there who's hurt. Get the first aid kit… and a stretcher."

The crewmen, Shaun and a couple of the leaders arrived at the house to see a man laying twisted on a heap of broken wood, unconscious. He had clearly come through the ceiling. There were bits of it everywhere.

"Looks like he's broken his leg," said Shaun. "And he's definitely hit his head. This is bad… what was he doing here?"

"Paparazzi," said Adnak, picking up a camera with a very long lens. "They follow us all the time. That's why we come here to this island. They can't take pictures from out at sea so easily with the beach tucked away in the inlet."

"How'd he get here and how long has he been here?" asked Shaun.

"No idea. But I don't think this happened too long ago," said Adnak. "There was no sign of him earlier in the day and there were no fresh footsteps up the stairs then. Look, the barricade has been removed. It was there when we arrived."

"I'm reluctant to move him, but we can't leave him here," said a crewman. He carefully felt the man's neck and back. "Seems to be alright. But his legs are both broken and I don't like the look of that head wound… OK. We have to get him onto his back. Shaun, that's your name isn't it?" Shaun nodded. "You hold his head and neck. Try and keep everything straight. Adnak you take that right leg. Careful where it's broken."

Between them they eventually, and very carefully, got the man onto his back on the stretcher and his two legs bound together with a splint padded with their clothes. The crewmen set off carrying him gently to the boat. Shaun and

Adnak stayed to check if there was anything else apart from the camera that might belong to the man.

"Probably upstairs," said Shaun.

"Well if there is, it can stay there," said Adnak. "I'm not going up there."

"No point," agreed Shaun. "If you hadn't left your binoculars that man could have died here. He's a lucky man."

"He is. I expect he was due to be picked up by his mates, but he would certainly have laid there some time before they came to look for him."

As they followed the stretcher down the path, Adnak said to Shaun, "You know what? Today's been great. He," looking at the man on the stretcher, "he wanted to get pictures of us half naked on the beach and put them in the local rag with some suggestive headline saying we are spoilt rich brats."

"Hope he didn't get any pictures like that – I mean us teaching the kids to swim. I wonder what he got?"

"Guess he went up the stairs to get a better view."

When they got back to the boat they checked the camera, which was remarkably undamaged. The last pictures were of the football match. They decided to leave it as it was. Thankfully the man hadn't witnessed the swimming lessons.

11

As the cruiser came into the harbour, Mr Pero, Jalli and Jack walked up to greet them. They were concerned to see an ambulance beside the quay and quickly ascertained that the captain must have radioed to say they were bringing in a casualty.

Jalli was relieved to see Kakko helping to hold back the children as a stretcher was carried off the boat and was put into the ambulance.

"I see Kakko," she whispered to Jack, "and Shaun, and Bandi." They breathed sighs of relief. It wasn't their children, then. But who was it? Then Kloa came over the gangway and the children started to file across. The first ones bounded up to Mr Pero, vying to be the first to tell him the news.

"A papzi," said Fran, "a man with a big camera. He didn't keep the first rule and went up the stairs."

"He didn't keep the second either. I saw him. He was got by a goof-adder," contributed a second child.

"And he didn't come for the picnic when the boat went…" said a third taking a breath and giving not a bad impression of the ship's horn.

"But none of *us* broke any of the rules!" said another.

"That's good," said Mr Pero. "I'm glad to hear it."

"And we learnt to play football. And Adnak saved the boys."

"He jumped a long way and stopped the ball. Kakko had hit it very hard."

"And then we went swimming. Shaun showed me how to float... when can we go again, Mr Pero?"

"Oh. I don't know. That's up to Mr Zookas. Perhaps if you all write him a nice thank you letter..."

"Oh we will."

"How did Adnak save the boys?" asked Jalli of one of the leaders.

"At football. He was... what did Shaun call him?"

"Goalkeeper?" suggested Jack.

"Yes. That's it. He jumped right over and landed on his side but his hand stopped the ball. He was very quick."

"So he didn't go off anywhere?"

"Only when we all did at the beginning, to look around," said Jeno. "But he wasn't allowed upstairs in the house and had to keep on the paths like the rest of us."

"Then he came when the boat went hoot and we had our picnic," added another.

"He kept all the rules," confirmed Fran. "We all did except the papzi man. But he wasn't there to hear Kloa tell us them."

"How did he get there?" asked Jalli.

"I expect he was dropped off round the back of the island to spy on us," replied Adnak. "He could have clearly read the first rule. The stairs were properly barred with a danger warning."

"But we kept all the rules and none of *us* got hurt," explained a little girl dying to contribute to the conversation.

"That's good. That's very good," said Jalli.

"Are you Kakko's mum?" asked Jess.

"Yes."

"She's very good at telling stories. She told us all about Gollocks and how she got to stay with the three furry people in the wood for ever."

"Oh. You mean bears?"

"Yes. There was Daddy Bear," said a little girl in a low voice, "and Mummy Bear…"

"And Baby Bear!" squeaked the little girl.

"Well, you have all had a wonderful time it seems. And now Kloa," said Mr Pero, "I think the house-mother and her team have got something cooking. So perhaps it's time to walk back to the centre."

They all walked back together.

"You had a good time?" asked Jalli of her daughter.

"Brilliant, Mum. And you?"

"I am pleased… Oh, we've had a quiet time visiting Mr Zookas in his great big villa and then had lunch at Paradise House." Jalli was cross with herself for allowing herself to doubt her daughter. She resolved to be less doubting in future. The teenage girl in Paradise House was right: coming from a loving home makes a difference.

Jack read his wife's thoughts, "I bet she behaves twice as grown-up when we aren't around. Away from us, our daughter is an adult…"

"I know, but she doesn't behave like that sometimes," sighed Jalli.

"Mostly at home where she has always been the child."

"I guess that's it. Perhaps we ought to trust her a bit more than we do."

★★★

That evening Mr Pero entertained them in his restaurant. It was good, he said, to sit with them and not have to concern himself with what was happening in the kitchen – but, of course, he did. But at the end of the meal he was satisfied. He had ordered the best for his guests and the kitchen had delivered. Of course he knew the panic that must have entered the hearts of the staff having to cook him, their greatest critic, the most complicated dish.

"By the way," said Mr Pero, "apparently, that photographer is expected to make a full recovery. I got a message from his family. They are very grateful to you all for saving his life."

"Let's hope he learned his lesson about spying," said Jalli.

"Doubt it. But he might have learned that you should obey the rules of the leader if you want to be safe. I don't think he has much of a sense of moral values."

"You never know," said Jack. "People change don't they? Look at Zookas. And now his children are being heroes for the Paradise children."

"True, you never do know the extent of change that is possible."

At the end of the meal Jalli called the waiter and said, "Our compliments to the chef."

"And mine," Pero added. The waiter beamed.

Then Mr Pero took his leave of them.

"It may be another twenty years," said Jack with a sigh.

"In that case I will most probably be in another dimension," replied Mr Pero. "Go well and have fun!"

"We will. We have learnt so much from you. But don't count on us not coming back. We never know."

★★★

The following morning the 'sun' shone just as brightly.

Kakko picked up the local newspaper. Their trip did not appear on the scandal page, but the front page. The headline ran, 'EX STREET KIDS GIVEN TREAT' which was followed by, 'Zookas' family and friends take Paradise Centre children for a picnic and swimming lessons.' The picture was of them all crowding round Adnak. There were other pictures but none of the later events of course.

Jack and Jalli resolved to get back to Woodglade as soon as they had eaten their breakfast.

"Do we have to go straight away?" complained Kakko. "Can't we go to the beach one more time before we leave?"

"We – ell," said Jalli, "we mustn't leave Grandma and Nan much longer."

"Oh, please," begged Shaun.

Jack put his hand on Jalli's. "Alright," said Jalli, "but we must not be late."

The sun was shining, the sea was inviting, and Kakko was ready to turn heads in her bright, brief swim-wear. Jack and Jalli settled under a palm tree on white plastic chairs and drank in the hot, spicy air that reminded them of the first time they had come.

"Last time we came I would have thought sitting in the shade very tame," observed Jalli.

"The idea of sitting never occurred to me," smiled Jack. "So what do you think of the Paradise Centre?"

"It reminds me of Wanulka, we had street children of sorts there. We don't know we're born, living on Joh."

"Today – this whole experience of coming here – has been a real eye-opener for the kids."

"Perhaps that's why we had to come."

"One of the reasons," agreed Jack. "It struck me just how much we are used as blessings for one another. You know, when people who really care get together they can strengthen and encourage the giving in each other."

For the second time in a few days, Kakko went home wet. At first, she had changed out of her bikini which she left in the sun to dry, but could not resist going for a last paddle, when, for some inexplicable reason, she got completely re-immersed. Her only option was to wear the evening dress (which she said was a totally naff idea) or put the bikini back on and cover herself with a towel. Jalli remembered that when she had got back to Wanulka twenty-plus years ago, she had worn her bikini too under her clothes, and had even scattered sand in the living room at home, so she said nothing. It would be good to get back and see her grandma and Matilda again. They might even have some of her grandmother's beans for tea.

Meanwhile up on the headland Zookas was congratulating his children. "This, son, is the best thing you've ever done," he said to his second born. "Keep it up."

"I intend to," said Adnak. "We've all volunteered to help them at the Paradise Centre. They're starting up football and they want us to help them get going. Kakko and Shaun have told us all the rules and how big a football pitch is meant to be. So, Dad, all we need is a bit of flat land to play it on. Can we use that field by the river where the animals are?"

"I can't see why not."

"We'll have to move the animals and mow the grass."

"Oh. Is that all?"

"Not quite," said his sister as keen as her brother. "Kakko has explained that the people in each team need different colour uniforms. She calls it a 'strip'. Can we buy shirts and shorts for them?"

"Why not?" said her father. "But that's it. No more!" But Zookas thought to himself, *If this helps my children become better and more respected citizens then it is not only Pero and his kids that will benefit.* Zookas was happy.

And Adnak, reflecting on the past unexpected and unplanned day, felt happy too.

12

Jalli took a last, long look at the bay over-looked by the Zookas' villa, as she ushered her family though the white gate that led back into the cottage garden. She stepped through the hedge, the setting seaside sun on her back, and then was suddenly caught in a burst of torrential rain. Matilda would have said it was coming down like 'stair-rods'. Shaun and Bandi had run across the lawn and had already reached the cottage door. Jalli adjusted her eyes just in time to see an almost naked horizontal figure, face down, limbs splayed, long dark hair streaming out behind, slithering rapidly through the puddles on the water-logged grass. Kakko's left hand was still firmly clasping the corner of her towel, which followed behind like a long, blue fish.

Jack strode out through the rain and headed in the direction of his sons who were banging on the cottage door. He was unaware of Kakko coming to a halt between him and his objective. Jalli went to shout, but before she could utter a sound Jack's right foot had hooked itself under Kakko's leg and he went down face first with a momentous splash. Kakko got to her knees and sloshed over to her father. Jalli grimaced.

Jalli covered the distance with more care than Kakko and joined her bending over Jack. He could easily have planted a heavy shoe somewhere painful on Kakko, or done himself a serious injury, but both seemed relatively unscathed.

"So," said Jack, lifting his head and getting his hands under him, "welcome home!"

"You alright, Dad?"

"*I* am. What about you? What on earth were you doing laying down in front of me in a puddle?"

"I slipped."

"So it seems. You OK?"

"I am." Looking up into her mother's face now framed in wet rats' tails, she added, "Sorry." Then she saw the funny side of it. Her mum was kneeling on the grass in a puddle and her dad was wiping mud off his face, and Kakko began to laugh. Gathering his breath her father joined her and, then, reluctantly, Jalli allowed herself a slight smile. She took Jack's hand to tug him up.

"What are you lot playing at?" barked Shaun. "We can't get in!"

"Nan and Grandma won't be out," shouted Jalli. "Knock."

"We have," replied Bandi. "No-one's in. The door's locked."

"The greenhouse," said Jack.

"What! We have to all pile into the greenhouse? I'm perishing," said Kakko, the humour gone. She was now cold and felt herself decidedly under-dressed, her brief bikini was totally inappropriate. She had suddenly become embarrassed.

"No," said Jack, "I mean there is a spare key in the greenhouse... at least there used to be. We haven't ever needed it."

"Yes," said Jalli, "I remember. It was a long time ago – before Bandi was born. We put it there in case anyone came home and I had gone to the hospital to have the baby unexpectedly."

"I remember," said Kakko. "It was under the last brick on the left at the far end. You showed me when I was a little kid. Will it still be there?"

"I expect so," said Jack. "No-one has moved it. Go and look."

Kakko stepped with care around the side of the house. The path was rough under her feet and there were stones on the flags that led to the greenhouse. *Why me?* Kakko thought to herself. Water gushed off the greenhouse roof and ran in a little stream down to the hedge behind. The rain was not making any sign of letting up. With difficulty Kakko slid open the glass door. It moved reluctantly but eventually she got it open and put a foot carefully onto dry soil. Inside Kakko smelled the sweet scent of the plants and vines that lined the glass walls. In here it was dry, warm and welcoming, Kakko felt she had wronged the little glass house, and then thought, *Why not me? I did say I remembered where the key used to be. And it's nice in here.* Making her way to the end she lifted the little brick her mother had shown her fourteen years before and there it was. The key was caked in soil, but, when she picked it up and knocked it on the brick, most of the dirt fell away.

***

Once inside the house the young people rushed upstairs and began stripping off their wet things. Kakko made a beeline for her bedroom, gathered the first top and jeans she could see (most probably not clean) and was in the bathroom and had locked the door before anyone could do anything to stop her.

"At least she could have let us use the toilet," despaired Bandi. "She'll be in there an age now."

"Doubt it," said Shaun, "the boiler's off. There will be no hot water. Where are Nan and Grandma?"

Downstairs Jack and Jalli were sitting around the kitchen table. The kettle was on. Jalli found a short note that had been put in the middle of the table under an empty fruit bowl.

"They've gone to hospital," she said.

"Hospital?" queried Jack.

"Yes. Listen. Your mum put a note on the table. It says, 'Grandma took a bad turn in the night. I rang the doctor and he sent for an ambulance. We're going to City Hospital straight away. Grandma needs tests. She's not in pain but she looks very unwell and can't walk.'"

"When was the note written?" asked Jack.

"She's put, '2 a.m.'"

"That could be last night or the night before."

"No, it's last night. They brought in post and put it on the side. That means they were definitely here the first afternoon. If it had been yesterday the post would still be in the box."

"Anyway, that's still over fifteen hours and they haven't come back. They must have kept Grandma, and Mum has stayed with her."

"Or she's gone to Ada's. That's not far from the hospital. That way she can be on hand. She knows we'll go down to the hospital as soon as we get in."

"You're right," said Jack. "I wonder what's wrong? We'd better get changed and get down there."

"Aren't you hungry?"

"Jalli. We need to get to your grandma... I don't want to panic you but if they've kept her in..."

"You're right. I'll make this tea and go and change."

Kakko was screaming about the lack of hot water. The boys had changed and weren't really bothered about getting washed. Jalli explained what they had read in the note. They would leave in half-an-hour. Kakko emerged from the bathroom.

"What's up Mum?"

"Grandma's in hospital. Your dad and I are going straight there."

"I'm coming too!"

"No. There's no point. They won't let us all in. And," she smiled, looking at her daughter in a scrunched top and dirty trousers, and with her newly towelled hair looking like something out of a horror movie, "I doubt they'll let you in like that and we need to get off. I made some tea. Come down when you're ready boys. Shaun you're in charge of seeing you and your brother and sister eat."

"Shaun?" said Kakko. "*He* can't cook!"

"Now, I don't want you to fight," sighed Jalli, as the thought of her sick grandma flooded over her. "Not now!"

"Sorry, Mum," said Kakko, truly seeing the point and enveloping her mother in a cuddle. "We won't. Tell Grandma we'll be in to see her tomorrow."

"Or bring her home," said Bandi quietly.

"We'll ring you when we've seen her," said Jack coming down the stairs. "Don't forget the tea. It's ready to drink."

★★★

The hospital stood glistening, clean and bright in the last rays of the sun now emerging from behind the clouds that were clearing over the mountains that flanked the coastal plain to the east. The storm had passed and Jalli felt hope rising in her chest as she sucked in the clean, soft air.

Inside they were directed to a first-floor ward. They pushed open the double doors and approached the nurses' station and asked to see Momori Rarga.

"You say you're her daughter?" asked the nurse.

"No, her granddaughter. She brought me up. My parents are dead… and this is my husband."

"Glad to see you. You are aware of your grandmother's condition?"

"No. We… we've been away for a couple of days. We just got this note saying she was brought in last night."

"I'm afraid Mrs Rarga is very ill. Come this way and I'll explain." The nurse took Jalli and Jack into a little room with soft chairs. "Mrs Rarga has some internal bleeding. We've done tests to see if we can identify where it is coming from, and we're still not sure. The bleeding isn't stopping. We're giving her a lot of blood, and that is keeping her alive. If she is going to recover from this she will need an exploratory operation, but even then they may not be able to do anything. It will depend on what they can find. And I'm afraid there is a significant chance that she will not survive the operation."

Jalli fell into Jack's arms. As long as she could remember she had always had her grandma. She was there when her parents died. It was she who took Jalli to school on her first day. It was she who had kept Jalli going after the dreadful events in Parmanda Park. And it was she who had conspired with Mr Bandi to get Jalli to see how stupid she was behaving towards Jack and had encouraged her into a relationship with a boy from a completely different world and let her be married at a ridiculously young age. And it was she who had been there as Jalli's children had been born. They had never lived apart in all that time.

"She is not in any pain. None at all," added the nurse. "I'll take you to see her."

The nurse conducted them to a private room with a view across the ocean. Jalli saw an ashen-faced lady in a hospital nightdress slumped against a pile of pillows and thought there must be some mistake. This woman was not her grandma. But then she saw Matilda spring out of a chair to greet them.

"Jack, Jalli. I'd no idea how long… I was worried…"

Jack put a strong arm around her.

"OK Mum, we're here now. We came as soon as we got back."

Jalli was leaning over her grandmother, "Grandma."

Momori open her eyes and smiled.

"Jalli… Sorry."

"Sorry, what for? You sound like Kakko."

"Do I? I'm so tired. But now you're here…" Momori clasped her granddaughter's hand and closed her eyes once more.

"She keeps calling Dang," said Matilda. "I've never met him of course."

"Dang. I am going to meet him, and my son, your father… and all of them," murmured Momori.

A nurse came into the room and checked the cannula beside the bed and then Momori's pulse.

"Who is this Dang you keep calling?" she asked.

"My husband, my dear husband," said Momori, summoning strength.

"Grandfather died along with my parents and brother, uncle, aunt and cousins in a flood," explained Jalli. "Only me and Grandma survived. She was all I had."

"But now," whispered Momori, "she has this wonderful man and a beautiful family."

"And a good friend in Matilda," added the nurse.

"She's my sister."

"Sister-in-law," said Matilda. "Jack here is my son. But Momori and I have lived together for over twenty years. Our children saw to that."

"But now I must go," sighed Momori.

"You're not going anywhere Grandma," asserted Jalli, "not yet. You have to get better first."

"No. I am going to Dang, and…"

"Grandma. No. Don't give up. They'll get you better…"

"Oh I *must* go. I must. The time has come. I am looking forward to it. I want to be with him again… where are your children?"

"Oh. At home. Hopefully behaving themselves!"

"They always behave themselves," smiled Momori.

"Grandma, they are going to do an operation and make you well," said Jalli.

"No. No operation. The time has come…"

"Grandma," wept Jalli. "You must…"

"No, Jalli. It is the way it should be. I have a future to go to. They have been waiting for me long enough. You no longer need me. You have Jack, the children, and Matilda here."

"We *do* need you, Grandma," sobbed Jalli. "*I* need you!"

"No… you *want* me, but you don't *need* me."

Jack came around the bed and took her other hand.

"I'll look after her, Grandma!"

"You'd better!"

"Nothing I want to do more."

"Of course not. You were destined for one another forever, as I am for Dang."

There was a slight tap on the door. It was Pastor Ruk from the church.

"Hello," he said. Then to Momori, "I heard you were here and thought I would come and see you."

Momori summoned up more strength to smile.

"She says she doesn't want the operation," complained Jalli.

"What operation?" asked the pastor.

"To find out where the bleeding is and stop it."

"Ah, I see." Jack stood up and made way for him. "…and you don't want this operation?"

"No. I'm too tired. My time has come," and Momori closed her eyes and sighed.

"Can I say a prayer?" said Ruk. Momori nodded. "Dear Lord God, we thank you so much for Momori. We ask you to bless her now, bless her with healing, and new life and all that she needs. Grant peace to her and all her family. Give the doctors and nurses here wisdom. Show them what it is you want for Momori and be with her, always. Amen."

"Thank you," said Jack.

"No operation," murmured Momori, and she drifted into sleep.

Ten minutes later the ward sister appeared and asked to see Jalli. Jack rose to his feet and Jalli took his hand.

"I will stay here, you all go and talk to Sister," said Ruk.

Back in the little room, the sister explained that the nurse had reported that Momori had consistently refused to have an operation.

"We cannot make her if she doesn't want to. And I must be frank with you, the doctor isn't happy with it either. The chances of her coming through are fifty-fifty at best, and they really don't know if it would help even then. If she wants it, we would do it. But she seems to have made up her mind, and I think if I were in her place," she added, "I would do the same."

Jack took hold of Jalli's arm, "She's happy and content. She wants to step into her new world. She can see her white gate."

"But this one is one way," wept Jalli. "I have never been without her... ever."

"No. But you've always known that she would move on one day. And maybe that day's arrived. It's Dang's turn now, and her children and her mum and dad and *her* grandma."

"You're right. I know you're right. But I just don't want to let her go ..."

"Of course not," said the sister. "You love her."

Jalli nodded.

Matilda spoke, "Can I ask a question?"

"Of course," said Jalli.

"Sister, if you decide not to do the operation, what happens then?"

"She is being sustained by the drip. There is only so much

of that we can do. One or two more bags and that will be it. Then she is on her own."

"…and then she will die," stated Jalli.

The sister nodded her agreement. Jack pulled Jalli closer to him.

"The children, they must be here, she cannot die without them seeing her!"

"That was what I was thinking," said Matilda.

"We'll send a taxi for them," said Jack. Then to the sister, "That's alright isn't it?"

"Of course. The bags will last an hour or two. I think you have made the right decision. You are very brave."

Back beside Momori, Jalli took her grandma's hand. Momori opened her eyes and smiled again.

"You sure you don't want the operation?" asked Jalli. Momori nodded.

"You'll be alright. Your grandma's done a good job. You're a brave girl… sand," she said, moving her hand towards Jalli's neck. "You've been to that beach again haven't you?"

Jalli smiled. "Can't keep anything from you, Grandma."

"Did a good job, didn't I?"

"Sure did, Grandma," said Jack.

"Oh, you. You're just prejudiced!"

"And so are you?"

The sister came in to say she had a message that the great-grandchildren were on their way.

Twenty minutes later, evening visiting had begun and the noise level in the ward had increased. It was fortuitous because it masked the sound of Kakko bursting through the doors of the ward demanding to see Grandma. The life and zest of the younger generation poured in. Their energy was in contrast to the stillness of the ward. A stillness that was, nevertheless, powerful and pregnant. As Shaun and Bandi caught up with their sister, a nurse hushed them and took them into the gentle silence of Grandma's room.

Momori was instantly aware and seemed to make an attempt to sit up. Kakko threw her arms around her.

"Gently," pleaded her mother.

Inside the doors, Shaun and Bandi held back. They were timid and confused. Matilda went across to them.

"What are they doing to make her well?" asked Shaun.

Matilda explained. Shaun protested, but Bandi was more philosophical.

"She believes in heaven," he stated.

"Of course, she has never had any doubt about that. You know the disasters in her life have led her to her faith. God is with her, she knows that. She keeps telling us she is going to see her husband. And I believe it."

★★★

Momori died as the sun rose. The room was flooded with the dawn light and the sun's rays highlighted the tops of the waves on the sea, all the way to the horizon.

★★★

Pastor Ruk conducted the funeral in the local church, which was nearly full. Over the past twenty-two years, Momori had made a big impact on Joh. She had brought many people to the freedom of faith through her quiet witness. The pastor retold her story. Her happiness as a child and mother and young grandmother in a small village that no longer existed, and how her faith had brought her through that and subsequent traumas. Now Momori had accepted God's invitation to sail over the horizon into a new dimension where there was freedom and love beyond our wildest imagination. There, freedom and love, beauty, goodness and justice, peace and joy exist unsullied, unspoilt. And there Momori had gone, where even she would need to be cleansed and forgiven in order to enter. Momori was open to God.

"Meanwhile," Pastor Ruk concluded, "back down here we have to get on with things. We have to be patient until *our* time comes and look after one another, and with God's grace be as good as we can be. Let us look forward to heaven while we enjoy the wealth of this planet – oh, and for those privileged ones among us," he looked towards Jalli, Jack, Matilda, Kakko, Shaun and Bandi on the front row, "whatever planet God takes you to next!"

As Momori's body left for the crematorium, the congregation set out the party food. "We are sharing in Momori's heavenly banquet!" declared Ruk as he prayed over the heaps of sandwiches, pastries and cakes that Momori's friends had produced.

Somehow, to her surprise, Jalli did not cry that day. It was in the middle of the night that she wept silently into her pillow and then felt Jack's arm around her. She was safe, and so was her grandma – they were just not together. One day they would all be in the same place again. She knew that. You couldn't come through all that she and Grandma had done just on wishful thinking. She remembered what Momori had said to her in the hospital that evening, "You *want* me, but you don't *need* me." She was right. And what's more she knew she wanted Jack now more than anything in the universe – but she didn't need him. She was, in one sense, already on her way to heaven. That's where they all belonged. Their real home, for all of them – Grandma, Jack, the children – was beyond all the horizons in all the universes.

13

It was an odd feeling – Momori not being in the cottage. It wasn't just that everyone missed her; it was that up until now they hadn't really understood how central she was to the family. There was a sort of vacuum in their home. A big Grandma-shaped gap. She had been the one who had quietly and naturally presided over them. They hadn't quite realised it before. Momori was just being herself. She hadn't been a dominating person, just wise, thoughtful and loving – the person that had kept everything together in times of crisis and who had naturally been the 'doyenne' ever since.

Matilda felt awkward. From the beginning, Momori had drawn her into everything – been her friend and 'sister', but now Matilda felt superfluous somehow. There was no way she could slip into Momori's role as a kind of matriarch; she wasn't that sort of person. Of course no-one rejected her or anything – it was just so different without Momori. Life was entirely transformed for her as much as any of the others. The others had jobs, college or school. But she and Momori had spent endless hours together, just the two of them, while the others were all busy.

Gradually over the following weeks, Matilda got into going to various events, and then, at the instigation of Ada Pippa, she went on outings with other ladies at the church and social clubs. She and Ada spent more and more time together with Matilda calling on her for afternoon tea at first, then morning coffee too, which gradually led into lunch. Ada almost never came to White Gates Cottage. It was much more cosy in Ada's little two-bedroomed town house. Her sitting room was *hers*; unlike Matilda, she didn't share it with a young family.

One day the two of them booked to go on an outing that got in late and Matilda stayed over with Ada. The grandchildren joked about Nan's 'sleep-over', and teased her about the single men they went with on the trip.

"Nothing like that!" said Matilda horrified. "I gave up on men a long time ago."

"So what about Ada?" laughed Kakko.

"Kakko. It may come as a surprise to you, but dating is not something that we are looking for. Ada had a good husband who has now gone on, and she's content with the knowledge that one day she will meet him again. Until then, we are more interested in the sea, the mountains or whatever else they are taking us to. And I am company enough for her. We don't need *men*! No offence intended to you of course," she added, indicating Jack, Shaun and Bandi.

★★★

One day, about a month after Momori's funeral, Shaun came in from football practice looking really excited.

"What's got into you?" demanded Kakko.

"I'm in the first team next match!" he declared. "I've been selected to play in midfield."

"But you like it up front?"

"I know. But there is no way I'm going to dislodge Rad or Gollip is there? They're brilliant."

"Midfield though. It's different," said Kakko.

"I spent this evening practising. I can come up front a bit when we're attacking. And I can score goals from deep."

"But you've got to get the tackling and passing right," said Kakko, "as well as fall back into defence. I've tried. I'm far better up front."

"Yeah. But you wouldn't say no if you were offered a place in the first team?"

"I *am* in the first team!"

"Yeah, well. It's *my* first chance. And anyway, I *can* tackle. I'll practice on you!"

"Will you?" said Kakko ruefully.

But he did, over and over again on the lawn. Kakko was good but Shaun was getting better. He even persuaded Bandi to run around the 'pitch' and laid off the ball to him after a successful tackle.

★★★

The day of the match came and all the family went to support Shaun. He looked resplendent in his red and yellow shirt.

"Nice colours," observed Jalli.

"What? Claret and blue?" said Jack.

"No," said Kakko knowing her father's history. "It's not West Ham United. You haven't followed them for ages. You've no idea now whether they're in the lower league of something!"

"They won't be. Not West Ham… but that's one thing I

do miss being away from Planet Earth. I always followed the football… so what colour are they?"

"Scarlet with yellow under their arms. They look really clean and bright now but it won't last. Not if they play properly!"

The first half was rather scrappy by both sides, but as the game went on Shaun's team was beginning to make an impact. In fact, to the Smith family's delight, Shaun had made a couple of decent tackles and then landed an almost perfect pass that forced a great save from the goalkeeper. At the beginning of the second half Shaun had the measure of the opposition's forwards. The score was still nil-nil however, but most of the game was in the opposition's half. Coming forward Shaun connected with a lay-off but his shot was far too high, occasioning some jeers from the supporters.

"Keep your head over the ball," advised his captain as they retreated for the goal kick.

"Thanks," replied Shaun. "Just give me another chance!"

But then their rather clumsy centre forward broke through. He wasn't fast and Shaun came across to tackle him on the edge of the area but as soon as Shaun arrived next to him, he went down like a skittle and began rolling around in feigned agony clutching his foot. Shaun stood mesmerised as the referee awarded a free kick against him. He hadn't touched the man! Shaun was livid. He turned to the referee and protested his innocence but the referee just waved him away. Shaun pursued him, indignant, as the forward got up affecting even more pain. The referee took his position ten metres from the ball he had placed, and beckoned Shaun and his team back to his mark. They formed a wall with Shaun on the end.

Surprisingly quickly, the same man who had gone down so heavily recovered to take the free kick. It wasn't well taken. Shaun jumped as the ball was struck, but his arm was too far from his body and the wayward ball connected with his lower arm.

"Ball to hand," yelled Kakko. But the referee was already pointing to the penalty spot.

The goalkeeper dived the wrong way and Shaun's team were one down against the run of play. Then Shaun did something rather silly. He again chased after the referee to complain the injustice of it all and, predictably, the ref produced a yellow card and warned him that more such behaviour would see him sent off. Shaun's captain came racing across and told Shaun to cool it.

After that, the reds struggled and Shaun's passing was not a patch on what it had been. His concentration was shot. After a poorly-timed tackle that could have got him a second yellow and the inevitable red, the coach pulled him off and substituted him. They lost one-nil.

The journey back to White Gates Cottage was not an easy one. Shaun was more sullen than Jalli had ever known him. He did not say a word and no-one else dared to either. Even Kakko thought better of complimenting him on his purple patch. She had been really impressed and felt that her brother seemed actually cut out for midfield, but she knew he wasn't ready to hear that – even from her.

That evening began equally painfully. Jalli couldn't help feeling that her grandma would have done something to ease the situation; she couldn't help remembering her weeks of depression following the Parmanda Park thing and how patient Grandma must have been with her. But Momori was no longer there. Shaun took himself to his room and Jalli resolved to break the tension and get them sorted for the evening meal. When it was ready she called for Shaun. When he didn't come, Jack decided to be firmer and demanded Shaun come for dinner.

"Even the street kids are not allowed to miss a meal," he reminded him, "and besides it is your mum's attempt at beans the 'Grandma way' and she needs your support." Shaun came, but still wore his pout.

After various congratulations to Jalli on her beans, which were good but not the same of course, Kakko thought she would open the subject. She rushed straight in.

"That ref was totally out of order," she stated. "It was clearly a dive. He needs to visit the optician."

"It makes no fucking difference though does it?" swore Shaun.

"Shaun!" exclaimed Jalli. "I didn't know you knew that word!"

"Well, I do. And I'll use it again! The fact was that I got a *fucking* yellow for doing *fuck* all!"

Jalli began to cry.

Jack reacted. He was shocked to hear his son swear, and he was instinctively protective of Jalli. He rose to his feet…

Matilda tugged his arm, "Surely, it's only a game isn't it? It's not as if it matters."

Shaun stood up clattering his chair against the cupboard, and stormed out of the room.

Jack put his arm around Jalli who now was really crying hard. Matilda sat stunned; she seemed to have stopped breathing. Bandi put his hand on hers and Kakko explained:

"That's what happens when you live in a world full of cheats and injustice. They generally win. I bet that stupid centre-forward is even claiming the credit for that goal. If Shaun hadn't jumped so well he would never have connected with it and the ball would have trickled out to the corner flag."

Bandi said nothing. He was thinking, *What would Grandma do here?* He reasoned to himself, she would leave it twenty minutes and then go knock on his door with a cup of tea. Shaun would have opened to *her* and she would have just smiled at him. She might have said, if she had said anything, "Actually Shaun, the swearing apart, you are right. And your football's quite good," and then leave him with the tea and say, "Your dinner's on the side when you feel like it. The others are all in the front room."

Jack made to go to the door in pursuit of Shaun but Jalli held him back, "No leave him!" she said.

"But he can't…"

"Leave him!"

Jack relaxed, angry but obedient.

"Finish your dinner," she ordered. Bandi picked up the chair.

After several minutes of silent eating, Matilda sighed, "Did I say anything wrong?"

"No," said Jack. "It's the elephant in the room isn't it?"

"The what?" spluttered Kakko, her mouth full of beans. "I can't see an elephant!"

"That's the point," said Matilda understanding exactly what

Jack meant. She hadn't heard the expression since she had left England. "It's so big, but we're all trying not to see it."

"You mean... Grandma?" ventured Bandi.

"Yes," said Matilda.

"You mean Shaun is missing Grandma?"

"You could be right," said Jalli. "He has been trying so hard to look after the rest of us that he's not had a chance to... to..."

"To grieve?" finished Jack. Jalli nodded.

"Everyone has been looking after me, and then Jack and Nan. That's what Ada's been doing isn't it?"

"Yes," said Matilda. "She just lets me talk."

"But Shaun has had no-one to talk to. Kakko says exactly what she thinks and I bet you've told all your friends about it."

"Yes. And Bandi talks to God," put in Kakko. "I've heard him pray. He even tells Grandma what he's been up to at school!"

"Kakko," said Bandi, "you shouldn't be listening!"

"Well, it's hard not to when you pray so loud! But I bet Shaun never talks about his grandma with his football mates. They'd think him a wimp."

"What are we going to do?" asked Matilda.

"Leave him... for a bit. I can't take any more just now," said Jalli and began to cry again. Jack gathered her up in his arms and kissed her wet cheek. Bandi checked the time.

After the washing up was done it was almost twenty minutes later. The family moved to the sitting room with their mugs and Bandi quietly mounted the stairs. He took a mug of tea as if to take it to his own room, but instead knocked lightly on Shaun's door.

"Do you want some tea?" he asked softly. "I've got some here."

To his surprise Shaun opened the door. A mug of tea was exactly what he wanted. "They've all gone to the sitting room. Your dinner's still in the kitchen if you want it. Do you want me to fetch it?"

"No," said Shaun, and then, "thanks."

"No trouble. I... I didn't get a chance to say this, but today you were actually quite good. Kakko thinks that too. She says you're a natural midfield player. And... when the coach pulled you off he said to get you off because he doesn't want you banned for next week..."

"The coach said that? All he said to me was to stop being stupid."

"Because he wants you in the team next time, I suppose. Drink your tea before it gets cold. I've got mine downstairs." Bandi turned to leave.

"Thanks," said Shaun.

Thank you, Grandma, said Bandi to himself as he skipped down the stairs.

★★★

The following morning Shaun was in a sweat about having to face his family. He had spent the middle of the night seeing his behaviour of the previous day from the outside. His indignation on the pitch, his stroppiness in the changing room and, above all, his behaviour towards his family. He kept seeing himself send the chair flying and storming out of the kitchen... and the look on his mother's face! He had really hurt her and none of it was her fault. He had taken out his anger towards that cheat of a so-called football player on his family. What his nan thought of him he dared not imagine. At first he told himself that hers had been an uncalled for remark. It *wasn't* just about football; it was more than that. It was the principle! Didn't she see that? But then around three in the morning it struck him. When his father was a year older than Shaun was now he had been a footballer, but then some monster had kicked his head in and stopped all his football and lots of other things, utterly changing his life. Perhaps that was what she was thinking. How did being the victim of a cheat on the pitch compare with what happened to his dad? He felt cold and bad.

He walked nervously into the kitchen, head lowered.

"Hi Shaun," said Kakko cheerily. His nan also looked as if she had had a good night. His mother was humming a tune over preparing some batter to stand for the evening meal. Bandi was reading a paper.

"Hi," muttered Shaun. "Nan, sorry about yesterday."

"Oh, don't worry about that. Better out than in. Do you want some cereal?"

Had he imagined what had happened? Shaun was confused.

Kakko smiled at him.

"Kakko," whispered Shaun sitting next to her at the table, "I made a fool of myself last night. I'm sorry."

"No problem. Someone had to do it."

"It isn't just about what happened on the pitch…"

"No. You made us see the elephant in the room and now we can talk about it."

"Elephant?"

"Big, grey animal on Planet Earth One."

"I know what an elephant is. But if there were an elephant here we'd see it."

"Exactly. But we were trying to ignore it. It's a saying Dad came up with. It means avoiding the thing we are all aware of but don't want to talk about."

Shaun began, "What...?" Then, "Grandma?"

"Got it. But you led us to understand that. We all felt cheated... the whole thing about Grandma going so suddenly didn't seem fair."

"But that's the way it is," said Jalli coming over. "And if being angry helps then we need to be angry. Last night we all got angry. It wasn't with you, or that idiot of a cheating football player. So we had a night of complaining."

"To whom?"

"Oh, God of course!"

"But He didn't... didn't kill Grandma."

"Didn't He? In Grandma's case He might not have sent a thunderbolt from heaven, but it is God who has made us, taught us to love and then rips us apart when people die. Is that fair?"

"Well, if you put it like that, no. So you all got angry with God?"

"Last night after you had gone to your room we said everything we had been bottling up, sometimes for years. Grandma had helped us do that with her patience. Jack and I, we thought we had got over that monster in Wanulka, but we hadn't. We called it the 'park thing' if we mentioned it at all, but we avoided it most of the time. I hate that bastard, and I hated God for letting it happen. Last night you got into trouble for your bad language. After you had gone I used all those words and more, and so did your dad …"

"And me," said Nan.

"Totally shocked," smiled Kakko slurping on her cereal.

"But we got it all out!" stated Jalli firmly.

"So it's God's fault?"

"Partly. That rapist has to take some of the blame. We all have to take our share. But, yes, God has to take His bit too."

"So does that mean we can't worship Him anymore?"

"No, quite the opposite," said Jalli. "You see, God is big enough to take the blame. Ever since He made us He has worked to get things right. He has not walked away. He has never asked to be given five stars for His creation. He wants justice and knows that that applies to Him as well. It is He who has also created love, justice and perfect goodness and is subject to those too."

"But God doesn't suffer. God doesn't have to do without Grandma, or put up with evil people. He's in heaven."

"But, he isn't just in heaven," said Kakko.

"If you love someone, where does your heart belong?" asked Jalli.

"With the one you love," answered Shaun.

"And if the one you love suffers… what then?"

"Then it hurts."

"Sometimes more than the one who suffers."

"So if God loves us, He suffers too?"

"All the time," said Kakko.

"So we get cross with Him, but all the time He is suffering as much as we are. And He has all the universe, perhaps universes, shouting at Him and He hurts for all of them too. Who would be God? Someone worthy of our praise! Last night we started by blaming Him and ended up by praising Him."

"And you know what?" said Nan. "I've never felt so blessed. We brought out all the elephants in the room and some of the skeletons in the cupboards too."

"Skeletons?" Shaun was again confused.

"Same as elephants only they're inside us. Hidden in secret compartments in our heads," explained Kakko, who had only just learned what that meant herself.

"Right. So what I did last night…"

"Was the catalyst. So don't be sorry."

Just then Shaun's phone vibrated in his pocket.

"It's from the coach. I'm in next week's match. He wants me in for extra training. Am I free tomorrow?"

"Told you you were good," said Bandi. The first thing he had said all morning.

14

"Tam," yelled the climbing coach, "red ones only! Ignore the blue ones, I want you to be more ambitious. You can do it! That's it, swing your right leg, let go on the left and propel yourself across." Tam resolved to attempt what was required; he had determination, but lacked confidence. It was not really about fear for his life – his *life* did not depend on him making this leap because he was suspended on a rope and knew that he could not fall. And in any case he was not that high up and the mats below him at the foot of the climbing wall in the gym were thick and soft. But on the bench opposite watching him were the other members of the club and, in particular, Kakko. He was determined to impress her... although in his heart of hearts he doubted if he ever would – but a devoted suitor like him would never admit that to himself.

Tam swung his right leg as instructed and grabbed for the red hold. He managed to touch it but it slid from his grasp and he swung out into empty space... again. Watching from below, Kakko sighed. He was such a wimp. He *could* do it, she was sure. The problem was that he didn't believe in himself enough.

Kakko had joined the climbing club six months before and had made rapid progress. *She* put a smile on the coach's face. *She* was the star of the Sports Centre and coach had already spoken to her about entering competitions with other centres. But Tam was different. He had struggled from the beginning, even with the simplest yellow holds. When the blue eventually came within his ability he just about managed, but the red level was defeating him. In truth it was only his devotion to Kakko that kept him at it. But unless he managed to make some better progress he was not going to impress; yet to give up would leave him no hope at all. He must succeed, he told himself.

Tam and Kakko had met in high school and he had always admired her. He thought it a privilege at times that she even condescended to talk to him. They had been the only ones from Woodglade, so they had got to travel to and from home on the bus together and they became friends. But that was as far as it had gone. At sixteen, Kakko had left school for the Agricultural Vocational Institute, and the following year Tam went to study law in the university. For longer than he dared admit, he would have liked it to have been more than just a friendship between neighbours. Tam didn't disabuse his male mates if they thought he and Kakko were dating, but in truth he had nothing to show for it. Kakko was not unaware of his interest of course, but had decided to keep it low key. He was a good friend and she didn't want to spoil that – she liked him – so she had just ignored his subtle advances. When Kakko told him she was going to see if she could join the climbing club, Tam suggested he came too. Kakko had not been enthusiastic about it, but she couldn't stop him if he wanted to (after all Joh was a free world she told herself) but she didn't go out of her way to encourage him. Now his failure to make progress on the walls confirmed her belief that even though he was quite attractive in some ways, he was a wimp. She was adventurous and daring, while Tam was naturally rather cautious, a quality that she saw as weakness.

Tam began again at the wall, determined to get to the top using only the red holds. He studied the wall carefully and knew where he wanted to go, but achieving it was another matter. Smothering chalk on his hands he went for it, but this time failed even before he got to the most challenging part. His strength was failing; he would have to rest.

In the next quarter of an hour, Tam watched Kakko hanging upside down under an overhang, at times only having two holds under control, and he cheered with everyone else as she hauled herself over the ledge and quickly attained the top.

"OK folks, that will do for this evening," announced the coach. Tam was not going to get another chance at the red holds. He was disappointed, but secretly relieved.

"Don't forget," continued the coach, "those of you who are coming on the abseiling trip on Saturday, the bus is leaving Woodglade at 6 a.m. Don't come here, the centre will not be open and there is no early public transport. Chak, Zebby and Tionga, I will pick you up from your homes in my car and leave it in Woodglade. Kakko, Pol and Tam (you are joining us, Tam?) you will be outside White Gates Cottage, when?"

"6 a.m.," returned Pol.

"Cate and Girly be outside your house at 6.10 a.m. Marvellous. See you Saturday. The weather forecast is good but bring something a bit warm… and climbing boots of course."

Voices echoed around the centre as the young people all

began talking and laughing at once. They were excited about the abseiling because it was good to be outdoors, up on the ridge above the coastal plain where they lived.

"Hey, you two," the coach called to Kakko and Tam, as they packed their kit. "Will you take a bag of tackle with you and some rope ready for Saturday? I'll have a struggle getting everything in my small car with three other people and their kit. It will help enormously. It's a bit heavy but it'll help strengthen those arms, eh, Tam!"

Tam smiled away the jibe. It didn't do any good getting cross. He shouldered a hank of rope and took one handle of the bag filled with abseiling equipment. Kakko took more rope and the other handle. Between them it was not more than a bit awkward and they made their way successfully to the bus stop.

"A bit of good teamwork," suggested Tam. "On Saturday when I fall you can come and rescue me."

"Don't talk like that, Tam! It's all in the mind – that's what's wrong with you."

★★★

When they got off the bus there wasn't far to walk to White Gates Cottage. But right opposite the gate, in the gathering dusk, Kakko spotted something strange. She turned and, the bag being between them, Tam turned with her. Kakko stared.

"What are you looking at?" asked Tam.

"There. Just there. The hedge seems to bulge. See? It's as if it is folded over on itself, and in the middle of it there is a shiny white gate!"

"Yeah, I see it. In the hedge. A strange white gate. And above it there is a kind of fold in the whole world!"

"Exactly." Kakko turned and looked at Tam, staring in front of him.

"It's strange," Tam closed his eyes, rubbed them and looked down. Then back up to the hedge. "It isn't an illusion is it?" he whispered. "I am sure it's real... you can see it too, so it is not just my imagination."

"I can see it, and I know what it is."

"What?"

"It's a portal: a door into another world. It's the way we go to other places with my mum and dad. This is the same thing."

"What should we do?"

"Go through the gate, of course. We are being summoned. We are needed in the world beyond."

"We?"

"Yes, we. Strange as it may seem, you are being called too."

"We can't go anywhere now. We're expected home."

"Oh, they'll understand. At least, my family will. We have to go when we are asked to." And with that Kakko slipped her phone out of her jeans' pocket and called home, even if it was only a few metres away. "Hi, Mum, we've seen a white gate just outside the cottage... we have to go through it... but, *Mum*, you *know* we can't wait... well, you can come out and see if you can see it and if you can you can join us. We're going now, OK...? OK... Oh, and Tam – he's seeing it too. Can you call his family? Bye Mum!"

"Wow. I couldn't talk to my parents like that," said Tam.

"I'm not being rude. What's wrong with being assertive? After all I *am* eighteen."

"My mum says you're headstrong and tells me to be careful."

"That's exactly what's wrong with you. You're *too* careful. You'll never achieve anything without calculated risks."

"But Mum worries that you don't calculate enough."

"Mums are like that. But they have to let their kids go. Now, are you coming or what?"

Jalli arrived just in time to see Tam's trailing leg disappearing through the hedge. There was no doubt they had gone. But she herself saw no white gate – the hedge was as solid as it had always been. The only reason she had seen anything at all was because Tam had been hesitant and had stood for a while in the gate and Kakko had had to yank him through with the handle of the bag they were both holding. The fact was, Kakko was determined to get through the white gate before her mother arrived. And she was a bit sore at being called headstrong by Tam's parents, which made her even more determined to be independent. Her nan sometimes said things like, 'Nothing ventured, nothing gained' and 'the one who hesitates is lost'. These expressions, Kakko told herself, were apt, and justified her actions. Too many people missed out on things because they were too slow, or too nervous. People's insistence that they approach life cautiously could be dangerous, she believed. Even her parents, who had been noted for their adventures in the past, had seemingly lost their willingness to really 'go for it' and pondered things too much.

★★★

In their new world, Kakko and Tam found themselves surrounded on three sides by trees, but in front of them was a narrow track which they followed. Here, it seemed, it was daytime. Emerging from the trees they realised they were on a cliff-top path with a beautiful view across an ocean. The sky above the horizon was almost indistinguishable from the sea below it. In the middle distance the water became a richer, deeper blue. Inshore, they could see white surf rise and fall where rocks broke through the waves. The sun was hot and the air was full of the rich scents given off by the bushes mixed with the tang of salt from the sea and the fine spicy dust of the path. At first, the only other sounds they were aware of were those of the sea-birds screaming as they hovered on the thermals rising up the cliff, but they became quickly conscious that among the screams of the birds were those of a woman.

They dropped the bag and ran in the direction of the sound. A group of people had gathered at the top of the cliff and were peering over the edge.

"My son, my son!" the woman was shouting. "My son ran too near the edge and he's disappeared! Ron! Ron!" she called again. But below all was silent.

"There! There he is!" yelled one of the men. "He is there on that small ledge. He is not all the way down… he doesn't seem to be moving."

Kakko approached. "We have ropes and equipment. Let me go down to him. Tam let me have your rope, and fetch a metal descender needed for abseiling. You know the one." Tam moved to obey without question – he was still taking all this in. He went back up the track and searched in the bag among the collection of abseiling tackle for what looked to be the right piece of equipment. He had never been abseiling before, but he knew what Kakko was looking for. He reappeared hoping he had the right thing and was relieved to see her happy with what he brought her. Kakko arranged the descender so that it locked when she slid the rope through it. This would enable her to descend on the rope a bit at a time safely. She looped Tam's rope around a small tree close to the edge of the cliff and pulled. It seemed good. Then, using a bowline knot, she tied one end of the rope around her waist and turned her back to the void and leaned back, allowing her weight to tighten the rope. She carefully checked that her own hank of rope was secure around her shoulders. Kakko looked the super heroine; her long dark brown hair tied in a ponytail blew upwards. "I am going to tie my rope around the child," she explained, and when I am back we can pull him up." She let out a little more rope and took a step down the cliff. Step-by-step she descended the cliff, getting ever closer to the child.

Then, as Tam watched Kakko making her steady way down, the rope made a sudden jerk. He heard a gasp from the onlookers. The roots of the small tree to which Kakko had secured the rope were coming away from the rocky cliff-top and it began to lean over the cliff edge. Kakko's weight was tugging it out of the insecure soil. Tam shouted to Kakko, but at that same moment the tree and the surrounding soil and rocks seemed to leap into the air and then hurtle down the cliff. Kakko fell some four metres onto the same ledge as the child while the tree and loose soil and stones clattered over and around them. She was covered in dirt as the tree just missed her and hurtled to the bottom with a series of crashes. It was followed by the sound of small debris settling, and then silence. Kakko was lucky. The rope had come free of the tree as it fell and was hanging limply from Kakko's waist. Kakko moaned.

"Kakko! Kakko!" yelled Tam. "Are you all right?"

"Yes… no. Ouch!" she said, barely audibly.

"Hold on Kakko, I'm coming," shouted Tam. "Don't move!"

He had no rope – Kakko had them both – and no equipment. One false move and he would either join them on the ledge or fall to the bottom. Tam studied the cliff-face. He decided not to climb directly down. He could dislodge a stone or fall himself and that would not be good news for the people on the shelf below.

Gingerly Tam stepped over the cliff edge. The on-lookers seemed confused to know what to do. Some clearly wanted to stop him. The mother was in a distraught heap on the ground. But Tam ignored everything except the footholds he was seeking. Carefully, inch-by-inch, he descended the cliff-face. It took him ten long minutes but eventually he found himself above and to one side of the ledge. He sized up the available holds. He thought he could just make it in six without too much of a stretch. He imagined himself just using yellow holds. He could do those. He swung out his right leg and took a hold with his right hand cleanly enough. One move. Lowering his right leg he found a projection, which he tested. It held. Two moves. Then he put his left hand down to his waist level and felt for a hold there. Three moves. Tam followed that with his left leg. Bending his right knee he felt for the step he thought he had seen from above. He found it and it, too, seemed good. He transferred his weight. Four moves. Kakko looked up. "Tam," she croaked.

"Don't move!" he ordered as he brought his right hand down about forty centimetres. Five moves. And finally, Tam lowered his right leg onto the ledge about half a metre from Kakko. He was down. He stepped along the projection and bent down over Kakko who was face down with her right side against the cliff. The child was lying limply barely fifty centimetres from her.

"You OK?" he smiled. She nodded.

"But I reckon my right arm's broken above the elbow, and I think I've done some ribs or something. It hurts. When you said you were coming, I decided it best not to move. You climbed down?"

"Yes."

"But I have both ropes."

"I know. Greedy aren't you?"

"How did you do it?"

"Carefully," he smiled.

"What are we going to do?"

"I'm going to take your rope and loop it around the little boy like you intended. Then," he said gently, "we've got to get you up without doing any more damage... OK? This is what I'm going to do. I shall loop the rope around you so that when we take your weight you will come up... bum first. Not very dignified, but it should work. As you come off the ledge, I want you to hold your right broken arm with your left. Hold it into you to support it... then as soon as you are up and free of the ledge kick yourself round so that your damaged side is away from the cliff. Got it?"

"Got it," said Kakko. "I see I'm in good hands."

Tam felt the compliment. "I'm going to get both you and the

kid up. OK…" Tam eased Kakko's coil of rope over her head and passed it over her left arm. She winced, but did not cry out. Tam carefully stepped over her to the child and examined him. He had a contusion on his forehead but otherwise did not appear to have any broken bones. It was amazing how children could fall without breaking anything. Tam took a length of rope and tied the end with a bowline under the boy's armpits. He was just beginning to stir. This was both good news because he was glad the kid was recovering, but on the other hand, he did not want him to wake before he had proper control of the rope. Tam prayed. It occurred to him that he had been praying since about the second step on his way down! He uncoiled the rope letting it lie loose on the ledge until he got the other end, which he tied around his waist. Turning back to Kakko, Tam pulled gently at the rope around her waist. To his relief it came up freely. He pulled it up until it, too, was coiled on the ledge. Then, taking the end looped around Kakko, he passed it under her left thigh, then looped it up between her legs, over and under the other thigh and back between her legs, and tied it with a bowline firmly to the rope encircling her at her back, arranging it so it pulled her up from the waist where, he guessed, was her centre of gravity. He pulled on it and her back lifted slightly. She was going to come up right, he decided. When he was ready, he tied the other end to his own waist along with the one around the child. Tam stepped carefully back over Kakko and bent down so she could see his face.

"OK," he whispered. "I'll see you later."

"Take care," urged Kakko. "Be careful!"

"You sound like my mother," he laughed. "You can be sure I will only take the yellow ones!"

"I'm glad," sighed Kakko.

Then Tam did an unplanned thing. He did it without thinking – instinctively. He bent over Kakko and gave her a light kiss on her forehead, and smiled into her sky-blue eyes. Immediately he thought that perhaps he should not have done it. He had never kissed her like that before. But to his relief, she smiled back and her eyes seemed to say, 'Thank you!'

"Don't rush. We're OK."

Tam straightened up and studied the cliff-face. Going up was definitely going to be easier than coming down. He was not going to take any risks. He arranged both ropes so that they hung down the back of his legs. As he went, Tam tested every hold before he transferred his weight. To his amazement it only took him five minutes to reach the top. It was definitley easiet going up than down. As he dragged himself onto level ground arms came out to take him while others applauded.

Standing up straight he stated authoritatively, "All right everyone. Listen. I am going to tie these ropes around that big tree over there." It was a long way from the edge. Tam walked around the tree and untied the first rope from his waist.

"This one is tied to the child." He pulled it until there was no more slack and looped it around another stump. "Now, you two, take the end of this one and do not let it go! This one is tied to my friend. If there is slack here, pull it around the tree until the slack is taken up. Keep it tight but do not pull at it. OK. You three we are going to pull the first rope up, slowly, very slowly."

Tam leaned over to see that the rope was straight down to the boy. "OK pull! Gently." The child slowly came off the ledge. "Take up the slack over there! Great. Again, pull!" The child lifted another half a metre. "Great," encouraged Tam. "Now, ve-ee-ry carefully." After what seemed a long time and many pulls, Tam ordered, "OK easy now, gently... gently! Be careful with him in case he has broken anything...", and he and two others leaned down and eased the child over the edge. He was clearly alive but semi-conscious. Tam undid the rope from around the boy and his mother scooped him up. Tears flowed.

"You need to get him to a hospital straight away," Tam declared. He need not have worried, someone had already sent for the emergency services. Someone had headed off running to the village as soon as the emergency had begun. The ambulance would not be long once he had found a telephone.

Tam turned his attention to the other rope. "You OK Kakko? We're pulling you up now!" Three men arranged themselves as before. "Pull, slowly," ordered Tam. Kakko was a different prospect from the boy, her back rose upwards. The two men on the end of the rope took up more slack. "Again! That's it. Now wait... Kakko, hold your arm like I said." He saw her do it. Then he ordered again, "Pull! Gently." Kakko lifted completely free of the ledge and thumped into the cliff face.

"Ooww!" she exclaimed.

"Turn yourself with your foot!" Tam barked.

Kakko pushed at the cliff-face with both feet and managed to make a one hundred and eighty degree turn. It was easier than she had imagined. Her damaged side was now away from the cliff wall.

"Great," yelled Tam, "fantastic. OK. Ready... pull!" and

slowly, bit-by-bit, Kakko was winched up the cliff. Tam ordered a final pull which brought Kakko to the top and half a dozen hands reached down. "Watch her right side," shouted Tam. "Very, very gently!" But he needn't have worried, so many hands quickly had Kakko lying on her back on the level turf without any part of her being unduly strained.

The mother came to Tam and gave him an enormous kiss on the cheek. "Thank you, thank you. You have saved my son's life. Where are you from?"

"Not near here," said Tam rather embarrassed, "we are visitors," and he again ordered her off to the hospital. She left along the path with a man holding the child in his arms.

Tam bent down to Kakko. "How do you feel?"

"Very relieved… and in pain."

"Let me check you properly," he said and one by one he checked her limbs for damage, removing the rope as he went. He felt each leg from top to bottom, being careful to test the ankles to see if there was any swelling. Her legs and left arm were fine. He even checked her fingers, which she thought was surprisingly thorough and caring. He decided that, as she thought, she had fractured her upper arm, and probably her right collarbone and a number of ribs on the right side.

"Better get you home. Do you think you could walk? We don't want you whisked off to the local hospital here. Let's see if we can find that white gate before the emergency teams arrive." They could already hear the sounds of sirens in the distance.

Tam supported her from the left side and Kakko stood up. It hurt but, leaning on Tam, she was OK to take a pace, then another. They entered the little copse and Kakko almost fell through the white gate. Tam followed and Kakko sank to the dry road outside her home. It was dark but the stars were bright.

Tam called. "Hello... anyone?"

Jalli was there in an instant. She had been waiting for them on her garden bench.

"Right side," yelled Tam, "careful!"

Jalli assessed the situation and saw her daughter was in pain. Kakko rolled onto her back. Jack arrived and Jalli ordered him to phone for an ambulance.

"What the hell have you been doing?" she demanded. She was frightened and cross.

Kakko didn't know what to say. In her pain she couldn't think of anything to say to mollify her mother. Eventually she uttered, "I'm alright." Which was clearly not true.

Jalli looked daggers at Tam. Tam opened his mouth to speak, but Jalli barked. "You stay back! Stay away from my daughter! Can't you see you've hurt her enough?"

"Mum! Mum! Listen! He saved my life. This," Kakko indicated her wounds, "is all my fault. I was too quick. Tam's brave and careful and so gentle!"

"Kakko went to save a little boy," explained Tam apologetically. "I think he's safe. They took him off to hospital."

"And that's exactly where you're going now, young lady," asserted Jalli.

Jack turned to Tam. "How about you?"

"Oh, I'm OK!"

"Apart from bleeding knees and chapped wrists... and there's some blood coming from your head," remarked

Matilda who had just arrived on the scene. Tam remembered that a small stone had hit him from above. That was why, under normal circumstances he should have been wearing a helmet. But he hadn't had one on… he should have used the helmets in the bag. And then he remembered. The equipment, the ropes and the bag of tackle were still the other side of the gate. He turned but the gate had gone! Whatever was he going to tell the coach…?

★★★

They arrived at the hospital just after midnight. It was situated a couple of blocks from the Sports Centre where they had been earlier. Tam was treated for his superficial scrapes while Kakko was wheeled off to the x-ray department. After a couple of hours Kakko was on the ward and Tam was sent home.

15

As day broke the following morning, Tam rang the coach to explain, as simply as he could, what had happened and apologised for the loss of the equipment. The coach just seemed to grunt a bit but said no more. He asked where they were and Tam told him Kakko was in the hospital and he was going there to catch up with Kakko as soon as visiting was permitted that afternoon.

★★★

Tam hurried into the ward as soon as the doors were opened to the visitors. He was pleased to see Kakko send him a beaming smile. She reached out with her good arm and took his hand in hers.

"You OK?" she asked, looking deep into his eyes.

"Fine. Didn't sleep much of course. What about you?"

"I feel a wreck but nothing hurts much because they have pumped me full of pain killers. They dosed me with something that made me sleep too. When I woke up I asked for you and that strict looking sister over there said that I would have to wait until visiting time. Then I wanted to ring you but they wouldn't let me use my phone and you have to have money for the ward phone! Sorry."

"No problem. I didn't expect you to ring."

"I am so glad you are here now. Mum and Dad are sure to come soon so before they arrive I just want to say how brave and level-headed you were. You did a fantastic job, and you know how to look after someone. While I was lying there, scared to move and not knowing what to do you just took control of the situation. I knew I was safe; I knew you had things covered. I knew I could trust you. And look, I *am* safe! I didn't think properly. I should have known that tree was not secure. I was in so much of a hurry, but you were careful and sure."

"I didn't do it right. I took risks I shouldn't have."

"No. You did *everything* right!"

"No, Kakko, I didn't. There were helmets in the bag as well as a lot of other stuff which I completely ignored. I should have taken the belt with the pin things and the hammer and secured us to the cliff. When I got to you I had two ropes. I should have used one to make sure that if I slipped I would have been safe. There are so many things I should have done with the stuff we had, and I didn't use any of it… I've been going over it all in my head last night. All the things I should have done."

"Perhaps in hindsight. But at the time it's not so easy is it?"

"No. I just wanted to get to you."

"And so you did. All I could think about was how brave and caring you were. You even kissed me… here." She touched the spot on her forehead where he had brushed her with his lips before he started back up the cliff. "You could have been cross with me but all you did was care."

What Tam saw in Kakko's blue eyes was more than the

gratitude of a girl he had rescued. He leaned over the bed and kissed the spot again. Kakko encircled his neck with her left arm and held his face against hers.

At that moment Jalli led Jack through the door of the ward. Jalli saw Tam bending over and Kakko's arm around him and stopped. She whispered, "I think something special happened between them out wherever it was. Tam's kissing her!"

Jack smiled. "Faithful devotion is probably more to her liking now than adventure," suggested Jack.

Jalli led him across to the bed and Kakko looked up. "Mum, Dad!" she exclaimed. "How long have you been there?"

"Long enough," laughed Jalli. "So the hero has rescued his princess!"

Both Kakko and Tam went the colour of beetroot.

"So no permanent damage it seems," said Jack as he felt for the side of the bed. "Which bits are safe to touch?"

"Left side only," whispered Kakko.

"Can *we* have a turn?" asked Jack of Tam.

"Sure… I mean…" he dried up with embarrassment.

Jalli took Tam in her arms. "Thank you for doing what you did. From what Kakko told me last night you saved her life. And you were very brave. I am sorry I barked at you last night, I was too upset to think."

"Th… thanks," stuttered Tam, even more embarrassed to be hugged so comprehensively by Jalli.

They sat together for a few minutes around the bed. It's a funny thing sitting beside a bed when there are other people sitting around other beds in close proximity. There is little privacy and it's not easy to know what to say. A nurse came round and took Kakko's pulse and her temperature while everyone sat still and Kakko smiled obediently. The nurse completed her chart and said a doctor was expected soon and she would decide whether Kakko would have to stay or could go home.

Then, the door to the ward opened and admitted the large, strong frame of Coach Jim.

His expression was difficult to interpret.

"So," he said to Kakko and Tam together, "you survived."

"Yes," replied Kakko. "Tam used all his skills to rescue me. He was very brave."

"So I hear."

"So – sorry about the stuff, I mean the equipment," said Tam quietly.

"I don't care about the tackle," said the coach crossly, "that can be replaced. People can't! *What the hell do you two think you were doing, eh?* You've had no training whatsoever to go down a cliff-face. You could easily have both been killed and endangered others too."

"But," protested Kakko, "there was a little boy..."

"I don't care if it was the President of the Galactic Federation! You were not qualified to use that tackle. I trusted you with it. I thought you were responsible! You know if you had been under eighteen *I* could be put on a charge, and *the club* closed down! As it is I think I might be allowed the plea that two people over eighteen might be expected to be trustworthy. I am *disgusted* with you, *and I don't want to see either of you near the club again!*"

"But it wasn't *Tam's* fault!" pleaded Kakko. "He saved my life. It was all *my* fault."

"You *both* acted badly. You," the coach spoke to Tam, "may have got away with this, but you do not have the skills. I did think, though, you had a natural sense of caution. I was wrong. *You are both banned!* You understand?" Tam nodded. And with that Coach Jim turned and strode to the door. You could have heard a pin drop in the ward. No-one else was talking. All the eyes from every bedside were on him. Coach Jim turned at the door.

"Oh, I am glad you have escaped relatively unscathed. But I hope it hurts. It'll be a lesson!" And with that he left.

Kakko sobbed. "That is just *so unfair*! He had *no right* to speak like that! OK so I made mistakes. But he wasn't there. And how could he say those things to you Tam? All you did was to rescue us and you probably saved that little boy's life too!"

"But he's right," sighed Tam. "If you made some mistakes, I made lots."

"He's in shock," said Jack. "He's blaming himself for giving you the tackle. He's a frightened man. Just imagine what he would have felt if either of you had not come through this as well as you have. It would have been on his conscience for ever. As it is, it's on his record. I doubt he'll let any tackle out of his sight again."

"But it's not fair that he should blame Tam," wailed Kakko. "And he doesn't understand that if we are invited into another world we are there for a reason. It wasn't just by chance that we arrived just after that boy had fallen."

"I agree with you," said her father trying to mollify her,

conscious Kakko had had enough criticism for one afternoon. But Jalli added, "Exactly what you were meant to do there, however, is another question… and as for Tam taking some of the blame, I don't think he feels it is quite so unfair."

"Not at all," admitted Tam. "I wasn't thinking properly."

"But you rescued me!" exclaimed Kakko. "You did it for me."

"Yes, and I am glad I did. But whether I did it a *sensible* way is a different matter. At least I could have used the stuff we had."

"Exactly," agreed Jalli. "Why take a whole bag of stuff if you were only going to use one thing from it? And what, precisely, do you think God wanted you to do?"

"Obviously," said Kakko, "rescue the little boy!"

"Did you ask God that?"

"There wasn't time!" Kakko was feeling angry again.

"There is always time to pray," replied Jalli. "You didn't have to hold a prayer meeting. It doesn't take ten seconds to ask God to guide you."

"*I* prayed," said Tam, "I prayed he would help me get back up that cliff safely, and after that I kept asking for his help."

"And he did," said Jalli.

"I felt him with me. Somehow I knew that, whatever happened, I was safe."

"But afterward you felt you should have done things differently?"

"There were so many things. It was the stuff that got me thinking. We had a whole bag of stuff and we didn't use it. It took two of us to carry it."

"So, it might be that God was not asking you to go down

the cliff at all," continued Jalli. "Perhaps all he wanted you to do was take the bag and the ropes. You said there were some other people. Could they have used the equipment?"

"I don't know," said Tam. "I never asked."

"And someone had already sent for the emergency services. It may be *they* could have needed them."

"Maybe," agreed Tam. "I never thought of that."

"Or maybe you *were* meant to use the stuff. But not the way you did."

"Or didn't," said Tam.

Kakko had been quiet throughout this exchange. And it was Jack who was first aware that she was crying again. "Kakko," he said reaching for her hand.

"It's all so confusing," she spluttered. "Why are things so complicated?"

"It's because you are young and full of life," whispered her father, "and, thanks to God and Tam, you still are. Put this down to experience. Whatever you do, even if you get into trouble for it, the most important thing to remember is that if your motives are pure, you will be able to live with the outcome. You may have made mistakes but only because you cared for a little boy and thought God was asking you to rescue him. That makes me proud of you. I could have the most sensible daughter in the world, but unless she cared about people, she would not please me so much... and," Jack said to Tam, "I am... we are," as he took his wife's arm, "going to be eternally grateful to you for your bravery young man. We are very delighted that you kept a level head even in your lack of experience." And Jack stood and clasped the young man in his arms.

Once again the ward had gone quiet. This family was extremely entertaining!

The doctor came – a young woman who didn't look a great deal older than Kakko and Tam. She asked the visitors to wait outside as she drew the curtains around Kakko. "So," she said, "having some adventures it seems."

"You could say that," sighed Kakko.

After a full examination, the doctor said that all was fine but she wanted Kakko to remain on the ward for another night just to make sure there were no complications.

In the corridor, the young doctor spoke to Jalli. "I think it best you leave her to rest a bit now," she suggested. "She will still be in a slight state of shock."

Jalli, Jack and Tam went back in to say goodbye.

"You rest now," said her mother.

"Forget everything but that we love you and we are proud of you!" added her father. "Come on Jalli, let's leave these two to say goodbye in the way you saw them say hello!"

Alone, Tam held Kakko's hand.

"That was hard," said Tam, "I'm sorry."

"Don't be. I deserve it. But I am so glad you rescued the little boy. He *was* OK wasn't he? He was being taken care of by his mother. He had been unconscious a long time but was coming round."

"I don't think he had broken any bones."

"Good!"

"Now, I must leave you and let you rest."

"Thanks for coming. Let me kiss you!" She did, only this time it wasn't on his forehead.

Outside the hospital, Jack and Jalli were waiting for him.

"We really want to thank you, Tam. We don't want you to feel bad about anything," said Jack. "I thought the coach was a bit strong under the circumstances. He should have let you both get over the shock, and allowed his anger to calm a bit before he said anything."

"You alright?" asked Jalli. "You look a bit queasy!" He didn't seem to hear anything Jack was saying.

"She kissed me! Really kissed me!" muttered Tam.

"Come on. Let us take you home," smiled Jalli.

"Er… yes. Thanks. Kind of us… I mean *you*. Sorry," replied Tam tugging himself back into the world. "I want to go and see Coach Jim. I need to really apologise."

"I wouldn't do that just yet, Tam … not yet," suggested Jack. "I know, why don't you write him a letter? I think that would be the best thing."

"A letter?"

"Old fashioned, I know. But sometimes there are still occasions when a hand-written letter means something."

★★★

"Kakko has him wrapped around her little finger," observed Jalli after they had dropped Tam off. "He's besotted with her."

"I know. He's a good lad. I know he thinks she's special and I don't blame him. But he may learn from this that Kakko is not perfect… and I hope Kakko reflects on the danger she led him into."

"I do hope so. I do hope so," breathed Jalli. "If she learns from this, it will be such a good thing."

"I agree," said Jack. "And she could go a long way to find another as good as Tam. He kept his head."

"I'm glad they've found each other. Love is a wonderful thing!" laughed Jalli. "And I should know."

"*I* would never have come down a cliff for *you*. You know how much I hated heights."

"What would *you* have done, then?"

"Got the stuff and found somebody else to use it, I suppose. Some 'intrepid hero'."

"Someone good looking, tall, debonair… and strong," added Jalli, tweaking Jack's thin biceps.

"But I would have hit him if he had kissed you when he had got you all alone on a ledge."

"And then I would have seen just how ungallant a man you were, and I would have disappeared with the 'intrepid hero'!"

"No you wouldn't, you love me too much!"

"Don't be so sure!"

"You would never have got into that situation in the first place, though! *Your* kind of adventures – *our* kind of adventures – are different. The Creator asks each of us to do different things."

"Exactly. So you can still be my hero." She cuddled up to him. How she loved her Jack! They were silent for a few minutes and then Jack said:

"But I still wish I had been a match for… for that… you know, that idiot by the hives."

Jalli raised herself up and took her husband's face in her hands.

"Jack, you were wonderful. What you did took guts… and love! You gave your sight for me… and, by the way, I thought we had got over the regrets. "

"I didn't think about it. I just rushed in. You didn't deserve what he did to you."

"We said that before, when Grandma died. A lot of things in the universe are not fair. You loved me. That poor man, evil though he may have been, probably never knew love. He was doomed from the start. When it comes to justice we still have everything compared to him. He had nothing... I hope and pray that he has had a chance to choose life in the next world. If God is just, he should give him that... and, you never know, there might be a cure for your blindness one day."

"I don't think about that. I have got used to not seeing. As long as you point me in the right direction, I can manage everything else. The brain compensates. I can hear and smell how people feel. I never used to smell people's feelings, but I do now. Like, I knew Kakko was crying. I smelt it. I felt her stillness, heard her silence."

"That is a gift."

"A gift I have only gained through being blind. And, in the end, I have you. And through *you* I have got to know God. You can't get better than that."

16

Kakko's enforced stay in the hospital was brief. She was assured that things seemed to be going on well and all she needed to do was recover. Easier said than done for a girl determined to do things without a lot of patience. After a week she was complaining that she was still sore.

"Of course!" said an exasperated Jalli. "What did you think? It takes months to mend broken bones."

"Months?"

"Yes, months. You heard what the doctor said. There is no rushing this, Kakko. I think you are doing remarkably well at getting around, all things considered."

"Not months, weeks! The doctor said six weeks."

"Six weeks till the pot comes off. But that is only the beginning."

"Six weeks for the pot! My skin will have rotted away in that time! It itches so much. There must be a better way than putting a broken arm in plaster."

"Kakko. There is no way of hurrying the healing process. It takes time because that's the way nature works. I'm afraid you will just have to be patient. You are fortunate that you can do so much with your left hand. Most people are not so ambidextrous."

"Be patient. Be patient! That's all that I hear!"

"So if you hear it so many times, it might just be the right advice."

"But what am I going to do with myself? I can't do most of the practical things at college, which is pretty difficult if you're on a 'hands on' course. I have to stand and watch and make notes while other people are getting in and doing it. How can I learn that way?"

"You're a lot brighter than you give yourself credit for. Don't be afraid to use your brain. Concentrate and you will still learn... why don't you do something extra just using your brain? Take your mind off things."

"Like what?"

"Like... like finding out about something you've always wanted to know the answer to."

"Research! That's, like, sooo boring!"

"Kakko!"

"OK. But all I really want to know is why things are so unfair? That's all I can think about. I mean Tam got into so much bother. His mum and dad have said that if he had been younger they would have grounded him for a month! And Coach Jim has sacked him for good. I mean, all he did was rescue me. That – what happened – was definitely all my fault."

"But his parents don't mind him seeing or contacting you?"

"No."

"I wonder why not. I mean if it was all your fault, I guess his parents would definitely tell him you were bad news."

"They wouldn't. They *couldn't*! He's twenty."

"And you are eighteen. So stop complaining like a child to your mum."

"I'm *not*!"

"No? You stop behaving like a hard-done-by-kid and I'll try and stop behaving like a bossy mum. Let's be adult to adult... deal?" Jalli raised her left hand, palm up in a high-five, and Kakko ever so slowly softened.

"OK deal," she said, exhaling noisily. She patted her mum's hand and sighed again. "You're right. But what would an adult with more experience than this one," she pointed to herself, "suggest I do with my time?"

"If you're really keen on finding out why things are unjust, why don't you take up Pastor Ruk's suggestion and join the church study on 'God's revelation to the worlds'. You know the one he suggested but you couldn't do because it was going to conflict with Coach Jim's club."

"It sounds like hard work."

"It might be, but it'll give you something to think about while your bones heal."

"OK. I'll think about it. Do you think he might answer the question why everything's so unfair?"

"From my experience, Paster Ruk approaches his sessions by asking what the participants would most like to talk about. He knows so many of the stories of God's revelations of Himself to the inhabited worlds we know about. He has a wealth of knowledge, but he tries to begin with the questions people come with."

★★★

A week later both Kakko and Tam took the bus into the city centre as usual but this time, instead of going to the Sports Centre, they entered the suite of rooms associated with the worship hall. After the excitement and the smell of the climbing walls this place seemed quiet and drab. Even the neat potted plant someone had tried to brighten the place up with seemed rather forlorn. But soon, despite the surroundings, a lively group of people began to gather. They were of all ages – although Kakko and Tam were definitely the youngest. Kakko recognised most of them. A number of ladies around the age of her mother came up to her and asked her how it was going with the pot and everything. They seemed genuinely concerned. One of the men, a small quiet man, whispered to Tam, "You must be the brave fellow I have heard about," as he nodded towards Kakko.

"Not *so* brave," protested Tam. "I didn't plan to be brave."

"Anyone want coffee, tea… or sodas?" yelled a woman leaning out of a hatch that she had just opened. Tam made his way back from the hatch with the Joh equivalent of a couple of cans of cola. Kakko took the can in her left hand and, in an effort to get into it, sat down and was about to put it between her knees when Tam passed her his open one. Kakko first reacted with a 'how dare you' look, but then relaxed and smiled. Tam was just naturally caring and she saw that he did it instinctively. It was his way. But Tam caught Kakko's expression and realised he had deprived her of a bit of the independence that she was fighting for – perhaps he should have been more thoughtful and quickly apologised.

"It's OK," whispered Kakko, "I'll let you."

"Let me what?"

"Be my slave."

"Get your drinks everybody and come and sit down and we'll introduce ourselves," announced Pastor Ruk.

There were about twenty-five people present and the pastor wanted them all sitting in a circle. He began with a prayer. After he had finished he explained, "I believe in prayer. God is always present with us. We cannot do anything as well without Him as we can when we invite Him to help us. In fact, some things we can't do at all outside of Him, but that'll come out in our discussions as we go along.

"OK. Let's introduce ourselves. So I'm Ruk and I live right next door in the plot over there. I have been pastor here for ten years. My favourite food is parsnips! Who are you and what's yours?" he asked the man to his left. And it went on round the circle. By the time it got to Kakko and Tam there was quite a feast of different foodstuffs. Kakko went for strawberries and Tam for ice-cream and that confirmed to everyone that they were an item.

Pastor Ruk then explained that the purpose of the first session was mainly to help people see where they 'were coming from', as he put it. "Not necessarily where you were born," he explained, "but discovering where your heart is. What occupies your thoughts? What questions you have got. There are no forbidden questions," he added. "There are no questions that should not be asked. The Creator, I believe, does not want anyone just to be resigned to accepting anything without questioning. And there are no 'pat' answers because every tidy theory actually begs a lot more questions than it answers! So, if you have come here to feel safe and secure thinking you will get certainty about your faith, then you are in the wrong place. But if you want a spiritual adventure – exploring beyond the horizons into regions in which many fear to tread, then you have come to the *right* place. The one thing I can promise you is that the more you question, the more of God you will discover. The blessings of God, of course, extend far beyond words, but words can take us a lot further than most people think. Once we have set out on the path of spiritual discovery, leaving behind religious theory and doctrines that can only take us so far, there is no going back – the only thing that will bear you up is the very presence of God himself in your heart. We must not use Scriptures, including our own, as an end in themselves – they show us a way to travel, a series of stories that tell of God's revelation, and an invitation to your own relationship with Him (or Her if you prefer). When we have come to know Him, then we can throw ourselves solely on Him. Scriptures are God's way of leading us forward – ever deeper into the life he has for us. We have our own Scriptures here on Joh, but there are others from around the universe – each of them talking of the encounters with the Creator experienced by different cultures down the ages. They all have insights. The purpose of our little gathering here is to discover if some of these can help each of us on his or her own spiritual journey. We have not yet arrived, we are nowhere near becoming who we really are; in this universe we are only beginning. Most of us are still only packing our suitcase with the things we need for the journey. Some of us are probably carrying much more baggage than we need, and it may be that what we have to learn is to dump some of it. That's hard because it may be stuff we have become attached to – the older we are, the harder it gets sometimes.

"If you do not think you are ready for this yet," Ruk

concluded, "then please do not feel you have to stay. No-one will think ill of you for being honest."

There was a moment's silence and some shifting of feet and people looking down at them. Roast beef (Kakko couldn't remember their names only their preferred food) asked, "You're not going to tell us that all we learned at Sunday School is wrong?"

"No. What I *will* say though is that if what you learned there was pitched at a child's level, then as an adult you are going to be able to go deeper."

"Some say you are dangerous!" smiled the quiet man (cabbage). People laughed nervously, but he added, "They think your way of teaching undermines people's faith."

"Yes. I suppose that is true if that faith depends on a series of doctrines. But if your faith depends on the presence of God in you, and you in Him, then nothing can separate you from Him. You will discover that your faith is even more firmly rooted."

"There's so much that doesn't make sense about God," volunteered 'apple and custard'.

Ruk looked at her and said gently, "So then you're asking questions already, and you are ready to explore."

Then a couple who had been fidgeting and whispering to each other got up. "I'm sorry," said the gentleman, "but this all sounds as if you want to criticise our religion. We don't mind talking about God in the least, but questioning centuries of tradition and even the Scriptures must be wrong. We were brought up to believe in what it says, and not doubt it."

"Please be assured," said Pastor Ruk, "I am not questioning that the Scriptures contain truth. They are all true in the way the writer intended, in the context in which he (or occasionally she) lived. They are Scripture because they are genuine testimonies to an encounter with God by whatever name. But each of us needs to look deeper within ourselves. It may be that what we have believed for centuries is actually preventing us from knowing all we can know."

"You are saying that other people's Scriptures contain truth, but we know that we have the only true Scriptures. We have our traditions and our teachers and they are the *only* ones with the true revelation."

"They are immensely valuable and to be respected greatly," said Ruk, "and many of those teachers would rejoice that we can stand on their shoulders and discover more, as they did their forebears."

"You dare to doubt we have the complete revelation of the Creator in the Johian Scriptures?"

"There is fullness. I believe our Scriptures contain *all* the elements – but there is much we have yet to grasp because we haven't fully understood them. We can think that the way we have looked at them is the only way, but there are many ways of interpreting the Scriptures."

"Not where we come from," said the man forcibly.

"I don't think what you are doing can be God's will," said the lady. "His words are to be trusted and we shouldn't twist them to mean something other than what they plainly mean."

"But is it so plain?" suggested 'apple and custard'. "The more I read it, the more I think I am missing something. I know people who have rejected the Scriptures entirely because they seem out-dated and contradictory. I am relieved to hear the pastor say they can still lead us to the truth. I want to hear more."

"Well, *we* are going home," stated 'roast beef', "and unless you have already sold out your faith as this lady sounds to have done, I recommend you all do too." And he and his wife walked across the room and left. You could hear a pin drop... no-one else moved.

Pastor Ruk kept silent, his eyes lowered. He was clearly praying. Then a youngish man with an interesting red scarf who liked red currants sat up straight and broke the silence. "I've been stuck with trying to make sense of the Scriptures for years. I agree with you," nodding towards 'apple and custard'. "Please Pastor Ruk, please continue." There were calls of agreement from others too.

Kakko was hooked. The whole idea of having an adventure (albeit a spiritual one) and exploring had grabbed her attention, and before anyone else had a chance she blurted out.

"What I want to know is why everything in the universe is so unfair! If God truly loves us all, then why is life harder for some than others? And why do people get the blame for things they haven't done while others get off scot-free?"

"An excellent place to begin!" affirmed Pastor Ruk. "Anyone got any suggestions of how we might tackle the question of injustice in the universe? Is God a God of justice?"

Everyone was silent. Then, after a few moments a quiet man (cauliflower cheese) sitting next to Tam, said, "If you can give a satisfactory answer to that one, Pastor Ruk, everything else we might ask would be comparatively easy. Our young people don't intend to let you off lightly."

The pastor smiled.

"Let me tell you a story that comes from Planet Earth," he began, "as it is told in their Scriptures. It goes like this. A couple of millennia ago, God decided the time was right to be born as a 'human being on Planet Earth'. Actually we share our DNA with them – they are our close cousins and we have had actual contact through the portals we sometime hear about that God, very occasionally, has set up for an individual. In fact some here have come to live on Joh by this means even today. It is through these people that we have gained our knowledge of their Scriptures and the story of the events in which God revealed himself."

Kakko moved uncomfortably in her chair. Her parents spoke to very few people of how they had arrived on Joh, although it was no secret. The people of Joh did not engage in gossip. The only way in which a person's origins would be discussed is if it had a direct bearing on a situation. Kakko wondered if she should say that, in fact, her father was from Earth One. But she was too interested in what the pastor had to say and did not want to interrupt at that moment.

Ruk continued, "Human beings are noted for their tendency to become aggressive, some of them actually believing that attack is the best means of defence. Also a few are obsessed with selfish ambition, and others are driven by *fear* to engage in wars and violence. They have, nevertheless, a huge capacity to love and this generally wins out in family relationships, which are mostly, but not always, peaceful. They long for peace but fear of the enemy (who is usually characterised as less than human) drives them to violence. The production of weapons on an industrial scale characterises the species."

"The Earthlings are a pretty cruel lot then," commented 'mango chutney', a large middle aged woman with a 'tea-pot' smile.

"Like all human species, they are a mixture," explained Ruk. "And so God decided to come to his own creatures as a fellow human being. He was born a child on Earth One. As he grew, this child learned his mission – to reveal that God, who is love, loves everyone on that planet whatever his/her language or group. As a young man, he witnessed to them that in God there is no darkness of evil. He was immensely popular among the ordinary people, but those in authority feared they would lose their hold on power and plotted to rid their planet of this young man who was also God. They chose not to believe he was from God – probably because that was inconvenient for them. So they arrested him on trumped up charges and then had him executed by nailing him to a cross of wood, which they set upright in the ground on top of a small hill so all could see who was in charge."

"Yuk," shuddered Tam. "Why be so cruel? That's an awful thing to do!"

"Apparently it was a pretty common thing to do with your enemy in those days on Earth One."

"But he hadn't been violent himself?" quizzed Kakko.

"All he had done was reveal God's love. He wouldn't let his followers fight – not even to defend him. So now, tell me, where is the justice in that?" asked Ruk.

"There is none," said Kakko. "He was all love and he was tortured and killed just because he was too good for those who held power. I have heard the story, he was called Jesus Christ.

Nan Matilda often tells it… because actually she was born on Planet Earth One."

There was an audible collective gasp that rippled around the small group.

"Your grandmother is from Earth One?!" exclaimed 'apple and custard'.

"Yeah," said Kakko slowly.

"I know her," she said, "she's a friend of my mum. I never knew she was born on Planet Earth One."

"No need to know really," said 'mango chutney'.

"No. It's never made any difference, but actually I'm half Earthling," said Kakko.

"Wow," said 'apple and custard'. "Do your friends know?"

"Some of them. Tam knows. We don't go around talking about it. It doesn't seem to matter who your ancestors are. Does it matter, Pastor Ruk?"

"Only in what you might be able to contribute to society. A diversity of backgrounds makes us rich. The more the merrier. It helps us look at things from different angles and get a clearer picture. You can probably tell the story of Jesus better than I."

"Nuh. I only know what Nan told me."

"You should ask her more… OK. So what might this story tell us about God and justice?" Ruk asked rhetorically. "It tells us that it is the nature of the Creator to suffer injustice as well as His creatures. God is not above it all, but comes into His creation and suffers hatred He does not deserve. So when we think something is not fair, it isn't because God doesn't care (like some kind of landlord sitting above it all looking down on us from some great height). He cares enough to suffer alongside us, bearing the injustice too."

"So," asked the quiet spoken man, "God allows injustice?"

"No, not exactly 'allows'. He has no choice," said the pastor.

"Surely," said a woman from across the circle, "God has the power to do anything? If He doesn't like it, He doesn't have to put up with it."

"We like to think that," replied Ruk, "but in practice He cannot because He is so bound up in the universe and He has to travel along with it. Not even God can make a star cold. A cold star is not a star – He has to obey the laws of physics. He cannot give his creatures the power to choose love, and at the same time make sure they choose it. That is no choice at all. What He *can* do, and has done, is build love into the system – and demonstrate what He wants us to choose, but then it is over to us to make the choice. If someone is bent on evil and injustice they can block God out, and the laws of the universe mean there is nothing God can do about it. That's not to say that He cannot act to restore and heal, but only when people let him."

"I don't get that,"retorted the woman. "If God is God, no-one can exclude him!"

"Yeah," came in Kakko. "Why doesn't He just zap the evil ones and do away with them? Why does He put up with wicked people killing him? That would be fair."

"But there's good and bad in each one of us," said the quiet man, "once He had started He would have to zap everyone."

"Yeah," added Tam gently, " and God loves even the most wicked. His love prevents him from destroying them. All He can do is show them the way. He won't give up on them as long as there is a chance they will change. I agree God is not able to do everything in the universe as it is."

"Right," said Ruk, "God's power is not the zapping sort. That's the way the Earth people thought of power. That's the way we sometimes do here too, but God's power is the power to transform, heal and restore. That's what being love means."

"Nan says the story doesn't end with Jesus dying," explained Kakko. "He is raised from the dead and goes up to heaven in glory."

"Exactly!" said Pastor Ruk. "In the end justice *is* done, God wins, but not always in our time, but in His. Thank you so much for that question Kakko. And God bless your nan for sharing that story with you. I would like to come and talk with her sometime."

The discussion went on. The pastor brought in other people and many struggled to get their minds around the nature of God's power. Kakko couldn't follow everything. Tam seemed to do better and explained a bit afterwards. But what she did take away from the little group was that God cared about injustice – and she felt better about it. She was also proud of her nan and was glad she had told her the stories of Jesus.

"I'm going to get Nan to tell me more," she told Tam on the way home. "Do you want to go again next week?"

"Yeah," said Tam, "that pastor's cool. I guess he's in trouble though. That couple will probably give him a bad report."

"That's unfair!" declared Kakko. "So many people get put off with the traditional stuff which doesn't work for them. It begs so many questions. And they didn't stay to hear him properly. They were against him from the start."

"Agreed," said Tam. "And, as for the unfair bit, if it's unfair for God, I'm sure Pastor Ruk will cope with it."

Kakko laughed. "He didn't dodge anything did he? He's cool… thanks for being patient with me Tam."

"Why? I don't want you to be any different from what you are. I like the way you speak out. You know I've always admired you."

"But I've been so arrogant!"

"Not *very* arrogant. But I must admit I didn't think you would ever really like me."

"I was too obsessed with myself to see your qualities."

"Thanks. I'm chuffed."

"Come here," said Kakko, swinging her good arm around Tam's neck. "Let me kiss you."

"What here? In the street."

"I don't care," she said.

"No you don't, do you? And," he whispered looking into her sky-blue eyes, "neither do I!"

"Hi Sis!" It was Bandi right up behind them. "Never thought my sis could get so cheesy," he laughed. They looked round and saw both Bandi and Shaun with an expression that betrayed a combination of triumph and guilt.

"Bandi!" exclaimed Kakko. "What are you doing here? Pesky little brothers. Sorry, Tam."

"We've just got back from the match," said Bandi. "Guess what?" indicating his brother, "two goals and two assists. Ta-dah!"

"Wow! Brilliant!"

"Love midfield!" exclaimed Shaun.

"Congratulations," said Tam. "Seems you have a fan in your brother at least!"

"We saw Nan just now," said Shaun. "She went home

earlier and found a note to say Mum and Dad have gone through another white gate, so she's come back to town again with her things and is going to stay at Mrs. Pippa's."

"A white gate?" quizzed Kakko. "Where?"

"Usual place, in the hedge next to the real gate."

"No, I mean, where have they gone to?"

"You mean where through the gate? No idea. Apparently there was only stuff beside the gate for two, so they guessed it was only for them. Nan couldn't see anything. We are to check when we get back."

"The note said to look after Nan," added Bandi, "but she rang her friend and arranged to go and stay with her."

"Like we're not up to looking after her," said Shaun.

"No. It's not like that. She's never been really happy since Grandma died," said Kakko. "She'll get bored with just us around."

"She gets bored anyway," said Bandi, "we're all out at school, college or work for a lot of the time."

"And you know how she likes to talk," said Shaun.

"Anyway, now she's with Mrs Pippa, no doubt telling her what wonderful grandchildren she has, or not," said Shaun. Their bus approached the stop and Tam put out his hand.

"Are you going to sit with us, or do you want to carry on snogging on the back seat?" asked Shaun.

Kakko went an odd shade of purple. "Come on Tam. I guess we'd better sit with these pesky brothers of mine. *So* immature!"

As they walked towards the bus stop, Tam squeezed Kakko's hand and smiled.

Back in Woodglade, there was no sign of a white gate for them. Although not surprised, they were at first disappointed, but then the thought of having the cottage all to themselves cheered them up. Perhaps they could have some friends over?

17

J ack and Jalli were sitting together on the bench in the garden under the tree where they had first sat twenty-two years before – then two strangers from different planets. The weather was almost the same as that first time, and the time after that, when they pondered the question of whether they should enter the cottage. Jalli still put a space between the syllables: 'cot-tage', even though she had learned to speak English very well for herself. She no longer needed to have it translated inside her head by the 'Owner'. They spoke English a lot – for Matilda mostly. And the children were fluent. Wanulkan, however, was not so easy for Jack. Not being able to see meant he couldn't do any written learning. He couldn't refer to the dictionary Jalli had brought with her. Nevertheless he had persisted. There had always been Grandma to give him practice, but now it was left to Jalli. The children understood it, but they were less competent at speaking it.

That day, however, Jack and Jalli were using Wanulkan. Jack was getting his tongue round it rather well. The lovely day reminded them of the Municipal Park and the Wanulkan City centre just through the hedge beyond the white gate that was no longer there. It did not seem so far away – although they knew it was somewhere on the other side of the universe. Jalli had realised one night, gazing at the stars, that she did not even know in which direction to look. She had tried to see

the cluster of three stars that shone down on Raika, but Jack
told her that, even if Joh was on the same side of the same
galaxy as Jallaxa, Suuf and Shklaia, from Joh they would look
like one star. And Planet Joh was not even likely to be in the
Elbib-Andromeda galaxy anyway. Yet sitting on the old bench
and speaking Wanulkan, the city in which Jalli grew up didn't
feel so *very* distant. They began to talk about Mr Bandi.

"I wonder how he's going on?" mused Jalli.

"Must be retired by now."

"Coming up for it."

"And your school friends?"

"All married to handsome, rich bankers, I suppose... "

Jack laughed. "And they all have kids who prefer the beach
to their school work!"

"Except for the occasional one inspired by the biology
teacher... Jack!" Jalli was staring across the lawn.

"What?"

"A gate! It's just this minute appeared. A white gate in the
hedge where I used to pass through to Wanulka."

"It's the reminiscing. You're imagining it."

"Jack, I know a white gate when I see one!" she declared
in English.

Jack scanned his brain and then nodded.

"Got it. I was feeling so lazy here! When are the rest due
to come home?"

"Nan's with Ada. Kakko is with Tam so God knows when
she will be back. Shaun is playing away isn't he? So he and
Bandi will be really late."

"So do we wait for them? Are there any things?"

"No... I mean, yes..." Jalli went over to the hedge. She

called back, "Two sun hats with, what's this, a wallet with what looks like money. The writing on the bank-notes is Wanulkan! They are different from what I remember but it says, 'Bank of Wanulka'. Wanulka! Jack we're invited into Wanulka. We're off to Wanulka! Jack, we're going to my home city!" Jalli bounced up and down with excitement. She was seventeen again. "We're actually going back, right now!"

"I'm so pleased for you to be going back. The place you grow up stays with you deep down. Especially if you were happy there for most of the time."

"I *was* happy. Grandma made sure of that. It'll be strange without her though... the notes have changed design but it definitely says, 'Bank of Wanulka' in Wanulkan... and we're rich. There's three hundred Wanulkan units. I've never had so much cash."

"Inflation. You haven't been there for over twenty years."

"Guess so."

"There are only two hats?"

"One for you and one for me. The others are not meant to come, then. Mine is lovely. It's Wanulkan ibon straw," Jalli smelled it, "and it has a broad brim with a pale blue ribbon."

"Sure that's not mine?" teased Jack coming over to her.

"No. Yours is a smart fabric hat. Worthy of a dapper man." She put it on his head. "Thank you my kind sir, I would be honoured to have you walk me through the Municipal Gardens." She did a little jig. "I wonder, perhaps we can go and find Mr Bandi."

"Maybe. It'll depend on what the Creator has lined up for us of course... better leave a note for the others."

Jalli fell silent.

"Jalli, what's wrong?"

"The last note anyone left in the cot-tage was from your mum saying Grandma had been taken to hospital… I'll miss her especially in Wanulka."

"Of course. But remember Grandma is happy. She is with all those you don't remember meeting even if you did meet them when you were little. People she had missed for forty years…"

"Yes, you're right. With or without Grandma I can't wait to go to Wanulka."

"I tell you what. We'll pin the note to the door so it doesn't look the same. We won't put it on the kitchen table."

"Good idea… Jack, I'm quite excited."

"I love you, my beautiful wife." Jack caught her up in his arms and kissed her passionately. It was the most passionate embrace they had shared since Momori's death. Jalli responded to Jack's lips, her arms around his waist and clutching her new hat with its blue ribbons.

"I'm going to put on my Jallaxa T-shirt!" she exclaimed. "I feel young again. And it will go perfectly with this hat ribbon."

Jalli decided against a handbag. Instead she put a few things into a beach bag. She elected to wear a pair of shorts she had not looked at for years but which she had often worn with the T-shirt.

They stepped through the gate and out onto the street exactly where Jalli had originally found her way into Woodglade for the first time. There was the bus-stop where Jack had seen her onto the bus when she was struggling to walk.

"Let's go into the park," said Jalli.

They walked down the outside of the wall and in through the main gates of the Municipal Gardens. The suns shone more strongly than on Joh. All three of them were above the horizon, Jallaxa high in the sky. Their new hats were not just fashion items. At that moment Jalli did not feel old enough to have an eighteen year old daughter! To her amazement (and delight) she was aware that men were giving her a second glance. She was turning heads like she did when she walked through the park as a seventeen-year-old. She had despised them then. But now, with Jack's hand in hers, walking among the sweet-smelling flower-beds she quite liked people looking at her – she still despised them though!

They traced their way up the slight incline that led deeper into the park. Jalli was half-consciously heading towards the far gate that led to the Wanulkan high school.

"Where are we now?" asked Jack.

"In the middle of the park."

"You're walking as if we're going somewhere."

"Am I? This is the way to Wanulka High School. I used to walk this way every day."

"Are we going to see Mr Bandi?"

"I guess that's what I want to do."

"Fine. But he's probably not there. Is the school in session?"

"I don't know. We'll find out."

As they got near the far gate Jalli stopped. Something had caused her to exhale sharply.

Jack squeezed her hand. "What is it?"

"School kids. At least the uniform has not changed much. Took me back."

Jalli led Jack through the school gates and up to the main doors. She pressed a button and a door lock clicked. Pushing the door they found themselves in a small lobby in front of a receptionist's desk.

"This has changed," said Jalli. "Never used to be a reception here."

The woman behind the desk looked up. "Can I help you?"

Jalli stammered in Wanulkan. She hadn't spoken it to any Wanulkan except Grandma for so long it seemed odd. "I'm… Is Mr. Bandi in?"

"Mr. Bandi. The biology teacher?"

"Yes."

"No. Sorry. Mr. Bandi retired last year. Are you an ex-pupil?"

"Yes. I'm… we're in Wanulka just for a short time and I was wondering where I might find him."

"Well, you could try Parmanda Park. When he retired he went to work there part-time. He loves his insects. Do you know how to get there?"

"Yes… yes, we… we do."

"You could take the new bus. It goes by the park. The bus-stop is right outside. If you go now you might just get the bus before the students come out. Being on the bus with them is rather crowded."

"Yes, I remember," smiled Jalli, recalling when she was a school-girl. They all used to get packed into the bus so tightly that the other passengers were squashed and sat on.

Outside the school Jack turned to his wife. "Parmanda Park. *Are* we going to Parmanda Park? Do you really want to go there?"

"Perhaps that's why we're here, Jack."

"What. To go to Parmanda Park?!"

"I think… I think it will help. Jack I do really *want* to go to Parmanda Park!"

"Right. We go to Parmanda Park. Where's this bus-stop?"

"Jack, I wasn't thinking. *You* don't have to go. *We* don't have to go. Not if you don't want to. What happened there was worse for you than for me."

"Let's not go into all that again. You know I don't agree with that. All I care is that *you* are comfortable. If you want to go, we'll go. But I'm not leaving your side this time – not for a minute!"

They didn't have to wait long for a bus. Jalli felt odd getting on a bus in such a familiar place and yet having no idea how much the fare would be. Jack had warned her about inflation but it did not stop her from having to apologise for offering the driver a note that did not cover half the cost for two single tickets.

"I could have travelled all week for that when I was at this school," she murmured to Jack as they made their way down the bus. "Do you think they've had a financial crisis?"

"Probably not. Just a small percentage adds up over twenty years. It really doesn't matter. What matters is the ratio of income to prices."

"Right, I'll remember that Mr Economist," said Jalli with a mocking tone. "It doesn't stop things sounding expensive all the same."

"You're showing your age," laughed Jack, "but," he added, "I guess you don't look it!"

"Stop teasing! If you really want to know, I feel quite young today." Jack pulled her towards him on the seat.

"Are you sure about this? Parmanda Park, and everything?"

"Yes I *am*. Actually, I am *really* ready to go there. I think that perhaps now is the time to face the memories. I can't say I'm not nervous, but I really think I can deal with this now. How about you?"

"I'm fine about it. You know I can't remember too much about the bad bits. The last thing I remember seeing is the parmandas' dance. You called out and the rest is a blank. So hang on to me and don't let me go…"

"I promise I will keep hold of you… all the time."

The bus went through districts of Wanulka that simply hadn't existed when Jalli was last around. New estates of brick houses and bungalows had sprung up all along the route to Parmanda Park, but the park itself was still quite unspoiled and unchanged. They got off the bus opposite the entrance and Jalli led Jack through the wrought iron gates that had stood there for over a century. They crossed the car park to the Visitors' Centre through which people had to pass to enter the park itself.

Inside Jalli spotted a notice and read the admission charges. She resisted the temptation to remark on how high they seemed to be. Season tickets, she noted, were only three times the cost of a single visit and life members were free. They were directed through a series of channels where people were showing passes, cards or proffering cash. Jalli counted out two adult single entries and asked the man for two tickets.

"ID," he demanded.

"ID?" repeated Jalli.

"Identity card, or driving licence. Guess you're too old for a student card?"

"Sorry," said Jalli, "we don't have them with us. They never used to demand ID cards. It's been some years since we were last here."

"Well, it's a *really* long time then. Years ago we had a man damage a hive and then get killed. We have to protect the parmandas and people. But that must have been, what, over twenty years ago. You must have been only a kid then."

"I was seventeen then... when we last came. That was twenty-two years ago." The man did his mental arithmetic and then looked at Jalli again in her bright T-shirt and shorts. She clearly looked after herself.

"The one who broke the hives," asked Jack, "Is that the one that attacked a girl too?"

"Now you mention it, I believe it was. Clobbered her boyfriend too. Then days later the bloke was killed by the parmandas. Never happened to anyone since but we have to be careful."

"But *he* didn't come through the entrance did he? The man who broke the hive. He came in round the back."

"Might have done then. Not now he couldn't. He would risk being fried on the electric fence... now if you don't have ID you need to go over there and get your prints checked... next please."

Jalli led Jack into a space away from the desk. "So, what are we going to do? If they take our finger-prints they'll find out we don't have identity cards."

"Maybe. But we might still get in. The worse they can do is send us away. I'm sure they are not out to catch people without passes – it's just about not letting the wrong people in."

"You mean like what happened to me in your country on Planet Earth? No. Everyone here has an identity card automatically. I had a student card. If I had still been here it would have just become a standard ID card. I guess that hasn't changed."

"Nothing ventured, nothing gained. If they don't let us in we can always ask for Mr Bandi. So let's try it."

Jalli led Jack over to the desk indicated by the official. A young woman sat reading what looked like a novel. No-one else it seemed had forgotten their passes. But she looked up as Jalli addressed her.

"We've come without our ID and the man over there directed us here."

"Press the fingers of your right hand on this plate," she stated.

"Like this?" The woman nodded.

Jalli did as she was asked. "Now your thumb."

"Perfect … oh, you're a life member! You should have said. No charge then." Jalli did her best to hold back the amazement she felt.

"Now you sir." Jalli took Jack's hand and directed him to the plate. Jack had never had Wanulkan ID. Clearly this devise was connected to some central computer and would show him up as unregistered.

"Confirmed," said the girl. "Life membership. I'll issue you with day passes. If you've lost the life membership passes then ring the number on the back and they'll replace them."

"Thank you," said Jalli. "Excuse me, can you tell me where I can find Mr Bandi."

"Yes. He's in today. He might be in the park with a group,

but his office is through that door into the park and then turn left. It's right next to the coffee shop. You can't miss it."

"Thank you. Thank you very much," said Jack in his best Wanulkan. The woman didn't seem to register his odd accent. She probably thought it went with his blindness. (Jack always said that being odd in one way meant they allowed him to be odd in everything else. It might be annoying, but if used to advantage, it was sometimes helpful!) The girl became engrossed in her book again as they took their day passes and continued through into the park. Mr Bandi's office was easily identifiable. Apparently he was responsible for organising group bookings and tours. Jalli took Jack by the hand and pushed open the door. Then she saw him. He was older but hadn't changed a lot in the essentials. He appeared to have altered much less than the city!

"Mr Bandi," said Jalli timidly.

He looked up from his desk.

"Can I... it can't be! Jallaxanya Rarga?" Jalli smiled. "My, you haven't changed a bit! Wow, it's so good to see you!" Coming from behind his desk he took her hand. It's been so long! Where have you been? How are you? You look fantastic! And this is your boyfriend, er..."

"Jack."

"Jack, yes, of course."

"He's my husband now. Has been for more than twenty years!"

"Never! Has it been that long?" Then turning to Jack he said with concern, "What about your eyes? Can you see at all?"

"Nothing at all. Quite useless," said Jack lightly. "I have put the brain to other uses."

"I'm sorry about that… they instituted a lot of security after you left… here in Parmanda Park, I mean. I have never quite forgiven myself…"

"Mr Bandi," broke in Jack quickly. "We have decided the past is the past and there will be no regrets – and that includes you!"

"You are so sensible. You are right. So what brings you here now?"

"It's just a short visit. But we wanted to see you. And come back here to this park."

"Well you've found me and the park in the same place. Do you want me to take you round – unless you want to go off by yourselves of course?"

"No. We'd like having you with us," said Jalli. "I have so much to catch up on."

"Just give me five minutes. I'll see you by that red post over there." Mr Bandi pointed to a group of benches beyond a sturdy wooden route indicator.

"I'll just go to the loo, Jack," said Jalli.

"Will you be alright?" Jack looked concerned.

"Jack, I know I promised to not let go of you, but I didn't think that would include taking you into the ladies! I'll be OK. I'm sure it's safe in there with all these people." She led Jack to the entrance of the gents. "Excuse me," she said to a kind looking elderly gentleman. "Can you conduct my husband into the toilets? He's blind. All you need to do is direct him to the cubicle door." She had done this many times.

Jalli was waiting for Jack as he emerged. They went over to the red post and were soon joined by Mr Bandi.

"I don't have a group for a couple of hours so now is a

good time!" he declared. "Which way do you want to go? The park hasn't changed much."

"Take us back to… where it happened. Can you do that?" asked Jalli.

"Of course… but…"

"I'm sure," said Jalli in a firm voice.

They walked down through the hollow where Mr Bandi had been flattened by Jack the day before the attack.

"Do you remember Jack knocking you over here?" asked Jalli.

"Never forgotten it. Felt so foolish at the time."

"I know where we are, then," said Jack. "I can picture it."

"It hasn't changed much," said Jalli. "And Maik Musula, do you remember him?"

"I do indeed. Strange man. He was banned from the park. But not long after you left – a couple of years I guess – he got married."

"Married?"

"Yes. They have eight children. I've taught some of them."

"Eight kids! His wife must like him then."

"I guess she can't get away from him!" smiled Mr. Bandi. "But, yes, they seem happy enough. He was always a one girl man, if I recall correctly."

"She must have 'interesting eyes'," laughed Jalli. "What does she see in him, I wonder?"

"Some girls," explained Mr Bandi, "seem to like their men utterly obsessed with them."

"But not if they are insane!"

"Well, we're all different. What constitutes insanity anyway? I've been told I am a bit insane at times."

"You. You're the most sensible and lovely teacher I ever had!"

"Yes. But, don't forget you like biology too. You enjoy the creepy crawlies whereas some people can't stand them. *My* wife has to be special. Not every woman will put up with dead insects in her bedroom."

"Dead insects?" asked Jack.

"My specimens."

"I never knew you were married," said Jalli.

"Oh I wasn't when you were here. I got married about fifteen years ago. You know my wife."

"Do I?"

"Yes. Do you remember the literature teacher, Miss Pammy Falminta?"

"Yes. I think so. I didn't have her myself. She wore short skirts and some of the boys pretended to fall over and tried to take naughty pictures. One got caught! But she's much younger than you."

"She is. I think it was my maturity that attracted her."

"You mean you didn't try and take pictures up her skirt in the staff room."

"Quite the opposite. It was I who dealt with the boy who did. She thought I was such a gentleman. We went out for a drink and, well the rest is history. You must come back to our house. We have a little girl. She's nine now. I... we... called her Jallaxanya."

"A beautiful name!" said Jack.

"I am so happy for you!" declared Jalli and planted a big kiss on Mr. Bandi's cheek.

"Steady on! Someone might rush out and knock me down." Jack laughed.

Jalli breathed in the fresh Raikan air. A hint of ripening ibon was drifting in from the surrounding fields. She looked across the clearing. "It's there... over there. That's the way to the hive where... it happened," breathed Jalli. "What happened to those parmandas? I never asked – I was too engrossed in my own troubles."

"Oh, they rebuilt the hive."

"So, we can't *all* go there, *together*," remarked Jack.

"The rules were changed after what happened to you and the problems that led up to it. At first they wouldn't allow anyone to go alone without a qualified park ranger. Now we even allow small groups and, because we never go too close and we're always still and quiet, the parmandas have got used to it. They seem to know the park rangers will keep them safe."

"The parmandas haven't ever gone for anyone else?" asked Jack.

"Never. What happened then was very rare. But it wouldn't be if we damaged their hives."

"So we can all go up there? Together?" asked Jalli.

"We can."

"Let's go," said Jalli. Jack detected the quaver in his wife's voice. There was both fear and determination. Holding her hand he also detected doubt and urgent excitement. She gripped him tightly and pulled him forward. Jack was not afraid. He had not been all those years ago. He was angry. He had this overwhelming need to protect his Jalli. It was the sense of failure all those years ago that came back to him. Despite more than twenty years of Jalli telling him otherwise, he still felt he had failed her.

They reached the spot and Mr Bandi beckoned to them to keep quiet.

Jack heard it first and squeezed Jalli's hand. The parmandas were active inside the hive. They listened for several minutes. Jack detected a subtle change in their tone. Jack put his arm around Jalli and held her.

"I think they're going to display," he murmured into her ear.

Then Jalli heard it too. After some minutes, few at first and then more and more insects emerged from the hive and began flying upwards and outwards. Others came from the trees and bushes to join them. Soon they were swirling and diving, swooping and dancing.

"Wow!" whispered Jalli. She felt Jack pull her close and then tense. He had detected another slight change in the sound that emanated from the swarm. They were spiralling down towards the hive. Then, with a crescendo of sound that was really loud, they suddenly disappeared, each insect knowing exactly which of the three entrances belonged to it. As they moved across each other they made a sound like a slurp and then it all ended suddenly with a plop.

Then there was silence, and all they were aware of was the calling of a bird in the distant woodland.

"Wow!" exclaimed Jalli again, quietly. Mr Bandi exhaled, "Best I've ever seen. And I've seen quite a few."

"They were waiting for us," said Jalli. "This was for *us*. They put this on for *us*. I know they did!"

"They were fantastic," said Jack as they walked back to the centre.

"It's a pity you couldn't see them," sighed Mr Bandi.

"No. But hearing them was fantastic enough."

"You knew what they were doing before it happened," said Jalli. "I could feel it."

"I could sense them. There is a really special smell. It's sort of sweet, like a flower, only more delicate. It increases when they are about to come out or go back in. You must have smelled it. It was really powerful at the end."

"I guess so," said Mr Bandi. "I've never really thought about it."

"Jack can sense things with an intensity that sighted people often miss," said Jalli. "You knew exactly what I was feeling up there didn't you?"

"Well, sort of. It was all mixed up. You're glad you went though, aren't you?"

"I am. Those parmandas, they wanted to give me a *good* time. They wanted to heal my memory."

"They know you love them," said Mr Bandi.

"Oh, I do! They, Jack and me. We were all victims."

"And now you are bound up in the dance of love," said Mr Bandi.

"The Trinity," said Jack, "God. That's what Christianity says about God on Earth. It's a divine dance of love. And God suffers when we suffer."

"And he rejoices and dances with us when we are set free!" exclaimed Jalli.

"Free," echoed Jack, his sightless eyes streaming with tears. Jalli saying they were *all* victims had struck a chord deep down. As victims they were bound together in something even more profound than the all-consuming delight they had experienced as young lovers. Love is something that underlies all existence and suffering is part of it. She who loves, suffers.

That's why Jesus had to die. The force of that verse that was so often said or pasted outside of churches in Jack's England hit him. What was it: "God loved the whole of the world so much that he sent his Son to die for us," or something like that. And then Jesus rose up and joined in the dance of the Trinity taking everyone with him.

"Jack," it was Jalli, "will you now forgive yourself?"

"Forgive myself?"

"That you let me down. You see when you came to rescue me, you loved me so much. You might not have overcome that man physically, but you towered over him spiritually and emotionally. He wanted me because he was empty, but because you did what you did he went away even more empty. He even knew the parmandas were on our side. If he had looked back he would have seen me bending over you. Perhaps no-one had ever bent over him and loved him. Poor man. Even the parmandas hated him. He had absolutely nothing. And I and you and the parmandas, we know we are loved, for ever."

"Caught up in the divine dance," said Jack.

"You two are such an inspiration. A breath of fresh air," said Bandi.

"Sorry, Mr Bandi. But this time is special to us."

"No need to be sorry. I'm privileged. You were decidedly my favourite student, but don't tell the rest that."

"And you were definitely Jalli's favourite teacher," said Jack. "You should really hear about all the things she has been doing in Woodglade."

"I would love to. You must come to my house this evening and meet Pammy."

"And Jallaxanya. We'd love that."

"What time are we thinking of going home?" asked Jack.

"Oh. Not today. I told the kids – on the note – not to expect us."

"But we need to check in somewhere if we're going to stay overnight."

"You must stay with us. We have a spare room."

"But Mr Bandi. You haven't asked your wife."

"I'll phone her. But she won't mind. In fact she'd love to see you. I'll phone her now."

"You must tell me about your children. Only," he said glancing out of his office window towards the red post, "I had better go now as I have a group waiting to be conducted around."

"Tell us where you live and what time," said Jack, "and we'll come to you."

"Just hold on…" Bandi took out his phone and held it to his ear. "Pammy, you'll never guess. I've got Jallaxanya Rarga here… I know, a real surprise… Yes. I can't talk now, I've got a group waiting, but can they come to us for dinner…? Sure." He turned to Jack and Jalli, "Is there anything you don't eat?" They shook their heads. "No… that's fine… seven?" he looked up and Jalli nodded, "seven it is… sure. And, Pammy, they haven't booked in anywhere yet… I agree… the room is made up? Great, Pammy. Must rush… love you… bye."

"OK, we eat at seven, and the room is already made up. So that's settled. Where are you going now?"

"Back to where I used to live," stated Jalli. Jack concurred. He had half expected her to want to go there straight from the municipal park.

18

The number of the bus from Parmanda Park to where Jalli and Momori had lived for so long hadn't changed. It took them through the middle of the city and on to the road leading west past Momori's old house. This same road continued on into the countryside, eventually leading to the village of Zonga where Jalli was born – a village that had never been rebuilt after the devastating deluge that destroyed it and so many of its population.

They got off the bus at the stop nearest the house and traced the same few metres that Jalli had done so many times as a youngster. She stood and looked at the house. It had changed. Subsequent owners had added an extension and put in new windows. Windows that Momori would not have liked. The curtains were chunky and bold and there was a big vase on the windowsill that Momori would have considered grotesque. The garden had been re-designed and there were little brightly coloured statues all over the grass. It was not at all Momori's thing. (*Her* garden had been neat but soft.) In those days the house had been painted a pale cream. Now it was a vivid pink.

"Not home?" asked Jack, as he stood next to his silent wife.

"No," she said. "It's a house. A strange house with no Grandma."

"Grandma's gone to her real home," said Jack.

"Yes. Pastor Ruk was right. I half thought of bringing her ashes here. But I'm glad I didn't. When we get back I'm going to take them on a boat, and when we are out of sight of land, I'm going to tip them into the ocean."

"Beyond the horizon."

"Yes. She's not in her ashes of course, but it will be a kind of sign that she has journeyed on. No-where in Wanulka, or Planet Joh, or anywhere in this universe can hold her any more."

"She's dancing with God."

"Yes. She's at home."

★★★

They found the Bandi's house at a-quarter-to-seven. They thought they would walk on and come back nearer seven, but before they could do so, a little girl of nine years came bounding down the path that led to the front door.

"Hi! Are you Jallaxanya?"

"Yes. And *you* must be Jallaxanya too."

"Yay! You're the lady that Daddy named me after."

"You were named after *me*?"

"Yes. Daddy said you were his favourite student, and you were very brave, and very clever, and… and you liked insects like him. All except worms!"

"Worms?"

"I hate worms too. They're so wriggly when you tread on them, because they come out when it rains and go on the path and you can't always see them. Anyway, Daddy says that the lady I was named after didn't like worms either – not like parmandas. *They* are my favourite insect. You went to Parmanda Park today. Daddy said… he likes ants too… and beetles…" Little Jallaxanya was swinging on the front of the gate facing outwards with her hands over the top behind her. *She is clearly not a shy little girl,* thought Jalli. She wondered if little Jallaxanya ever stopped talking.

"…And …and," she continued trying to think of something else to say.

"Jalli, don't keep our guests outside the gate! Let them come in," called Mr Bandi. "Sorry, my little girl has really been looking forward to meeting you ever since she heard you were here in Wanulka. Do come in."

"Mummy, Mummy," shouted the girl as she rushed ahead of them. "Mummy, they're here!"

"So I see," said her mummy.

"Hello Miss Falminta. It is nice to meet you again. I do remember you – just. You came as a teacher around my final year but you never actually taught me."

"I do remember you. Call me Pammy. And it's Bandi now. I stopped being called Miss Falminta a long time ago."

"Pleased to meet you, Pammy," said Jack extending his hand. "I'm Jack."

Pammy took his hand. "You are very welcome. Come on in." Pammy ushered them into the sitting room and offered them a comfortable upholstered settee. "Paadi tells me you have children."

'Paadi'. Jalli reflected that she had never really heard Mr Bandi being called by his first name.

"Yes, three… the youngest we named after your husband."

"Did you? What a remarkable coincidence!"

"If it weren't for your husband we may never have got married," explained Jack. "he is very dear to us."

"I was having a… well, a bad time," explained Jalli, "…and he came round to my house and told me not to be stupid."

"It wasn't quite like that," said Paadi Bandi. "I don't think you would have listened if I had said that."

"No, you were much more subtle. But it boils down to the same thing. I was not thinking straight. I didn't think Jack wanted me…"

"And *I* thought it was *she* who didn't want me," added Jack.

"So God sent us both a wise person to put us right," went on Jalli, "and for me it was Mr Bandi. So you see, we named our first son after Jack's dad and our second one after you."

"But you have three children?" said Pammy.

"Yes. The eldest is a girl – Kakko."

"Who is just like you?"

"Hardly," said Jack. "She is very impulsive."

"*Something* of her mother in her then!" exclaimed Mr Bandi.

Jalli rolled her eyes at him.

"But she finds studying tedious," added Jack, "and is quick to jump in. Quite extrovert."

"So only *some* of her mother. You were an excellent student, Jalli."

"But Kakko is very caring," said Jack. "She has brought us much joy."

"I am sure," said Pammy. "So tell us about Bandi, and Shaun."

Kakko, Shaun and Bandi would probably not have approved of being the subject of conversation, even with people on another world. But all parents want to talk about their children. The conversation that evening covered the present day and the past. Their families, the school, the biology department, the new head teacher set on change, the way things were with young people, what Jack and Jalli were involved in in Woodglade, the church they belonged to…

Pammy went to see to the cooking. After a few minutes she reappeared.

"Paadi, would you watch the vegetables while I show our guests the spare room?"

Pammy led them upstairs pointing out the bathroom on the way. "I hope you will be comfortable here," she said. "I hope you don't mind a double bed?"

"Not in the least, we use one at home," said Jalli. Seeing herself in a mirror and becoming aware that not only did shorts not seem the right thing for an evening indoors but that there was a brown smudge on the side of them (and perhaps more round the back she couldn't see), she added: "I am sorry we haven't brought anything to change into."

"I can lend you something. We are about the same height I guess. Come on, let's see what we can find." Without time to object, Jalli followed her host into her bedroom.

"What would you like? A dress might be easier. My trousers might be a bit baggy on you. Let me see."

She pulled out three and laid them on the bed, then added two more. Jalli was taken with the colour of a green dress, not dissimilar in style to what she used to wear. It was sleeveless with a fitted bust but then flared free from a high waist. Jalli picked it up and put it against her. It was shorter than she originally thought, quite a bit above her knees. Yet Jalli had good legs. If she could get away with shorts she would have no problem with this, she surmised. But perhaps she should wear something longer. Pammy smiled.

"That suits you. You would look good in that. It's a good colour."

"Perhaps something longer," ventured Jalli. She picked out a couple of the others.

"Not as good as the green," suggested Pammy. "Why don't you try it on?" Jalli slid out of her shorts. When she saw them off, she felt ashamed. The back was marked by the brown dust from Parmanda Park. How could she have sat on Pammy's settee! She should have guessed, she thought, as she remembered sitting on that log watching the parmandas; the Wanulka dust got everywhere anyway.

"Sorry," she said, "about your chair. I had no idea I was quite so dirty!"

"No problem. Paadi comes home covered in dust every time he goes out. I sometimes think he crawls inside the insects' holes after them! Give the shorts to me. *And* your top. I'll put them in the washing machine. They'll dry overnight." Then Pammy held out the green dress for Jalli to put on. It fitted nicely. "Perfect! It was made for you!"

"It's lovely. Are you sure?"

"Of course. Go and show Jack… oh, sorry, I forgot!"

"Don't worry. Jack has his own way of looking," Jalli laughed. She walked out onto the landing and called Jack.

"Jack. Check this out on me." Little Jallaxanya came bounding up the stairs to look too.

Jack coloured a little at being watched. He glided his hand lightly down the sides and back, then her front and to the hem."

"It fits well," he said. "But you haven't worn anything this short in years."

"I went into longer stuff when I was carrying Bandi and never reverted," explained Jalli.

"But I like it," said Jack. "What colour is it?"

"Leaf green, with bits of pink."

"Nice."

"You look very pretty!" exclaimed Jallaxanya.

"You keep it," said Pammy. "It's yours."

"But I couldn't possibly…"

"I haven't worn it for years. It was never quite my thing. I don't know why I kept it. It must have been for you."

"I don't know what to say."

"No need to say anything. It gives me pleasure to give it to you."

"Hello-o," shouted Bandi up the stairs. "Are you people coming? The veggies are about done!"

"Coming!" replied Pammy. She ushered her daughter down the stairs leaving Jack and Jalli to follow.

"She's so kind," said Jack. "Happy?"

"I love this dress, but…"

"You've made her day just by being happy in it. What about me? Am I scruffy?"

"No. Your jeans don't pick up the dust like my cotton shorts." She patted his bottom. "You'll do."

"And my top?"

"No. Not dirty," Jalli giggled.

"What's up?"

"Just thinking of you borrowing something from Mr Bandi's wardrobe. He's one third shorter and two thirds wider than you!"

"You make him sound square!"

"Well, no. He's not exactly fat. Just well made."

"While I'm skinny!"

"Tall and slim and quite gorgeous," she said pressing up to him and kissing him firmly.

★★★

"Tell our guests about what you do at school and church," said Mr Bandi to his daughter. At the age of nine she was happy to oblige and kept them amused throughout the first course.

"Our daughter Kakko likes climbing," said Jack, "do you like climbing?"

"You mean mountains?"

"Yes. Eventually. At the moment she likes climbing walls in the gym."

Little Jalli gave a sideways look as if to say that that sounded like a stupid thing to do. "Doesn't she fall off sometimes?"

"Often, but she has a rope round her waist."

"*I* can do the hula-hoop in the gym," said the girl.

"Your daughter is very sporty then?" Mr Bandi returned to the subject of Kakko.

"Yes. She plays football too. If it's physical, count her in, if it's mental, she loses patience."

"Is she not clever like you?"

"I'm not really clever, sir!" laughed Jalli, "It's only you who thinks that because I like insects… Kakko's OK, but she's not academic. It's Bandi who is the studious one."

"Biology?"

"Not really. He's more into arts than science."

"I like science!" declared little Jalli. "I am going to be a biologism when I grow up."

"A biologist," corrected her father. "She is my little helper."

"But I don't like *worms*!"

Jalli laughed.

There was so much to catch up on. After little Jalli had gone to bed (reluctantly), they talked of their adventures and of how they never knew when the gates would appear. And they spoke of Momori and how they were just about coping without her.

Then the phone rang.

"That's rather late. I wonder who that could be?" queried Mr Bandi. Pammy picked up.

"Yes, they are… Really…? I'm sure… I'll put him on. Just let me explain… Jack, it's a consultant from the hospital, an eye specialist. He got wind that you were here – his brother works in Parmanda Park." She passed the phone to Jack who wore a look of surprise.

"Hello. Yes…yesterday…we plan to leave tomorrow… I don't understand…that was more than twenty years ago… really…? I see…tomorrow…? Well, it would have to be early… OK. Nine o'clock in the ophthalmology department… " he reached out to Jalli, "got a pen?" he whispered. Mr Bandi passed her a pen and a notepad. "OK. Mr. Barn, Department of Ophthalmology, Wanulka General Hospital. Nine o'clock… thank you…yes, I'll be there… thank you." he held the phone out and Mr Bandi took it."

"Jack?" said Jalli, intrigued.

"He's an ophthalmic consultant. He heard that I was in town. (He was a junior at the time I was in Wanulka Hospital and remembers my case.) They are trying out a series of new cutting edge procedures and he says he has been trying to find me for a month. He'd just about given up when his brother saw us yesterday. He says I might benefit."

"What, see again?" exclaimed Jalli.

"Well, perhaps a little bit. He can't promise anything, and I wouldn't have to mind being a bit of a – I didn't get this bit – a striped mouse."

"He means he wants to experiment on you," explained Mr. Bandi.

"Oh, I understand. A guinea-pig."

"A guinea-pig?"

"We say that in English when someone tries something new on you. A guinea-pig's a bit like a mouse."

"Yes. That's what he means. So you've agreed to go tomorrow," said Jalli with concern.

"I have agreed to go just to talk to him. To listen to what he says. Nothing more. Anyway it's unlikely that we can return. It will all depend on the white gate."

"But it may be why we are here," considered Jalli.

"Maybe. But I think what has happened so far is reason enough. It is great just to meet your wonderful teacher and his lovely family. I really am so grateful to you, Mr Bandi, for talking to my obstinate girlfriend, as she then was. Being blind was bad when I was in the hospital, but it was not having Jalli that hurt so much. I thought she was cross I hadn't done a better job in rescuing her, and she wouldn't want a blind boy…"

"Oh, let's not go there again," said Jalli, "it makes us sound so silly."

"No. You weren't silly. You were young and traumatised. What happened to you both was not something small," broke in Mr Bandi. "It would take anyone time and effort to come to terms with it – even sensible and level-headed people like you two."

"I agree," said Jack, "and I don't think we need to try 'to put it behind us' now. It was the right thing once – but now, here, I think we can really face up to things – properly."

"You are so brave," said Pammy. "But you are so happy together."

"We are," said Jack, and Jalli squeezed his hand.

Then they went on to tell the Bandis about their recent adventures, and how the younger generation were becoming involved.

At last, Mr Bandi said, "I don't know about you, but I think I am ready for bed."

"Yes, me too," said Jalli. "It's been a wonderful evening."

"Your clothes are drying on the rail by the boiler," said Pammy. "We can iron them tomorrow."

"Thank you. Come on," said Jalli, "let's go up and let these people get to bed."

Jalli led Jack up the stairs.

In the bedroom Jack took Jalli and kissed her. She responded quite passionately as Jack explored the dress in more detail.

"You look lovely," he said, stroking her hair.

"Jack, I want you to make love to me. Make love to me now!"

"What, here?"

"Yes, here. In Wanulka. We have never done it in Wanulka. But today I think I have finally put an end to the hurt. I am mended Jack. What that man did has not taken away my spirit because he took nothing. He wanted me because he wanted my life, my energy, my passion. But he got none of that because, all the time, all I could think about, was you. He went away empty. He had no life. We have called him a monster, but he was not, he was an empty, weak shell of a person. Sure he had physical strength, but so does a metal bulldozer. He had no heart, no soul. And today, properly for the first time, I felt sorry for him. I hope that God has caught him up, built him up, restored and repaired him. I want him to be the person God created him to be. Full of life in his heavenly home."

"Heaven is for good people."

"Yes. But none of us are good enough for heaven. God has to *make* us new – forgive us when we realise we need it. No. I believe, heaven is for *everyone*. I don't believe God forces people into heaven, but I would hope – expect – a loving God would give people like that man a second chance – a chance to claim life. God wouldn't be love if he didn't. No matter how bad my children might be I wouldn't turn my back on them – not if I loved them – and neither would God. So now, Jack, make love to me. I'm free! I have *you*, and I want you!"

"But Jalli, we… we haven't brought anything to – "

"I don't care. If I get pregnant we'll call him Paadi," she laughed.

"But, Jalli – "

"Stop talking and come here!" Jack put up no resistance. He had been aware of the scent of his wife's passion building through the day, just as he had smelled the mood of the parmandas when they were ready to display. He rejoiced in the honour to be this wonderful woman's husband.

19

Jalli woke. The first of the Wanulkan suns was already rising in the sky. It took her a couple of seconds to decide where she was, but then it all came flooding back. She was naked, cradled in Jack's arms and she smiled as she recalled her intense, unfettered climax the night before. They had fallen asleep, satiated and exhausted. Jalli's abandonment had taken them both by surprise. For the first time in her life since those dreadful events in Parmanda Park two decades ago she had experienced real freedom.

Breathing deeply, Jalli rejoiced in the familiar smell of the Wanulkan morning. It brought back the happy, childhood years with Grandma… yet, weren't they supposed to be going somewhere?

"Jack, Jack it's getting light."

"Umm…"

"Jack. You said you would go to the hospital for nine."

"Urr… what time is it?"

Jalli reached for her watch. "Five-past-seven."

"Seven. Already? Wow, Jalli! Last night… you were really alive! You sleep well?"

"Very well. That's how it *should* be Jack. I think – I know – after all these years, I'm truly free. Perhaps this morning the same might come true for you…"

"Right," said Jack thoughtfully. "Do we have to get up? I

mean, right now. I like this newfound freedom of yours!"

"So do I! Better shower though. I think Mr. Bandi and Pammy are already up."

"They will be, with a little girl."

★★★

Pammy had laid out Jalli's shirt and shorts, nicely ironed, on the side of the towel rail. They dressed and appeared downstairs where they saw a wonderful assortment of breakfast things.

"Sleep well?" asked Pammy.

"Yes. Very well indeed. Thanks for washing and ironing my things."

"That was nothing; don't mention it. Now what are you going to have to eat? Paadi doesn't have to be at the Park before ten, so he will drop you off at the hospital for around ten-to-nine. That OK?"

"Marvellous. Thank you."

"And then I will come and pick you up."

"That's alright. You don't have to –"

"Paadi and me want to know how things are. And you are welcome back here for lunch. What time do you plan to leave?"

"It'll have to be sometime in the afternoon," said Jalli.

"Good. So have some lunch with us before you go."

★★★

Jack had never seen Wanulka General Hospital but he had had a lot of experience of it. It had a unique smell that hadn't changed since he was last there. Jack felt the hairs rising on the back of his neck. The pain and frustration, anger and despair of that time came flooding back to him.

Mr Barn was waiting for them in his consulting room. He introduced himself and showed Jack and Jalli to a seat.

"I am very pleased to see you. If I may say so you have worn well. I was a junior when you first came in and now I am the leading consultant in this department. I'll get straight down to my proposal. We know exactly what happened and what treatment you received from us before you left us. The damage was then, given the treatments available to us, irreparable. However we have now pioneered a whole new set of techniques to repair the kind of damage you sustained. If you had come in to us today with this as a new injury we would definitely recommend it to you. But I need to be frank. This is very pioneering and I do not want in any way to build up your hopes. We have had some slight success in restoring a tiny bit of sight in a dozen or so new patients. We have never tried it before on people who have had a long term condition. We want to try it on such people as yourself without knowing what, if anything, we can achieve."

"But if it did work," asked Jalli, "what is the best Jack could hope for?"

"What we are aiming at is to help your brain get a message, of sorts, from one or both of your eyes. This may mean you will be able to distinguish light and dark which makes a lot of difference to new patients. The world is not so dark and they are able to get around and some of them make out shapes – people for example. You will know where someone is in front of you. Some patients have been able to see where they are putting their hands…"

"Not actually see again, properly, then," clarified Jalli.

"Not at this stage, no. We still have a long way to go. As I said this is new, pioneering technology. If you were willing to go through with this it would help us in our research. Of course, it will not cost you anything. We will pay all your expenses, and accommodation for you, too, Mrs Smith (he pronounced it 'Smitt') if necessary. We will also compensate your employer for the period you are away from work. You do have work?"

"Yes. I do. But not here in Wanulka."

"That doesn't matter."

"Well, I don't even live on Raika."

"This is the bit that I still find confusing! Where else could you live? There are no other planets to hop to. We could not refer you on when you left us last time and we have been trying to contact you without success. Then you suddenly turn up at Parmanda Park where my brother is deputy warden. Mr Smith, where exactly *do* you live?"

"I… Jalli can *you* explain? It would be easier for him if he heard you in Wanulkan."

Jalli explained in the same way they did on Planet Joh. "We do not know how it happens but we are taken around the universe. Sometimes there are portals that are open for us to step – literally step – between planets located in different parts if the universe. It must sound strange to you. In fact it still does to us! But that's how it works. Where we live it has happened to other people too. We live on a planet called Joh. It cannot be seen from Raika. Jack is not from there but a planet called Earth One. I am from Raika. As far as I know, myself and my grandmother are the only Raikans to have gone through one of these portals – ”

“So you are here just because your portal happened to open up after more than twenty years.”

“Correct,” said Jack, “we have not been back since.”

“So if you can help Jack it’ll depend on the white gates (our portals) to be there – and that’s something *we* can’t decide,” finished Jalli.

“I don’t understand,” sighed the consultant, “but I’m willing to take your word for it. The important thing for us now is whether you would like to undergo this… if you can. We will need, of course, to check your general health and the current state of your injuries first.”

“Thank you,” said Jack. “I appreciate your contacting me. And your offer. And I would like to help you, but I need to think about this.”

“Of course. I think you have got the point – this is probably more about benefiting the research than about helping you. You don’t have to decide today; take your time and phone me when you’re ready… is there anything else you would like to ask me at this stage?”

“Yes. Those bits of my brain that used to be connected to my eyes. They haven’t just been sitting there doing nothing for twenty years have they?”

“No. They haven’t. They will have been employed in other ways. That’s one of the things we would want to test.”

“So, if you, say, flood them with a signal, even an indistinct one, what happens?”

"That is precisely why you'd be a striped mouse. We don't know. That is what *you* could tell *us*."

"I *could* get a bit of my brain wiped clean of other things just so I could see shapes if I were lucky?"

"I wouldn't say 'wiped clean' exactly. You would still have a functional brain zone."

"But maybe a confused one that can't think straight?"

"But one that can see enough to help you get around and know where things are. I am not trying to persuade you either way on this, Mr Smith. It's your choice."

"Thank you," said Jack again. "I'll think about this. I'll get back to you."

"Take your time. I can appreciate that this is a very big thing after so many years."

★★★

Jalli took her husband's arm as they left the hospital.

"How far are we from the Municipal Park?" asked Jack.

"A couple of blocks. Do you want to go there?"

"Let's go to that café we passed yesterday, and sit in the sun and think."

"What café?"

"The one not far from the main gate. It's on the right opposite those strong scented flowers."

"Oh. You mean the stall that sells hot drinks and things."

"Yes. I smelt it. It smelt like the stuff your grandma gave me once. It was nice."

"Right then, straight down the hill… We will pass the white gate, if it's there."

"We could pop home for a cuppa then? But no, while we're here let's do the Wanulkan stuff. I want to think. And I'm not ready to talk to Mum and the children at the moment."

They passed the white gate, which was reassuring, and found the stall and sat at a table.

"Nice stuff this," said Jack.

"It's a kind of tea made from a local shrub. We call it 'bru'."

"Bru it is. Easy to remember… good thinking stuff. OK. So this is the deal as I see it. That doc has a new procedure he wants to try out on people. They're already doing it on new cases. At first when you can't see a thing, when it's pitch black, it's very scary. Back then I would have done anything just to have that darkness lifted. But now, for me, the darkness is normal. I don't need to see shapes to know someone's there. I did at first. But not now. I know where and who. I know if they're on their feet or sitting down. Take that doctor. He was sitting behind a desk. He had a pen and a computer on it. The computer was on his left (my right). It was a desk-top computer with the fan, under the desk. He was sitting in front of a window which was open at the top. There were blinds not curtains – the up and down sort (they make a distinct noise when they blow backwards and forwards). The man himself was as tall as me, slim, and about fifty-five years old, I guess. He was married (or at least he was wearing a ring). He had a cotton mixture jacket, probably a suit of good quality and he had hard bottomed shoes. The chair I sat on was made of leather, rather worn. Yours was a bit wobbly…"

Jalli laughed. "You know that?"

"Every time you moved the legs rocked. It was especially

distinct when you were talking. I don't think about this most of the time. I just build up the scene from the clues I get. But as you and he were speaking I was thinking about what I knew and why. How wrong am I?"

"You 'saw' more than I did! You've got nothing wrong as far as I can tell... So, what you are saying is that you do not need to see with your eyes again?"

"Well it might help to see light and shapes – but it's the trade off that worries me. How much would I lose of the acuteness of the rest of my senses?"

"And you think you will?"

"That's why I asked what I did. I think it is bound to. The doctor knows that too, but he doesn't know how much or in what way. That's why I'm the perfect striped mouse. I could stand to lose a lot. The real benefit is for them – what they will learn from me for their research."

"So, what are you going to tell them?"

"I don't know yet. I'm going to have to sleep on it. But my immediate instinct is that I am alright as I am. But then, I don't just want to be taking the easiest option... or the selfish one. It's not what's in it for me. If I thought I could be able to see enough to be able to see our children, I might think it worth all the hassle, but I won't be able to. As it is, in the end, it won't be me but science that gains – and other people, but that's a good reason for saying yes."

"Jack. I... I don't want you to have any operation that can't make things better for you. It's a big risk."

"As I said, let's sleep on it."

"But we're going back today, you said so. We mustn't leave the kids and Nan too long."

"We will go back. Before we do I'll ring the doctor and say I'm sleeping on it. I'll explain that if he doesn't hear from me within, say two weeks, then the answer's a definite 'no' because it means we haven't been able to get back. In the end, it may not be that the decision is in my, I mean, *our* hands... Do you want another cup of bru?"

"How do you know I have finished this one?"

"Beca-ause," said Jack playfully, "you always put the cup down more firmly when you've finished and kind of move back a bit in you seat. You always do."

Jalli laughed. "OK. You've really got so used to being blind haven't you? Jack, I just want you to be happy. If you are, I am."

"I know. I can't say I like being blind. It is very frustrating at times. I miss not seeing you and the children. I'd love to know what they really look like. And it's hard work whenever we go somewhere new. I really have to concentrate as I build up the pictures. I find myself counting steps all the time. And I couldn't do so much without you or someone to guide me. Around home it's fine – most of the time... but right now, I would very much like a second mug of bru."

"You like this stuff?"

"It reminds me of Grandma."

"I know," said Jalli thoughtfully.

"There's the frustration. I doubt I could get a cup on my own and I'd have no chance with this money. I'd be alright after a couple of times, but I can't remember an instance when I didn't have you or someone to help me."

"That's to do with your charm, kind sir," teased Jalli. "We'll have another and then it will be time to walk through the park to the Bandi's."

★★★

"You're so brave," said Pammy over lunch. "I've not heard you complain at all about being blind."

"Oh, I did at first, believe me, but I haven't of late… mostly. Not so much since I got my Jalli back."

"But don't you ever think that what happened to you wasn't fair… I mean, don't you question God?"

"The whole *universe* is not a fair place. Unfair things happen all the time. I guess you could question why God made it that way, but I don't believe working out whether we should blame God or not gets us anywhere. The question I ask is, 'Is God trying to do something to make things fairer?' and, in my opinion, the answer to that is definitely yes."

"But things keep going wrong."

"They do. And the Creator keeps working to build people up again. But not everyone lets Him. That's the main problem. That was *my* problem. But now I see over and over again how God finds a way through. Another question to ask is, 'Does God think things are fair when they aren't?' I am sure He doesn't any more than we do. He knows exactly how unjust they are – and wants to change them. And He can, if we let Him; and He can't if we don't."

"Like finding this doctor to make you better?"

"Maybe. But he has already given me all I need. I already have so much more than most people. Of course I want to see again, properly, but the doctors can't really do that yet. This procedure is very much in it's infancy."

"So what are you going to do?" asked Mr Bandi.

"Phone the doctor from here, if I may, and tell him I'll sleep on it."

"A very good idea," stated Mr Bandi. "Big decisions should never be made in a hurry."

★★★

It might not have been more than mid-afternoon when Jack and Jalli reached their white gate but they were tired. It had been an emotional day.

"What an exciting time we've had," said Jalli. "Wonder what the weather's doing in Woodglade?"

They stepped through and were immediately conscious of the sweet gentle Joh air… and Kakko and Shaun sitting on the garden bench.

"Wow! Cool shorts, Mum," said Kakko.

"Yeah," agreed Shaun. "Bet that turned them all on in… where was it you went?"

"It did," said Jack, "and we're tired. Move up." He and Jalli sank down on the bench between their children.

"So what've you been doing?" urged Kakko.

"Give us a chance!" said Jalli.

"Welcome home. I'm putting the kettle on," called Matilda from the front of the cottage.

"Good idea," called Jack.

★★★

That evening Jack led a family debate on the question of his treatment. They all sat around the kitchen table and he went from person to person allowing them to say everything that they could think of. Then he took small pieces of paper and got them all to write down all the 'fors' and all the 'againsts' – each on a separate piece of paper. Then he told them to put all the 'fors' in one pile and all the 'againsts' in another.

When they had all finished, the pile of 'againsts' was the bigger one. Jalli said, "That seems pretty conclusive, Jack. But it's your decision." She read out all the comments. For themselves and the family, the decision was pretty much that they couldn't imagine Jack being any happier than he was. Even Matilda was nervous about the outcome of interfering with what she thought was working. Jack was a good son, husband and father. He had a steady job and brought stability to a household that had already gone through a lot recently. Bandi made an interesting observation. While it might help the development of a new treatment for people in the future if Jack could see, even just a little bit, it would change things in his school. It would be harder for the students to look up to him if they thought his dad was, as he put it, 'cheating a bit'.

Jack thanked them all and declared he would sleep on it as he had told the doctor. Kakko sighed. Tomorrow sounded a long way off. Jalli said, "Your father's right. 'Big decisions should never be made in a hurry'." Kakko relaxed. Her mum and dad were no doubt right – but it was pretty obvious to her which way the decision was going to go.

★★★

The following morning Jack was up early. The white gate was still there.

"Definitely your decision, Jack," said Jalli

"I know. I was hoping that the decision would be made for me."

"God doesn't seem to work that way. I think He's neutral on this one."

"Jalli, if I say, 'Thank you, but no', do you think I am letting anybody down?"

"No. I've thought about that. It is important for them that they have someone who really wants to go through with it. Someone with determination – someone properly frustrated. They'll find someone else that's more suitable."

"Then I am not their man. As long as I have you…"

"*I'm* not going anywhere as long as I have anything to do with it."

"I know. I am so lucky. Let's go to Wanulka after breakfast and contact the hospital. Then we can do whatever we like."

"I'm glad we have been back to Wanulka. It has put so many things right. But now I want to move on. If you're sure about the doctor."

"Certain."

"Then let's go and tell him your decision, ring and thank the Bandis, and then come straight back here."

★★★

The doctor quite understood. He was not surprised. He acknowledged that the procedure needed a high degree of interest on the part of the participants for them to put up with all the challenges that it posed, and Jack should not become a striped mouse unless he really wanted to go through with it.

However, should Jack ever change his mind all he needed to do was phone. He wished Jack well, and Jack thanked him for his work. He really wanted to encourage him and wished him success.

★★★

The moment Jack and Jalli re-entered the cottage garden the white gate melted away.

"Any regrets?" asked Jalli.

"No. More like relief really. What about you?"

"I'm happy Jack. I feel just so free! Mended."

"And I do too. I have not just accepted my lot, I have now embraced it."

20

As the weeks passed Kakko slowly recovered from her broken bones. Not, of course, as quickly as she would have wished. The days in the pot had dragged by, but the hospital was pleased. One doctor commented that she had good healing properties. "Excellent progress," he told her. It didn't feel like that, but Kakko 'had her tail between her legs', as Matilda kept saying, and she was remarkably patient with the doctors. Her nan did not mean to be rude. Apparently on Earth One the expression was a metaphor that referred to a dog trying to keep a lower profile in the pack, at least whilst injured. *Guess that's true,* thought Kakko to herself. *I don't want to make a fool of myself.* She wondered if it would always be like that. Would she ever get another chance at a white gate for instance? Anyway, one good thing had come of it: Tam. He really cared for her no matter what, and her opinion of him had changed. Her enforced retreat was helping her to see that he had many qualities she hadn't noticed before. Behind his outward quiet persona, there were many hidden treasures.

But gradually things began to improve for Kakko. The plaster came off. Her ribs felt less sore. And, to her amazement, the climbing coach from the Sports Centre actually came all the way to Woodglade to check on her, *and* to invite her back into the fold when she was given the say-so from the doctors. He had decided that she was probably going to be safe in the future. She said she would consider coming back. She hadn't given it a thought because she had assumed he had banned her for good. "What about Tam?" she had asked. Coach said he was welcome back too.

She phoned Tam. "Would you really come back to the Sports Centre with me? You never actually enjoyed it."

"I didn't enjoy learning to swim, either, but some things are useful to know how to do. If *you're* going to go on climbing then you might need me on hand to help you."

"To rescue me, you mean."

He laughed. "Perhaps. But I hope not. I don't want to go through all that again."

"But, if you don't enjoy it, it might be more dangerous."

"Maybe, but let's see. If you go back to it, I'll give it a try."

"You really love me, don't you? I can't imagine why."

"Don't give up on yourself, Kakko. No-one else has. Not even Coach it seems. And, yes, I *do* love you."

"Thanks. Do you want to come round?"

"Sure, later. But first I must finish my essay."

★★★

Tam came over to White Gates Cottage later that day. As he walked through the gate, though, he spotted another to his right. It was clean and white and crisp against the dark green hedge. He went over to it and touched it. *Oh dear,* he thought to himself, *it seems like the Creator hasn't given up on us either. Well, at least not on me.*

At that moment Kakko came out of the door and called over to him.

"You can see it too then?"

"Yes. So it's you and me. Anyone else?"

"No. I thought of texting you, but I knew you were on your way. Anyway, it wouldn't have gone away in fifteen minutes."

"You've slowed down then?"

"I guess so. I have to prove to Mum and Dad that I'm not 'impetuous' as they put it. I wish they wouldn't keep using that word – it's as if it was only invented to describe me."

"Well, they can't use it this time you've seen a white gate can they?"

"No. But, Tam, I guess now I've made the point we'd better get going!"

Tam laughed playfully. "Let me phone my mum."

"She won't be happy – especially if she knows you're going with me. Come inside. Then when you've told her, you can get my mum to talk to her. It might help."

"Are there any things we should take?"

"Not that I can see. I guess what we've got on is all that we're going to need."

Inside the cottage Tam rang his parents. To his surprise they were less antagonistic than he had anticipated. He passed the phone to Jalli who chatted on to his mum and said she was sure that they would be sensible this time. It was unlikely to be rock climbing again. She did not tell her about the times when she found herself in a war zone or aboard a spacecraft about to be boarded by hostile space pirates, or, indeed the exploding arms factory. Jalli knew from her own experience that you can't protect your children when they get to eighteen, or in her case seventeen; you just have to let them go like her grandma had done her. What a wonderful woman Momori had been. She must have been so brave. Jalli hadn't really appreciated it at the time. Now she had learned that simply letting children go bit by bit at the right time was a part of parenthood that took courage and a lot of patience. It was also painful, a kind of bereavement.

★★★

Kakko and Tam took their leave and stepped through the gate with a mixture of apprehension and anticipation. The apprehension disappeared in a wave of excitement as they found themselves inside a large hall with seating around a brightly lit stage. There was a big banner in the centre-rear bearing words in zany letters that they could not read. They found themselves in a line of young people like themselves dressed in a huge variety of casual clothes – the girls in tights, trousers, shorts or skirts with every description of top from skimpy to fully covered; the boys in baggy jeans or narrow legs and T-shirts. Whatever you were wearing was fine it seemed, and Kakko and Tam felt not at all out of place. An attendant gave them each a single sheet folded programme written in what looked like the same script as the banner.

"I reckon it's a pop concert," said Kakko. The line led them into rows of seats and they filed in and sat down. As they waited, loud recorded pop music emanated from large speakers front, side and back. The atmosphere was buzzing with expectation. This was a real groovy place to be.

"Cool," shouted Tam in Kakko's ear. "So what've we got to do here, then?"

"No idea. Enjoy ourselves I guess."

"Go with the flow?"

"You got it."

"Just sit."

"Just do what the rest are doing."

After everyone was seated, a compère in a posh suit appeared on stage-left with a mic. The audience cheered and whistled.

"Is anyone out there?" he asked in a hugely amplified voice. The audience made an even louder noise. Working up this crowd was not going to be difficult; they were already hyped to the brim.

"Oh. Hi!" thundered the man on the stage. "Welcome to the Galuga Talent Competition!" More cheering. "Tonight we have for you twelve of the best talented unknowns in Galuga. And who gets to choose the winner?"

"We do!" shouted the audience in unison. It was clearly an established formula.

"How you gonna do it?"

"On our zap-pads!"

"Yoo-u got it. 'One' for 'yuk', 'eight' for 'ace'! Just score each act out of eight on your keypads." Tam and Kakko located theirs on the back of the seats in front of them. "When you hear this you've got ten seconds." A loud cymbal-clash followed by nine drum-beats thumped through the speakers. The audience counted down: "nine, eight, seven, six, five, four, three, two, one, zero!"

"OK. First up, we have the Fuggs, a talented boy band that's going to tear your hearts apart..."

"Ugh," groaned Tam. But Kakko had bright eyes. She

appeared to be up for a sexy boy band that would 'tear her heart apart'!

Actually, they weren't that bad – musically – and Tam gave them a six. *Funny,* he thought as he saw Kakko give them a five. Clearly not up to her expectations. But the people around them were all clapping and whistling and the lads took their bow with satisfaction.

Five more acts followed. A couple were like heavy metal – one a decidedly better group than the other. *How do you award points to stuff that isn't really your thing?* thought Tam. They found it interesting that Kakko was into it more than Tam, who only gave them four and five respectively. There was a pretty awful ballad attempt that was decidedly out of tune that they both marked down.

At the interval the group of teen girls next to them, all leapt up and pushed past brusquely. Whatever they were after they were not going to be down the queue. Tam and Kakko had no money and decided it best to remain where they were.

The second half was the same format as the first. There was one exceptional singer. He had a fantastic voice and sang with soul and passion, hitting high notes with ease and power. Everyone leapt to their feet. The girls next to Kakko were whistling and shouting. There was little doubt that this artist was going to get eights from most of the people.

"How do you follow that?" yelled Kakko in Tam's ear.

After a more muted announcement, a rather timid-looking dark-skinned girl with a guitar crept onto the stage. She was dressed in a pale blue T-shirt and a green and blue rah-rah skirt over navy blue tights. She sat on a high stool, flicked back her long, fluffy hair with blue highlights and began to sing. It was a melodious country song – gentle and deep. There was only polite applause at the end of her song. She failed to manipulate the young audience like the boy who had preceded her. *He* had been all power and charisma. It was an unfortunate slot, thought Tam. Had she followed the poor heavy metal band she would probably have come over better. He gave her a seven, but Kakko was moved and pressed the eight. The final act was a girl-band. Kakko remarked to her boyfriend that they couldn't have worn much less if they had been on the beach. Tam just shrugged. They looked pretty cool to him.

When the girls had finished and the final ten-second countdown had been completed, the compère returned and invited all the acts back on the stage. He explained that he was about to get the results through his headset. After a delay punctuated by a few of his terrible jokes, he announced the results. The better heavy metal band came in third, the boy-band that had opened the show, second and the solo male artist, first.

"You can't argue with that," said Kakko in Tam's ear as the applause resounded around the theatre.

"Guess not. The female acts didn't stand a chance with this audience," he grunted as the teenagers next to them trampled them to get out of their seats. "The girl country singer with the guitar was good, I thought."

"That's because you like that kind of music."

"Sure. I know I am square. She didn't stand a chance after that boy. He was always going to appeal to this audience."

"You are about four years older than most of them."

"An old man!"

"Yeah. At twenty you're definitely past it," joked Kakko.

"So what now?"

"Follow the crowd, I guess."

"Go with the flow. Better hold on to each other in this crush."

As they left the theatre, the crowd pushed and pressed in on them and Tam and Kakko were forced closer together than they had ever been.

Outside the air was cold. Some of the young members of the audience were going round the corner to the stage door. Kakko and Tam watched from across the street as the rest of the crowd gradually melted into the bright lights of the coffee shops and bars. The girls at the stage door let out a scream as the bands and, finally, the single male singer were ushered through them into waiting cars. Then they, too, dispersed, and the lesser sounds in the city centre were all that remained.

Tam and Kakko looked at one another.

"Our white gate was inside," murmured Kakko.

"I was thinking the same thing. The doors are locked to us now. Guess it's time to trust again. What next?"

"Let's just walk," said Kakko. They chose the street with the lights and the night-life and walked past brightly lit shops, a discotheque, several bars and a gaming arcade in semi-darkness with flashing colours and the rattle of coins against a backdrop of up-beat music. As they had no money, none of these places were open to them. People – mainly young – jostled about, intent on having a good time. Some looked happy, some didn't. Kakko couldn't remember herself ever being quite so on the outside of things. All they could do in this strange place was observe.

"You notice so much more when you're just watching," said Kakko.

"Yeah, 'people watching'. Looking at these faces, I reckon there are a lot who are not happy here. They've come for a good time but so many are sad." They stopped outside a particularly popular arcade. Young folk were feeding greedy gambling machines with an intensity new to Tam and Kakko.

"That's ugly," said Tam.

"But they don't know that."

"No. I suppose they can't afford to admit it. They are keeping the blues at bay with the drink and the bright lights and the crowds… and probably drugs too, some of them."

"They'll know it tomorrow. I bet they will all wake up depressed with painful heads."

"They aren't thinking of tomorrow; they daren't."

"We don't have many people like this on *our* planet," remarked Kakko.

"Oh. We do! You haven't lived in the city. Downtown we do. Kakko, have you ever looked into the eyes of some of the kids? When you get to college you see it. Some of them are decaying from the inside. They have no sense of purpose and no sense of self-worth. I was once invited to a party in one of the halls. The air of depression and a lack of any kind of hope just hit me. All I was expected to do was get drunk and make passes at the girls. I tried to get into conversation with one of them but she quickly got upset with me and told me to give up talking and thinking and just snog her."

"And did you?"

"What do you think? I hardly knew her! All I could think of was getting to the bathroom before I puked. Honestly,

Kakko, the place just stank. I got outside and I could smell the night scented flowers and the clean, fresh air and thought…" Tam hesitated.

"What did you think, Tam?" asked Kakko impatiently.

"If you must know, I thought of you."

"That's nice. So what did you do?"

"I texted you. But you didn't reply."

"What did you say? I can't remember that one."

"Oh. Something like, 'How u doing? Missing u.'"

"But I wasn't ready to be missed, was I? All I could think of was passing my exams."

"Quite right. But I'm not missing you *now*. Here we are stuck on a foreign planet goodness knows how far from home and our only means of getting back there is behind locked doors."

"Yet you're not sad?"

"No, for two reasons. First, because I'm with you of course…"

"You're so romantic! And second?"

"Because the Creator is here too. And wherever She is, we are in Her hands…"

"Home is with God?"

"Ultimately, yes. So if the worst comes to the worst and we are dissolved into oblivion we'll still end up with Her in our home dimension."

"With Grandma," sighed Kakko.

"Oh. The welcome party will be tremendous. But for now, I don't think that's God's plan. Let's keep walking."

After a couple of hundred metres the shops and lights ended but the road headed on into darkness. They had come to an unlit bridge with iron railings. It spanned a large river that was pitch black except for the glint of lights reflecting on its rippled surface. A cool but sweet breeze struck their faces and fresh air cleared their lungs of the fug of sweaty bodies, stale perfume, alcohol fumes, smoke and who knows what else they had encountered only a few metres back.

"Peace at last," sighed Kakko. "I guess this place is quite pleasant in the daytime."

As their eyes got used to the darkness, Kakko and Tam made out the shapes of the occasional person coming towards them – people walking with purpose, going somewhere. It crossed Tam's mind that there may be muggers about in a strange city like this at night, but he didn't say anything. Then about twenty metres in front of them they saw a lone figure, sitting on the paving stones, back against the railings but hunched forwards, head lolling. They stopped, hand in hand. The person appeared to be asleep … or something. There was a dark object on the ground just beyond the body. Kakko recognised it as a guitar case – and then she made out a skateboard too.

Somehow these things seemed to make this figure less threatening and Kakko approached dragging Tam behind her. The figure moved and looked up, alarmed and yet resigned at the same time.

"It's OK," said Kakko hurriedly. "We won't hurt you."

Then Tam recognised the pale blue top and the long hair with blue highlights.

"You. You're the girl that sang in the talent contest just back there. You sang a country song. Danni… or something," said Tam.

The girl nodded dejectedly. "Da'yelni." She struggled to get up but Kakko had already got down on the pavement beside her.

"You OK?"

"Yeah… I guess."

"What do you mean, you guess?" asked Tam who was crouching on his haunches in front of the girls. "What's wrong?"

"Well, it's all finished, ain't it?"

"What's finished?" asked Kakko.

"You saw it, if you were there. They don't like me. Nobody voted for me. I ain't got no talent!"

"But you have. We voted for you. I gave you a seven."

"And I gave you an eight," smiled Kakko.

"Thanks. But it didn't stop me coming last. The compère, he didn't say who came last but I saw the scores. I was twelfth."

"But that's to do with the audience," said Tam. "They were bound to be into the boys – most of them around us were not really discerning the music but just who was hot. At another kind of gig you'd be at the top."

"But there ain't no other kind of gig is there? Not around here."

"But you don't need loads of fans. Do *you* think your music's good?"

"Nah. I guess it ain't. I thought so, but now I know, it ain't. That's the problem, I really ain't got no talent."

"So are you going to try and sing some of the songs the others sang?"

"Nah, course not"

"Why, because you're not good enough to try?"

"I don't *wanna* try. They're crap. That boy who won, did you register them lyrics? There was only three lines which went over and over, 'Baby I'm into you. I'm into you big time. You're oozing all over me...' What kind of song is that?"

"So what you sing is better, right?" said Tam.

"I think it's not only better, it is *good,*" said Kakko. "But you have to believe that yourself. As long as *you* think it's good, that's fine. If the rest of them don't recognise that, who's fault is it?"

The girl hesitated.

"Theirs," affirmed Kakko. "They're the ones that are missing out."

"Guess so. But it don't feel like that."

"What about your folks? Won't they be looking for you?" asked Tam. "Won't they be worried about you out here in the dark all on your own?"

"No. They're back in the village. I'm a student here. All my flatmates are down there getting pissed. No-one's giving me a second thought. When I got out the stage door they were all trying to get to that boy-band so I just sloped off."

Kakko was beginning to understand. Da'yelni felt that even her so called friends had deserted her to swoon over some slick, male pop singers.

Tam had got to his feet and was looking across the road to the other side of the bridge. He stopped to take in what he saw.

"Da'yelni. Are you adventurous?"

"How d'you mean?"

"Can you see anything over there?"

"Where? It's dark. What am I supposed to be looking at?"

"Straight across… there," he pointed to what was, for him, a clearly defined white gate.

"What's that doing there?"

"Describe it to us," commanded Kakko who had also seen it.

"A garden gate, all shiny… in the railings."

"Da'yelni, you say your music is not appreciated *here,* but it might be the other side of that gate!"

"You mean kill myself? Walk off the bridge? Who *are* you – some kind of angels from heaven? I'm not ready to die… not yet! I mean my life might suck, but that's extreme!"

Da'yelni got to her feet and looked at Kakko and Tam as if they were harbingers of death. She was ready to run.

"Wait Da'yelni. You will *not* die. We promise," said Kakko. "We are not from the 'other side'. We are from *this* universe. We're… we're space travellers. I know that that might sound strange but that gate doesn't lead to heaven but to another planet. And I'm guessing a planet where they want you to sing. To sing your stuff."

Da'yelni hesitated.

"I've heard of this before. Some people say we, our race, came from another planet thousands of years ago. They just walked through some kind of door. Some people reckon it still happens, but nobody wants to hear that because it means having some sort of belief in God, and that ain't cool."

"Do you believe in God, Da'yelni?"

"No… yes… I don't know."

"Would you mind if God did exist?"

"Course not."

"But you say others don't want to believe in Him."

"That's because a God would stop you doing things. Take away your freedom."

"So without God people are free to do what they want?"

"In some ways, but not really. There's always someone ready to set themselves up in his place. No. There's always someone trying to dictate and control – making laws and rules and stuff… if it ain't God, someone else will step in. Sometimes my songs are about that."

"But what if God was not about making laws and making you do things? What if God was really about setting you free?" asked Tam.

"Free? How do mean? How can anyone give you freedom? If the law says you have to do something and you don't, then you get done."

"God sets *me* free," said Kakko. "Free to think, free to explore *inside* me, *and* out there." Kakko threw her arms about in every direction. "The God I believe in doesn't *make* anyone do things. It's people that do that. God invites us to choose. We are always free to be ourselves. She wants it that way."

"She?"

"Oh, I often think of God as a 'She'. I know God is neither male nor female but somehow the universe She has made… well, has a feminine touch. It's not so much mechanical as artistic… but that's to do with how I feel."

"You have a feeling for God?"

"Yeah. It's a sort of… kind of thing we have. A relationship."

"And your God. She makes you feel free?"

"Sure. Those in authority might tell me what to do – but

they can't tell me what to think or feel inside… with God. And she tells me I can do my thing… be me, even if that gets up people's noses."

"You mean God will get you out of prison if you get into trouble?"

"No. It's not that kind of freedom. There will always be people who make rules for us. But with God we're free inside ourselves – whatever anyone does to us."

"You really believe in God, don't you? You're from Her, ain't you?"

"I suppose we are," answered Kakko. "When people are in a jam we just find ourselves talking about Her… that gate. It'll be two-way. You'll get back here. We've always managed to get back home. We've learned to trust the Creator on this one." Kakko held her hand out to Da'yelni. She swung her guitar case on her shoulder, picked up the skate board and crossed the road as Tam led the way. The girl checked over the railings. They were above one of the bridge supports and at this place one step was not going to take her plunging to the river below, even if the gate failed. Kakko was relieved to see the gate was positioned like this because she knew Da'yelni would probably not have had the faith to step through her first white gate if it appeared to lead her into an abyss. Faith and trust grow with experience. Still, Da'yelni hesitated.

Just then a blue car with yellow stripes turned onto the bridge.

"Police!" exclaimed Da'yelni. "So, are we going, or what?"

Tam stepped through and disappeared. Kakko took Da'yelni by the hand and pulled her through. She had been contemplating taking just one careful step, but in the urgency of the situation she almost leapt. They found themselves in the midst of a neat garden with green grass, shrubs and trees. The sun was high in the sky. Da'yelni just stood and stared. The place was beautiful.

"I *must* be dead," she said slowly, "but you know what, I don't care!"

21

Despite it being full daylight, Tam, Kakko and Da'yelni felt tired. They had just got to the end of a demanding day and now, here they were on another world with bedtime apparently some way off. And, God only knew where they were going to find a bed anyway.

"That's the first time I've heard of a white gate inside a white gate," commented Kakko.

"What do you mean?" asked Tam.

"I mean travelling from one place to another without going back home to Joh. When we went through that gate I was expecting to get back to the cottage."

"I was too. But this *is* Joh isn't it?"

"I'm not sure. It doesn't smell quite right."

"Now you mention it, I agree. So, I wonder what comes next."

"I don't know about you but I'm going to rest," said Kakko.

The grass was lush and soft and the three young people found a comfortable place under a tree. They lay back and closed their eyes. Kakko slipped her hand into Tam's. She asked Da'yelni why she wanted to avoid the police. Were they dangerous? Had she committed a crime?

"Nah, I ain't done nothing. And they're not exactly *dangerous*. They probably wouldn't actually hurt us. But they would want to take us in just because they could. I mean out there on the bridge, it would have been easy for them."

"For our safety?"

"Nah, they might say we were loitering with intent or something. They just pull young people in to get their parents to give them money to release them."

"But that's kidnapping and extortion!"

"Not if you're the police. It's *expenses*. They're always after what they call a 'recognition'."

"Couldn't you report that to a lawyer?"

"Only if you had a friendly one. Otherwise you'd just have to pay *them* over the odds too. They don't want to keep you, but everyone knows they won't let you go until they feel 'compensated for their trouble'."

"So there's no justice on your planet then?"

"Oh. There's justice. It's just different for the rich and the powerful – those with connections have one sort, and the rest of us – well it depends on how much we can pay."

"And country singers? What's it like for you?"

"We're part of the underground mostly. There's kids I know who write protest songs. They see us as being against the authorities."

"Do you write all your own stuff?"

"You have to really. You can't go round nicking other peoples'. You can only sing that if you pay."

"Do people cover *your* stuff?"

"Sometimes. They don't pay nothing though. They might do a swap, but, generally, their songs are not what I like. I don't hardly ever sing anyone else's stuff."

"Will you play something for us? We can't pay you though. We haven't got any money."

"Maybe… what do you live on if you've got no money? You don't sound poor."

"My mum and dad both work," answered Kakko.

"Mine too," said Tam. "It's just we don't have any of your type of money on us."

"Where you come from, what about them without parents?"

"The State pays. But there really aren't many poor people on Joh. Some people don't have parents but the State steps in and helps them with the taxes the rest of us pay. It seems to work OK," replied Tam.

Kakko continued, "On the planet where my dad comes from, Earth One, there are some very poor people. He says that millions and millions of kids never get to school at all. And in some places on the planet a girl is more likely to die giving birth than to finish primary school. In that place there are few schools and no hospitals. And it's not so much better for the boys, Dad says."

"That ain't fair."

"That's what I said. Dad says that on this side of death, life isn't fair. What is important is that we try and do something about it. The more people that try, the more progress we will make. But the problem is so big. And then some people don't help themselves. They get something and then they spoil it by starting wars, or cheating… they don't think of others."

"Like on our planet. Most of the money is in the hands of a small minority. To get anywhere you've got to get recognition, get connections."

"And that's why you entered the talent competition."

"Yep. But to come bottom of everyone means I've mucked up any chance I had."

"But you're at college. You could get another sort of job."

"Yes. But you won't get anywhere in it if you haven't got friends, connections – that's what I keep telling you."

"You could meet a rich boy," suggested Tam.

Kakko squeezed his hand and thumped it on the grass.

"Get lost! I want the recognition for myself! Besides the rich work that all out among themselves. If any of their boys dared look at me he'd get it in the neck… no, unless I have some status that can't happen. I ain't going to marry anyone for their money. I don't want a creep who's rich but got nothing else."

"How'd you mean?" asked Tam.

"Well, *if* I had a boyfriend he'd be someone who wasn't just out for an easy life. Someone with a passion for something; someone who wants to make the world better. You know, someone with real character."

"I know exactly," said Kakko.

"So I won't find anyone because there ain't many like that to find, that ain't already spoken for. But I ain't wasting my time looking for one. If he comes along fine, otherwise… well, I don't suppose anything will work now – not now I've come bottom of the list… Anyhow, what're we doing *here*?"

"Waiting," said Kakko. "To tell you the truth I don't want to do anything but lay here for the moment. Something will turn up in God's time."

"You really do believe in Him… Her, don't you?"

"Course. Tried once or twice doing things without Her. I

am learning to wait for Her. When She's in it, you know what you have to do. Otherwise best wait."

Tam smiled. Jack and Jalli would have been amazed, and delighted, to hear their daughter speaking like this about waiting.

"She keeps you safe. She stops you getting hurt."

"No, not really. Sometimes perhaps, but mostly not. Mum and Dad got hurt bad. Things can still happen, but if they do, it won't be your fault and God's always picking you up. That's what Mum says, and what Grandma always said even when she was dying."

"I *ain't* dead then?"

"No, Da'yelni, you're not."

"I can't be. I'm whacked. You can't be whacked and dead… by the way, call me Dah. All my friends do."

Tam had already succumbed to sleep. Kakko lay still listening to the birds. Before long all three were fast asleep. It had been an exhausting few hours.

★★★

Exactly how long they slept the three young people were not sure. They were woken, however, by the sound of voices. Kakko felt a sudden embarrassment. She thought of Goldilocks, but it seemed that no-one had seen them. A party of elderly people were making their way down a paved path towards a large building at the end of the garden. Some were on crutches, some used frames and a couple were in wheelchairs. There were younger ladies with them, all of whom seemed to be shouting.

"Mrs Gillespie, are you sure you don't need help?"

"'Eh? What you say?"

"Are you sure you don't need help?" yelled a younger woman in her ear.

"You don't have to shout! I'll tell you if I can't manage."

"Good."

"What's that? Speak up, can't you? Don't know why people have to mumble everything these days."

"Never mind… just keep going," she shouted.

"That's what I *am* doing!" protested Mrs Gillespie.

This group were followed by another. There was one man in a self-propelled wheelchair. It had three wheels and he seemed far too large for it. He proceeded down the path but the chair got out of control and one of the rear wheels ran off the edge of the path onto the grass. Then, slowly but surely, still clutching the handlebars, he went over sideways and fell onto the grass with the machine on its side.

Tam was across the lawn in an instant with Kakko not far behind. They were too late to catch him but fortunately he didn't seem to have hit the ground very hard. He lay there helpless, the machine tucked behind his large frame. Kakko gently took his hands that were still gripping the handlebars and Tam dragged the chair clear and upright. Then between them, Kakko and Tam lifted the gentleman into a sitting position.

"Oh, Bert!" exclaimed one of the helpers rushing up, "I told you to wait! You hurt?"

The man grunted a negative.

"He should be able to take his weight on his feet," declared the helper to Tam and Kakko. "Do you think you can get him up?" she said, looking at them hopefully. They each took a side.

"One, two, three," said Tam, and Bert was upright. "The chair," said Tam urgently.

Dah was already dragging the chair to line up with Bert. The helper swung the seat out sideways and Bert took hold of the handlebars with his right hand and lowered himself. Dah put all her weight onto the other side of the chair to counterbalance it.

"That's it, steady the chair," said the helper as she manhandled Bert's right leg forwards onto the platform. Bert then dragged his left leg after it and sat squarely once more on the machine.

"Thank you so much. I don't know what I would have done without you. You came just at the right time. A Godsend," said the carer.

"Yeah," whispered Dah to Kakko, "so God doesn't stop accidents. He just sends people to pick you up when you need it."

"That's generally the way of it," said Kakko.

"It was Him… Her… who sent you to me," affirmed Dah.

One of the ladies came from the building and fussed over Bert as he navigated himself up the path. He seemed to have already forgotten the incident.

"I am so glad you were around," gushed the lady, who seemed to be in charge, "but I'm sorry you have had such an introduction." Then she noticed Dah's guitar case. "I see you have an instrument. I was wondering how we were going to manage for music – our keyboardist was taken sick yesterday. I hope you found us OK. Mrs Merton explained that you hadn't been here before, but that you were keen to help us with our little party. My name's Mrs Higgins." She took each of their hands in turn. Kakko tried to explain that they weren't from Mrs Merton.

"I don't think –" she began, but the lady kept going, seemingly without a breath.

"You will find we are a happy bunch here. Our clients, we are supposed to call them – but I prefer to say, 'our ladies and gentlemen' – are all elderly; some of them live alone; I can't imagine how they manage, they get ready mostly by themselves, they must start very early, although we have a few who have to be helped of course, like Bert here, can't dress himself at all, always on the floor too; has had to have a side put on his bed; he has a man go to get him into bed and another gets him up every morning, this is about the only time he gets out – to our gatherings – and they say he's exhausted at the end of it. Well, so am I and I can't say how happy I am to see you. We need the help of young people and so glad you have music too… come on, what are we standing here for? Come inside. Is there anything you would like to ask?"

"Yes," replied Dah, "have you got a toilet?"

"Oh, of course. How silly of me. You should have said right away. How have you got here? Oh, on foot. Of course you *must* be wanting to use our rest rooms. They're new you know. Put in last year with a grant. Very proud of them. Never thought we would get it – all the paper work. Come in, come in. What are you waiting for?"

Mrs Higgins led them into the entrance hall and pointed to doors at the end of a corridor. "On the right, belles first door, beaux the second. Should be everything in there you need, just –"

Dah didn't wait for Mrs Higgins to stop. Perhaps she might not have. She just headed for the door with the symbol of a person with long hair and a ball-gown. The other symbol had short hair, trousers and a bow tie.

Kakko had been wondering how she was going to ask where they were in the universe without alarming anyone. And people were expected from Mrs Merton and she was anxious to tell Mrs Higgins or someone that they were not these people. However, right at this moment getting to the loo was the most immediate thing.

As she dried her hands she thought she recognised the script on the hand-dryer attached to the wall. She recalled some of the stuff her nan read. It was English, she was sure of it. Perhaps they were on Earth One.

While they were still in the 'rest-rooms' some people from Mrs Merton arrived. But they were welcomed with even more delight by Mrs Higgins. She was so pleased so many had come. These other young people had no idea how many were to be expected and just took the presence of Kakko, Tam and Dah in their stride. They were no more able to get many words in edgeways than anyone else. After a while Kakko and Tam decided that they were not going to get a chance to explain anything and they decided to just 'go with the flow' as usual. Mrs Higgins was fussing over everybody. She was clearly enjoying herself with so many people to talk to.

"I bet she's exhausted at the end of the day," said Dah.

"Probably has no one to talk to all week," suggested Kakko.

Dah went back into the garden and collected her guitar, but she decided to leave the skateboard outside. She propped it on its side against the hedge.

Inside Mrs Higgins was calling everyone to order.

"Ladies and gentlemen," she struck a block with a gavel. She was enjoying herself. "Ladies and gentlemen, welcome to our weekly gathering. Today is party time!" The helpers cheered. "And a special welcome to our newcomer, Mr Larry Williams, who has recently moved to New London to be near his daughter and their family. I believe you lived in Georgia, Mr Williams?"

"Lived in Atlanta all my life," shouted the old man. "An African-American like me can be free in these northern parts, can't he?" he inquired with mock confidence.

"No matter you're black, Mr Williams. We're all friends here. We'll soon make you feel like a true Nutmegger like the rest of us … and welcome to our young people who have come to help us. They've already earned their supper looking after Bert even before he got through the door."

Some people looked at Bert but he didn't seem to notice. Mrs Gillespie was fiddling with her hearing-aid. "Damn thing!" she said in a voice loud enough for anyone not deaf to hear. But again people just ignored her.

"And one of them has brought along her guitar to get us all singing." A little lady down the front clapped. "You like singing, Mrs Smith?"

"Ye-es, I do."

Smith, thought Kakko. *It is Earth then. New London? Hadn't her nan talked about London?* Even though she had never ever been to Earth One before, hearing her own name made her feel that she, somehow, belonged although all this was foreign to her. She wondered if she and this bright old lady who liked singing were somehow related. She would talk to her later if she got a chance.

They did 'birthdays' and Mrs Higgins got all the young people to confess to their ages. Dah turned out to be nineteen. Kakko was relieved to find that she, herself, wasn't quite the youngest – there was a young girl who admitted to being a 'high-school sophomore' whatever that meant, it did mean that she was a lot younger than Kakko – but otherwise they were all as old or older than her. She felt annoyed about this, but then, she told herself, it wasn't age that counted, but experience. And as far as that went the experience represented in that room must have been huge. She was sat next to a lady who had just had her eighty-first birthday. She couldn't imagine what it must feel like to be her. She didn't want to. But the lady seemed content enough.

After a few more preliminaries Dah was invited to the front.

"I didn't know I was going to sing for you today," she began. "I'm afraid I don't know any of the songs you know. I generally write my own."

"That's wonderful," declared Mrs Higgins, "teach us some of yours."

Dah tuned her guitar nervously, then struck a chord. She cleared her throat and said, "OK. This is about a boatman who has sailed a river boat up and down his river doing trade all his life." She began to sing. The effect was wonderful. In this context, her rich, sweet tones were gripping. As she sang she saw every eye on her and she warmed even more into the song. As she got to the third repeat of the chorus, Mrs Smith began to join in. It didn't seem to matter that no-one else did, she was enjoying herself. Kakko smiled. One day she would be an old lady by the name of Smith. She glanced at Tam. He was enthralled by Dah and her music. Kakko felt a twinge of something. *Was it jealousy? It couldn't be, could it?* For all her natural confidence she hadn't any of Dah's gifts. Dah was talented and under-estimated herself. Kakko thought about herself, and wondered whether, in comparison, she was just an empty extrovert.

At the conclusion of the song, there was loud applause. Tam applauded too. He turned to Kakko and whispered, "I wish I could sing like that! We really were meant to bring her here." And then he put his arm around Kakko's waist and she wondered how she could have doubted his devotion. Whatever he saw in her it was far more than any talent she might or might not have – his love did not depend on her being anything else than who she was. And the pang of jealousy brought home to her how much that devotion had become mutual.

"That was beautiful, Dah," said Mrs Higgins. "Have you any more?"

Dah sang another song and, as she did so, she saw tears in some of the old folks' eyes. As it finished there wasn't immediate applause; rather there was a silent pause. And then Mrs Higgins started to clap loudly and soon the whole room was joining in.

Mr Williams called out, "I see you come from the South, young lady. You may not be as black as me, but you've got a black soul. I haven't heard anything quite like that for years. So commercial these days. You keep singing like that my girl! Don't you ever let anyone tell you to stop!"

Dah sniffed, "Thanks."

"It's almost time to eat now, ladies and gentlemen, but

Dah, we would all like another song before we go. Have you made a record?"

"Nah," said Dah, flattered and embarrassed.

"You should… now folks, the food is coming to you."

The helpers collected food from the kitchen and distributed it among the tables. Kakko and Dah were given the task of taking round cups of tea, coffee and cans of cold soda. Larry Williams took Dah's hand as she served their table and smiled at her. "What's your name… I mean your last name?"

"Lugos," she said shyly.

"That's an unusual name."

"It isn't where I come from."

"You don't come from the South then?"

"Nah. I ain't from your country."

"You could a fooled me. You got black soul, girl. Mark my words. It's in there somewhere."

"Thanks," smiled Dah.

"That's my girl!"

After she had finished serving, Kakko went and sat at the same table as Mrs Smith.

"You and I share the same name," she smiled.

"Common as dirt," said Mrs Smith unexpectedly.

"What's that?" asked Kakko.

"The name. Common as dirt. I told that to my Jim before we were married. Now *my* name – *my* family name is different. It's Prendergast. Now that's a special name if ever there was one."

"I was wondering," said Kakko, "if your husband might have been related to my father in some way. He's called Jack and his father was Shaun."

"Where they come from?"

"Persham. Well that's where my dad grew up."

"Persham?" said a lady from the same table. "Persham. That's in England isn't it?"

"Yes."

"I *thought* you were English. My husband's mother was English. I think she came from somewhere like Persham. Met during the war they did, his ma and pa. He was a GI stationed over there. Met her at some dance. He gave her chocolate and silk stockings and that was it. They didn't have those things because of the war... not that she didn't care for him. She loved him all her life. A good woman."

"Most of us here came from Europe though, didn't we?" said another. "I mean in the beginning. Even if you can trace your line back to the very early days in America, you come from Europe. My family were Dutch. Could be I am a direct descendant of the original settlers."

"Could be," said the lady proud to be born a Prendergast.

"All of us. Except him," she said theatrically, "the new one from Atlanta. His ancestors would have been African for certain."

"Now, then. Don't talk like that. We're all equal these days. We won the war so they could be free."

"That was when your husband's father met his mother?" queried Kakko.

"No dear, not *that* war. The *civil* war. The war we fought here, among ourselves."

"How many wars have there been?" asked Kakko.

"So lucky you young'un's today. You take peace for granted. There's been *hundreds* of wars over the years, dear."

"And there's hundreds going on today in different parts of the world that we don't know about," said Mrs Smith.

"Hundreds?" queried Kakko amazed.

"Hundreds. They don't bother putting them on the news any more. My son says that if you look on the computer you can learn what's really going on. But the news, like you get on the television, they only tell you the bad stuff from around here, and the stuff about the big boys like China and Russia – and the Arabs, of course."

"Sometimes it gets over here though, doesn't it? I mean we had 'Nam didn't we, and then the 9/11 lot…"

There was so much Kakko wanted to ask her father and her nan when she got home. She listened as the old folks on her table went through war after war that they had lived through or heard about.

"Why do people want to fight wars?" she asked. "I mean so many people getting killed and so on. I mean isn't there a – "

But Kakko never got to finish her question. Dah had let up a scream, threw her chair back and was chasing a man out of the door. Mrs Gillespie was shouting, "He's got my purse! That man, he just came in and stole my purse!"

Dah was after him, but the man had rollerblades on his feet for a quick escape. He whistled down the path and was at the gate before Dah could catch him, quick though she was. Kakko was on her feet too and Tam instinctively followed. The thief had not anticipated being pursued so immediately, but he clung on to Mrs Gillespie's bag as he pulled the gate open and skated off down the hill. Dah dragged her skateboard from the hedge, threw it through the open gate, leapt on it and was in hot pursuit as Kakko and Tam got to the gate themselves.

"Not just a musician," declared Tam. "She can handle that thing."

"It could be nasty if she catches him," breathed Kakko as she tried to run. Her chest hurt and she slowed up but Tam was in hot pursuit. He rounded a bend and saw the thief and Dah below him. She was keeping up with him, possibly even gaining slightly. Suddenly the thief leapt to his left off the road into a wood. He stumbled and fell down a steep slope, got to his feet and tried to run across an open clearing. Here the wheels on his feet were an encumbrance, as with each step he strained the ligaments in his ankles just to keep his feet upright, but if he made the cover of the trees on the far side of the open ground he would have a chance to hide from his pursuers.

An instant after the thief had left the road Dah had reached the same spot. She took a quick glance and saw the challenge but she had enough speed to take her and her skateboard up and over the edge and the slope. Crouching on her board, Dah landed upright in a mass of undergrowth on the edge of the clearing. She was now only metres away from her quarry, only she was on *foot* over the springy turf.

As he reached the trees, the thief spun round and threw Mrs Gillespie's bag at Dah, just missing her right ear, and then plunged through the undergrowth. Dah continued in pursuit but Tam had now arrived at the top of the drop from the road and saw what was happening.

"Dah," he yelled. "Leave him! Dah, if you catch him what're you going to do? Leave him!"

Dah stopped. Tam's call had quietened the adrenalin coursing through her veins and she stopped, breathing hard on the edge of the clearing. She couldn't see the thief, he had dived for cover somewhere, but he hadn't taken the bag with him.

Tam and finally Kakko caught her up.

"He's in there somewhere," said Dah.

"I guess they will have called the police," puffed Kakko. "Let them find him. He can't get far without being seen. Anyway, we've got Mrs Gillespie's handbag which is the main thing. Let's get it back to her. She'll be able to relax then. She was really upset."

Tam picked the bag out of a thorn bush. "The way she reacted, you'd think she had the family jewels in here."

"Probably has," said Kakko, wheezing. "Sorry, I'm not quite fully mended."

"You OK?" said Tam with concern.

"Yeah. I'll be fine. Just give me a minute."

Dah had retrieved her skateboard from the undergrowth.

"You can really use that thing," said Kakko.

"Thanks. I've had one for years. I got this one for my eighteenth. Loads of parents were buying their kids wheels – only they had cars. My mum said she reckoned I would prefer this kind of wheels, she says she was lucky I wasn't actually born with a board attached to my feet."

Kakko winced. "Sounds painful!"

"But she's right," said Dah as they climbed back up to the road, "I reckon I was using one of these as soon as I could walk."

As they got back to the gate a police car pulled up. Kakko was aware of Dah flinching.

"It's OK, Dah," said Kakko. "You're the hero!"

Tam walked up the path with Mrs Gillespie's bag in his hand. As soon as she saw it she gave a whoop.

"My purse! Oh thank you, thank you!" she grabbed his wrist and pulled him to her and planted a huge kiss on his cheek.

"It wasn't me," explained Tam. "It was Dah. She was so quick on her skateboard."

Dah and Kakko were talking to the police and showing them which way the man had gone.

"I reckon we'll need helicopter back-up," drawled one, and he got back into his car and began to talk on his radio.

The other motioned to Kakko and Dah to go back into the hall. "We'll need you to make a statement," he explained.

Dah looked at Kakko and Kakko nodded, "No problem, officer."

As they stepped into the hall the old folk applauded them. Mrs Higgins came over to them all effusive with congratulations and praise, which Tam and Kakko immediately directed towards Dah.

"We really, really are so grateful to you. You were so fast. One minute all was peace and joy and the next Mrs Gillespie's purse was gone and you were in hot pursuit. She really shouldn't put all that money in there. Two thousand dollars," she said. "Imagine. Two thousand dollars in your purse! She was scared to leave it in her apartment. Well, I don't blame her but it's no safer with her is it? I mean she could get mugged anywhere, couldn't she?"

"She was!" said Dah.

"Yes. Well, all's well that ends well. That's what I say. I do hope they catch the man. It was a man, wasn't it? Mrs Gillespie said he had a scarf over his face and sunglasses. Gloves too so there won't be any fingerprints. Didn't have a gun, did he?"

"Nah," said Dah, "at least I didn't see one."

"He could have one tucked away somewhere. What you did was very brave. I was just thinking of that report I read in the New York newspaper the other day. Terrible things happen in New York City, you know, and this man could have come from there. I tell them, don't think that because you're across the state-line that you're safe. I mean it's not just New York is it? We're not that far from Providence, or Boston come to that. I heard about this gangster who hitched a ride in a truck…"

As Mrs Higgins was talking on, Kakko started to panic inside. Suppose this man did have a gun! Because people in Joh didn't go round toting weapons it didn't mean that they didn't in other parts of the universe. And apparently it wasn't unheard of in this place.

"Miss." Kakko woke from her musings to see that the police officer wanted to talk to her.

"If you can tell us what *you* saw, Miss?"

"Er… nothing much at the beginning. I was over there talking to those people when I heard Dah – Da'yelni – scream and Mrs Gillespie shouting and then I saw Da'yelni run out after someone. She was almost at the gate behind him when we got there. He had rollerblades but Dah has a skate-board. That's how she got close to him."

Dah described the events and the police officer noted them down.

"Mrs Gillespie," he said, "is everything still in your purse? Is there anything missing?"

"No, it's all here officer. Thanks to this young lady."

They were then aware of the sound of a helicopter. The officer left them and he and the other policeman drove off down the hill.

"Well, what a to-do!" declared Mrs. Higgins. "And it's now about time we should be rounding things up. We'll have the draw, and then I did suggest that our young friend led us in another song before we all head off home. Are you still up for it, or have you had enough excitement for one day?"

Dah recognised that she could not disappoint these old folks. She had made something of an impression on them in more ways than one.

"OK," she said. "But this time you all have to join in." And line by line she taught the assembled company the chorus. And nearly everyone *did* join in and Mr Williams struck his knee in time. Needless to say, Mrs Smith was in her element.

"Do you know, 'Be Not Afraid' by Bob Dufford?" she called out when the song had ended.

"No, sorry – " began Dah.

"I do," Kakko found herself saying. "It's my dad's favourite."

"Can you sing it for us, Kakko?" asked Mrs Higgins.

Tam looked at his girlfriend and nodded to the front. "Go on," he said, "be not afraid!"

"I can't sing," she hissed, "not like Dah."

"That doesn't matter," said Tam. "You've told them you know the song. You can't let them down now."

Kakko screwed up her face at him, she was wishing she had not jumped in, but she was already on her way.

"I have to explain," she said. "I can't sing like Dah. But my dad taught me this when I was little. He used to sing it to me when I was scared of something. Like when I had a nightmare. Dah will you me give a good note to start on – not too high and not too low."

Dah twanged a G. Kakko nodded and cleared her throat. She tried humming it and Dah twanged again and smiled as Kakko got on the note. Kakko began to sing.

After the first line she thought of how relevant the next lines sounded now she was here on a strange planet. For the first time she understood one of the reasons the song appealed so much to her father.

"You shall wander far in safety though you do not know the way. You shall speak your words in foreign lands and all will understand," she sang. Her dad had explained that it came from the Scriptures from Earth. God had spoken them to a man called Jeremiah, or someone, when He called him to go out and take on the corrupt leaders of his planet.

By the time Kakko had finished the third line she found that not only Mrs Smith and Mr Williams, but a number of the others were joining in with her. Mr Williams had a lovely voice, deep and rich. As Kakko reached the chorus, *"Be not afraid. I go before you always. Come follow me, and I will give you rest…"* he had virtually taken over. Mrs Smith was now in full voice too. Kakko was grateful to them for keeping her on course. Then Dah started to pluck the tune and by the third verse was playing full chords and even twiddly bits here and there. Even Tam was joining in.

"That was brilliant," he said to Kakko as she rejoined him amidst the applause. "Well done!"

As Mrs Higgins brought the gathering to a close, Mr. Williams stood and declared: "The Grace of the Lord Jesus

Christ, and the love of God and the fellowship of the Holy Spirit, be with us for evermore!" and, despite the gathering not being a religious one, there was a resounding, "Amen!" One thing was sure, noted Mrs Higgins, this new Mr Williams was by no means a shy character. She was going to have to watch him, but his antics this time had not seemed to cause offence.

As the old people got to their feet and walked, hobbled or were pushed towards the exit, the young people did what they could to help. The three people from Mrs Merton gathered themselves together to leave too and Kakko, Tam and Dah took their leave of Mrs Higgins.

"Whoops," said Kakko. "No gate!"

"No," said Tam. "I had just noticed that. Looks like we're stuck here for a while."

Just then a minibus drew up with the words, 'New London YWCA' in bright orange on the door and a young woman jumped out of the driver's seat.

"Hi, Hermione," she said approaching Mrs Higgins. "How's it all going?"

"We have just so much to thank you for, Amy. These six young people you sent are such a wonder. Not only did they lead us in a singing session second to none – I don't know how I am going to get Mr Jones accepted again – oh dear, I mean he tries hard but he never got everyone going like these young people, and then, as I say, it was not only the singing but they also rescued dear old Mrs Gillespie's purse that some man stole from the table by the door right in front of everyone – just came in all covered up and took it, as large as you like, thought we couldn't catch him, but then Dah here, she went after him on her skate thing and got it back, these two as well, and the police are after him right now. You can hear the helicopter…"

"But Hermione, I don't recognise…"

"Sorry," said Tam, fighting to get a word in. "We never said we were sent by you. Mrs Higgins just assumed it and…"

"It was too late to explain properly," sighed Kakko, "by the time we got out of the loo…"

"You don't need to explain!" laughed Mrs Merton, "I can quite understand. Anyway, you seem to have made an impression. Where *are* you from?"

"To tell the truth," Kakko spoke up, "we had come a long way and we were tired so we lay down there under the tree. Then a gentleman fell off his wheelchair and we just came forward to help rescue him…"

"Oh, I had quite forgotten about that!" declared Mrs Higgins. "What a day! We are just so glad you were here. Without them it would have been a disaster from the beginning. They had poor Bert back in his seat pronto, and then the music thing with Mr Jones being ill, and of course the thief… excuse me, I have to say goodbye to Mrs Smith and make sure Mr Williams comes again. My, can he sing!" and she was off.

"Where are you staying?" asked Mrs Merton.

"Nowhere. I mean we haven't got anything sorted out yet," stuttered Kakko. "Is there anywhere we can stay in New London?"

"There is room in the hostel," said one of the other three young people, "they can stay with us can't they?"

"Well, I don't see why not."

"I'm afraid we haven't got any money," explained Kakko. "It's a bit embarrassing really."

"I've got some," said Dah who produced two fifty-dollar bills.

"Where did you get that?" asked Tam alarmed.

"Mrs Gillespie gave me one of them. She just pushed it into my hand… said I had to take it. I had saved her bag. She wouldn't take it back and while I was trying to tell her I couldn't take it, Mr. Williams gave me another one. He said I have a black soul and I should take it to buy strings for my guitar. I was too afraid to argue with him… I thought I would give it to Mrs Higgins."

"Well now, one hundred dollars will get you all full board for one night at the YWCA," affirmed Amy Merton.

"And you can play for us tonight. Teach us some of your songs," suggested one of the other young people. "You were brilliant in there," she said gesturing towards the hall.

"In this YWCA place," asked Dah, "are they all young like you?"

"Mostly," answered Amy, "the 'Y' stands for 'Young'. We began as the 'Young Women's Christian Association.' Don't worry," she said, seeing Tam look a little worried, "we have some rooms for men. You won't be on your own. There is John here."

"Thanks," said Tam.

"But if they're young," said Dah, "they are not going to like the stuff I sing."

"Garbage!" exclaimed John. "You were brilliant. What you sing is good for any generation!"

"Careful!" yelled Kakko, looking past Mrs Merton and

charging forward just in time to prevent Bert from repeating the same mistake as he had on the way in. "I reckon you should have a line of people along your route like a president to make sure you keep straight," she said.

"Keep on the straight and narrow," repeated Bert. "Keep on the yella brick road… heh, heh…"

"Come on then," said Amy Merton when all the elderly people had departed and Mrs Higgins had retreated inside to 'straighten things up', "get your things. All aboard."

Dah collected her skateboard and shouldered her guitar case. Kakko and Tam just stood and looked sheepish.

"Is that it then?"

"Yep," said Kakko, "we forgot to bring anything!"

"Stranger and stranger! I expect you'll want a toothbrush and some soap."

"That would be great."

"Oh. We'll give you something to make sure you smell nice… for all our sakes. Come on!"

22

Amy drove up to the hostel. They bundled in through the main doors and their new friends showed Tam, Kakko and Dah to the dormitories and found them some soap and tooth paste.

"You will need a change of clothes – well something while you get those things you are wearing clean. It looks as if you have been dragged through a hedge backwards!"

"I suppose we have," sighed Dah, "chasing that thief."

"OK, we'll find you something to wear while you take those things to the laundry."

Amy Merton produced a variety of stuff to choose from. It was mostly jeans and T-shirts.

"You'll be decent at least. Take a shower. We eat at six-thirty."

***

Kakko and Dah emerged into the dining room rather self-conscious in things which were too big for them, but no-one seemed to notice. In fact most of what the young people were wearing seemed rather shapeless. Tam was already there helping to set the table.

"Apparently there is an all-comers concert in town tonight," he said. "Some of these people have come specially for it."

"Good job they ain't expecting me," remarked Dah.

"Oh, they *are*. John has been telling everyone you're special. They want you on the programme. Kakko too."

"Me!" blurted Kakko

"Yes you. You're to teach them all 'Be not afraid'. Mrs Merton – Amy – says that it is important to keep reminding themselves of the 'C' in their name, the 'C' in 'YWCA'."

"That's Young Women's *Christian* Association, isn't it?" said Kakko. "'Christian'. That's for Jesus Christ."

"Yes. Pastor Ruk told us the story. Mostly, these people still follow Jesus Christ who promised never to leave them whatever happens – spiritually that is. Hence 'Be Not Afraid'. It's a Christian song."

"Oh. I see," said Kakko. "But I really couldn't sing…"

"I can play the tune," interrupted Dah. "Sing it to me again so I can get hold of it properly and we'll do it together. You have a nice voice. It ain't bad."

"It's not like yours!"

"It's different, but I reckon we can make a good duet. I'll teach you one of my songs and you can help me with it. You said God sent you to help me."

"Well, I hadn't thought about singing!"

"But that doesn't mean God hasn't," laughed Tam.

"So I don't have a choice?"

"Oh. You have a choice," said Tam. "You can say, no. Nobody, especially God, wants to *force* you to do anything. But it's pretty obvious what we all want you to do. Besides you did it for the old people, what's the difference?"

"Most of them were deaf. And besides that, Mr Williams was brilliant. He saved me… Tam you've got to sing it too!"

"Me!"

"Yes, *you*. And don't tell me you don't know it. If Dah can learn it, so can you!"

"OK. Why is it you always win? I mean you always seem to have the last word!"

"I don't know. I didn't mean... sorry."

"No, don't say that. Don't apologise for being you. You needn't worry, I can stick up for myself. Trouble is, you're right. There really is no reason why I shouldn't join in with the singing..." But Kakko was upset. "Kakko, it's OK, it really is."

"But I don't want to always have the last word!"

Dah took over the table laying, instinctively knowing that her new friends needed space.

"You're making too big a deal of it. The thing is, I love you as you are. I promise, if I thought you were going to do something dangerous I *would* stop you *now*, because I know you wouldn't despise me for it."

"You mean, you *knew* I was making a mistake on the cliff?"

"Well, yes. I wouldn't have been so quick myself. But, honestly, if I had told you to slow down, think, what would you have done?"

"Probably told you not to waste time. Told you that you were only saying it because you were a wimp."

"Right. So it never *occurred* to me to say anything. It wouldn't have made any difference – except that I would have been right off your list of friends; and I didn't want that, did I?"

"But I wouldn't do that *now*, not after you saved my life – saved me despite my stupidity."

"So we have both learnt things. You have learnt to think

twice and I have learnt to be bold and to say 'slow down' if you forget."

"And I have learnt something else. I have learnt that you really love me, and that you're not a wimp – never was and never will be."

"Now, don't overstate your case. There is definitely the wimp about me in lots of things! But I do really, really love you… and I *will* learn your song. It says that whatever happens God never leaves us. I believe that. One day we will move on from this universe – we don't know how or when. But the God who made me has got me and won't let me fall."

"Scary, all the same… dying! Guess that makes *me* a wimp."

"No, it doesn't. You're not ready to die. When it comes to it, you won't be a wimp. You'll be saying, 'OK God. Bring it on!'"

"Like Grandma."

"Yeah. Anyway, doing something when you're really scared means you're certainly *not* a wimp. The opposite – you have to be really brave!"

"Like Tam rescuing his Kakko."

"Yep! I still wobble at the knees at the thought of it," he laughed.

The YWCA volunteers rolled into the dining room in ones and twos.

"Hi, I'm Sue."

"I'm Peter."

"Tam and Kakko."

"Love those names. West Coast?"

"Joh."

"Oh, right," said Peter doubtfully. He didn't want to admit he hadn't heard of Joh.

Dah was already engulfed in a group on the far side of the table. She didn't seem too perturbed at meeting so many strangers but John from the old people's party was in the group and was behaving as if he had known her for years rather than just an afternoon. He was proudly relating the dramatic events of the day.

The assembled people took a place at tables of six. Amy called them to order and began the meal with a grace:

"Lord, bless this food to our use and keep us mindful of the three 'p's. We remember those who will not eat today. Amen."

"Amen," repeated everyone and then fell back into conversation, while the person at the end of the table got up to fetch the first course from the hatch.

Everyone on Kakko and Tam's table introduced themselves. There was Zoe in a white, loose-fitting T-shirt like Kakko's, Lucy in a very close-fitting top that just met her low-rise tight jeans, and Beth with long brown hair wearing a green and white cheerleader's uniform – sleeveless top with a short, flared skirt. It was adorned with large red stars, one above her left breast and a second at the top of her right thigh. The other was Jane who was just reappearing with a tray of food. Jane was smartly dressed in a blue trouser suit and white blouse.

"What are the three 'p's?" Kakko asked Beth.

"Oh. It's from Grace Dodge. Eighteen hundreds or something... Grace became the first combined president of the YWCA in the US. I know it, but I keep forgetting it exactly..."

"Profanity, promiscuity and porn," said Zoe.

"Zoe!" exclaimed Jane. "We are in mixed company! Please excuse our Zoe," she said, "The three 'p's are 'purity, perseverance and pleasantness'."

"Right," said Kakko. "That represents a challenge."

"Impossible I would say," said Zoe. "Jane. You have to choose just one for me. Which one shall I be today?"

"Right this moment, Zoe, I reckon you should at least be pleasant," said Jane, "but there's no reason any of us can't manage all three with God's help."

"OK. I'll try and be pleasant," replied Zoe, "but I'll leave the purity to Beth. Had a good day with your hunk, Beth?"

"What hunk? I was with the girls."

"Sure you were, being thrown up in the air showing off your panties to all the guys – especially Joseph McArthur from the engineering department. We know you fancy him," said Zoe.

"I was not showing off anything to anyone. It's part of the cheerleaders' routine that's all! And anyway, they're not panties, they're briefs."

Tam found himself wondering whether Beth's 'briefs' actually matched the rest of the outfit, and then contemplating if he was going to get a chance to find out!

"Same difference," said Zoe. "And you want me to believe cheerleaders aren't showing off! Tell that to Grace Dodge. No sweat Beth, I mean *I* don't mind. You show what you've got and catch your man. Joseph McArthur's quite fit. Good luck with him."

"But it's not like that! I…"

"Methinks the lady protesteth too much!" teased Zoe.

"Zoe, you said you were going to try and be pleasant," reminded Jane.

"Sure thing. But I'd do the same if I had Beth's figure. I don't blame her for showing it off!" Beth's face had gone the colour of her stars, and even Zoe thought it was time to change the subject. "Kakko," she said. "That's a good name. Where does it come from?"

"Kakko? Oh, I was named after one of my parents' friends. Someone they met right at the beginning of their relationship."

"She an American?"

"No. This is our first time in America. Are you all Americans?"

"Sure are. I'm from Texas, Jane here is from Massachusetts (you can tell can't you?)."

"And I'm from Michigan," said Beth looking a little less red.

"California," smiled Lucy.

"Yes. And who is this? Your brother?" asked Zoe.

"No," Kakko declared, "he's my boyfriend."

"Oh, shucks. That's a shame. He *is* rather cute. What do you call yourself, honey?"

"Tam," answer Tam timidly.

"Oh. You don't need to be scared of Zoe," said Jane. "She's committed to 'purity' in this hostel."

"And perseverance! Yeah. You're safe with me, Tam. I don't mess with people already taken. Still, it's a pity you ain't her brother all the same…"

"Erm, compliment accepted," smiled Tam.

"So, tell us about what happened this afternoon," said Lucy. "I mean with the old people. You chased down this dude who stole a woman's purse."

"It was Dah. He would have got away if she hadn't used her skateboard," explained Kakko.

"Tell us about it. She sounds cool."

So Tam and Kakko recited the story once again. The imagination of the others embellished the story for them. Zoe would have preferred to have had Dah chasing the man up a tree begging her not to hurt him.

"Some of us watch too many movies," said Jane.

"Movies?" asked Kakko.

"Films, I think you folk from England say," explained Jane.

Kakko was still not sure what she was referring to.

"You *are* from England aren't you?"

"No. Not exactly. Nan and Dad are English, but Mum is from Raika."

"Scotland?" asked Lucy

"No."

"Wales? Ireland?" added Zoe.

"No. It's complicated. Nowhere on Earth."

"You mean to tell us you're *aliens*?" asked Beth, astonished.

"If you mean, do we come from a different planet then the answer is 'yes'."

"Shut-*up*!" exclaimed Lucy. "I don't believe it!"

"It's true. I'm afraid. But we're human like you."

"You ain't, like, shape-shifters?" asked Zoe.

"You mean we make ourselves *look* like this? No. This is how we are. We have one hundred percent human DNA like you."

"Go on!" said Lucy. "How's it all work then? Are you here to take over the planet?"

"Hardly," said Tam, "there's only two of us. And I doubt

if I am a match for, what's his name, Joseph Mackathy."

"McArthur, Joseph McArthur," corrected Beth.

"So, you *are* keen on him then. I knew it!" said Zoe.

"Quiet!" ordered Lucy. "Don't interrupt them. How come you came here?"

"It's a long story," began Kakko. And she explained how the white gate had led them to the garden outside the hall. She described Planet Joh and how it had been settled many years ago by people like her parents who had arrived through portals. Planet Earth One was probably the mother planet, although the original memories had been lost in legend. Her family were the only ones currently connected through portals as far as they knew – and now Tam of course. She finished by saying they were really privileged and really wanted to listen and learn – and help where they could. The Creator always seemed to have a task for them, something where they could make a difference for the people they met.

"So you believe in God, then?" Zoe concluded.

"Yes," replied Kakko, "because of all the things that have opened up for us. My mum and dad reckon She introduced them to each other. And Grandma died a few months ago certain that she was in Her hands."

"God is a She?"

"Well, I generally call Her 'She'. Sometimes we say 'She' and sometimes 'He'. God is neither really because God is God – which incorporates all there is of both masculine and feminine."

"That," said Jane, "is an idea that would have intrigued Grace Dodge. I like it."

"But," said Zoe, "it's OK believing in God when He…

She… gives you free trips to another planet or matches you with some cute man… sorry honey," she added to Tam, "but it's not like that for most. For some of us, life sucks."

"Agreed," said Kakko. "We are privileged. But it has not been all plain sailing for our family. Some pretty awful things happened to my parents on the way."

"Like what? My aunt's town was hit by a tornado. She used to be a leading member of the local church until it was flattened. The pastor was a broken man. My aunt gave up going anywhere to worship after that. Mom always believed God looked after his own, but now she doesn't give Him house-room. The minister said something about punishment for sin and my mom said, 'What sin?' My aunt was so faithful, always kept the ten commandments. She would give her last penny to support that church and what happened? God flattened it in just one minute! What had my aunt done to deserve that?"

"I'm sorry for what happened to your aunt. That must be hard for her."

"So do you think if that happened to you, you would still believe in God?"

"I don't know… except it's hard to say someone doesn't exist, or doesn't care, if… if you kind of know She's there. My mum says it's like you're cross with God but She doesn't stop loving you. Maybe… well, I don't think God actually does the bad thing Herself."

"But He doesn't stop them! Isn't that the same thing?"

"Maybe God *can't* stop them."

"But God can do *anything*! He's 'almighty, King of kings, Lord of lords, God only wise etc., etc.,'" chanted Zoe.

"I don't think my mum and dad believe God can do just anything She wants. She wants to make things and does, but I don't think She can always stop things, or stop people breaking what She has made. They have always taught me that God is there to love us when we hurt. And that is what I have found."

"But what if your parents went through something. Something really horrible. It's OK being on beautiful Planet Joh!"

"But they *have* had bad things happen. Life wasn't really easy for them."

"Like what?"

"My mum is an orphan, all her family except Grandma were killed in a flood when she was three… and she was raped when she was seventeen. Dad was blinded at the same time… it was pretty nasty for them. But they came back to believing that God loves them. In fact, Nan and Dad never did believe in Her much *until* then. It is the hard bits that got them to know God, not the easy bits."

There was a stunned silence around the table.

It was Jane who broke the silence. "So you don't just believe in God because you were brought up to?"

"I did when I was little. But not now. It's not about believing what other people tell me. It helps of course to hear about other people's stuff, but you've got to try and meet Her yourself. I'm not very good at it, but then it's really just doing the best you can and She kind of says, like, 'I know what you mean, I just need you to come with your heart open, don't worry about the words…'" The table was silent again. "Sorry am I boring you?"

"Far from it," said Lucy. "It's like, having angels from outer-space, like in the Bible. You really do come from another planet don't you?"

"Yes," said Kakko.

"I'd love to travel the universe!" said Lucy.

"She loves sci-fi," said Beth. "You should see some of the books she reads. What've you got now, Carl Sagan or someone?"

And so the subject lightened as Beth and Lucy started to talk about the various merits of authors past and present.

Zoe reached across the table and took Kakko's hand. "Thanks," she mouthed.

Amy Merton called over, "Beth. There's someone looking for you. Out in the corridor."

"Oh. Who?"

"Don't know. Didn't give his name."

Beth got up and went to the door and they caught sight of a well built young man that Beth quickly pushed out of sight.

"Joseph McArthur?" asked Lucy

"The very man," said Zoe. "Ain't he a hunk?"

After a few minutes Beth returned with a look that was a mixture of pleasure and embarrassment.

"So," said Zoe, "the sight of your panties paid off then!"

"Zoe, take these plates back to the hatch will you, and don't be rude!" said Jane.

When she had gone Jane apologised to Kakko and Tam, "I am sorry, Zoe is a bit outspoken. Not really a good advert for the YWCA. She's what you might call 'a rough diamond'."

"What you see is what you get with her," said Beth. "I don't mind her. She's exactly the person to have around if something bad's going off. And actually if it hadn't been for her, I wouldn't have noticed that Joseph liked me. And don't believe her underwear comments. He's not like that."

"Perhaps she wouldn't say it if she thought he was," suggested Tam.

"Wise words," said Jane. "I see that for all your quietness you are quite deep."

"Oh, he is," said Kakko, "and lot's of other things. But now I know he's also 'cute' it seems…"

"Cute," said Zoe as she came back with a tray full of the sweet course, "who're you talking about?"

"You," said Tam with a cough.

"Why thanks," she said making a pose, "I may be a lot of things but I ain't cute!"

★★★

Meanwhile Dah was getting on extremely well on her table. It was pretty obvious that John was taken with her.

"Just you wait until you hear her sing," he said.

Dah smiled. She liked this boy. Yet he was a bit young for her she thought. A bit too cosseted too. Anyway, she did not expect or want to stay on a strange planet on the other side of the universe. No way. But to have a young fan, just one young fan, from outer-space, well that was something to put on your bio!

★★★

That evening after dinner, in the dormitory Zoe approached Kakko.

"I have been told to come and apologise," she said. "Apparently I was rude to you – and Tam – at the table... I didn't mean to be."

"Nonsense," said Kakko. "How were you rude?"

"Well, using three bad words beginning with 'p' and then saying it was a pity Tam was your boyfriend among other things."

"Goodness! There was no way I thought you were serious."

"I wasn't. Except that Tam *is* rather good looking."

"To tell you the truth, I thought you were rather fun. Mrs Dodge sounds a bit stuffy."

"'Miss', she never married. She fought for women and girls – demanding men respect them. So I guess we must give her credit. But things are different now. It's no longer just about respect, it's equality and freedom from people who want to put us in a special 'female' place. And sometimes that includes *women* who insist on outward appearances of 'purity'. I can't stand them – all lah-de-dah polite and reckon sex is a bad thing... while they still cheat and deceive if they get the chance."

"But with you, Zoe, you get what you see?"

"I hope so... most of the time. I guess I'm not perfect – no-one is."

"I see you as a young women who wants to be herself. The so called 'rudeness' is defiance of those who want to restrict you."

"I suppose it is. Anyway I've to apologise to Beth too."

"Me?" asked Beth.

"Yeah. I'm sorry I teased you about Joseph."

"Garbage! If it weren't for you, I'd never have noticed him. OK, I was embarrassed perhaps, but you're right he *is* a hunk. I got a date with him! Yay!" She danced around in a circle and did a high kick. (Her briefs *did* match her skirt – although Tam would never know!). "It's Jane isn't it? She's the one who got you to do this apologising."

"Yeah."

"Oh, don't mind Jane. She can be rather sad sometimes… look, Kakko, would you and Dah like something a bit more, like, colourful for the concert this evening – seeing as you're going on stage? Perhaps Zoe and I could help out."

23

The concert venue was just across the road. It was being hosted by the YWCA to raise funds for their work among disadvantaged girls in New York City and it was a sell out. The only thing that had concerned them was that they hadn't managed to attract the usual numbers of talented performers as in previous years. They had delayed finalising the programme hoping for something to turn up. At the last minute their prayers had been answered as Da'yelni and Kakko arrived out of the blue.

"We've put you in for two slots," explained Amy. "Dah, can you find two songs to end our first half? Then if you and Kakko – "

"And Tam," added Kakko.

"Yes, and Tam. Can you lead us all in 'Be Not Afraid', that's by Bob Dufford is that right?"

"I'm sorry I don't know who wrote it. My dad taught it to me."

"I'm sure we've got that correct. You OK with that?"

"Yeah," said Dah. "We've been practising. Just as long as Bob Dufford ain't here."

"No. But we're covered for copyright. I've checked that… I see you've been helped out with some new clothes. Great. Tonight is going to be fabulous!"

***

When they got to the venue they found it already busy. Unlike the concert just a few hours before, the audience was a mixture of ages and cultures. There were men in tuxes and women in black dresses, boys in jeans and tank tops and girls with tattoos, bejewelled midriffs and short skirts of all colours. There was a high stage on the back of which was a large, orange logo with the letters YWCA on the left and on the right, the words:

Pursue justice
Rescue the downtrodden
Defend the vulnerable.

"What does that say?" asked Dah. Zoe read the words. "I like that."

"I reckon it comes from the Bible somewhere – Isaiah, I think. Jesus said something like it too."

"You follow this Jesus?"

"Yeah," said Zoe, "there was nothing lah-de-dah about him. Stuck up for the weak, demanded equality, set people free from oppression and got done in for it."

"Done in?"

"Yeah, killed... nailed to a cross... executed by those who controlled the world."

"Tell me those words again," said Dah. "I'll try and put them into my songs."

"Sure. You're amazing! It says: 'Pursue justice; Rescue the down-trodden; Defend the vulnerable'. That's what the YWCA is trying to do in New York City. You really are an ET ain't you?"

"ET?"

"Extra Terrestrial. Alien from another planet."

"I suppose so. But in many ways it doesn't feel that far away. We have down-trodden and vulnerable people on my planet. And we certainly need justice. My songs are about that. But most young people ain't interested – they just want the rock bands and the sex symbols, and the old folk despise me because they don't want to hear my message. It requires *them* to change, to think of poor people, but they would rather believe that it is the poor people's fault that they are poor."

"I know what you mean," said Zoe, "they think that God has blessed them because they have worked hard and deserve what they have, forgetting that most poor people also work hard – with their backs up against the wall because the rich people have gotten all the goodies first… but the people here tonight, some of them may be rich but they really want to make a difference. They believe those words, so I guess they'll like you."

And they did!

When Dah came onto the stage you could have heard a pin drop. Everyone was fully attentive. Dah strummed her first note and introduced her song.

"I ain't from these parts. I don't speak your language, but I know what these words mean. I mean I *know* what they mean – I've seen the poor cheated, and the corruption of those in authority and only a few hours ago I knew what it was to be left out and unwanted. But since then I've found new friends, good friends that have made me feel special. So tonight I don't care whether you like what I sing or not – I got friends, and no amount of cheating, corruption and oppression is going to give you friends. So… let's sing…"

Out of the silence as she was about to begin a lone voice shouted from half way down the hall.

"You got soul, young lady, black soul. May God bless you!"

Some people turned to shush the old man, but Dah called.

"Mr Williams, is that you?"

"Sure is," said the voice from the darkness.

"Then I ain't going to be singing alone! After the break when I do my next session, will you come up here?"

"Sure."

Dah strummed her first chord again and began to sing. Her rich voice filled the hall and when she incorporated the words from the stage into the melody people applauded. When she had finished, some people at the front stood up and then everyone was standing.

"Please sit down," she requested, "I have another one. This is my favourite song."

The contrast between the reception she got from the concert on her own planet and this one was enormous. Dah fled from the stage and almost fell into Kakko's arms.

"I'm tired," was all she could say as the people from the other acts crowded around her.

"Is there anywhere we could go and rest?" Kakko called to Amy.

"Follow me," said Amy, and led them into a small room back stage.

"You OK?" asked Kakko as she and Dah sank into a comfy love-seat. "Can I get you anything?"

"You can get me some water. I'm OK. Just tired. It doesn't seem possible that that disastrous concert was only twelve hours ago; and I haven't been in a bed since."

Amy called for water.

"You OK for the second half?" asked Kakko, concerned.

"Yeah. No problem. It's your song this time. I invited Mr Williams to come up. Was that OK?"

"Perfectly," said Amy. "You must have met him this afternoon."

"Yeah. He's got a lovely baritone. I don't know what this 'black soul' business is really about; I hope that's OK."

"He's a proud black man who has come to live in New England having spent all his life in the South. I guess he's looking for allies, and your music moves him – resonates with his culture."

"I don't know why. I never thought of myself as 'black'. We're all about the same colour in my world. We don't have people with pale faces like yours or black ones like Mr Williams'."

"It's not so much your colour as your songs. It's the style that counts – and the sentiment. That goes for most people here. We're mostly here because we want to provide more opportunities for disadvantaged young people – in this case New York City – and they will be of many colours and languages."

"Is that far from here?"

"Not so far. A couple of hours by road without hold ups."

"Is it a big place?"

"New York City? Eight and a half million I believe."

"Eight and a half million in one city!" exclaimed Kakko.

"Nearly twenty million in the metropolitan area."

"Amazing, we only have a few hundreds of thousands on the whole of our planet! So the money you get here, this evening, won't make that much difference."

"A drop in the ocean!" replied Amy. "But hopefully it will stimulate other things. It's an attitude shift that is needed. Even if we don't raise much money, we will have helped to raise awareness. Look what the YWCA has achieved since the nineteenth century. We need to keep at it."

"But you still have poor people?" said Kakko.

"We do. More than ever. But that doesn't mean we have to give up. If we can give just one person a life changing opportunity that they otherwise might not have had, that is worth it – but the truth is, we achieve more than one. And girls are far more likely to be disadvantaged than boys in the US. We are really grateful to you Dah for agreeing to sing tonight. Some of those people in evening dress are quite influential."

"Thanks. I'm getting a second wind now. When are we on again?"

"About fifteen minutes. I'll call you. I'm going to arrange to get Mr Williams on the stage."

★★★

In the privacy of the back room Dah, Kakko and Tam practised 'Be Not Afraid' once more. Dah discovered Tam picked it up very quickly. "Can you harmonise?" she asked.

"What's that?"

"Sing the low notes. You could sing this." Dah played a base line in Tam's range. He sang it.

"Now sing it while Kakko and I sing the tune."

"What, at the same time?"

"Yes. It'll complement what we sing. That's what harmonising means."

They tried it and Tam got lost.

"Listen again," said Dah. Tam sang his bit three times without fault.

"Got it in your head?"

"I think so."

"Let's try it again from the top." To his, and Kakko's, amazement it worked and sounded great.

They were practising it for a third time when Amy came and asked if they were ready.

"I think so," said Kakko.

"We're ready," smiled Dah confidently.

As they came onto the stage again the audience applauded with anticipation. Mr Williams was helped up and given a chair. He sat beaming. Dah explained that the song was Kakko's and handed over the introduction to her.

"I learnt this from my dad," she explained. "It means a lot to him and mum because it reminds them that God is, like, there for them... erm, whatever..."

Dah began to play and the trio hit the first note spot on. After that it was plain sailing. Mr Williams joined in the first chorus with the tune and never stopped. At the end Kakko invited the audience to sing too. Many of them already knew the words it seemed and soon five hundred people were belting out the chorus. Standing next to him, Kakko was impressed at just how well Tam stuck to his bass line throughout.

"Didn't know you could sing!" she shouted in his ear as the audience applauded.

"Neither did I," he mouthed.

When his carers came for Mr Williams, he reached out and grabbed hold of Dah. "One day you'll be famous... change the world my girl. You change the world!" He was helped off the stage and the trio dived for the safety of the little room.

"I want to sleep," sighed Dah.

Tam looked out into the corridor and spotted Zoe.

"Zoe, we're really tired. Do you reckon we could get back to the hostel?"

"Sure," she replied. "You know where to go. There'll be someone on the door. They'll let you in. Sign the book to say you're in. I'll let Amy know you've gone... that was really, really brilliant. Dah," she called, "you're a star!"

"Thanks," said Dah.

Zoe ushered them to a back door. Go left, down the alley. Never had a strange bed felt so welcome.

Meanwhile, back at the venue, everyone was looking for them. People wanted to know everything about them. They were clearly just as impressed with Da'yelni as Mr Williams had been. Was this girl a member? Where did she come from? One man said that he would welcome her to sing in New York at his club and another leading personage from the YWCA wondered if she would front a national campaign.

Lucy told them that she would pass on the cards and that her agent would be in touch. No, she didn't know who her agent was but she was sure she would have one.

On their way back to the hostel Zoe asked Lucy how she knew that Dah had an agent.

"I don't. But what I do know is that with her talent she will need one. There are a lot of people out there ready to exploit young people. You gotta be smart."

"But suppose she ain't got an agent?"

"We'll find one."

"Who're you going to get? Do you know someone who could be her agent?"

"No. But *we* can do it to start with. Us. You, Beth, me. We'll watch her back."

"And be paid for it?"

"No! That's just it. *We* won't rip her off. And, I've been thinking, we'll have to keep all this extra-terrestrial thing in check. I mean, we don't want Homeland Security sending them to 'Area 51'."

"Ouch! Got ya! If they haven't got proper visas that'll be bad enough."

"They won't have. You saw them. They don't have *any* luggage. Not even a purse between them – unless they've got their passports sewn into their underwear…"

"They haven't. I shoved the whole lot into the washer when they were in the shower. Nothing."

"So. When these folk come snooping tomorrow we'll give them my number and get them to ring me. I'll pretend to be their agent from the West Coast."

"Sounds cool. We'd better check it out with them first of course. They're proper jet-lagged. They'll be out for the count tonight."

★★★

The next morning seemed to come round very quickly. Their new friends woke them.

"Breakfast finishes at eight-thirty," called Zoe. "You getting dressed?"

John was up with the lark. He was determined not to miss Dah and hung around all through breakfast until she and the others staggered in, still half asleep but feeling rested.

"Needed that," said Tam. "Slept like a log."

"Me, too," yawned Kakko, kissing him on the cheek.

"Morning," said John bouncing across the room. "You OK Dah?"

"Yeah. I'll do. I'm hungry."

"Sure thing. Help yourself – there's all sorts of breakfast things. Do you want some toast? I'll make you some fresh."

"Toast? What's that?" said Dah half to herself. But John had already gone in his eagerness to please. Toast with peanut butter and jelly appeared to be the standard fare at breakfast.

"What's this?" asked Kakko.

"Peanut butter and jelly?" smiled Zoe. "You never had PBJ before, honey?"

"Of course not," said Lucy, "you *know* they are not from around here. Strange as it may seem, most of Planet Earth has not even heard of peanut butter and jelly."

"Now, that does sound strange. But I guess you're right… you can put on whatever jelly you like – strawberry's the best in my opinion," declared Zoe.

The three extra-terrestrials did as they were bid but each of them secretly decided that this concoction was an acquired taste. The fruit seemed far more appealing. Dah couldn't get over just how nice passion fruits were. All the fruit was new to her.

"Listen," explained Lucy, "last night, after you had gone, this dude and a woman from HQ – that's YWCA headquarters in New York City – came up and wanted to offer you gigs and stuff. They left their cards." She went on to explain her idea to her, Zoe and Beth acting as their 'agents' – just to give them protection from those out to rip them off.

"But we won't be staying," cut in Kakko quickly. "We must be getting back to our own planets. We need to get back to the hall on Galuga where we were yesterday. That's where our portal will be."

"Look don't worry about money to stay here. I'm sure that won't matter. And we can get you to the shops."

"Thanks," said Dah, "but if I stay away too long I'll be missed. No-one knows I'm here. Kakko's right. I have to get back today."

"That's such a shame!" said Zoe genuinely. "You've cheered us all up."

"And Joseph offered me a bet that you would get a track in the top twenty within two years. I didn't take the bet of course. I'd a lost."

"He ain't a gambling man is he?" worried Zoe.

"Hope not. I don't think he really meant it."

"Avoid the gambling types. You'll never have anything – ever."

"Don't worry, I will."

"He's a real hunk though. Glad I told you he fancied you? He'd got that look. The one that makes a great big footballer look like he's gonna melt."

"Thanks. Zoe. He's certainly a lot bigger than any other guy I've known."

"Big enough to sweep you off your feet," laughed Lucy.

"That's what my mum says!" exclaimed Kakko. "She said Dad swept her off her feet when they first met."

"And they're still in love?"

"Of course," said Kakko. She had never imagined it could be otherwise.

"So what do you say about us being your agents? You might come back again. You never know."

"Sounds like an excellent idea to me," said Tam.

"We must get back to the hall. Can anyone take us, or is there a bus or something? I guess it's too far to walk."

"Let's ask Amy," said Lucy.

Amy Merton agreed to take them in the minibus in the late morning when she was free for an hour. Kakko, Dah and Tam's new friends decided to skip their usual activities that morning because they were, "responsible for them as their new agents", they said. Neither was John going to be parted from Dah as long as she was around. So at the appointed time, the seven, plus Mrs Merton, all piled into the bus and headed off back up towards the hall of the previous day's gathering.

After half an hour they were climbing the hill past the wood through which the thief had attempted to escape.

"I wonder if they ever caught him?" said Kakko. As she said it, she spotted a policeman guarding the roadside. They edged past him and John leaned out and asked, "Everything all right officer?"

"Nothing to worry about. The wood is out of bounds for forensic investigation. Please move along."

"Did you catch him – the thief who stole Mrs Smith's purse?" persisted John.

"I know nothing of the incident," replied the officer, "please move along."

They continued on up the hill only to be flagged down by another policeman a hundred metres further on.

"I see you were in the vicinity yesterday at around four-thirty in the afternoon ma'am," said the officer checking a clipboard. A note must have been taken of the van's registration number.

"Yes, officer."

"Did you or any of your passengers see a man dressed in a white T-shirt and blue jeans on rollerblades?"

"Yes," called John, "Dah here, and Kakko and Tam chased him and got Mrs Smith's money back."

"Pull your vehicle over to the side here, please…" and as Amy was doing so he spoke on his lapel radio. When the engine had been turned off the officer mounted the bus.

"I have radioed for the lieutenant in charge," explained the trooper. "You're best staying put. He won't be long."

"Have you caught him?" asked Kakko.

"Keep your questions for the lieutenant," he said and got down from the bus.

"What the hell's going on here?" demanded Zoe. "We seem to have driven into a swarm. Best keeping your mouth shut," she warned John.

"Sor-ry…" drawled John. "I just wanted to know…"

"Alright you two!" barked Amy. "Listen. I think this is more serious than just catching a purse thief. So keep calm and – "

"Go with the flow," sighed Dah.

"Excellent words. Answer their questions. Don't volunteer any opinions. Right?"

"Right!" agreed John still feeling a bit hard done by, but at the same time getting really protective towards Dah.

True to the trooper's word, the lieutenant was soon on the scene. He climbed aboard the bus.

"My name is Lieutenant Harper, Connecticut State Police. I believe some of you witnessed the incident yesterday."

"Yes, officer," spoke Tam. "A man dressed with a tight fitting hat and dark glasses stole a lady's bag and headed off down the road on his rollerblades. Dah chased him on her skateboard. Kakko and I followed on foot."

"You didn't catch up to the man?" The question was directed at Dah.

"I nearly did. He left the road down there near where that other policeman is standing. Off the road his rollerblades hampered him. I chased him across a clearing and then he threw Mrs Gillespie's purse at me and Tam shouted to leave him. I think he thought he might be dangerous."

"Very wise of you. This man has been on the run for several days. He skipped a courtroom last week in Philadelphia. He was last seen in Grand Central Station getting on a train headed for New Haven. This man is regarded as extremely dangerous. He was on trial for a series of murders."

"How'd he escape?" asked John.

"That need not concern you young man. We think he had accomplices. The important thing is that he is now behind bars. Your calling us as quickly as you did, and the actions you took have helped us to apprehend him. Did it ever occur to you that this man might be armed and dangerous?"

Dah, Kakko, Tam and John shook their heads.

"Well this time you got away with it. Drive up to the hall. I want all of you who witnessed the events to make statements."

"Certainly officer," said Amy in her most efficient sounding voice.

As they entered the hall, Kakko checked around the corner of the hedge and to her relief the white gate was visible.

"It's there," smiled Kakko to Tam. "When can we get away?"

"I don't know, but we'll have to go through with this because we'll leave the others in trouble if we just disappear."

"Right," agreed Kakko.

The lieutenant and a master sergeant took the statements of the trio and John, who also witnessed the incident although he had not taken up the chase. They signed the statements giving their address as the YWCA in New London. They also agreed to be called as witnesses if necessary, but the lieutenant thought that that wouldn't be for several months if at all. The murders for which the felon had been on trial for in Philadelphia might get him the death penalty. Only if he was acquitted of these would they prosecute for the purse theft. The lieutenant left with an admonition to keep out of the woods until the forensic team had completed their work, and next time to be much more careful whom they took on. Dah nodded mutely. She had never considered the risk that this man was anything more than a petty thief. It appeared that the possession of fire arms by the public was very common in this place. That was not so on her planet. Certainly there were some, but they were very rare. It was illegal for a member of the public to own a firearm, let alone carry one. But, if this man had noticed that Mrs Smith had actually had a small revolver in her purse, he would almost certainly have used it. That was another shock. The fact that a little old lady who was clearly somewhat confused carried a loaded handgun was a complete surprise.

"But," explained John who had seen Mrs Smith relieved to get her bag back, "I think she was even more determined to keep it." It was her right as a citizen to bear arms. "It's enshrined in the second amendment," he explained.

"All I can say is," declared Tam, "that if Dah hadn't been so quick, he would have had time to have looked into the purse and find it. I reckon you and your skateboarding could have saved someone's life!"

Amy Merton had busied herself in the kitchen in the hall and had managed to rustle up some coffee.

"Why thank you, lady," said the lieutenant. The mood changed. "I reckon now we have these statements the job is done, Ted," he drawled to the master sergeant, "as soon as they're done in the forest we can go back to base."

The coffee drunk and the police departed, Tam asked, "What did he mean. The death penalty?"

"Judicial execution," said Lucy.

"You do that here. You kill people for doing wrong?"

"Not here, not in this State, not in Connecticut," explained Amy, "but they can and do in Pennsylvania."

"But it's wrong to kill people, right?"

"Yes. Unless it's self-defence or in defence of your homeland," said Zoe.

"So how is killing a person, even if he had killed someone else, right? I mean two 'wrongs' don't make a 'right', do they?"

"Welcome to the United States of America!" said Zoe.

"My State does, her State does," she indicated Lucy, "but Amy's State doesn't."

"So if this man had been on trial here, instead of… where did you say?"

"Philadelphia – Pennsylvania."

"Then he would *not* have been facing execution?"

"That's correct," said Amy.

"The man might be sick," suggested Dah.

"Then the courts should take that into consideration when they sentence him."

"But I still don't think it's right that anyone can be killed in cold blood. It makes the law as bad as the crime. On Joh if we said, 'We will kill you if you kill someone else' people would think the law was a nonsense. We know it's wrong to kill. But on this planet it seems people are killing each other all of the time. You don't seem to think it's so wrong."

"I agree," said Zoe, "we don't. We 'say' it's wrong – but we have so many exceptions. I tell my parents I don't want to have anything to do with guns, but they think I'm stupid. They wouldn't hesitate to blast off at someone who tried to break into the house. But I don't agree with that. You can't do that in Europe – and people ain't busting into your house any more often there. It's the other way round. Having a gun makes people do things they wouldn't otherwise. They don't think of the consequences to them if they get caught – they don't reckon with that."

"I'm glad I didn't know that… I mean, about guns and all that," said Dah. "If I had known that I would have hesitated and that might have given him time to find the gun. And then someone would have got hurt."

"It's a scary universe," said Kakko, "I'm glad I don't have to live here on this planet all the time. It must be tough for you people," she said to her new friends.

"Our country is one of the safest places in the world... I think..." muttered Beth.

"Actually," said Amy, "you are three times more likely to be murdered in the US than in Canada and ten times more likely than in Japan. But you are right, it is still safer than most."

"We ought to be going," said Kakko interrupting the conversation. "We must return Dah to her Planet Galuga. Our gate awaits us."

"Where?" asked a disappointed John. He had been hoping the whole thing was a set up and that Dah was not going anywhere.

"Round there by the hedge."

"Yep," said Tam, "I see it."

"Me too," agreed Dah. "It's the same place we came in."

"Where? I can't see anything," said John.

"Only those invited through can see the white gates," explained Kakko. "If you're not meant to go through you won't see them. In our family not everyone is invited each time. This time it was only me and Tam."

"And me when you got to my world," added Dah.

"So, thank you everyone. It has been fun," said Tam.

"Sure has," said Zoe.

"We shall miss you," said Amy, but still secretly thinking this was all a hoax.

"Do you have to go?" protested John.

"Sorry," said Dah. "You've been so nice to me. But I need to get home. If I stay any longer I will be missed and my parents would ground me for sure if the police get involved. The 'expenses' for a false call could be enormous."

They took each of their friends in their arms and accepted the invitation to look them up if they were ever in the US again. They stepped up to the hedge. Tam went first, Dah followed with just a little look back and Kakko followed.

The four earthlings stood stunned.

"They were telling the truth!" affirmed Amy Merton.

"They sure were," said Zoe. "You could tell they meant what they said. What you see is what you get with them."

Beth put her arm around John who was frozen in a state of shock. "She was special wasn't she?" she said. "First time?" John nodded.

"Tough," said Lucy, "love at first sight and she turns out to be an extra-terrestrial! One day you should write a book about it – trouble is no-one would believe you! Perhaps Area 51's full of good-looking alien girls?"

"Don't joke!" said Beth. "He's hurting."

"She's left still wearing your pants!" remarked Zoe to Beth.

"I know," said Beth. "I swapped her. I've got her tights and skirt. I possess clothes from the other side of the universe!"

"Shut-UP!" yawped Lucy. "That's really something!"

"Do you think… one day," said John, "we would be able to go too? I mean, travel the universe through invisible white gates?"

"John," said Amy, "I don't think you should live in hope of that. You have to let it go."

"Don't tell him that now," said Beth, taking his side. "Tell him next week when the pain has eased."

24

"Parting is hard, ain't it?" said Da'yelni after a short pause. They were standing on the bridge in her home country again.

"It's the hardest thing of all," agreed Kakko.

"I expect you will want to be getting on home, back to your planet too."

"Yep. Better get back. We must go and see if we can get into the theatre where you performed."

"I can't believe that was only yesterday!" said Dah. "So much has happened in such a short time! It's nearly five o'clock here though. I'd better contact someone," and as she said it, her phone rang.

"It's my mate from the hostel. Hi Zay… yeah, I've been on a trip, I was out of range… you haven't reported me missing or anything have you…!? That's a relief! Thanks for caring Zay… look, I'm with friends at the moment. We're on our way to Main Street Theatre… no, just seeing them off… Oh. I'd forgotten about that… yeah. I can help out some – I'm a bit tired though… wouldn't you just like to know! I'll tell you all about it later. I did this gig… fantastic. See you then. Bye.

"That was my room-mate, Zaynayi," explained Dah. "She was going to get in touch with my parents if I didn't show for evening meal. But it's OK. I told her we were going to the theatre and she says they're sorting the food and toys for the families on low incomes. That means the theatre will be open. I had forgotten. We could go in as volunteers. Zay says she thought she might go. She and I will go and eat together somewhere after."

"That's great," said Tam. "You can see us off and spend the evening with your friend."

"I'll miss you guys. Less then twenty-four hours ago I was sitting on this bridge thinking I had run out of chances to do anything with my singing and stuff – and now I am back I know I don't have to mind if they don't like me here. I have fans from another planet that none of them have."

"And you still have Beth's trousers!"

"Yep. Swapped her. Cool, ain't they? No-one here has got anything quite like these."

"You'll stand out?"

"A bit. Not much. It's not as if no-one wears things something like these. But the point is, *I* know that they are from another planet. That's cool."

"And I expect Beth is just as happy. She likes skirts like yours. She was wearing a skirt when we arrived at the hostel."

The trio walked off the bridge and made their way to the theatre. The doors were open and they walked in to find most of the seats folded and several rows of tables stacked with toys and tins. People were carrying in still more in cardboard boxes and bags of every description.

"Hi," said a woman who met them inside the door. "You come to help?"

"Yeah. What do you want us to do?" asked Dah.

"Put your things over there so they don't get mixed up with the stuff."

"I've only got my guitar and my skateboard."

"Fine. They'll be safe in that corner."

"Can you see your gate?" asked Dah as they walked over to the corner to deposit her things.

"I'm not quite sure where to look," said Tam. "The place has been so re-organised. I can't see anything at the moment."

"Ah, more volunteers!" a middle aged woman approached them. "Come with me. I'll set you on to toys."

The three young people followed her down towards the front of the hall beneath the stage.

"Here. See the various tables? They range in age and sex. We begin with babies over this side and go up to teens over there. All you have to do is decide where each of the toys belong. In my experience young people are better at it than us oldies. Grandparents are the worst! No idea when children stop liking things. Probably never grew up themselves, or have entered their second childhood…"

There were cardboard boxes and bags of unsorted toys – some used, some new, and a couple of other young people were already wading into them.

"Oh, good! Help has arrived," said one.

"I don't know how good I'll be at this," wondered Kakko.

"Oh, don't worry. Just guess. If it's not obvious it probably won't matter."

Tam took a small box from the pile. He opened it up and saw a variety of pastel shades and a selection of brushes.

"What's this?" he asked Dah.

"Make up set for someone about eleven I would guess," she replied.

Tam passed the box to her and headed for some stuffed

toys. They would be easier, he reckoned. As they got stuck into the work they kept looking around for a white gate.

"If it's in here," said Kakko, "it would be pretty obvious. We can see all the back of the theatre, and both sides too…"

"Clearly not time to go, then," agreed Tam. "More work still to be done."

"What about my assignments? I have a submission in three days!"

"When," smiled Tam, "have you ever worked on an assignment more than twenty-four hours before the deadline?"

"Not often. I'm usually doing it the night before."

"Usually? You mean *always*."

"I did *one* early. I took a week over it – and got my worse marks for it. It's always better if it's fresh."

"Well, then. You wouldn't be doing your assignments anyway would you? And besides, there is nothing you can do about it. GWTF."

"Go with the flow… I wasn't exactly getting impatient… *honestly*. I wonder what our Creator has got for us now then?"

"If it's anything like the last twenty-four hours it'll be pretty cool."

A boy with a tray hovered behind them. "Tea?"

"Lovely," said Dah. "Thanks. I recommend our Atiota tea. I really couldn't take to that sweet chilled variety they gave us at the hostel in New London."

"Neither could I," agreed Kakko, "tea has to be hot. Nan says what we call tea on Joh isn't the same as on Earth, but she never suggested she ever drank it cold with ice in it! Thanks," she said to the boy. "Now this is *really* good," she acknowledged after taking a sip. "Mum says they drink something they call 'bru' on her world. She and Grandma really missed it. Nan said she liked a decent 'brew', but she meant her kind of Earthly tea, not the Raikan sort."

Dah spotted her friend. "Zay!" She waved to a tall girl who had just been set on to sorting a stack of tins. The girl waved back but they were too far away from each other to talk. "Don't tell her about our adventures," Dah warned her extra-planetary friends. "Too complicated. She'll never give up on it. She likes to talk."

"Got you," said Tam.

At that moment the organiser called for attention: "Hello everybody. We'll take a meal break in an hour. We'll send out for cold food for everybody. If there is anything you can't eat, let me know."

"We haven't got any money," hissed Tam.

"Don't worry," whispered Dah, "it'll be free to the volunteers."

"Better earn it, then," said Kakko putting down her cup and rummaging in another cardboard box. "There are loads of toys here. Some people are very generous."

Dah texted Zay across the hall. "*Tlk meal time. Hv 2 new frnds – Kakko & Tam.*" Dah watched as Zay checked her phone. Then, as she looked up, pointed out Kakko and Tam. Zay gave her a thumbs up sign and got back to her tins.

★★★

At the meal break Dah introduced her new friends to Zaynayi.

"So you did another gig last night?"

"Yeah. It was great."

"Made many new fans," put in Tam.

"Is it far from here?" asked Zay.

"You *could* say so. Near in some ways, but the other end of the universe in another."

"How do you mean?"

"I mean I can't go back there."

"But they liked you?"

"Yeah. But it wouldn't work."

"Why?"

"It just wouldn't. You know me."

"Dah, at one moment you want to get recognised and the next you want to hide. You can't have it both ways."

"I know. An introvert musician is not an easy thing. I think I will keep to writing songs and leave it to others to perform them."

"But your lovely voice," said Kakko, "it's so unique. No-one could sing your songs like you do!"

"I guess not. But you have to be tough to stand up on a stage. The one *here* proved a disaster," said Dah nodding towards the stage behind them.

"I told you," said Kakko, "it was the audience, not you."

"Yeah. Well, it hurt all the same… but I ain't giving up. Just not going to try to do gigs where no-one wants to hear me."

"I suppose that makes sense," said Tam.

Just then, a woman came across to them.

"Aren't you the girl who sang here last night? Da'yelni Lugos?"

"Yes," said Dah.

"I spotted you and thought, where have I seen that girl

before? Then it registered. I thought you were very good."

"Thanks. But I didn't make much of a hit."

"Oh, don't think about *that*. You were never going to with that turnout. Most of them were here for that boy-band. They were already fans of them. I think they are too shallow though – all sex appeal and no real musical talent. I give them less than a year – if they don't fall out with each other before that. You were far too deep for their fans."

"Thanks for the compliment."

"I mean it. If I might say so, you shouldn't have come expecting much here last night. Don't give up."

"I ain't. I am going to carry on writing."

"Good," said the woman, "and performing too, I hope…"

"Da'yelni Lugos!" gushed a woman striding over towards the group. It was the organiser. She had just been told they had a musician in their midst. "I have heard all about you, and how you performed so bravely last night." She took Dah's hand and shook it vigorously. "You are most welcome. If I might… if… would you condescend to sing for us, here, this evening? I mean at the end of the break. Remind us of why we are here and what we need to do to help those least able to help themselves…" she tailed off nervously.

"Go on Dah," enthused her roommate. "It'll be cool."

Dah looked taken aback, then glanced around the room.

"But they ain't expecting anyone to *sing*."

"Oh. Don't worry, they'd just love it."

"You've got to get your message across," said Kakko, "you don't just write songs to entertain. You have something to say and people need to hear it. You see, it's *here* as well as… the last place."

"It is so encouraging to us more mature people when we have young people around with vision," explained the organiser.

"Go for it!" said Zay impatiently. Dah looked at the cautious Tam who smiled and nodded.

"OK. But I want Kakko and Tam up with me."

"By all means," smiled the organiser looking very pleased with life. "That would be even better!" She went off with a happy expression on her face to find a microphone, which she began to tap vigorously.

"Ladies and gentlemen," she announced. "If I might break into your meal for a moment. Everyone happy?" There were muffled sounds of assent from full mouths. "Da'yelni Lugos here," she gestured towards Dah, "has just agreed to sing for us." There was light applause. "For those of us who have not come across her yet she is a talented young woman from the university who writes her own songs about the injustices in this world. I am sure you will be pleased to hear her. Finish your meal and we will have a couple of songs before we get back to work... you are all doing very well. I doubt we will have any more deliveries this evening so it's just finishing up what you already have... and, while I am on my feet, I want to thank you all and everyone who has given so much stuff so generously. It is a tribute to our society that, though we still have far too many people on incomes below the poverty line, we also have a lot of people who care. Finally, our thanks to Mr and Mrs Zol and their helpers for organising our refreshments." There were many hear-hears and hand clapping.

At the end of the meal the organiser came bustling over to Dah again. "Can you be ready in about five minutes?" she asked.

"OK. Where do you want us to do it from?"

"Why, up on the stage. I have organised a microphone for you."

Dah glanced up to the very same stage she had fled from less than twenty-four hours before. Tam took her hand.

"Forget about anyone listening. Just do your song. Don't think about them," he said. "Me and Kakko, do it for us."

Dah gave him a smile and went to find her guitar.

On the stage, sitting in a chair just like the one she had sung from the previous time and before the same microphone, Dah spoke:

"Hi. These are my friends Kakko and Tam." She didn't wait for any response but continued to introduce her song. Needless to say this audience were hugely moved. The song and Dah's special voice filled the hall with a quality that was not so discernible on the previous evening. The lesson: that no-one can expect to be appreciated or understood by everyone, everywhere, every time, had not just been learnt by Dah but also by Tam and Kakko. The contrasts of the last twenty-four hours had brought that home to them so clearly. *And*, Kakko contemplated, *I suppose that applies to God Herself too. There are times when I get a rush of appreciation for Her greatness, Her love and Her generosity, but so much of the time I just take Her for granted. I don't give Her a second thought. She must get fed up with me. But God doesn't give up on me. She just waits so patiently. And it's not just me but the whole universe! What a patient God we have. She makes such a difference. Yet the irony of it all is that the people of the universe spend most of their time totally ignoring God and trying to do everything without Her. That is the ultimate injustice.*

TREVOR STUBBS

Dah introduced 'Be Not Afraid' and the trio wowed the audience again with their harmonies. Tam was thinking how Dah had shown him that he could sing. At the end of the short performance, as they were making their way back to the toy sorting, he told Dah how much he appreciated her drawing out this little gift he hadn't realised he had. "We could do with you on Joh," he said, "you're such a great singing teacher."

"Thanks," said Dah, "but I'm not ready for any more interplanetary travel right now. I'm happy that I have found confidence to be me here in Galuga on Atiota."

"Wouldn't you like to go back to Planet Earth sometime and meet up with John again? He quite liked you."

"Yeah, he was sweet wasn't he? He was attracted to me I think because I was different, but he would soon have found out that I am not that different, not inside… anyway I am not ready for a special relationship with anyone right now. I'm still finding 'me'."

"Look!" announced Tam. "A white gate. Our time has come."

Kakko looked up. At the back of the auditorium there was indeed a shining white gate.

"We must finish our shift!" stated Kakko firmly.

"Agreed," said Tam.

They worked another hour until all the cardboard boxes were emptied and the toys from each of the tables carefully repacked and labelled. Many children were going to have a happy time in the next few months as they were distributed. Kakko thought about them, and gave thanks to God that she had been useful to someone. To be able to make a difference, even a small one in someone's life, is a tremendous blessing.

She resolved in future not only to help, herself, but to find opportunities for others to contribute too.

"Dah," said Kakko gently, "we have a white gate at the back of the hall." Dah looked up.

"I see nothing," she whispered.

"If you could, it would mean more adventures," smiled Kakko.

"I ain't wanting any more of them quite yet. But… but it would have been nice to meet your folks and see where you come from."

"You never know," said Tam, "you might one day. But for now we must take our leave. It was really good to meet you… and thank you." Tam gave her a hug.

"It is *I* who needs to thank *you*!" exclaimed Dah.

"Let's *all* thank our wonderful Creator," said Kakko. And they just stood in a circle, the three holding hands, their heads bowed in silent prayer. As they looked up they saw Zay coming over.

"We're off," she said, "you coming?"

"Not us," said Tam quietly, "I'm afraid we've got to go home. You two go on and have a great evening."

"Thanks," said Dah again, "hope to see you sometime."

"Sure," said Kakko. "Bye!" They hugged again and then Zay took Dah's arm and they made their way through the crowd to the doors where other young people were waiting. Kakko saw Dah retrieve her skateboard and then she was lost from sight.

"Come on," said Kakko, "let's get through that white gate." She took Tam's hand and they headed through the crowd but before they opened the gate and stepped through, Kakko leaned up and lightly kissed her boyfriend. "I like having adventures with you," she said.

They emerged in the cottage garden wearing broad smiles.

"Why, hello!" It was Matilda crossing the lawn. "You are home at last. At least this time you seem to be in one piece. And you've had a good time – you're glowing."

25

Nothing remarkable had happened for more than a week, and Kakko was bored. She had completed her assignment and handed it in days ago and was now looking forward to something to help with the tedium of the long college holidays. But then something did happen. A space shuttle came in to land at the city spacedrome down the coast. This was always an event because Joh was not a space hub with regular flights. This was the first landing in over a year. But it was not just because this was a rare event, but because this one was unscheduled and unexpected.

The shuttle had come from a gigantic inter-sector freight-liner in low orbit and clearly visible as the largest object in the night sky. The pictures of the craft circulating on the news channels were of an impressively sophisticated ship. The pilot of the shuttle parked his vehicle where he was directed and he and one other crew member descended the stairway. They were not of human origin, their large flat faces above tall spindly bodies were rugged and ridged, but they were smartly dressed and almost suave in their demeanour.

The news reader had explained that they were believed to be Sponrons from the Planet Ramal in the neighbouring Medlam System. They had travelled far but their state-of-the-art intrahelical drive had reduced the travelling time from their home-world to Joh to less than ten standard years. The purpose of their visit, they explained, was trade. They had quantities of rare minerals including rare magnetic silicates, only found on two planets in the galaxy, used for antimatter conversion, as well as processed helicates necessary for intrahelical propulsion. They also had diamonds and gold, much prized in the universe not only for their beauty but for their use in mechanics. (Kakko, for example, was always extolling gold conductors which she rated far higher than copper ones.) Joh was not rich in gold or diamonds – most had to be imported from outside the system.

The potential buyers, however, were suspicious of these pedlars. The traders on Joh were used to doing business with people they had known for years. Supplies were usually ordered – they didn't just appear from outer-space without notice.

Shaun, Kakko and Tam were, however, among the young people whose interest was not primarily about interstellar trade. They were intrigued by the appearance of these strangers, or to be more precise, their vehicles. They caught a bus which passed close to the spacedrome and joined the crowds watching through the perimeter fence.

The space shuttle was of a design that had not been seen on Joh before. They saw it gleaming in the sunlight. It wasn't metallic – 'opalescent' would be a better word. Its iridescent lustre made it appear luxurious as well as truly other-worldly. The smell that wafted across to where the young people were standing was also from beyond. There was fuel technology here that told of advanced space travel.

"I'd love to get aboard that," announced Shaun.

"And I bet you, Kakko, are dying to get inside the engine housing," said Tam.

"What I would really like to do," said Kakko, "if you really want to know, is to get to see the engines of the mother ship. This shuttle has only a simple antimatter propulsion system for short tripping."

"Correct," said a man standing just behind them. He wore an identity tag that indicated he came from the local scientific institute – Prof Rob Nivriks. "The mother ship will have to have at least an interhelical, or even the latest *intra*helical drive."

"What's the difference between an interhelical and an intrahelical drive?" asked Tam.

"How technical would you like me to get? They're both dark matter vortex engines, of course. They both draw on the polykatallassic particles in the dark matter clouds as they pass through them, but an intrahelical system recycles the exhaust combining it with alpha particles of standard matter and condensing it, making it nearly twice as efficient. A very powerful engine – it's state of the art."

"Thanks," said Tam. "I *think* I get the gist…"

"*I* do," stated Kakko. "They've only been around a few years but most interstellar craft are undergoing upgrades – if the structure can take it, I gather. The significant thing is that an *intra*helical system can propel a ship at up to nine-tenths the speed of light compared to the *inter*helical's six tenths. This enables them go anywhere they please in this sector of the galaxy."

"Have we seen one here before?" asked Shaun.

"These ships were first built in the Mintu System by the Minians," explained the scientist, "but the interhelical engines and onwards have been designed across the sector by scientists and engineers in permanent contact through the

Interplanetnet. We have done a little bit here on Joh towards it, but this is the first time we will have actually witnessed the finished project."

"Wow!" said Shaun. "So I bet you want to go up there even more than my sister."

"I guess you could say that. What are your names?" The three young people told him and he noted them down. "Wait here. I'll be back."

The scientist pushed his way to the gate and waved his ID in front of the guard who opened a side pedestrian gate. He walked across the tarmac and into the terminal building.

Ten minutes later, a young woman in uniform came across to the gate which was opened for her. She approached the gathered crowd and called out Kakko, Tam and Shaun's names. They presented themselves and she told them to follow her. She issued them each with a pass to put around their necks and ushered them through the gate and across the tarmac into the space terminal building.

The three young people stood in awe as Prof Rob beckoned them across. He explained what was happening. The government authorities were interviewing the Sponrons to ascertain their status.

"When they come back out," smiled Prof Rob, "it is proposed they take me and my colleagues up to the mother ship. Want a trip?"

"Wow! You mean that?" marvelled Kakko.

"Of course. We need to keep our young people better informed about the progress of science. Too many of us have our heads in our research and do not pay enough attention to the up and coming generation."

"Thanks Mr... er..." said Shaun.

"Call me Prof Rob."

"Thanks Prof Rob."

A few minutes later the Sponrons emerged onto a mezzanine balcony with some officials of the Joh immigration department. They looked rather stern, but then so did the Joh officials. The head of the department, Director Ylah, called attention and she began to address the gathered company.

"Colleagues and representatives. Thank you for waiting. I have ascertained from our Sponron friends from the Medlam System that they have salvaged the ship in orbit, and its cargo, and are anxious to dispose of the cargo to local planets at a fair price in order to lighten the ship and ease the repairs. You will understand that this is an unusual request and the authorities are looking carefully at the legalities of the situation. Our president is consulting the lawyers in the field and is in touch with the United Bureaux of Interplanetary Transport in our sector." There was a murmur of approval from the gathered representatives. "However, in the meantime you will be pleased to hear that they have consented to a party not exceeding twenty-five persons – the capacity of their shuttle – to visit their ship to inspect the damage and the cargo bays. It is not that we don't trust you," she said, turning to the Sponrons, "but you will understand that your visit is unexpected and the community would want us to ensure the safety of all our citizens." The Sponron who appeared to be the most senior grunted.

"Mr Gallok, I believe, is the person delegated to select the team." She looked in the direction of Prof Rob who nodded his assent.

Gallok stepped forward and addressed the gathering. "I have twenty on my list from various departments. If others would like to join us please approach." People began moving in his direction. Prof Rob looked in the direction of the young people and gave them a thumbs-up. They were already on the list.

★★★

Thirty minutes later Tam, Kakko and Shaun found themselves in a meeting room where the strategy of the visit was being discussed. Twenty-five, including them, were lined up to face others who were voicing questions they wanted answered. Prof Rob and the others were noting these down on their e-sheets. Shaun regretted not having his with him but would ensure he took it when they departed.

After the meeting the twenty-five made their way to the lounge where the Sponrons were being entertained and were introduced as the delegation. It was clear the atmosphere was a bit prickly. The residents of Joh were generally open and relaxed. These people were introducing a dimension not usually found in local discussions and debates. Perhaps it was simply to do with them being from a different place thought Kakko. She was soon to be less patient. The Sponron leader scanned the party, then declared, "No females. In our culture it is forbidden for females to board a ship." A gasp went around the room.

"I don't understand," said Prof Rob. "What can anyone's gender have to do with their scientific ability or experience?"

"In our society," continued the Sponron, "a female does

not conduct science, unless," he smirked, "she does it in the kitchen."

Tam felt Kakko rail. She was going to let fly and he felt that it would be better to leave the reply to Prof Rob. He grabbed her arm and pulled her towards him. She fought him but he whispered into her ear an insistent, "Not now Kakko, later! Let Prof Rob deal with this."

"Cool it, sis!" added Shaun from her other side. "Wait…"

But Prof Rob was already saying, "We would find this hard to accept. Perhaps my senior colleague in the university physics department, who happens to be a woman, would like to comment."

"Thank you, Prof Rob. People have been on Planet Joh for five hundred years. From the beginning, equality between the sexes has been accepted as an unwritten norm. Unlike other planets we have had no need for legislation or making provision in our constitution to ensure the rights of women and girls. You will understand, captain, if our people find this difficult – even abhorrent. However, in negotiating with people of different races and cultures, I believe we have to accept that not everyone has the same norms, no matter how objectionable they may be in our own society. But the most important thing is that we send a *qualified* delegation to your ship, captain, to ensure the safety of our planet. You have agreed to this and we are grateful. Therefore, I am going to nominate my deputy, who happens to be male, to take my place. Perhaps other departments would consider doing the same if they have properly qualified male members."

"Thank you," said Prof Rob, with a stern face. "I just want it noted on Joh that I adhere to the term 'abhorrent', but nevertheless, for the reasons stated by my colleague, I am also willing to compromise. Let us adjourn and reconstitute our party." The people began to leave the room in clusters, many engaged in rambunctious, if not heated, discussion.

Back in the meeting room, Prof Rob called for order.

"I apologise for this," he began.

"No need," said a female physicist, "we appreciate your use of the word 'abhorrent'. You have stated your opinion in the strongest terms and I know you find it as upsetting as we women. However, we are all aware now of what we are up against. These people, or at least their spokesperson or leader or whatever he is, may be trying to engage in as many spoiling tactics as possible. We should be aware that they may be out to deceive, divide, deflect and weaken us. I expect they are hoping that right now we are having a heated row over this. We must not fall into that trap. Let us not be perturbed here but focussed on our objective, which is to inspect their ship as thoroughly as possible. We need to check the damage and the state of repairs. Clearly the engines and space-frame are functioning well enough to have enabled them to get here. We need also to check the condition and the status of the cargo and it's origin and intended destination. There has to be a manifest – let us inspect it and photograph it. And let us talk to the other members of the crew and snoop around. So now let us decide on our twenty-five males and allocate our tasks."

The women all nominated replacements. Kakko just had to accept she was to be left out. The female scientist approached the three young people.

"You must be disappointed, young lady. I am so sorry, but this experience has been a lesson to us all. We cannot take for granted that the freedoms we enjoy here pertain throughout the universe. And we must not be deflected from our primary goal in this task. You understand that?"

"Yeah, I suppose so," muttered Kakko, "but it's just not right."

"It isn't. *You* know that. *Joh society* knows that, and I hope our Sponron friends are beginning to know that too. No matter how much you tell yourself that you can make up the rules against natural justice, somewhere there are things that come back to discomfort you. What happened today is just another case of someone having to defend injustice – and deep down that drains energy. Those who insist on discriminating have to be on the look out for people discriminating against them. Those who deceive have to be constantly aware of others trying to deceive them. Nothing is certain in such a culture – it is a constant drain on energy. It hinders the growth that accompanies openness. But those who accept natural justice, as we do in this matter, find themselves invigorated and free to develop."

"You mean it's, like, anarchy?" volunteered Tam.

"Well, not quite," replied the physicist, "anarchy means 'no laws'. They have their laws I suspect, but they are probably laws organised to favour the few. Law, for it to be just, needs to be based on the *universal* values of right and wrong. Justice requires an equal distribution of power and access to well-being. It demands freedom for exploration of the self and of the environment so that each individual can attain his or her potential. Justice demands that we make education universal, for example, and the best possible medical care accessible to everyone in need regardless of their age, sex, race or anything else. I doubt the Sponrons lack laws, what the Sponrons lack is a commitment to natural justice."

"But doesn't giving into him mean they have won? The wrong has overcome the right? Shouldn't we stand up to him?" asked Kakko strongly.

"A wise person chooses her time and her battlefield," replied the scientist. "As I said, in this case it is probably a spoiler to try and deflect us. Now is not the time."

"But the right time will come?"

"Undoubtedly. In their case it might take generations, but it will come. Look how long it took for our ancestors on Planet Earth One."

"My father is from Planet Earth One."

"Yes? Interesting. So get him to tell you their history of the emergence of gender equality. What is your name?" she asked trying to read her pass.

"Kakko. Kakko Smith."

"Count you blessings, Kakko. Imagine," she smiled, "you could have been born on Planet Earth One and suffered some of their discrimination, or worse still, a Sponron. Pray for their women."

"I will!" stated Kakko vehemently.

Prof Rob came over. "Sorry," he said to Kakko. "Where do you work?"

"I'm studying at the Agricultural Institute, in the engineering department."

"An engineer! I shall send you an invitation to visit us at the university."

"But I only do agricultural stuff," said Kakko, not wanting to be misunderstood.

"There's no *only* about that!" said Prof Rob, "we all need to eat. And engineering is engineering. Come and see us."

"I will," replied Kakko. Things weren't turning out *so* badly perhaps.

"Now, you two. I have a job for you. I want you to try to talk to the other Sponrons on this ship. Because you are young they might not see you as posing too much of a threat. While we are looking at the technical stuff, why don't you ask them about just how they got hold of that ship. Find out how the command structure works. What plans they might have for the future. You know, just in 'innocent' conversation. Do you think you could do that?"

"We could try…"

"See if you can get them to give you a tour of the less technical parts of the ship – the living quarters for example."

"OK. I get it. You want us to, kind of, generally snoop around while you're all looking at the 'official' stuff."

"Yes, but do it 'congenially'. Just be natural. Just show your ordinary enthusiasm."

"You mean, like unsophisticated, inexperienced, excited young adults?" said Shaun.

"Like, be normal!" laughed Tam.

"Exactly," smiled Prof Rob. "Don't try and act. Just be circumspect and listen. Don't take notes, that'll put them off talking freely."

"Shouldn't I take my e-sheet?" asked Shaun.

"No. Let *us* look official. You just be informal."

"What should we wear?"

"Just come as you are. Be you."

"Thanks!"

"And, once again, sorry Kakko. I mean that. Many people over many generations of both sexes have fought for gender equality in the universe. That is established beyond question and is not about to change on Joh."

"Thanks, Prof Rob," said Kakko. "I think I understand."

"Be back in two hours," said Prof Rob. "Give me your passes, I will get them updated."

After a few minutes a secretary returned the young men's IDs. And as they left Kakko said, "Don't you two get any ideas."

"Wouldn't dare," said Shaun.

"I'll miss you," said Tam.

"Too right you will," concurred Kakko.

★★★

Two hours later, after a quick lunch in town and phone calls to Tam's parents and White Gates Cottage, the two young men presented themselves once more at the gate of the spacedrome.

26

The Johian inspection party were ushered aboard the shuttle-craft and directed to belt themselves in. They were all wearing insulation suits with iridescent strips that reflected brightly both in the visible and ultraviolet spectra. Each suit was fitted with a pencil torch attached to the cuff, which emitted a permanent beam of ultraviolet light. Wavelengths in the infrared range, longer than seven hundred nanometres, were detected through a night-vision devise positioned in the helmet that could be activated when called upon. "Knowing where you are and what is around you is the key to self-defence," the team leader had explained as they were instructed in the suits' use. Also sewn into the suits was a small flask of oxygen connected to masks if needed. In their left breast pockets was a first-aid kit containing syringes with medication against anaphylaxis and edema.

As they moved through the craft to the seats, it was clear that a cleaning crew had not been aboard the shuttle for some time. There was a background smell of sweat, oil and dust that contrasted starkly with the fresh air of Planet Joh. Cleanliness was not something that seemed to bother these Sponrons.

The shuttle's antimatter impulse engines, however, did not seem to lack the necessary maintenance and they were soon airborne. This was the first time either Tam or Shaun had seen their planet from above; it was an impressive sight. What a beautiful world they had to live on! How privileged they were! This encounter with aliens was helping them to realise just how much they had been taking the wonders of their Planet Joh for granted.

In a very short time the shuttle was approaching its mother ship. It was impressive. It was huge, almost half the size of the spacedrome they had just left. They were soon to learn that most of it was given over to twelve separate holds, each of them like warehouses. The value of these goods must have been staggering. They docked with a gentle jolt and almost immediately were assailed by the stifling "pong" of on-board air. Shaun reached for his emergency mask. However, a Johian brought along specifically to monitor the safety of the team, shouted out that the air was safe to breathe, but that did not prevent Tam and Shaun feeling sick.

"They will have technology on board for keeping the air fresh and avoiding this smell," said the man next to Shaun, "but they don't seem to want to use it."

Once on board, the team was addressed by the commander of the ship. He was curt but not unwelcoming. Dressed in a kind of uniform of a different cut and colour to the Sponrons standing to attention behind him, he explained that they were in possession of the vehicle because of a space emergency. The crew of Thenits – people from another planet in the sector – had sent out a distress signal. The intrahelical drive engines had malfunctioned and they were stranded in space with only their low-powered standard, antimatter engines and it would have taken beyond their own lifetimes for them to get anywhere where they could effect repairs. And, even more to the point, they had only a year's supply of antimatter for full-time operation. The antimatter engines were only meant for close-in manoeuvring.

That crew were desperate, explained the commander. "Fortunately we were on hand with a ship equipped with an interhelical drive and were with them within three months." He explained that the original crew were immediately conveyed to Planet Hegeh in their system and all their needs seen to. They then returned to salvage the vessel. Their engineers had worked for many months and were eventually able to get the engines turning again, but only in 'safe' mode. They were seriously curtailed in their ability to travel far without over-taxing the repairs. What they needed was, a) to reduce drag on the ship caused by the magnetic silicates they were carrying, and b) to take on more fresh food and water in case the engines failed again and they found themselves stranded for another extended period.

"Gentlemen," he continued, "you will understand that under galactic law those who salvage vessels have the right to any proceeds from their sale or repair to offset the cost of the rescue etc. You will understand that we have put in many months and used many men in bringing this ship back into some form of use. Your planet was among the nearest to us and we are turning to you to help us reimburse our costs."

The man next to Shaun whispered, "That sounds overstated. With all the helicates and magnetic silicates on board they wouldn't need to buy fuel. Besides, both inter- and intrahelical engines are 'chamilophagitic' – that is, they use very low amounts of fuel, and ninety-nine percent of that is collected from dark matter as you pass through it – and that doesn't have to be paid for! I can't see how they can be so very much out of pocket."

"As you go around the ship," the commander continued,

"ask to see anything you want. I believe you are most interested in the engines and the cargo."

"We are," stated Prof Rob. "Five of us will inspect your engines and the repairs you are effecting. Have you any other areas of damage you want to show us?"

"We have nothing that remains to be seen that is damaged. My crew have worked very hard on everything."

"Except the cleanliness!" muttered Shaun's companion under his breath.

"So the rest of you, please inspect the cargo and anywhere that seems relevant," ordered Prof Rob.

Tam and Shaun attached themselves to the group and were led off to the right. The five engine experts, including the man who had whispered to Shaun, descended some stairs with the commander.

The two friends hung back a bit and tagged onto the end of the line. They were followed by a crew member clearly instructed to bring up the rear and make sure nobody 'got lost'.

Shaun asked him if there was a pictorial layout. He looked around and, seeing no other Sponrons, nodded. He seemed young; not much older than Tam. He led them to a panel on the wall and touched it. A schema of the ship was immediately displayed with a red dot indicating where they were.

"These panels are every tenth section," explained the Sponron, "the ones with the green line above them. Using these you can never get lost. We also wear wrist bands that we can use, but they also tell the bridge where any of us are at any time. They are irremovable and remain on us at all times."

"Clever," enthused Tam. "So we are here. The cargo holds here and here and… here. The engines are located…"

"Down here," said the Sponron as he touched a stairway sign on the plan and a second desk was displayed.

Tam played with the panel, exploring up and down and examining different parts of the ship.

"We must go," insisted the young Sponron after a minute. "We must catch up with the others." He propelled them towards the back of the snake of inspectors. When they had reconnected with the line, Tam asked the young Sponron about the crew quarters.

"I saw on the schema that there are extensive living quarters towards the bow. Is that where you all sleep?"

"Most of us. The senior officers and their females have suites aft. They don't show up on the plan. They are restricted areas."

"Females! I thought females were not permitted on your ship. We had to comprise our team completely of men. The women were forbidden!"

"Come. We will talk... off the record... please. Just wait," whispered the Sponron.

The party came to the first of the holds and began grouping around a large window. The young Sponron spoke to one of his companions, indicating Tam and Shaun. Then they saw him do something quite unexpected. He slipped his wristband over his hand and passed it to his companion who put it into his pocket. He came quickly over to them and, looking up to see he wasn't being watched, whispered:

"When we move on from here, follow me *quietly*."

They made sure they showed interest in the piles of blue sacks stacked at one end of the hold. "Definitely helicate," murmured one of the team. "They are not telling us that of course, but I can read the markings and am familiar with the bags."

"You need helicate for the engines?" asked Tam.

"Yes. There is enough here to drive this ship for centuries. This is not for consumption. It is a consignment. We're going to ask to see the manifest."

They moved on but before they could get to the next hold, the young Sponron ushered them down a stairway.

"What I am going to tell you and show you didn't come from me, right?"

"Right. OK," said Tam and Shaun together.

"Good. My wristband is with my colleague. They will think I am with the party. You did not see me remove it, right?"

"Right. I didn't think it came off?"

"It doesn't. Or shouldn't. I have been working on getting it lose enough to come off for months. Now, first, ignore whatever you have been told, we *stole* this ship, which the Thenits called the Talifinbolindit (which we shorten to 'Tal' – we don't care for long names). The Thenits owned this ship but got into difficulties because there was a malfunction in one of the engines. It needed a replacement part but their three-dimensional printers both jammed and they did not have the parts and tools to repair them. They radioed for anyone in the vicinity to see if anyone could supply them with a 3D printer. We could. But they were not stranded. They still had one engine working. When our supreme commander on our own ship, the starship Zon, came within range he came aboard the Tal with weapons and we took it over. The Thenits were transferred onto the Zon and taken away and we were sent here to the Tal to replace them and secure the ship. The official tale is that the Thenit crew were conveyed to a planet without communication with the outside, the Planet Hegeh, but my friend saw what really happened because he was watching the shuttle with a telescope as it returned from the planet. They had been there about three days but they must have returned with most, if not all, of the Thenits. He said he didn't realise what was happening at first. He saw tiny bubbles coming from the shuttle and bursting in space behind it. He looked through the telescope he had for star gazing – it's the only good pastime we have, checking out all the beautiful stars – and he guessed they must have been the bodies of the Thenits exploding in the void, their atoms scattered into oblivion. Our officers did not tell us this, but we knew they were capable of it. There are three of them that run this ship. Please don't judge our race by *their* behaviour. Us Sponrons are not like that for the most part.

"None of us elected to come on this voyage. We are all from an orphanage. They came to our school and offered us jobs at our spacedrome when we got to sixteen, but they did not tell us we would be used as crew on a starship. We were excited at first, but we soon learned the score. They torture us if they see any sign of rebellion. One girl was even jettisoned for saying what she thought. They use our sisters as sex slaves. Come, I want to take you to see them. As they are in the restricted section there are no monitors."

"Thank you…er… what do we call you?"

"Call me… call me One. But I won't tell you my real name in case…"

"Your secret is safe with us, One. We won't quote you

publicly. We shall just report what we have picked up 'from listening as we went'," stated Tam.

"Come, let us go quickly before we are missed."

One took Tam and Shaun down another narrow flight of steep stairs and then to a door marked with small red letters. "The broom cupboard," said One. "Keep this secret too."

"Of course."

"The main door to the restricted section is kept locked and is only accessible with a pass, which I don't have. Our sisters are kept inside at all times but we have a secret entrance through this cupboard which leads into a wardrobe in my sister's room."

One opened the cupboard, removed a few items and knocked on the back wall three times, left a pause and knocked again. After a minute, there was a reply of two knocks which One followed up by another rhythmical knock. A low panel was then pulled open from the bottom three feet of the cupboard. One hissed, "I have guests from the planet," and signalled for them to squeeze through. He then replaced the brooms and closed the door.

Inside Tam and Shaun found themselves in what they described as "feminine space". After all the rest of the ship, this was immediately different. One introduced them, then said quickly to the girls, "Tell them your story. We only have a short time."

Shaun and Tam were led around the restricted quarters. They saw the luxury in which the three senior officers lived. The apartments were rich in art treasures – paintings, sculptures, and ceramics. The upholstery was ornate and sumptuous. The women were all young.

"The officers access their captive harem at will," said one of them. "They come and select one of us for each of them, sometimes more. They are cruel and inflict pain. If we get pregnant we are beaten until our babies leave us."

"One of our sisters," said another, "stood up to them and escaped into the main deck where she denounced them and told our brothers all that was happening. They forced her into the airlock and ejected her into space. We were all made to look out and see her die. Her body died, but her spirit lives on in us – and she is with God. She is more than material atoms."

"After that," said One, "we cut a way through the cupboard. We know everything, but we pretend we know nothing."

Tam said that he would report what he knew without the officers being able to guess how he knew until a rescue could be attempted. The girls wept.

"We will not dare believe we can be free until we see the outside of this ship and we are safe!" emphasised the first. The others nodded their agreement. "But we are grateful to you whatever happens. Now go. You must not be caught."

One squeezed through the wardrobe wall and waited in the cupboard listening. When he felt the way was clear he gingerly opened the door. No-one. Quickly the two from Joh stepped back into the corridor. The door was closed. The girls were safe from being seen to have had visitors. One led them back up the stairs and through a tiny corridor that opened out near the tenth hold. One held up his hand and they held back in the shadows until they could hear the inspection party with their guides pass the end. As soon as they had gone by they emerged and joined back up with the others. One's friend slipped his bracelet back to him and Tam and Shaun strained close to see into the hold being shown to the group.

"Interesting," said one of the team, and then smiled a welcome to Tam and Shaun who returned a relieved smile back, "there must be enough insulation material there for several domes. Rocks with these properties are only found on a few planets – these look as if they have come from Telba."

"Correct," said the guide. "You have need of them on your planet?"

"No," replied the scientist. "Fortunately our planet is one of the warm ones. We are very privileged."

"Very," agreed the Sponron.

No doubt, thought the scientist to himself, *you would like to get your hands on our planet too. But you will find that it is well protected!* Their inter-planetary alliance had been tested before and any attempt at attack was intercepted before the assailants could even land by disrupters beamed from ten other worlds.

The final hold on the Tal was the one kept at extremely low teperatures. It was shielded on all sides. The door-side had an automatic heat sensitive swivel drive that kept the opening pointing away from any heat source within the ship. Furthermore, anything above a few degrees Kelvin on the external skin of the craft above the hold would determine its positioning. Very near a star, while in planetary orbit, the orbit would be adjusted in such a way as to keep the planet between the craft and the star, and the whole ship would also rotate to ensure the hold constantly faced away from the planet into outer-space.

"Where was all this bound?" asked one of the team.

"I don't know," replied the guide. "You will have to ask the commander."

"Whoever it was is missing this stuff. They could even be starving!"

"Ask the commander," he insisted.

"Of course. I will."

Meanwhile the five engineers had asked enough questions and seen enough evidence to conclude that both of the engines would have had to cease to work to merit a mayday call. They witnessed a group of Sponrons who had the covers off one of the engines and who were hovering around with spanners. The engines were, of course, both turned off at present. The Sponrons were indicating that they had only managed to repair one of the engines and were still working on the other. (In fact, they discovered later, the one engine that had ceased working had been repaired by the Thenit owners when they had arrived with the 3D printer before they had been forcibly removed.) But the five Joh engineers, although they were not personally familiar with a chamilophagitic intrahelical engine, knew when people were only playing with things. In fact, these Sponron engineers were probably not engineers at all!

One of the Joh team looked meaningfully at his colleague, "Go and ask them some questions," he said. Their guide immediately intervened. "No-one is to disturb them. I have my orders."

I bet you have, he thought. "Fine, so can we talk to you?"

"Of course."

"What do you know about intrahelical engines?"

"Very little, I'm afraid."

"But you can tell us how long you have been repairing this?"

"Ever since we arrived on the ship."

"What about the other engine. You have repaired it? When?"

"Three months."

"Three standard months. Are you certain?"

"Yes."

"Thank you."

"Come. I will lead you to the briefing deck. Our commander and his team have prepared you tea."

"Very good. Have we all seen what we need to here?" The others nodded.

They all reassembled at the briefing room and were given some strange looking cake. It tasted even stranger but was pronounced safe by their protection man. The commander approached the engineers and asked if they had enjoyed their tour.

"Immensely. How long did you say you have been repairing the engines?" one of the engineers managed through a mouthful of Sponron cake.

"Four months. The second engine is not finished."

"We could see that. We did not disturb your engineers."

"Good."

★★★

An hour later the team was back on Joh at the spacedrome. The shuttle had been dismissed and the pilots told they would be contacted as soon as they had spoken to their superiors. They were all careful not to give any indication of dissatisfaction with what they had seen, but they were all aware that their inspection team had not been given the access they required. What were the Sponrons really up to? And if they knew, what could they do about it?

27

As soon as they were reassembled in private with Director Ylah and their other female colleagues, Prof Rob called for a review. They began with the engineers and their view on the engines. They all agreed that the maintenance job was staged.

"They were playing at it. They were just 'looking around with spanners'," they explained.

The other party had taken a full inventory of what they could see in the eleven holds they had seen, but they were sure there was a twelfth. Tam raised his hand and said that he had seen an interactive schema of the ship which showed twelve holds.

"Thank you," said Rob. "That seems to be conclusive then. What about the manifest?"

"Likewise incomplete. None of us are familiar with Thenitic but the translation and transliterations into interstellar terminology would indicate that two pages were missing. Some of the things in the holds are not accounted for on the manifest. There may be other items not listed that are in the twelfth hold.

"Could be weapons or ammunitions," suggested one of the team. "The ship appears remarkably clear of them."

"Noted," said Rob. "Now our young men, Tam and Shaun here, managed to go walk about. Shaun, Tam tell us what you found."

The young people related what had happened to them from beginning to end. The company was shocked, but not surprised, to learn of the fate of the Thenit crew. They explained about the danger that One had put himself in to take them to the restricted area and what they found there. On learning about the young female Sponrons and the abuse they were suffering, the meeting let out an audible gasp.

"So both deceiving *and* hypocritical," said the woman physicist. "But I am delighted to hear that our Sponron officers are not representative of their people. This is abuse wherever you are, but these abusers are doing it with a high hand. They have no excuse."

"We… er… said," stammered Tam, "we said we would try and rescue them."

"Did you now?" smiled Prof Rob.

"We have no choice!" It was Kakko, almost shouting from the back of the room. "How could you sleep knowing you have left innocent people to continue to be abused by bullies? You have to stop them!" Her righteous indignation spilled out, added to the frustrations she had already suffered. "You're not just going to leave them there! Are you?"

"Hold on young lady, don't read things into this that have not been voiced."

"But…"

"Miss Smith, no-one wants to leave them to suffer. Is that OK…? Now we need to keep calm and level headed here and decide exactly how to tackle this. At the moment we are still gathering facts and observations. We are very grateful to you two for your careful and circumspect work. It is often the case that young people can get into places that older people cannot.

You have done an excellent job. Thank you... now, we must turn to our lawyers. What is the legal situation here?"

A lawyer rose to his feet and referred to his e-sheet.

"The claim of the Sponrons to have salvaged the ship has been borne out by the United Bureaux of Interplanetary Transport (UBIT). They reported answering a call for help. When contact had been made it appears that their ship which they call... er," he checked his notes, "the Tal-i-fin-bol-in-dit, was stranded. The Sponrons offered to take them to safety which they did on Planet..." he referred again to his e-sheet, "Planet Hegeh. A radio link was established but after twenty-four hours, contact was lost. The Thenit commander appeared to be reading from a script but there were photo-shots of a makeshift camp being set up on the ground. He said they were trying to make contact with the local people, but to our knowledge Hegeh is not currently inhabited. The Thenit commander said that the Sponrons had put into operation some sort of salvage plan but he was not sure what that entailed."

"Could be reading that under duress," observed Rob.

"Maybe," said the lawyer, "but there is no hard evidence for that. What we know the Sponron commander has done is, so far, only the testimony of some of his crew and our own gut instinct."

"And we cannot name our informants, or, indeed that we have met others on the ship at this stage," added Prof Rob.

"Quite. Anyway, the upshot of all this is that the UBIT accepts the Sponrons' right to the ship and its cargo. We have no right in law to impound the ship or arrest the crew."

"Unless we can prove they have committed murder and are detaining people against their will," reflected the director.

"Agreed," said Prof Rob. "But we can't at this stage without invoking evidence we have gleaned from our visit – evidence that would endanger the innocent Sponrons on-board. Any ideas?"

"The law is an ass!" grumbled Kakko.

"In this instance, it might be, but if we disregard the law we end up in chaos."

"Agreed," said Tam, as a law student. Kakko scowled at him.

"Thank you. Our young people keep us on our toes. But there *will* be ways forward that break no laws. We just have to find them," said Prof Rob.

"Er… um… excuse me," said one of the engineers. "I have to confess to having already broken the law."

"Explain," said Prof Rob.

"I noticed the engines' control panels were set to operate *only* from radio signal remote control from the bridge, not just the engines but the engine room computers too. The commanders don't seem to trust the crew to operate them independently. So, for that to work there has to be two RCCs (remote control couplings) plugged in."

"Understood. So?"

"When they want to restart the engines it will have to be done remotely from the bridge. The programme protocols will default to having to be controlled remotely. If the link with the bridge is absent, the system cannot be operated from the engine room."

"And how have you broken the law?"

"The two RCCs have to be plugged in. They are very small – each only about one centimetre square. And they have… er… become… sort of, er… displaced. I… er… have to confess, I was examining the couplings and they must have accidentally slipped into my pocket…" and he placed two small devices each no more than a centimetre square on the desk. "I know my actions are quite out of order, but, the thing is that when they try to fire the engines they will not be able to do so, unless they can hack into the system – a system that they set up specifically to *limit* access and resist overriding."

"A heinous crime indeed!" declared Prof Rob. "But, don't blame yourself too much," he said with a smile, "these little incidents can just happen sometimes. I'm sure we can restore the RCCs in due course. But for the moment the Tal is grounded it seems." A rustle of satisfaction rippled around the room and the 'culprit' clapped on the back.

"They can't make a quick getaway now," continued Prof Rob, "even if they don't care for our more searching questions. So then, colleagues. Since our Sponron friends cannot leave, I propose the following:

"At this juncture, the Sponrons' commander suspects nothing. Our knowledge of his deceit must remain a secret. A communication should be sent telling them that contact has been made with the United Bureaux of Interplanetary Transport in the sector and they have confirmed the Sponrons' claim to the salvage rights of the Tal. We will invite the commander and those engaged in the commercial trade to come to our spacedrome with a list of what they are wanting to sell and their price. Once they have arrived they will be told that an application for asylum has been received from members of their crew. No deal can be reached until this has been investigated. The law demands that the crew must all be asked whether they wish to stay on Joh or continue with the ship. We tell them we have to be seen to be acting in accordance with the law."

"I have two concerns," said Director Ylah. "What if the commander radios orders to his henchmen on the bridge to discipline or intimidate the crew – or worse?"

"The commander is aware that all transmissions to the Tal can be monitored," suggested the lawyer. "If he radios such orders, or attempts any transmission in code, then that will be ground for his arrest."

"How he takes the news," suggested Prof Rob, "will depend on the manner in which we inform him that we have had an application for asylum. I recommend that we do it intimating that we are frustrated by the request and apologise to him. We can make him think we do not intend to take such an application seriously."

"Especially if we kind of hinted that all we are after is a bribe," smiled a female officer.

"You mean," said Prof Rob, "pretend to be as corrupt as he is? That might work. We will request that he send for all their crew members to come to the planet."

"But he won't send for them *all* will he – only the ones we are supposed to know about," remarked Tam.

"That is easy," said one of the others, "we inform him we have the technology to read all carbon-based organic life-forms on the ship."

"Do we have such technology?" asked Rob. "You didn't tell us that."

"We haven't. But the Sponrons don't know that, do they? All we need do is draw up a CAD graphic of their ship and scatter it with red dots. So long as we cluster them a bit they won't be able to count them. We can ensure that there is a fairly dense cluster in the rear of the ship in what our young friends tell us is the restricted area. As soon as the Sponrons see that, they will think that as long as we have red dots on our screen we will know there are carbon-based beings still on board."

"What if they decide to kill the ones they don't want to admit to?" asked Shaun.

"That's easy. The dots show dead as well as living carbon-based beings. We can put a few smaller pink dots around the kitchen areas and joke about the meat they have in store. They wouldn't want any bright red dots suddenly becoming pink, or clustering around the airlocks."

"They might suspect we're bluffing," suggested a more cautious member of the team.

"They might. But if they don't think we are making much of the asylum request – if they think it is only a formality – then the risk of calling our bluff will be too great," suggested the director. "When we think we have all but the agreed two here with us, then we can go up and check out for ourselves to ascertain we actually have them all."

"And, at the same time, surreptitiously return the couplings," suggested the thief.

"After that," continued Director Ylah, "those who choose to stay here can, and those who don't are free to leave. No laws will have been broken."

"When we have the crew here we can arrest the officers and charge them with murder," said one of the team.

"That's a possibility," said the lawyer, "but it would be difficult. With no independent witnesses it would go to trial with no guarantee of success. It would be argued by their defence attorney that the crew have an axe to grind. In my opinion it would be better and cleaner to allow them to depart but then inform the UBIT that we are not accepting the goods because we are not convinced they were rightfully come by. We could recommend that they are taken to the original port of destination where the people are in need of them. This will be seen by the interplanetary community as just. The ship will, of course, remain the property of the Sponron officers; but since it will take them ten years to get to the original destination planet, the only place they can possibly dispose of the cargo and probably for very little, and then another twenty years or so to get back to their home planet – all this time without a crew and any female entertainment – it will add up to a life sentence anyway."

One man started clapping and was followed by general acclaim. This seemed to be a workable plan; it appealed. With the couplings in their possession, any chance that the commander decided to make a run for it would fail. It would take some time for them to realise what the problem was, and even if they did, they wouldn't be able to do anything about it.

★★★

Later, as the three made their way home, Kakko wondered whether a deception was ethical.

"The only really illegal thing," said Tam, "is holding on to the RCCs."

"I think," mused Shaun, "that if we are faced with a choice of two evils, taking the lesser evil is justified. I mean, we do have a request for asylum and we are obliged to act on it. We know the request is justified because we have seen exactly what is happening for ourselves. But if we are transparent with the Sponron commander and tell him the entire truth, then we are putting the applicants at serious risk. Therefore, we cannot be transparent – even about the reason why they cannot fire up their engines or how we have come by the request for asylum."

"I was just saying," said Kakko a little irritated, "you don't have to be so analytical. OK, so it's ethical. I agree with you."

Shaun held his tongue. He knew his sister was still sore at being left out.

★★★

In the event, the commander was more suspicious of them than they had anticipated. Devious by nature, he didn't take much at face value. When he was asked to return to negotiate, he replied that they knew what he had. All he needed to do was send a consignment down. When the director insisted on them coming, he decided to make a run for it. Rob and his colleagues didn't know that at the time. The command panels were locked. It was easier to conclude that there must be some external control exerted than detect that something as small as a coupling is missing, especially when he didn't trust the Johians any more than anyone else. The furious commander and his colleague entered their shuttle and came to Joh protesting. They were told that a jamming signal was a standard procedure to ensure the safety of the planet and they would be released when they returned to the Talifinbolindit.

The rest of the plan worked well. When only male crew members appeared in the first batches they played into the computer programmers' hands. They simply retained the grouping of dots in the restricted area. It looked convincing. The commander struck the desk with his fist and uttered an expletive that the translation program couldn't translate, but it didn't need to. The female Sponrons were conveyed to the spacedrome. The shuttle returned to the space-craft with a team from Joh, including women (to make a point), and inspected the Talifinbolindit for others. They found only one officer whom they bundled aboard the shuttle before replacing the couplings in the intrahelical drive control panels.

In the end, the commander and two officers were relieved to be allowed to return to the ship and within minutes it had disappeared as quickly as it had arrived. It was a matter of speculation just how long the three of them could live together with nowhere to go that would accept them within less than ten years worth of travel, without going mad.

Later when the three young people met together with Rob and some of the others, Shaun commented that he felt for them.

"I do too," said Prof Rob, "but I do not feel any guilt. If they had chosen to, the three officers could have asked to stay here too, and if they were to reappear now we would still grant them entry. Of course, they would be tried for murder, abduction, rape and theft, but prison here on Joh in the open air under our blue skies would be infinitely preferable to being cooped up in that ship, no matter how state of the art, with two other corrupt individuals.

★★★

The captive Sponrons were overjoyed to be on Joh. The clean air, the colour, the sound of the birds, and the fresh smell of the planet was amazing. They just stood, gazed and breathed.

None of them knew how they were related to the other members of their group except they had all grown up together in an orphanage. It would take months, if not years, perhaps never fully, for them to recover from their ordeal. But they knew what love meant, and they knew what hate was. They respected goodness and were determined to live lives different from that which their captors had imposed on them. Contact was eventually made with their home planet, Ramal, but it was in the neighbouring system of Medlam and would take at least sixteen years for a craft, even with an intrahelical engine, to reach Joh from there. And, of course, Joh did not own such a craft herself. Besides none of them wanted to enter another spacecraft in their lives. Provision was made for them in a hostel on the edge of town where they were given language lessons and training; they rarely went far. Kakko, Tam, Shaun and Bandi paid them regular visits and took them out for walks.

It was on one such walk, several months after the departure of the Talifinbolindit, that Kakko spotted a white gate. They all saw it, including the Sponrons. Kakko gave a quick explanation and assured them all would be OK.

"It's cool," she said, "we always get looked after. We don't need to be afraid. It's an adventure."

The Sponrons were doubtful about any kind of adventure but egged on by Kakko and without any opposition from the boys, who had no reason to doubt there was purpose in the white gate appearing, one by one they stepped through it. Kakko and Tam first (who was determined not to let Kakko act precipitously!) and the two brothers last after the Sponrons. They found themselves standing on a wooded hillside beside a road.

"Any idea where we are?" asked Kakko.

"No," said Shaun. "Could be anywhere."

They walked a few metres down the road and rounded a bend.

"A sign board," declared Kakko. "Not in any language I know!"

"It's Sponron. This our language," declared One. "It says Par, ten jaks, and Kat, fifteen jaks. It's Ramal! We're back on our planet! How can this be?"

"The wonder of the portals. You have been brought here!" said Kakko.

The party were all leaping in joyful abandon when a bus rounded the bend. It pulled to a halt unable to pass them.

"What's this all about?" mumbled the bus driver. An elderly passenger in a front seat stared at the group. They might be older, but they were definitely the children she had looked after for many years in the orphanage. They were the right age.

"I know them!" she exclaimed. "Wait."

She got down from the bus and began to call their names.

"Mrs Fan! Mrs Fan!" they all surrounded her.

"What are you doing here?"

"We've just arrived. It's a long story," said One. "Come. You must meet our friends, they rescued us."

Mrs Fan was introduced to the four from Joh.

"So where are you going?" asked Mrs Fan.

"We do not have anywhere to go. We've only just worked out where we are."

"Then you come back with me. All of you."

"Is anyone getting onto my bus? If not, clear the road!" demanded the driver.

"Bus!" they shouted like the children they had once been.

"Then get on," ordered Mrs Fan, "I will mollify the driver."

They went to mount the steps but then remembered their four friends. "You must come too."

"No. You are home, our job is done," said Tam decisively. "You go ahead with your lady. Our families will miss us if we don't return. We will try and stay in touch through the Interplanetnet somehow." The Sponrons all took it in turns to embrace them as they mounted the bus. And then it started up, descended the hill, rounded the bend and was gone. A minute later all that Kakko, Tam, Shaun and Bandi could hear was the sound of the wind in the trees and the hum of insects.

"Job well done," voiced Kakko quietly.

"Is that a compliment to Tam and me for our work on the Tal?" asked Shaun.

"It is indeed, you did remarkably well considering you did not have a woman around!"

"We did, didn't we? I guess you were praying, though," said Tam.

"I was," said Kakko. "That must be the answer then!" They all laughed.

"Imagine a planet without females," said Bandi. "It would definitely be different."

"Imagine a universe without God," said Tam. "That would be worse. And those Sponron officers have neither now."

"They don't have to be without God, though," said Bandi.

"Let's hope they find him," said Shaun. "I guess it won't be in a hurry though."

"They will, one day, when they leave this dimension. I believe God will take us all to himself whoever we are, wherever we might be, and whatever we've done," said Tam with conviction.

"Do you think so?" asked Kakko as they walked back up to the place where they had entered through the white gate. "How can you be sure of that? I can't see how God can take you into heaven if you are not good."

"I've thought about that. The trouble is, like Pastor Ruk said, there is some bad in all of us. We might not be really wicked but we're all a bit flawed, aren't we?"

"Speak for yourself," said Kakko.

"I do. And *you too*, Kakko. Even though I love you, I know that even you are a teeny bit flawed…"

"Definitely," laughed Shaun.

"Watch out!" yelled Bandi as Kakko swung an arm at her brother. "No violence allowed in heaven!"

"I see it's mended then," smiled Tam.

"What!" sputtered Kakko.

"Your arm. It's back to normal!" And then Kakko realised that she hadn't thought about it for the first time since the cliff, and felt good.

"So," Tam resumed, "if we aren't perfect, we won't measure up to heaven either. God has got to do some work on all of us – it'll just take a bit more work on those deceiving Sponron officers."

"You're assuming they will let Her," said Kakko.

"Yeah. God won't force Herself on them against their will. They could always opt out of heaven …"

"I wonder what it is like in the next world? What Grandma is experiencing, or those unfortunate Thenits. Do you think dying feels like stepping through a white gate that accepts only your spirit?" wondered Kakko.

"For some people, perhaps. For others it might not be so nice. Who knows?" answered Shaun.

"But when you get there it has to be good, really good – better than in this universe," said Tam. "Because if it wasn't it wouldn't be just. Our next stop beyond this universe, whatever it is, has to be a step nearer to ultimate justice."

"How can you be sure there is a heaven anywhere?" asked Kakko.

"If there is a just God, there has to be," replied Tam. "Otherwise God will not be true to Herself. If God is just, there has to be somewhere where the oppressed are set free, somewhere where wrongs can be righted, painful sacrifice rewarded – something for those poor Thenits for example."

"And I know God exists from all the other things She does for us," stated Kakko confidently. "So, therefore, heaven exists…"

"That's the logic – it all depends on whether you believe in the existence of a just and loving Creator God in the first place," said Tam.

"You're not bad at this sort of thinking," observed Bandi. "That makes sense. It fits with what we already know of God through our own experience – ours and those who have gone before us. "

"Next year I think I am going to combine theology with my law studies," said Tam, "Justice is more than law. Law is a tool – an important tool – but in itself it doesn't tell you what is right or wrong, good or bad. There *is* a universal justice. I mean those Sponrons had never been to Joh or any of the planets peopled by human beings, nor do they share any of our DNA, but they know what is right and what is wrong – their sense of justice is no different from ours."

"It's all to do with love," said Bandi.

"Yes," said Shaun, "and that comes from God. God has given us the gift of love. She is just. I want to learn more about Her and what She has revealed to us about the universe and ultimate justice. Our human law is OK, but it is only a human attempt at codifying what we sense to be just."

"So it's all common-sense after all?" said Kakko.

"Yes. It's all based on a common sense of justice," said Tam, "but in practice it can get complicated when one person's interpretation of common sense is not the same as another's – so we need to write it down and work from precedence. But you're right, law should always try to interpret universal justice."

They found the white gate where they had entered the Sponron world and within a very short time were sitting in the kitchen at White Gates Cottage eating Matilda's cake. Life was good.

"You know, we are so privileged to live here," said Kakko.

"I know," agreed Tam. "And what makes it even more special is that I've got you for my girlfriend. I *did* miss you on that shuttle. Honest."

"We need each other," smiled Kakko.

"You two are so lucky," remarked Bandi.

"Oh. There'll be someone for you too," assured Kakko.

"Duh! I didn't mean that! What would I do with a girlfriend? I'm quite happy as I am thank you!"

★★★

Decades later, the Talifinbolindit was found drifting in outer-space. Its cargo was intact and taken on to its original destination. It was empty of life – abandoned by its crew, who in their pain had probably elected to join their victims in the void of space. They may have thought that at least there, there was a kind of freedom perhaps, or maybe a dimension for the soul. They may even have become aware of the presence of God. There was no telling.

28

When Matilda noticed the new gate in the garden she was not so surprised. After years of stability, life had now become more of a roller-coaster ride. She didn't quite know how to break it to Jalli as she entered the cottage.

"Oh hi, Nan. How's Ada?"

"Oh, she's good. Jalli... there's a... a new gate."

"What? Let me see."

She looked out the window, then went into the garden. No white gate. "Not for me, Nan," she said and then called the children. Bandi spotted it straight away, but not Shaun and Kakko.

"It's not fair!" lamented Kakko.

"Oh. Kakko," sighed her mother.

Kakko heard herself through her mother's ears. "Sorry, I guess I'm acting like a spoiled kid. But why Bandi and not Shaun and me?"

"Maybe the Creator has got something else for you here," suggested Jalli.

Then Jack came in looking for his lunch. "A new gate!" he declared.

"Yes," said Jalli, "for your mum, Bandi and it seems you too."

"Just the three of us?"

"We'll manage," smiled Jalli. "But you'd better get yourself sorted. Your mum and Bandi are ready. Nan reckons it's Persham. She has found a reservation for the Red Lion Hotel there, some British banknotes and wet weather stuff including an umbrella!"

"Right …" whistled Jack. "I wonder how long for?"

"The reservation is for four nights."

"Right," said Jack again. "That long?"

***

When they stepped through the gate it was raining – on the Persham side that is. The season in Persham was early autumn and the yellowing horse-chestnut leaves of the park hung heavy with raindrops. As they descended the hill, the cars splashed along, spraying muddy water onto the pavements. Jack was glad that the Red Lion Hotel was on their side of the town. When they arrived, Matilda held open the narrow doors as Jack and Bandi staggered through with their luggage. They were greeted by warmth, and the beer-scented conviviality of the bar on their left. There was a small reception desk in front of them behind which sat a young woman in a tight, black blouse to which she had attached a shiny brass badge declaring to the world that she was called Angie.

"Hi," Angie grunted still beating the keyboard of a desktop computer.

"We have a reservation," said Matilda as she pushed the paper across the desk. The girl forced herself back into the real world – her Facebook friends would have to wait for the moment – and scrutinised the sheet.

"That's fine," she said. "You're foreign are yah?"

"From Persham," stated Matilda with dignified authority, "back for a few days… to see friends."

"That's great. You have two rooms for four nights on the second floor. No lift I'm afraid."

"'Course not," said Matilda curtly. "I can manage stairs without difficulty."

"But could you carry my mother's case for her?" asked Jack politely. "As I can't see, I need to keep one hand free."

"Yeah, sure," sighed the girl without conviction as she reluctantly tore herself away from the monitor.

★★★

The rooms were comfortable and old world. The Red Lion had once been a coaching inn and Jack wondered how many countless thousands had slept in his particular room down the centuries. It was Saturday. The three held a mini-conference about their next move and they decided that, as the rain had stopped, they would go for a walk around where Jack and his mother used to live, and see what had happened to the house. Then they would go on to the parish church and check what time the service was the following morning. They would make a beginning there, unless anything else came up.

★★★

As they turned into Renson Park Road, Matilda was immediately struck by the size of the trees that lined the pavement. When they had first moved in nearly four decades before, they were all so small. By the time they had left for

Woodglade they were certainly growing but, now, more than twenty years on, they were majestic. The whole street was dominated by them, but the really impressive thing was that the one outside number 68, where she and Jack had lived for nearly fifteen years, had also grown tall. It was still a little behind the others but was otherwise indistinguishable from them.

"Well, look at that!" exclaimed Matilda. "Our tree, it's huge!" She guided Jack so that he could place his hands on its trunk. Jack shuddered as the memories flooded back. He encircled it. "Well, that has come on! How tall is it?"

"Nearly as high as the house!" declared his mother. "It really struggled when we were here. It was always in the wars. Seemed to keep getting broken. The vandals were always at it," she said with a gentle irony – an irony Jack pretended not to notice.

"Did you ever see them?" he asked. Matilda answered that she hadn't; which was true. She was out when her son had demolished it for the final time that day in the rain – when he had vented all his anger and heartbreak on it as he despaired of ever seeing his beloved Jalli again. He remembered all that stupidity – and he was once again filled with gratitude that his mum had had the courage to arrange for the elderly Mr Evans to call. That had been the turning point between despair and the joy of his setting off to begin again with Jalli. It was good to know that his mistreatment had not prevented the tree from coming back and being almost as high as the house. Jack placed his hand on the bark as high as he could reach and whispered, "OK, you win."

"What you say, Dad?" asked Bandi.

"Oh. Nothing. Just talking to the tree." Bandi shook his head. Kakko was always saying their parents were a couple of tree-huggers.

The front of the house was also transformed. It had received a make-over from caring owners. The garden was a picture – all the old rubbish had gone. There was a border of bedding dahlias and fuchsias surrounding a carefully cropped little square of grass. All the former ill-fitting wooden-framed casement windows had been replaced with contemporary, white, PVC double-glazing units. The front door matched them. Below a semicircular piece of double-glazed stained glass were the figures "6" and "8" in carefully polished brass. Through the front window they could see the outlines of some high-class furniture and a standard lamp behind heavy, deep red velvet curtains. Matilda described what she saw to Jack.

"Better off than we were, then?"

"The whole street's different. It's quite grand. They've got some expensive cars parked outside and there are two skips further down where they are doing up another place."

Just then a young woman with two small children emerged from number 70 and saw the trio standing and studying.

"Can I help you?" she asked in an educated accent that was not Persham. "Sky come here. You know what I told you about the road – stay with Willow! Er, sorry they are quite full of autumn spirit."

"No, that's alright," replied Matilda, in her best posh English voice. "We used to live here at number 68 and were interested in how things were coming on."

"Oh. Your old house is in good hands," smiled the young

woman. "They are excellent neighbours… Sky! Put down those leaves. You'll mess up all your clothes. Sorry, must move on…" She forced a smile and charged after the child, beating bits of tree off the little girl's front.

Bandi laughed and imitated his nan's posh voice, "We used to live here…"

"Bandi," scolded his father. "That's rude!"

"Why can't they call their kids by honest-to-goodness Christian names these days? Willow and Sky! I ask you," remarked Matilda, ignoring her grandson.

"What, like Kakko and Bandi?" laughed Jack.

"Well that's different. You don't live in Britain."

"We'd have called them the same wherever we had lived," said Jack.

"You know what I mean!" said his mother, a bit peeved. "With names like that they're not likely to be churchgoing are they? They're not Christian names."

"Oh, I don't know. It doesn't follow. Names go in fashion. In generations when lots of people went to church they still called their children by names that weren't in the bible – Amy, Louise, Charles and William. Wasn't your mother's family all flowers: Violet, May, and Daisy?" Matilda shrugged.

"It's gentrification. That's what it is," mused Bandi thoughtfully.

"What's *gentrification*?" Matilda wanted to know. "That's a big word."

"I did it in geography last year. What's happened here to this street. Streets near the centre of towns become popular with yuppies who are not so interested in large gardens and garages. Small houses get done up and sell for much higher prices while the original occupiers end up moving away further out of town…"

"Where they have to spend a fortune on bus fares!" broke in Matilda.

"You've read the same geography book?" asked Bandi.

"Didn't need to. I've seen it happen."

"So we moved at the right time," observed Jack.

"*We* did. But I bet there are lots I grew up with who are not so lucky. Come on, let's go on down to the church."

They walked to the end of the street, past more evidence of gentrification, but the church building didn't seem to have changed any. St Augustine's, Persham, still looked the same as it had done when it had been built in Victorian times – at least from the outside. On the inside, however, it had been transformed twice since its birth. Once in the period just before the First World War when much of the Tractarian statuary and ornamentation was replaced with vast quantities of carved woodwork, including a chancel screen and a reredos all given in memory of some wealthy parishioner – his family desirous of making a splash. But then, in the minimalist early 1970s, these furnishings were mostly removed, despite a howl of protest from the descendants of the 'named' and the threat of a consistory court. The interior of the church building had then become more open and user-friendly, but its reputation had suffered with the local people. The message of Jesus had been drowned out by the controversy over the building at the very time in history that it most needed to be heard, when the rise of popular secularism was undermining faith by calling it 'unfounded superstition'. What the ordinary people saw was an unholy feuding about furniture, and that just confirmed what they were coming to believe anyway – that the Church was largely irrelevant in contemporary culture. The Church was chiefly about history and conservation. "Tradition" was becoming co-terminus with "living in a quaint period drama" which is nice at Christmastime and for weddings, but not in the rough and tumble of daily life.

The present vicar, however, was a person of vision and he and his congregation stuck to it. As well as opening up the space, the Christ-centred church-goers had also moved away from using the four hundred year old *Book of Common Prayer* for the main services. Slowly, the Church was beginning to relate the good news of Jesus to current needs and take notice of the prevailing postmodernism. St Augustine's was making a come-back. In the little garden in front of the church there now stood a giant notice-board proclaiming in large letters:

MESSY CHURCH
Every Saturday between 2 pm and 4 pm.
For children, families and those who have never quite grown-up.
No-one is ever too young or too old for Messy Church!

The time was now just after two o'clock on a Saturday and there was a wondrous noise from inside, a cacophony of sound. Those who had 'not quite grown up' were mixing their voices with children of all ages running up and down. The chairs had been moved to one side and people sat, perched or stood around large, bright-blue plastic sheets, carpets and islands of newspaper, while the kids were all doing something different at the same time. There was painting, cutting out and sticking. Lively children were darting backwards and forwards to large boxes in the centre full of colourful bits of cloth, crepe paper, pipe-cleaners, sticky-back shapes, and a myriad of other attractions the kids could seize on to decorate their masterpieces. Even some of the adults were engaged in painting some kind of mural, while a few ladies huddled in a corner in a sewing-bee-come-knitting-circle with material off-cuts, cottons and wool. (Matilda learned later they were constructing a child-friendly, knitted Christmas crib.)

The three visitors from Joh moved around the edge of the activity but were soon caught up by a group of children demanding they admire their frieze.

"Hi!" It was the same young mother they had seen emerge from number 70. She seemed to be very relaxed in the gathering. (So calling her children Willow and Sky hadn't meant she was resistant to coming into the church after all!) "Pleased to see you again! Welcome. We're doing something for Harvest Festival." Her Willow came up and seemed lost for the moment.

"What can I do, Mummy?"

"You can choose between making a frieze over here, help write a prayer (or drawing a picture for one) in the corner over there, or finding a song to sing, or just running around if you're not ready to concentrate – so long as you keep clear of the paint." The little girl swung her arms across herself as she rocked in thought, eventually opting to hover around the singing group. She was quickly absorbed within it.

"Sorry. Nice to see you," said the mother again.

"Well, actually, we had just come to see what time the

service was tomorrow morning. Does this happen every Saturday?"

"Yes, but we vary the activities. Sometimes we are more chaotic than others but we do our best not to look the same as school. Free expression is important if people are to find real meaning in their lives."

Jack was about to agree and suggest they move to the 'prayer corner' when a very elderly gentleman came up to them.

"Jack," he said huskily, "Jack Smith?"

"Yes!" Jack had instantly recognised the man to whom he owed so much. He reached out and took his hand, then the whole of him. "Mr Evans! How are you doing?"

"You remember me! Not so bad considering. I'm ninety-five at Christmas."

"Wow," said Jack.

"And how's it all going with you?"

"Very well. You know my mother, Matilda," the old gentleman took her hand, "and this is my youngest, Bandi."

"Your youngest! How many do you have?"

"Three."

"And they're all well and your girlfriend, um…"

"My wife, Jalli."

"Of course! How long have you been married now?"

"Twenty-two years."

"Time rushes by!"

"I have so much to tell you about," laughed Jack, "none of which would have happened if you had not come round and sat with me in the rain!"

"Are you coming to the Harvest Supper later?"

"To tell you the truth we just popped in to find out the time of the service tomorrow and discovered this hive of activity!"

"Yes, 'Messy Church'. I've been waiting for it all of my life. I've had my ups and downs with what I have now come to call 'Stuffy Church'. Now I feel a bit like Simeon when he met Jesus in the temple, 'Now let thy servant depart in peace, for I have seen thy salvation!' or in Messy Church words, 'Now I can kick my clogs with a smile because people in the church are at last having fun learning about Jesus!'" he laughed. "But really, you *must* come to the Harvest Supper. There is someone I would love to introduce you to, John Banks. John is a town councillor who has been struggling to get a specialist school for blind children going in this part of the county for years. It has at last got the go-ahead in principle. All they have to do now is vote on the money! You and he could have a very fruitful conversation. By the way, do you have a job where you are now?"

"Yes, I work in a school for blind children!"

"Perfect. This meeting is meant."

"I believe it is. I can now see why we had to come here today. I am delighted for the blind children of Persham."

"Good. So you'll all come tonight. It begins at 6.30 pm. Don't worry about tickets, I'll organise those."

Just then the old man stopped talking and put this hand in the air as high as his ninety-five years would allow. He had just seen the lady in charge do it. Then everyone stopped what they were doing and stood with their hands in the air too. The noise had been turned off like a tap!

"Five more minutes!" ordered the woman. "Start finishing off now."

When the five minutes were up the woman said quietly, "Now, sit down where you are." Everyone did so. "Chloe's people first. (There are some Chloe's people in the Bible too, in Corinth.) Now Chloe's people, do you want to show us your frieze?"

A long length of still wet wall-paper with drawings and cuttings of fruit and vegetables was extended. The leader called the others to move round to see.

"What have you got there in the middle? That looks like people."

"It is," said one of the older members of the group, "it's us because we should be part of God's harvest too. All safely gathered in like my husband Joe who passed away last year."

"Dropped dead in the Pig & Whistle over a pint," whispered Mr Evans in Jack's ear.

"Sounds the perfect way to go," replied Jack.

"No, he still had three-quarters of his bitter left. He died too soon!"

"Yes," said Joe's wife, who had picked up the last words. "Too soon. But he's getting me place ready for me when the time comes."

"Good!" said the activity lady quickly. "*We* are part of God's harvest too. And we don't have to wait till we die because we can all become part of the Kingdom of God now. How good is that! Good, what have we got from Peter's group working on the prayers?"

They went through each group in turn and soon they had prayers to say, songs to sing and a little playlet. Finally the lady leader asked, "So, are we ready to begin? Let's sit in a big semi-circle. That's it, spread out. Not too far, George, we need to see you!"

When they had all settled, she called them to their feet and announced the first song. Words appeared on a large screen above her head and a young man standing behind a keyboard began to play a harvest worship song which clearly the children all knew and sang with gusto. Then they were all urged to turn to the people on their left and right and greet them, saying: *Welcome in the Name of Jesus Christ. I'm (name).* The reply was to be: *I'm (name). Together we praise him.* Then a second hymn was sung. This one Matilda and Jack knew instantly: 'We Plough the Fields and Scatter.'

The worship progressed with all the elements being presented by the different groups and all too soon it was ended.

"Alright," said the activities lady. "The *sad* news is that today we have to finish early because the people who are going to set up the church for tomorrow's Harvest Service need to get in and get started." There was a polite boo. The lady raised her hand, "But the *good* news is that over in that corner there is orange juice, tea and coffee, aannnddd... loads-of-Mrs-Whittaker's-Dorset-Apple-Cake-and-iced-biscuits. Wait, waiiit for it...! I've still got my hand up, George! Let's finish with our prayer, together, 'The grace of our Lord Jesus Christ and the love of God and the fellowship of the Holy Spirit be among us, now and always. Amen!'" She threw her hands in the air and there was a mass rush for the goodies.

It was a very slick operation but within a very few minutes all the 'messy' kit had been gathered up, the floor swept and the chairs returned to their traditional rows.

"Ten minutes past the agreed time," sighed the activity leader checking her watch.

As soon as they had finished, a small army of people surged into the church with armfuls of greenery, buckets of dahlias and chrysanthemums and baskets and boxes of fruit and vegetables of every description. Jack was blown away by the smell of it all. For even the least churchgoing Englishman, the scents of harvest are laden with nostalgia – a nostalgia that is not just about the younger days of an individual but a cultural memory that extends back to Pagan days.

"Sorry Mrs P. Ten minutes late!" called the Messy Church leader. She was met by a scowl as a women bustled by her clutching special flowers for the sanctuary. The leader relaxed. It seemed that was all the trouble she was going to get into. But it was not to be.

"Since you seem to have persuaded the vicar and the churchwardens that you can move things, the least you can do is to restore the church to how it should be! Who put those chairs there?"

"Er, sorry," squeaked Bandi, "it was me. I wasn't sure of exactly where they went. I'll put them right. Where would you like them?"

"I don't know you, do I? Coming in and moving furniture before you've been here five minutes!" snapped Mrs P.

"I was only trying to help," sputtered Bandi, feeling cowed.

"I'll tell you who he is, Petunia!" spoke up Matilda. "He's my grandson, that's who he is!"

"Well," gasped Mrs P., "if it isn't Matilda Simpson. Where'd you spring from?"

"Yes, Petunia Greenbottom, it's me. I'd like to say I'd died and come back to haunt you! But I haven't, sadly, so you'll be spared that a few years longer. It seems you haven't given up bullying people then?"

A small group of people began to gather. No-one had ever dared take on Mrs P. before. The ladies squared up to each other as they had done in the playground of the Persham Primary School some fifty years before. It was soon evident that Mrs P. had met her match, perhaps her long lost nemesis.

"Now," declared Matilda, "apologise to my grandson and get on with your bouquet!"

"Flower arrangement," wheezed the woman in an effort to appear defiant, but without being at all convincing.

"Whatever!" barked Matilda. "I'm waiting."

"Sorry," said Mrs P. to Bandi. "I hadn't realised you were Matilda's grandson." And then, before any more attention could be drawn to her, minced off to the chancel step.

"Well, that sorted her out," whistled a small man in a royal-blue clerical shirt. "I gather you are Matilda. Welcome back. People have told me about you. I'm Dave, the vicar. Been here for eight years now and no way could I have faced up to Mrs P. like that. She still sees me in nappies, I fear."

"Pleased to meet you," smiled Matilda. "Petunia Greenbottom was a bully at school but I was a worse one!" People laughed.

"I never knew her maiden name – or her Christian name come to that," said the Messy Church leader.

"People used to call her Grassy Arse," smiled Matilda. Bandi couldn't control himself and began to weep as he laughed.

Partly to draw attention away from his son, Jack then introduced himself and explained that they used to live in the parish many years ago. They were back on a very short visit. Mr Evans then came over and explained that he would like to introduce Jack to Councillor Banks that evening.

Jack asked if there was anything they could help with.

"No I don't think so," said Dave. "It's all organised. Just come along to be seated by half past six. Thank you Mrs Simpson…"

"Mrs Smith. Simpson is the maiden name."

"Of course! Thank you. And, don't be put off this church by Mrs P. – I'm afraid her attitude to life is not so, so… exactly Christlike."

"No worries!" retorted Jack. He turned to help put the chairs in the right place but the leader had already done it.

"Five moves," she laughed.

"As easy as that?"

"As easy as that."

"So, Petunia Greenbottom married a man with the initial of 'P'," said Jack.

"She *was* married but I don't know what happened to the husband," explained the vicar.

"I know," explained Matilda. "He ran off with the floozy behind the bar of the Red Lion less than two years into their marriage. He and the girl emigrated to Australia…"

"Talking of the Red Lion," said Jack, "we'd better get back there. We'll need to get ready if we're to face a delicious Harvest Supper!"

"I love this Messy Church," said Bandi, "it's cool. The leader there has just told me that sometimes they have a guitar band in, and the teenagers do a drama. It's not craft-work every week."

"So, my home town is fun?" remarked his dad.

"The church is, anyway," replied Bandi.

"That," said Dave, "has made my day!"

They took their leave and wended their way back through the streets. As they walked, Bandi observed that he had seen a new side to his nan.

"There's lot's about me you don't know," she said.

"How'd I know you were going to say that?" laughed her son.

29

When they arrived in the Church Hall at a quarter past six the hall was almost full. Mr Evans met them and ushered them to seats he had reserved for them.

"Just sit here for now," he said. "I expect the vicar will try and mix people up anyway. But whatever happens those two tables will remain exactly as they are. They are the same every year. The only way anyone gets to sit with those people is if one of them dies or is sick and can't come."

Matilda surveyed the tables. "It was the same when they were at school. The very same people. Excuse me I'm going to sit over there while there is still a space."

"It'll be reserved for someone," worried Mr Evans.

"That may be, but I haven't seen Cynthia for thirty years." And she was off. Of course everyone remembered that Matilda was high in the pecking order from her school days. It turned out, as luck would have it, that the displaced person was none other than Mrs. P. There was nothing else she could do but sit on another free seat. As Mr Evans predicted, the vicar suggested that they all moved to sit with someone they didn't know so well, so that any new people would not feel so left out. That didn't apply to Karen and Tom, he joked, who had just returned from their honeymoon the day before! There was a roar of delight and people applauded them, while Karen and Tom went the same colour as the fresh beetroot on the side table. Tom stood up and took a bow.

"OK," said the Vicar, "let's do it!" People got up and started moving around including Mrs P. It was like a game of musical chairs. Before he knew what was happening, two pretty girls had swooped on Bandi and carted him off to a table populated by young people. Mr Evans signalled to Councillor Banks who plonked himself down in his place. The last person to find a chair appeared to be poor Mrs P. who had hovered around the table with the 'friends' but, of course none of them moved. They just continued to talk and totally ignored what was going on. This sort of stuff didn't involve them. By the time that Mrs P. had given up on getting onto a table of her own choice there was only one chair left – next to the vicar. That was not exactly a bad thing because she had been so battered that day, at least he could begin by helping her get over it by treating her with respect.

Bandi had never enjoyed vegetables quite as much. There was pork and ham as well as all sorts of different roots roasted and covered in gravy. It was all new to him. The others were amazed at just how much he didn't know about things everyone took for granted. In return they wanted to learn as much as they could about Joh. Bandi had gathered from the way his father did it that it was best not to speak as if Joh was a whole planet because it begged too many questions. He allowed them to think it was some exotic place on Earth. It was easier that way. They seemed to think he sounded a bit American and built him into their romantic view of California – Hollywood, sunshine, beaches and, following the song by Frankie Ballard, 'bunches of girls' in skimpy attire.

Meanwhile Councillor Banks was in earnest conversation with Jack about the school for blind children. It would be attached to the Middle School, he told him. Jack explained the nature of his job and how important he felt a school that taught blind children how to make the most of their world was to them.

Mr Banks asked, "Would you be prepared to come and address the meeting? It's Tuesday evening."

Jack realised their hotel reservations took them through to Wednesday morning. He decided that was why they, or at least he, was here.

Matilda was a having a whale of a time goading and stirring up the ladies on her table. Three of them remembered her from school but only one had seen her since. This was positive for Matilda because they didn't know about the dark years with, and then without, her husband Shaun Smith. She could return to her dominant rating in the school pecking order.

"So, you've not been to the church much before?" asked a dumpy woman. "How now?"

"We don't live in Persham these days but I did come a few times before I moved – but that was a long time ago."

"But you was never brought up to come to church. Never remember seeing you in Sunday school. Anyways from what I recall you were dead set agin 'organised religion' as your family called it."

"Oh, I was. I couldn't stand most of them vicars and priests that came to take assembly. Do you remember that one who called himself, 'Father Hopkinson'?"

"Yeah. He was a not popular. He got that young curate…

didn't look above twenty, but I expect he was… anyways he brings him along to the school and introduces him. He had the unfortunate name of John Christmas. But the worst was when Father Hopkinson tells everyone that he doesn't hold with calling priests by their Christian names – no matter how young. So he only goes and introduces him to the kids as 'Father Christmas'. Poor lad didn't stand a chance."

"Whatever happened to him?"

"I dunno. He didn't stay long. Went to another parish by all accounts…"

"I remember, my mother liked him. He was the one who organised her to help with the flower arranging. He allocated her a windowsill. It's the same one where I still do my arrangement… I can't stick this Messy Church on a Saturday afternoon. It really gets in the way of doing the flowers. We used to have all day to do 'em but now we can only do the 'top end' in the morning. We can't come in while they're on and if we want flowers in the nave we have to wait till after four."

"But you came in earlier today though," remembered Matilda.

"Well, today's different. It's Harvest. But I don't see why they couldn't hold their kids' thing in the Church Hall. Why does it have to be in church?"

"Because it *is* church," suggested Matilda, "and I don't think it is meant just for kids."

"'Cours it ain't church," one of the ladies was getting a bit high on something and she was speaking rather too loudly. "It's Sunday School – of a sort."

"Shh a bit Fiona," said Cynthia, "don't doctor your orange juice any more. You'll smell like a 'distillery'."

"But it looked like church to me," observed Matilda, "There was singing about God, harvest hymns even, prayers, a bible story and some drama. Next week they're having communion, I gather."

"But it's not *proper* church. Folk are not coming like they used to. Our numbers are going down."

"But Messy Church numbers seem quite high," said Matilda.

"Well, that's the point. Our congregation has lost the young people to Messy Church. They go there instead."

"Twenty-two years ago I don't really remember too many young families in the church," said Matilda. "How many of the Messy Church people ever came to the main Sunday Service?"

"None. Except the leaders, and they still come on a Sunday," said a woman who up till then had not said much, "and they want it on a Saturday afternoon because that is the most popular time for it. I think it's great seeing kids in church having fun. I reckon my son's daughter might even get confirmed this time – even though no-one in the family mentioned it to her. I was *sent* and *done* when I were thirteen. But she *wants* to be. She believes! I didn't until much later on."

"But she doesn't have to get confirmed like we did if she wants communion."

"No. She's been taking it since she were three. They've given up linking communion with confirmation it seems."

"Like living together before you're married," broke in Cynthia. But she quickly regretted the remark. Of all the people around the table she was the only one with a straight forward love-life. Still happily married to the man she dated when she was sixteen, she was the exception.

The conversation died, until Matilda picked it up again. "That's probably why I never came as a teenager. I was never sent, and I thought church must be the most boring thing in the universe from what the kids that went said."

"But you said you did come – just before you moved."

"I did," explained Matilda. "I met someone. Well two people really. The first was Mr Evans over there, who helped us all through Jack being blinded, and the second was Jesus himself. It was, like, Mr Evans introduced us. Once I started talking to him – praying to God, that is – I began to understand why church was so… important, even special. When it makes sense, it isn't boring. And all the decorations and all the ceremony – even the statues and the incense if you have 'em – make sense too. It all depends on whether it's about worshipping the Creator, or just decoration and ceremony for the sake of it."

The table was silent again. This was serious stuff. Then the quiet woman agreed. Jesus was what counted. She began to talk of her own experience of God 'in her life' as she put it.

"You've never told us about this before," commented Cynthia.

"No? Well, I didn't think you would be interested. But hearing Matilda talk it has made it sound like… something I could share."

"We're all very serious tonight!" laughed a woman with increasing hollowness. "We're not at a wake!"

"No," said Matilda, "but we are here to give thanks to the Creator for the wonderful gifts he has given us and to ask him to safely 'gather us all in'… *right now*…" she glanced around at a set of stunned open-mouthed faces, and then laughed. "I didn't mean *die* you idiots! Aren't we at the Lord's banquet here tonight? We can be 'gathered in' to his Kingdom *before* we die, can't we?"

"Indeed we can," said the vicar who had come over. "You're clearly having an enormously enjoyable conversation."

"Indeed we – hic – are," said Fiona with a slightly glazed expression. "Vicar," she called out loudly, "you'll know. Whatever ever happened to that gorgeous Father Christmas?"

★★★

The Sunday service was one that could not fail. All the traditional harvest hymns and the Eucharist in contemporary language. There are few things in the universe, thought Jack, to rival an English Harvest Festival with use of all five of the senses so intensely. Bandi was being helped to follow the service by an attractive young blonde girl. Matilda hoped that he would survive till Wednesday, but then realised she was the Vicar's daughter and scolded herself for not trusting these young folk. She recalled with horror how she had behaved at their age. By contrast this was tame stuff indeed!

★★★

Sunday lunch was enjoyed at the Red Lion. Jack asked Bandi how much he liked the young lady.

"What young lady!?"

"The one you've been cuddling up to most of the morning – and some of yesterday evening too."

"I haven't been cuddling up to anyone!"

"No, perhaps not. But you've got very close all the same. You smell of violets or whatever they call the perfume she sprayed on herself this morning. And you've got that wistfulness about you which means that something inside is a bit pre-occupied."

Matilda laughed. "And I saw her. Pretty, tastefully dressed in a not too revealing top and nice clean jeans. Blonde – natural perhaps – lots of it." And she picked a strand off of Bandi's shoulder. "Vicar's daughter I think."

Bandi shrugged. Why did he have to be blessed with detectives for parent and grandparent?

"OK. Good taste," said Jack. "Go for it. Only don't get heart broken in the next two days…"

"Her name's Abby," said Bandi blushing, "…and nothing serious is going to happen, is it?"

30

The next day, which was blowy but fine, the trio spent catching up with the changes in Persham. Bandi got a bit tired of his nan saying, "Oh look, the bakery's gone!" and, "Well, I never, they've changed the crossing arrangements *again*. I always said it wouldn't work. Should have listened to me before they did it," and similar remarks.

They had lunch in the indoor market and Matilda was happy that the standard menu hadn't altered, so she had the all-day breakfast she had usually ordered.

In the afternoon they went to the library beyond the middle school and explored the history of the children's blind school initiative. Then they wandered back down the hill and through the park just as the Renson Park High students were coming out of the school on the far side.

"Hi!" called out Bandi. He had spotted Abby's blonde hair as she crossed the park. The girl turned and saw Bandi running down the grassy slope and waited for him. She waved off her friends who were watching as Bandi gathered speed. They moved on, but reluctantly; they were curious to see what this vision of boyhood was like. "Not bad," said one. "Bit keen isn't he?" They giggled.

Bandi's feet slipped on the wet grass as he tried to come to a halt without running past. Fortunately he just managed to stay in an upright position and saved his blushes. If he had hit the mud he would have died of embarrassment. He stopped beside his friend rather flustered. He realised too late that his antics had drawn attention – he should have played it cool, but Abby didn't seem to mind. What her silly friends were saying was their problem.

"Bit steep that," Bandi motioned to the hill for something to say as he gathered his breath.

Matilda watched from the hill as she led Jack down the much more gradual path. "He seems to like that one," she observed. "I've never seen him keen on a girl before."

"Abby, the girl with the violets?" enquired Jack.

"The very one. She's sent her friends off so I think she likes him too. They're dawdling."

"Dawdling?"

"Yes, just mooching along so as to give themselves more time to talk to each other."

Eventually Jack and Matilda arrived at the road and waited for Bandi and Abby to get to them. Dozens of other school children in similar brown uniforms passed them, flowing to the road to catch buses in different directions or else disperse in ones and twos into the local area. It was like a muddy stream that just petered out. Eventually Bandi and Abby drew near.

"Dad?" enquired Bandi tentatively. "Can I… may I go to Abby's for tea? She says it'll be alright with her parents."

"Well, of course. I can't see why not. You know where we're staying?"

"The Red Lion Hotel."

"Where's home?" Matilda asked Abby.

"Oh, the vicarage. My dad's the vicar."

"No problem," said Jack, "Don't be -"

"...late. No I won't."

"I was going to say to take care walking through the streets on your own at night," said his father.

"That's OK. We'll see him back," said Abby.

★★★

When Bandi rolled into the hotel later that evening he was followed by Abby and her father. Jack and Matilda were sitting in the bar to the left of the entrance. They were almost alone, except for a man reading a newspaper and Angie, the receptionist, who doubled up as a barmaid.

"Dad? Dad?" called Bandi seeing his father and grandmother. "Can I go to Oxford tomorrow?"

"Oxford?" queried Jack. "Why Oxford? It's not just down the road from here."

"Oh, I know... Dad, Nan you know Abby's dad?"

"Yes," said Jack, extending his hand. "Come and sit down, Vicar. What can I get you?"

"Oh, call me Dave. Thank you. Just an orange juice. I don't drink and drive." He smiled as he dragged over an upholstered chair.

"Abby?"

"Oh, can I have a coke?"

"Course you can," said Matilda, "*I'll* get these. You just sit down. Ice?"

"Please."

"Dave?"

"Oh, no. No ice for me. Thanks."

"So," said Jack, "you've been getting to know my son?"

"Indeed we have. A fine young man. He has been saying some very complimentary things about his family."

"That's good to hear."

"So," broke in Bandi impatiently, "can I go to Oxford tomorrow?"

"Let me explain," laughed Dave. "Abby has an appointment with the orthodontist at the Radcliffe Hospital. It's just a follow-up to some work she had done in the summer. She won't be in there long but it means taking the whole day off and driving up. So, since you have no plans for him tomorrow – well, Bandi doesn't think you have – Abby wondered if he would like to come with us for the trip. The appointment's at 10.30 am. After that we could take Bandi into the city and show him the sights – the old buildings, the churches, the colleges and so on."

"And hire a punt!" put in Abby with some enthusiasm.

"…and, yes, hire a punt," agreed Dave.

"Well, we have nothing booked except my address for Councillor Bank's meeting in the evening," said Jack.

"We'll be back well in time for that. I plan to be there myself. We'll feed him and then bring him along to the meeting."

"It seems OK with us," said Jack smiling, "if you're keen to have a strange boy along with you when you have to see a doctor."

"Oh, no problem, he can wait outside. There'll be stuff he can read in the waiting room."

"And probably toys to play with," joked Matilda.

"We'll have to set off around nine though," explained Dave.

"Oh, that's not early. No problem."

"Well then, if that's settled we'll get along home, Abby. See you here tomorrow at nine."

"I'll be ready," said Bandi as he walked them to the door.

"It sounds as if you've made a hit there," said Jack when his son got back. "I *have* to say this. Don't be cross with me. I expect that we will return to White Gates Cottage on Wednesday morning. And after that we may never come back again. Look how long it's taken us this time…"

"I know, Dad! I know," said Bandi a bit vexed.

"Well, just so long…"

"*You don't have to say it, Dad!*" repeated Bandi with exasperation.

"OK." Jack held his hands up. "Make the most of it, lad. Have fun while you can."

"Now that's something *I* always wanted to do," mused Matilda.

"What?" enquired Jack.

"Ride in a punt. A punt propelled by a handsome man in a boater. All suave and debonair…"

"Sounds like a disaster. He sounds rather eccentric and likely to fall in," suggested Jack.

"Abby's Dad went to Birmingham Uni," commented Bandi.

"I always had this dream of a date in a punt," Matilda was going a little glassy eyed.

"But my dad never took you?" queried Jack.

"What? Who? Shaun. You must be joking!" she sighed. "And now my young grandson from another planet has got a real chance! Oh, well. I don't suppose I'm invited too?"

"Not unless you can find yourself a handsome, debonair young man by nine o'clock tomorrow morning," teased Jack.

"Well you can't have everything… now I'm going to bed. Goodnight!"

"I think that's a good idea," agreed Jack. "Time to dream. I'm tired. Goodnight, Mum."

Jack went to bed happy, but it didn't stop him wishing Jalli was with him.

★★★

For Bandi and Abby sitting in the back of the car, Oxford didn't seem very far at all. Time swept by as Bandi told Abby all about their life on Planet Joh and how his parents had arrived there more than twenty years before. He told her how they had had lots of adventures until the babies started to come along and the white gates stopped appearing. But now the portals had started up again. He described the fantastic week-end they had had in Pero's hotel. It was all a wonderful dream. "The only thing," he explained, "is that you can't decide yourself when, where or how long. It is all planned for you. So tomorrow I expect we shall be back on Joh and after that the white gate to Persham will disappear behind us – perhaps for ever."

"That sounds so dreadfully final," retorted Abby. "That's not fair. That's, like, mean. You just meet someone and get to know them and you can't even text them!"

"I know. But Dad and Nan, they used to live here and this is the first time they have been back in twenty-two years."

"But they are together. Your family isn't broken up."

"That's true."

"Yeah. I know people who are refugees who can't go home. Some don't know where their parents or children are, or even if they're still alive. That's really bad. We have this girl at school from South Sudan. She ran away when soldiers came through her village. She hid in the bush but her mum never made it. Her brothers had run in different directions. Her dad had already left to fight for the rebels and she has no idea where any of them are. She was only seven. Some strangers fleeing through the area picked her up. They took her to a refugee camp over the border but then abandoned her. Nobody claimed her. Eventually she ended up here in Persham. Her name is Rebecca but she doesn't remember any of her other names."

"That's terrible. Has someone adopted her?"

"Well, kind of. It's a long-term foster family she's with. They get money to look after her until she's eighteen and she's hoping she can stay with them at least until then. She works very hard at school. She's determined to be a doctor."

"What about you? Have you decided what you want to do?"

"No. Not really. Not a doctor though. It won't be anything with science or maths. What about you?"

"Well, I was thinking about computer science."

"Isn't that a bit boring?"

"Boring! No it's very interesting."

"But it's working with machines all the time. I'd get fed up with it unless I did things with people."

"I'm quite content not to have so much to do with people. I like thinking on my own."

★★★

At the Radcliffe, Abby was taken for an X-ray, after which she saw the doctor who expressed satisfaction with the way things had gone.

"How do you feel about it?" he asked as he prodded around in her open mouth.

"'eels ahK," replied Abby as best she could with his instruments in her mouth.

"Happy?"

Abby attempted a nod.

"Right, well I think we can discharge you. Come back if you have any trouble – but I doubt you will. Your jaw looks beautiful!" he smiled, and within twenty minutes of leaving them, Abby had re-joined her father and Bandi in the waiting room.

"Well?" asked her father. He had wanted to go in with his daughter but she had insisted that she was old enough not to have her hand held.

"He told me I'm beautiful – well, at least my jaw is from the inside. I don't have to come back no more."

"*Any* more," corrected her father automatically.

"Dad!" said Abby peevishly. Her father could be a pain at times. She didn't want to be corrected in front of Bandi. "You know what I mean!"

"That's good news, then. Now let's get the bus into the city centre and show Bandi around. I've discovered he likes thinking but has no knowledge of any philosophy – not the Earthly sort anyway – and I want to take him to a bookshop."

Abby could see that the two of them had had quite a

discussion while she had been with the orthodontist. They were getting on very well. She would have liked to have had Bandi to herself but knew that was not possible.

In the city, Dave pointed out the colleges and the libraries and told them some of the very long history of the university.

"I didn't study here though," he explained, "I'm a Birmingham man. I did my undergraduate degree in chemistry and then went on to Queen's College to do theology."

He asked Bandi if he had plans to go to university in Joh.

"Well, yes ... sort of. I thought I would study computing."

"Ah, very important,"

"But a bit boring I'm told," smiled Bandi glancing at Abby.

"Who told you... ah, I see. Abby that was a bit cruel, don't you think? Not everyone feels the way we do about things."

"No. But it's still boring."

"Come on you two. Let's go in here and have some lunch."

They went into McDonald's and Rev Dave asked Bandi what he would like. Bandi shrugged. "Whatever you recommend," he said. "I'll get my dad to pay when we get back."

"No you won't. It's our treat."

"Get him a double layer thingy," said Abby. "He looks as if he needs feeding up!"

She led Bandi to a table in the corner while her father stood in the queue. Bandi offered to help but Abby told him to sit down, her dad would get it all on a tray.

"Do you like Oxford?" she asked.

"It's very busy. I don't think I've been to anywhere as big as this city."

"What Oxford – big! Oxford's a tiny place compared to, say, London, which has houses and shops that go on for miles."

"I live outside a town in a kind of village, I suppose you would call it. We have a garden with a house in the middle of it. There are four houses like that in our lane. You have to get into the centre of town before the houses join up with one another like here."

"So you are a country boy?"

"I suppose so. I've never thought about it like that. Mum teaches entomology in an agricultural college and Kakko is learning about tractors and stuff. She likes engines and things she can get herself dirty with."

"What about you? You're not so practically minded."

"I guess not. I like computers and indoor things, and reading and just thinking about stuff. Kakko and Shaun are into sport but I can't really see the point of it. They get so involved in kicking a ball about or making something, they... they kind of miss things. I mean they don't ever think about the sand they are playing on, while I get to thinking about how it came to be there. I think about how the rocks were laid down under the sea, then rose up into cliffs, and finally got broken up again by the sea over millions of years. Every grain of sand has a tale to tell. Then I think about how *people* came to exist. I mean, where did people come from in the first place? I don't mean babies, I mean, how did it all start? I know we can trace our ancestry here, to Earth, but how did it all begin for human beings?"

"I hear the philosopher," Dave said as he put down a tray with burgers, fries and coffee. Bandi felt hungry. Dave placed a towering heap of bap, meat, cheese and trimmings in front of him.

"Wow! All that! It's twice as big as yours."

"I know my limits," smiled Dave. "Dive into the chips too. Now then, what's this you're saying about thinking?"

"He's just explaining that he sits and thinks while his brother and sister play football," explained Abby.

"Go on," urged her father.

"Well," said Bandi tentatively, wondering how he was going to get his mouth around his food, "so many people take stuff for granted. But I reckon you can't. Life is such a fantastic thing, and being able to think about it like we do is so incredible too. How come such unlikely beings as us exist? Like, Kakko gets excited about the most up-to-date technology that makes engines go, but I think that the *people* who can work all that out are even more wonderful. I mean, a tractor engine can do just one thing but my mum can do so many different things. And she's wise too. She knows how to teach, and she's got this enormous patience. And my dad, he's blind, but he can do all sorts of things and knows how to make unhappy people happy. And then we love each other. I mean, what is *that* all about? What is love and where does it come from? And then there is all this about our being sent to places just at the right time, and…" Bandi stopped, embarrassed. "Sorry, I am rabbiting on, aren't I?"

"No. Not at all," stated Dave emphatically, "I'm intrigued."

Abby had not taken a bite of her burger. She just sat staring at her new friend.

"And how does all this thinking compare to computers?" asked Dave.

"Computers? Well, they do things. People made them. They don't provide answers themselves – that needs people."

"Would you rather think about why things are as they are, or study computers?"

"Both. I have to think about things, I guess. But it's important to do something useful isn't it?"

"And asking about the 'why' of things is not useful?"

"Not like making things or working with computers."

"Do you know what I think, Bandi? I think you have the makings of a good philosopher."

"A philosopher? I don't know what that is."

"Don't you do any philosophy at school?" asked Abby. "Plato and stuff?"

"No. How would he?" replied her father. "Plato and philosophy is from *Earth*. It's *our* history. If this young man comes from a different planet then he's unlikely to have heard of Plato and the history of philosophy. His planet will have its own thinkers."

"I suppose so. I was forgetting that. Bandi kind of feels so like us."

"In many ways he is of course. He's human – just not from Earth. And his father and grandmother are from right here in Persham. The translation is very sophisticated and we can get the impression that he knows what we know."

"Until he gets in a mess with a McDonald's," laughed Abby as she watched Bandi struggle with his food. "You are allowed to use *both* hands," she explained, "but you're not supposed to take it apart."

Bandi laughed too. "It tastes great. What's it made of?"

"Dead cow… cheese (that's milk that someone's messed

about with) and bread. Oh, and that green thing is a slice of gherkin. You don't have to eat that if you don't want to." Abby never ate the gherkin.

"This is a special treat for days out. It is not recommended as everyday food, you understand Bandi," stated Dave.

"Tell me about, what did you call him, 'Play' something."

"Play? Oh, You mean *Plato*. Better ask Dad."

"*You* can explain, Abby."

"Nah. I'll get it wrong. Dad's the expert here."

"I am no expert but I *have* been reading philosophy a bit longer than Abby," Dave said. "Plato was a teacher who loved wisdom – that's what the word 'philosophy' means. It's Greek, as was Plato. He lived about two and a half thousand years ago and founded a special school in a place called Academia just north of Athens. Here he taught the philosophy of his teacher Socrates and contributed lots of his own ideas too."

"He told a story about a cave," put in Abby. "Tell Bandi about the cave."

"Well, it's really all about what is the *real* and what is only a *shadow* of the real. Plato was asking questions about 'goodness', and 'beauty' and 'justice'. Somehow we recognise these things. We have an instinct for what is good and what is not. Likewise we seem to know what is beautiful and what is ugly, and what is right and what is wrong. It's like there's a template of them outside of us that is eternal and universal. We can try and tell ourselves differently, try and convince ourselves that *we* can decide on what is right or wrong, good or bad and so on. We can even bring up our children to believe bad is good, but it doesn't work. If we try and adapt good and bad, or right and wrong, to suit ourselves then the world gets into a mess. So to Plato it seemed there were *ideal forms* of goodness and justice and beauty – real goodness, justice and beauty – that exist outside of us, outside of the everyday world we live in – somewhere that is eternal and perfect. But where are they? It's not somewhere we can naturally see directly."

"It's like, we can only see the shadow of justice or goodness. Plato's true 'forms' is the ultimate stuff – the real stuff, the original," contributed Abby.

"That's right. Ordinary people living ordinary lives don't see the originals – the forms – only their shadows. But Plato reckoned that using reason to find the forms was better than seeing them, because our eyes often deceive us. We can work out what the ideal world must be like from contemplating all the reflections or shadows of the ideal we encounter. In our everyday lives we only get clues to the nature of the true forms. But every new clue helps us to have a better understanding of the ideal." Bandi nodded. He was listening intently and was with the argument so far.

"So this is where the cave Abby is talking about comes in. It's as if we live in a cave, and all we can see are shadows of the true 'forms' outside the cave shown up by firelight on its back wall. Most of the people inside the cave don't realise that they are only seeing shadows. They are tied down and under servitude to their masters inside the cave and do not contemplate leaving it. But occasionally someone – a thinking someone, a budding philosopher who asks questions about 'why' and 'how' – will not be satisfied with the cave existence and will free him or herself and leave the cave and begin to explore the real world outside. When they see the true forms, they will see immediately what the cave is all about. If the person with this new and more complete knowledge then goes back into the cave and tries to explain to the others what they are missing, the cave dwellers may mostly choose to ignore the wise person or even think them mad, and some of the masters will even see them as subversive. In their world he or she is, 'upsetting the settled order of things and sowing seeds of discontent among the people', they may say. They may even attempt to silence them, intimidate them, disappear them and perhaps kill them. (That happened to Plato's teacher and friend, Socrates.) But some will listen, struggle free and get to leave the cave and travel into the real world where they, too, can explore what true goodness, true justice and true beauty are."

"...and that true goodness, justice and beauty is the same wherever you are in the universe?" asked Bandi.

"Exactly! The 'forms', as Plato calls them, are universal and eternal."

"So I can explore that truth even from Joh."

"From anywhere in the universe (or beyond it) because it doesn't belong to any one culture, or religion or school of thought – and it is not limited by space and time."

"I like that. This is philosophy?"

"Plato's philosophy. Since then, there have been some really great strides in exploring the ultimate questions of life. From Plato's pupil Aristotle onwards we have been considering different fields of philosophy. There is *'metaphysics'* with questions like, 'Who am I?' and 'Do I have a purpose?' Then we have *'epistemology'* – asking questions about knowledge such as, 'Can I know that things actually exist outside my imagination?' and 'How do I know I am real myself?' And *'logic'*: 'Can I deduce the truth of one thing from others?' and so on…"

"You've kind of lost me now," sighed Bandi.

"Dad, don't try to sum up two and half thousand years in, like, one breath!" pleaded Abby. "Bandi, you've really set him off now. He's into his 'big words'. He'll not stop all day!" she laughed.

"But I do want to understand. I want to know more about these philosophers."

"There are books. Many books. Come on, finish up the rest of those fries and drink your coffee and we'll go into Waterstones and we'll see what they have. I always like to start people on *Sophie's World* by Jostein Gaarder."

They went back onto Cornmarket Street and Abby took Bandi's arm and they followed her father into Broad Street.

"See, I told you computing was boring," she whispered. They were too close, her father overheard.

"Not for *everyone*, Abby. Don't make generalised statements. That is not good philosophy!"

"I am not generalising," she retorted. "I just know Bandi."

"After two days?"

"Yes!"

"I think Abby is right," agreed Bandi, "I mean about the computing. I have been going for what I could do as a job rather than what I most enjoy doing."

"As a matter of fact *I* think she is right too – from what I have heard from you. But I would rather emphasise the positive. You may enjoy *philosophy* – but that doesn't exclude you from enjoying *computing* as well. I am afraid my daughter is prejudiced. And, as a rule, it is impolite to tell someone that their chosen way of life is 'boring'. To say something is 'boring' is a very subjective statement. Only young people can sometimes get away with being quite so subjective because people make allowances. When she gets a bit older, our Abigail will find herself in hot water, I fear… ah, here we are, this is Waterstones."

Bandi was just amazed by all the books. There were floors of them – he had no idea how many. The shelves seemed to go on for ever. How Dave managed to navigate around and find the philosophy section he had no idea. He passed his hand along a shelf and, hey presto, there it was – *Sophie's World*.

"It tells the story of a fifteen-year-old who explores the history of philosophy. She begins by asking some of those ultimate questions we were discussing earlier, and her teacher very wisely explains in a very simple way how the philosophers through the ages came up with some answers – and, of course, the new questions those answers themselves raise. There are always new questions. I think you'll enjoy it. It will give me pleasure to get this for you."

"Dad will pay -"

"I wouldn't hear of it. No. It's a present."

"Wow. Thanks. This is great." Bandi opened it up at the first page. "Oh dear, it's all in English."

"Of course. What language would you like?"

"No Earthly one."

"No. I guess not."

"Nan would be able to read it, though. If she read it aloud

it might translate – like we are doing now. And Dad and Nan had to learn Johian from nothing. They might even be able to translate it themselves. Mum's own language, Wanulkan, is completely different but she managed too. They're clever. I don't think I could do what they have done."

"You could," said Dave. "If you came to live here you would learn quickly enough. But philosophy has its own language in any case. It's quite an exact discipline. Properly understanding the words in the way the philosophers meant them is the key to grasping their concepts. Words in common use are not so exact in their meaning, and their common meanings today are sometimes different from what they used to be, so even people who speak English as their mother tongue have to spend time learning the vocabulary. That is often the hardest part for them because the common meaning of the word keeps getting in the way."

"I know that," said Abby. "It's like when Plato uses the word 'form' or 'ideal'. It's like a new language. Grandma says 'ideal' reminds her of 'Ideal Milk', which has nothing to do with philosophy."

"Yes, Abby. It took you a bit to get that didn't it?"

"Not *so* long, Dad!" exclaimed Abby colouring.

"No. Not so long," agreed Dave hastily, "but some people never cotton on at all and that's difficult for us. I mean us clergy and people who want to do some disciplined thinking. They can think we're being deliberately difficult. But don't get me on to that…"

"Dad got told off by the leader of the Ladies' Guild last year," whispered Abby in a confidential tone, "for using big words, and he's still annoyed…"

"Abby!" It was her dad's turn to blush. "She wasn't willing to take the trouble to understand... I doubt *you* will have any problem, Bandi."

"I want to learn. I want to learn more words. Words are so interesting. They go back into history and the way they change their meaning sometimes tells us something."

"Hold old did you say you are?"

"Fourteen."

"Fourteen and already an intellectual. Your years on Planet Joh must be longer than ours."

"No. They are the universal standard years. Dad says they are based on the Earth One year. A year for us isn't related to anything to do with our planet. I get Dad to tell me about Earth sometimes. He never told me about philosophy though. There seem to be so many books!" said Bandi scanning the shelves.

"And this is just the current ones," reflected Dave, "not counting the electronic stuff which is as common as paper these days. Let's go and pay for this, then we'll go down to the river and hire a punt."

"Yay. Great!" Abby's face was a picture of delight. She had only been in a punt once before. Having Bandi around meant this routine journey into Oxford to visit the orthodontist had turned into a rare outing. Under normal circumstances, her dad would almost certainly have driven straight home again from the hospital.

★★★

The punting turned out to be great fun. At one stage, while they were changing places, Bandi had nearly fallen out, but

Abby had grabbed his belt and yanked him back. They both collapsed in the wildly rocking punt on top of one another roaring with laughter as Dave struggled to maintain his balance.

★★★

When they eventually got home there was only time for a quick meal before they had to leave for the Persham Middle School hall. Abby's mum had worked hard cooking something that they really needed more time to enjoy – but she was a patient woman. Her husband dashing in and out and coming home late was apparently part of the deal of living in a vicarage.

31

The Persham Middle School hall was packed. As Dave and Jack were ushered up onto the dais, there was a rumble of dozens of conversations and greetings and the clanking and scraping of more chairs being brought in to accommodate a larger than expected gathering. Jack got whiffs of his old school mixed with the smell of bodies, make-up and damp wool. He was in one sense 'at home' again in Persham but was overwhelmingly grateful that he was no longer trapped in the school as a pupil. Tomorrow he would step through the white gate to the freedom of White Gates Cottage and into Jalli's arms!

These, however, were not the thoughts of our two teenagers. Bandi was contemplating how much he would miss his new friend, while Abby felt it was quite unfair. They found themselves crushed together on a gym bench on the side of the hall – the chairs given to people of more mature years. Abby knew (or she thought she knew) that she would never meet anyone so wonderful as this boy from across the universe again. It occurred to them both in that moment that it might be possible for Abby to see the white gate and to visit Joh, but neither of them said anything.

"Welcome everyone," announced Councillor Banks calling the meeting to order. "Welcome to this meeting to acquaint you all with the latest developments of the proposed new unit for blind children to be connected with Persham Middle School. And today an especial welcome to our own Jack Smith, one time pupil of this middle school, who now works as a full-time teacher in a specialist school for blind children overseas. I heard Jack was in town and I am so glad I persuaded him to stay on for an extra day to come to this meeting. Judging by the attendance this evening, Jack," he turned and looked at his unseeing guest, "it seems as if my getting an announcement on local radio has drawn in some of your fans!" He continued to address the gathering, "But, whether you have come because you are interested in the plans, or just meeting your friend again after all these years, I hope you find this evening informative and enjoyable. Let me begin by summarising where we are with this project."

Councillor Banks went over the history of the proposal. It had long been felt by some that a specialised school for blind children was needed, although they had had to fight off strong objections. A compromise had been reached. Falling roles had made the three tier system in Persham precarious. It was uneconomical to run a pyramid with most schools not coming near their planned admission levels. Other councils had solved the problem by opting for a two-tier arrangement. But in Persham there was a particular problem because it would mean building a new secondary school on a new site from scratch – there simply wasn't room to expand Renson Park High in its current location. Then the middle school head had come up with a suggestion that part of her school could become a specialised unit for blind children – from reception to Year Eight when they could move on to the mainstream upper school. As they were associated with the middle school they could be gradually integrated into the activities and learning in the mainstream which would mean the transition to the upper school would not be as daunting. "Amazingly," Councillor Banks declared, "all sides have united on the plan. The blind children's unit will draw in pupils from across the county." The most enthusiastic people seemed to be the parents of the blind children, which was significant.

"Now," continued the councillor, "I have asked Jack Smith who has been teaching at a specialist school for over twenty years if he would tell us about his school. I know this school is not in Britain, but Jack grew up here and he is in an excellent position to explain how a school for the blind could work in Persham. Ladies and gentlemen, Jack Smith…"

There was a rattle of applause as Jack rose to his feet. He felt for the rostrum. "Councillor Banks, ladies and gentlemen, I don't know how many there are here this evening but the room smells quite full… I sense one of you is about to open a window." The whole room turned to stare at a man at the back just in the process of reaching for a window catch. As the window swung open Jack heard the creak in the silence and continued, "I am blind, but when one is blind you learn to use other senses you take for granted if you can see. This is the point of a specialised school for blind children in their early years. They need to be taught how to use and hone those faculties of hearing, touch and smell which mainstream teaching often puts into secondary place. Five-year-olds can pick up Braille very quickly, for example, but it is much more than that. Children can be taught how to touch faces and how to sense danger and a multiple of other necessary skills. But perhaps the most important thing of all is for them to relate to children like themselves from a young age – "

"Cheat!" yelled someone from the back of the room. "Jack Smith you're a cheat… and a liar."

The audience again turned; this time to look at a small man dressed in scruffy jeans and a dirty white T-shirt.

"I'm sorry," said Jack. "Should I know you?"

"Too damned right you should. My life has been shit because of your cheating, you arrogant prig!"

Councillor Banks stood up but Jack motioned for him to sit back down.

"It's OK, councillor… explain," Jack asked the man. Bandi watched his father, horrified but amazed at the way he was keeping his cool.

"Sure, I'll explain. When you were ten you cheated at the end of term tests. The daft teacher marked all the tests and then got us all to call out our marks while he wrote them down. He hadn't done it as he marked them. This was embarrassing for most of us, but Jack Smith just called out more marks than he had been given. You bloody cheated. You ended up in the top six and I was pushed into seventh place. The top six got special coaching, didn't yah? *You* got it and *I* missed out. Remember now?"

"Little Jim Carter."

"Less of the little. I'm big enough to give you what for."

"And I remember you tried that several times before I went on to sixth form and you…"

"Dropped fucking out at sixteen! That was all down to your cheating. Go on… deny it. Why don't you? You're good at lying so why don't you lie again?"

"I admit it," sighed Jack, "I cheated. And I did a whole lot of other things when I was young that I am ashamed of. I wasn't a happy child and I certainly wasn't a good one. I am sorry Jim that you still feel cheated. After this meeting we'll meet up and see if there is anything I can do – "

"Excuse me," broke in Councillor Banks, "this is all very interesting but can we get on with the business in hand. Mr Smith was explaining what his experience *after he left Persham* can offer us now. Please continue, Jack."

"I do apologise councillor," said Jack, "there is always a danger in coming back to your roots where you can't hide." There was a ripple of laughter.

"The school for blind children has been running in Joh where I live for the past forty years…"

"Rat!" It was was Jim Carter again. Jack ignored him and kept going. "It was the inspiration of two sets of parents who both had…"

"Prig!"

"…who both had blind children whom they felt were struggling in…"

"Shit-head!"

"Mr. Carter, if you can't be quiet, would you please leave!" roared Councillor Banks.

"No," said Jack, "I wronged the man. It might have been over thirty years ago. But he needs a proper apology. Jim, come up here!" The man did not hesitate. He got up and stormed onto the stage.

Jack stood in front of him and said, "Jim Carter, I am truly sorry I cheated you, the teacher and the whole class. If I could turn the clock back I would. In those days I was indeed a liar and often a cheat. If it's any consolation I was so horrified by what I had done on that occasion I never cheated precisely like that again. I am truly sorry you missed out because of me. You tried to get your revenge on a number of occasions but I was rather bigger than you were. But now you have me at a disadvantage. I cannot see you. So you can safely beat me if that's what it will take. Go to it!"

The room was stunned. Councillor Banks tried to intervene but Jim pushed him off the platform. "No Bandi," yelled Jack, "stay where you are!" He sensed Bandi was in the act of leaping to his father's defence. Jim Carter stared Jack in the eye but there was no emotion betrayed in Jack's unseeing eyes. Carter fumed and cursed. "Fuck you! Fuck you! Fuck…" Jack reached out and found the man's shoulder and then enveloped him in a bear hug. "Jim Carter, you don't know how much this means to me," said Jack, his eyes streaming with tears. "The guilt of what I did as a child has never left me. And I knew just how much you wanted to be in the top six… Dawn White," he whispered into Jim's ear, "you wanted to be in the same group as her, didn't you?"

"You haven't bloody forgotten then."

"No," whispered Jack. "She was rather good-looking, wasn't she? Whatever happened to her?"

"Moved to London."

It was clear the emergency was over and people were returning to their seats.

"I'm sorry… which is your local?" asked Jack.

"Pig and Whistle."

"I promise I'll meet you there after I have finished here."

Jim Carter nodded and slowly made for the door. People moved aside to let him through.

Councillor Banks had a bruise on his lower arm, otherwise he was physically in one piece, but he was in shock and his dignity was dented. He looked flustered and confused. Jack reached forward, "Bandi, will you find the councillor some water?"

Jack found the rostrum again and announced, "Ladies and gentlemen, if I had been blind as a child I would not be standing here now – I certainly would not have had the opportunities in Persham that I had as a sighted person. Even though the system in those days often failed Jim, me and others more than once, both he and I had so much more going for us than children with disabilities did. I commend the people of Persham that things have changed so much for the better. I am delighted that in Persham today you are united in seeking to give blind kids the best possible chance. Their parents know what they need. My own blindness has helped me to help the blind children in Joh – but so has my past. At times I was all those things Jim rightly accused me of. I was a rat, a cheat, a liar, a prig and lots beside, but I've learned from that and I hope I am a little better these days…"

Jack went on to explain the way they taught and encouraged the children in the school in which he taught on Joh.

Finally, he concluded, "I think the best thing for me to do now is allow you to ask questions, if there are any?"

"I have one," spoke up a woman on the left of the hall. "If you were a 'naughty' child, was it being blind that helped you improve?"

Councillor Banks had regained something of his decorum, "I don't think this the place for…"

"Let him answer," shouted someone else.

"I suppose, I suppose – and this might sound stupid to you – I suppose the change in me began when I stumbled into, well, a holy place. I was eighteen. It was *before* my accident in which I became blind. I was still kicking out at life, angry with what others had and feeling cheated most of the time. I realise now I shouldn't have been, but I did. But then I was drawn into a beautiful garden. It wasn't just beautiful to look at, it was deep down beautiful. It was holy. It was overflowing with the presence of its Creator. We have so many different misunderstandings around the word 'God' that I hesitate to use it even now. But I knew I was loved. I saw myself as if from the outside – selfish and self-centred. In this garden I saw hope, love, true goodness, and I met someone else there who helped me to discover that deep down *I* could be almost holy sometimes too. Basically, despite all the lies on the surface, the core of my being was still sound. I was loved by my mother, and despite my resentment, I discovered that I wasn't flawed beyond repair. And with the help of the Creator and other people – even people like Jim – I have learned to give love away. And when you start to do that – love others – all sorts of inner rubbish and mess gets flushed out. And you get huge amounts of love coming at you in return. Does that answer your question?" The room was silent for a moment as people were taking in what Jack had described.

Then, "How did you become blind?" asked another.

"Someone kicked my head in! I can't remember too much. I was unconscious for some time."

There was an audible gasp from the audience.

"Why did he do that?"

"Sometimes you meet some messed-up people."

"What happened to him? Did he get sentenced?"

"No. He died."

"Did you kill him?"

"No. I might have wanted to if I hadn't been unconscious at the time. No, he had died of natural causes before I came to." Jack wondered whether an insect attack was exactly 'natural causes' but he wasn't going to prolong this conversation. "Anyway, to cut a long story short, I discovered," he went on, "that, despite everything, my girlfriend still loved me. We married and I went to work at the school. Being blind was a real asset to hitting it off with some of the kids."

To Councillor Banks' relief they were now back on task. Some good questions about the way the children benefited from the school followed.

As the meeting came to an end, the councillor concluded, "All that remains is to obtain funding for the project from the town council. We want this in next year's budget," he declared, and he urged them all to write in.

Councillor Banks thanked Jack for coming. Jack apologised for the kerfuffle. He left the platform to applause. After some interesting conversations with parents, case workers and community leaders of various sorts, he and Bandi eventually set off for the Pig and Whistle.

★★★

Making their way along the pavement lit by street lights, Jack explained where the pub was and Bandi took his father's arm.

The street was familiar to Jack, the sounds, the smells and the feel of the autumn air were very much like he remembered. But this same place was utterly strange and foreign to his son who marvelled at his dad's ability to remember.

"I think it's the pub on the corner of the High Street and Hope Street," explained Jack. "It's not far."

"It's right what you said. Kids should have equal opportunities."

"I didn't say 'equal'," said Jack. "A blind person can never have an equal opportunity in life. They can never drive a car, for example, or climb mountains. And some sighted people find it hard to read through no fault of their own. The universe is not a place of equal anything. It's about giving kids a chance to make as much of the opportunities that come their way, developing what they've got."

"Growing their own gifts."

"Exactly. But that takes imagination when it comes to the ones on the margins of our attention. And it's not just about kids who are blind or deaf but everyone who's not mainstream. Society puts the emphasis on the majority, or to suit those in control. We can run away with the idea that giving people the *same* opportunities is fair. But if you have to be something you are *not* to take advantage of those opportunities, then that is *not* fair."

"Like, you could say that all kids have the right to be taught how to read and write but for blind kids that means teaching touch script which we don't in mainstream schools."

"Yes. But it goes beyond provision for disabled kids. It goes across the *whole* of society. For example, expecting women to turn away from their own feminine insights and become like men to succeed in life."

"That sounds feminist, Dad."

"I suppose it is. Haven't you noticed I *am* a feminist. Why should women have to stop being themselves to get on in society? I would much prefer Aphra Behn to Margaret Thatcher."

"Er, Dad?"

"Yes, Bandi"

"You're talking in riddles."

"Oh, sorry. It's British history. Planet Earth. Aphra Behn lived just over three hundred years ago and was a playwright, novelist and poet. She said it how it was. She did not flinch to write from the woman's point of view, saying how it feels like to be a woman. She has often been dismissed as outspoken and even bawdy – but she was not. She was feminine *and* strong. She stood up to men who expected women to be weak, meek, quiet and frivolous, but succeeded in doing it in a feminine way. Margaret Thatcher was a British prime minister in the 1980s who certainly was not weak or quiet, but she downplayed the feminine side of things. She stood up to men like a *man*. Some believe she sold out to male domination."

"Like Kakko is not girly-fantastic but yet is still feminine."

"Something like that, Bandi."

"Dad. Do you miss Britain? I mean, you grew up here."

"I can't deny the smell of this place feels like home. But as you have heard this evening, I was not a happy child. For most of my time here I wanted to get out. And I still do. If the gate is not there tomorrow, I shall scream. I can't be doing with being trapped here again!"

"Right. You *really were* not happy. That's sad. I don't think

I want to live anywhere else than on Joh… but I liked meeting Abby."

They walked a few more steps in silence then Jack said, "So now, Bandi, you know what a sad dad you have. A cheat, a liar, a rat, a prig and… what else did he say?"

"A shit-head."

"Yeah. I really was all those things."

"I knew you weren't always an 'easy child', as Nan puts it. But I hadn't realised you lied and cheated so much."

"Well, Jim did rather overstate his case, and he wasn't actually wanting the special teaching either. What he was really sour about was that I got to be with Dawn White instead of him. Little Jimmy Carter (we used to call him 'little' to distinguish him from the American president of that name) was not noted for his application at school. He had only tried on that occasion to get to sit with Dawn. And, don't tell him I told you this," laughed Jack, "*he* cheated too! He copied my work and other people's. If he had got into sixth place instead of me it would not have been because he was an honest, able scholar."

"So he was lying in that meeting?"

"I doubt if he remembers what he did that day because he did it all the time. What he remembers is being cheated at the final hurdle when he thought he had won. I regret cheating – that was wrong, but I don't think Jim Carter's problems stem from my dishonesty. All we have to do tonight is listen to his story. He will tell us how the whole of life has cheated him at every turn. It will make him feel better. Then we can discover some of the good things he has done despite all that and congratulate him."

"Can't he get on a catch up education course for adults?"

"Of course. That's one good thing about Britain, it's never too late to take up your opportunities. But, you watch, he'll have every excuse why that wouldn't work for him – unless he has changed a lot from when we were teenagers, which I doubt."

★★★

Leaving the Pig and Whistle an hour later, father and son took a taxi back to the hotel.

"Dad, you're clever."

"How come?"

"You knew *exactly* how that would go. It was as if Jim was reading your script."

"It's not rocket science, Bandi. It comes with years of listening. All he really wanted was a bit of attention. We all do."

★★★

The following morning it was grey and damp. The pavement slabs glistened, the moss glowed green in the cracks and the yellow lichen on the roofs and walls took on a dull greyish tinge. The chirping birds didn't seem put off in the park to their right, however, as the little group walked up to the school on the hill. Jack, Matilda and Bandi had been joined by Abby and her father who were coming to see them off. Secretly, Abby and Bandi were both hoping Abby would see the gate too, but neither said anything.

"I lived here for forty years," sighed Matilda. "It was good to see it again. But I'm glad I'm going home."

"Home is where the heart is," observed Jack.

"Indeed. And my heart is where you belong. The only sadness is that Momori is no longer there."

"You've got *us*," said Bandi.

"I have. And my very good friends on Joh. Ada and I and the others are going on a bus trip the day after tomorrow into the mountains."

"Sounds lovely," said Jack.

Matilda and Bandi saw the white gate glowing in the dullness of the day from some distance away. Jack sensed it too. "Home!" he sighed. Bandi looked at Abby as they walked up to the gate, but it was not there for her. She turned and looked at Bandi and, despite her resolve, a tiny tear formed in the corner of one eye.

"Here we are," declared Matilda. Dave stared at the middle school boundary; it was unchanged and uninterrupted. Abby stifled a snuffle in a tissue.

"It's not fair!" she exclaimed quietly.

"Abby," said Jack, "if you could have the past few days over again knowing that they could not last would you still have them? Would it have been fair if you and Bandi had never met?"

"No. I wouldn't change any of that. I just don't want it to end."

"But Bandi has his school to go to and his mother is waiting for him," said Dave putting his arm around his daughter's shoulders. "It's time to let them go."

"Thanks for the book," said Bandi, "I want to be a philosopher when I finish school. Thanks for taking me to Oxford."

"Yes. Thank you for all your hospitality," Jack added as he sought Dave's hand.

Bandi caught up Abby in a cuddle. "You never know," he smiled, "this may not be good-bye for ever."

"Come on you," cajoled his father. "Your mum's waiting for you."

"Bye Abby," said Bandi with as light a face as he could muster.

"Bye," said everyone together. Matilda turned and stepped through the gate. Jack pushed Bandi forward and followed.

The father and daughter just stared as their new friends disappeared from their sight. "*'Tis better to have loved and lost, than never to have loved at all.*" Dave quoted Tennyson's famous line to himself. But he didn't say it out loud as he led his tear-stained daughter back home across the park.

32

"It's been difficult," said Jalli that evening when she was cuddled up to her Jack in their bed. "Kakko missed you all more than I did. Shaun got on with his things. He had work to do for school and then a match in which he was once more on the winning side. But Kakko was unsettled. She tries hard but she's not made for studying, that girl."

"Bandi has found his calling," explained Jack. "He found himself in long discussions with the vicar there about philosophy."

"Phil who?"

"Philosophy. It's the Earthly name for the discipline that involves asking questions about life. Like, 'How do I know I exist?' and, 'Can I prove the existence of the Creator?' or, 'Is this right or wrong just for now, or for the whole of the universe in every dimension'?"

"What we call 'ultimates'?"

"Exactly."

"He was always that way inclined. He always wanted to know why."

"Well, he's right into it now. Says he wants to combine it with computing at college."

"Is there such a course?"

"Don't know. But he has to get his preliminaries first, then we can think about it. He also met this young girl called Abby. She's only fourteen too, but they were really into each other."

"That's probably why he's been a bit quiet, even for Bandi."

"The parting was hard with her saying it wasn't really fair. But *he* knew the score from the beginning – although he's still cut up about it."

"What was she like?"

"Vivacious in a thoughtful way, if that makes sense – intelligent, caring and polite... Mum says she's pretty – long blonde hair – not tall. It's difficult to know what she is like when she has to just get on with everyday school because life was rather exciting for her with Bandi and us around."

★★★

The following day when Bandi began to open up about some of the things he had done – without, of course, letting on how he felt about Abby – Kakko couldn't help showing her frustration. She wanted to know every detail of the punting but was not so interested in the book that Bandi was treasuring. *Is my sister stuck in Plato's cave?* he asked himself. He concluded she wasn't. Kakko would never be stuck anywhere. She *did* think, she *did* care about things, but in fitful bursts. She did not have his gift of concentration. Perhaps in some ways Kakko was far more 'normal' than he was, he decided. Kakko had been disappointed not to have been invited but actually she would have found it very dull – there had been a lot of sitting down and listening. He hoped she would get over her frustration soon.

★★★

As it happened he didn't have to wait long. Less than a week later, Kakko came bounding in to say there was a white gate on the other side of the road beyond the cottage hedge where the one to the cliff-top had been. It was excitement all round. Everyone rushed out to see, but only Kakko could make it out. Tam was sent for. He said good-bye to his parents ready to accompany his girlfriend into regions unknown. But despite studying the place carefully, he too had to conclude that it was not for him this time. This gate was for Kakko, and for Kakko alone.

Beside it was a shoulder bag and a small carrier which again only she could see until she touched them. They contained a sophisticated looking video camera and Shaun uttered a cry of delight.

"It's the latest model," he explained. "It is so easy to use. You can do all the settings manually if you want, but if you just put it on automatic… here, he indicated a green button, it does everything for you. Just point and shoot. It's got the long life batteries too so you should have hours of filming."

"And some spares," said Kakko pulling out a packet of more batteries. "So I have to take pictures. How cool."

Also inside the carrier bag was a long colourful skirt with an elasticated waistband and an old straw hat – that was all. She was wearing a loose top and shorts so she just pulled the skirt on over the shorts and donned the hat and she was ready. The family stood in the road and said the usual things about taking care. Kakko was excited but then realised that for the first time she was about to have an adventure all on her own, and became more serious. Her leave taking was reassuring for her parents.

"Don't forget to listen, and pray. Remember to just pass things through your brain occasionally before you act," said her mother.

"I will, Mum. I promise. I won't have anyone to rescue me this time will I?"

"No. But God gets into every corner of this universe. Don't forget to call on Him."

"She's calling on me now, isn't She?"

"I guess She is Kakko," said Jack. "We'll be looking forward to getting you back. Now, you had better go before we all start getting emotional." He could sense Jalli tightening up.

"Bye!" said Kakko and then, shouldering the camera bag, turned and stepped carefully through the white gate.

Kakko found herself standing in a cleft between huge, red boulders. She could see a streak of blue sky above her and made out the unmistakable sound of children playing. It was hot. Kakko emerged from the cleft and put on her straw hat against the sun. The long skirt was ideal in this heat, but there was no way to be cool. Below, the children's voices stuttered to a halt and all she could hear was the sound of a cicada and a bird somewhere behind her. The children stood stock-still and stared. Kakko waved to them and smiled. Then, suddenly, there was a crescendo of noise and a dozen screaming children, most clad only in a few rags, some entirely naked, rushed towards her. "Khawaja! Khawaja!" they shouted. "Khawaja!" The first children took her hands, her arms and then she was being gently touched all over. They spoke in a language she did not understand. They dragged at her, propelling her forward. One of the older children spoke in English. "Khawaja, you come. You take pictures. You come."

The excited children led Kakko over a short patch of open ground that still bore the marks of recent careful sweeping with a broom, to a couple of circular thatched huts with mud walls. Outside the first, a young woman nursing a baby sat cross-legged behind a cooking pot on a charcoal burner. She was staring at the gaggle of children and rose to her feet as Kakko approached. Soon other adult women appeared. Kakko introduced herself. It was clear her words had been translated into English because one of the women asked, "You from America?"

"No," Kakko replied.

"From UK?"

"No. I am from neither. I come from Joh."

The woman nodded. She could not have known anything about Joh but the answer seemed to satisfy her. Kakko gathered from their questions that she must be somewhere on Planet Earth.

"You come to take pictures? You come to tell the world about our suffering? That is good. We don't see anyone for many months. The bombing, it is very bad!"

Kakko noticed that there didn't appear to be any men-folk or older people, just these mothers and their children. "Where are your husbands?" she asked.

"In the bush," said the woman who spoke nodding over her shoulder. "They have gone to fight."

"So you are here on your own?"

"We wait until the harvest. Three, maybe four weeks. Then we go."

"Where?"

"Over the border. Safe place."

"Have soldiers come here?"

"Not yet. Just planes with bombs. You want to take pictures of the bombs?" She barked at three of the older girls to pick up some empty water jars to bring with them and then led Kakko off to a clump of trees about a mile away. It was hot and Kakko was glad of her straw hat but the girls wore nothing on their heads – they just balanced the pots on them. Kakko asked if she could try. She was amazed at how heavy they were, despite being empty! Even with two hands she couldn't balance it herself. The girls laughed.

They came in sight of what looked at first sight like a pile of rubble behind some spindly trees. But when Kakko got closer she realised it wasn't just any old rubble but four or five broken mud huts similar to the ones she had just seen. They were battered and torn. Pieces of light blue tarpaulin were scattered among the burnt remains indicating, she later learnt, that United Nations relief supplies had got this far sometime in the past. There were patches of ash where charcoal burners had been not too long ago. In among the scorched wood and mud there appeared to be pieces of broken furniture and torn clothing. The children went over to a water pump that was still working. A series of mounds looking like graves lined the edge of the site. Kakko held her hand out towards them.

"Twenty-two people, all dead. Some straight away, others over days. No medicine." The woman began to weep. "My mother," she said, pointing to the first. "My son," indicating a second. "My baby too. He was holding her to protect her but they both killed."

Kakko stood in shock. Then remembered she was supposed to take pictures. She pulled the camera out of its bag and set it on automatic. She panned the scene and then pointed the camera at the woman and asked, "What is your name?"

"My name Miriam. I am Miriam Ishmael."

"Miriam, tell me what happened?"

"Two weeks ago an Antonov came from the west. He went round and round and then went away. We thought he had gone, but then he came back suddenly and dropped three bombs. Bomb, bomb, bomb. Twelve people dead. Some in many pieces. Ten injured. These tukls all destroyed. We sent one for help. She not came back. You meet her?"

"No," replied Kakko.

Kakko was surveying the scene. It was not till then that she realised that all the bits of twisted metal strewn about over a large area must be shrapnel from the bombs.

"I am sorry," admitted Kakko. "I have no food, no medicine."

"But you have camera. You can tell the world what is happening to us."

"I will! I will tell the world and everyone. I promise," said Kakko vehemently.

"UN don't come. They are frightened to come."

"I don't understand."

"UN have soldiers but they don't fight for us. They run away. Now the enemy plane has come our enemies they think we are all dead. Maybe they won't come again. When we have food," she indicated a few storks of some kind of grain, still green, growing on the periphery of the destruction, "we will leave. We will go south over the mountain." Kakko panned over to the crop and then the mountain. "This is what they want, the people with the planes, they want us out. They want to take our land. They want to kill our children. We are not like them. Our ancestors are not theirs. They have been our enemies a very long time – long before my grandparents were born. *Then* they didn't have planes – not like now. But our husbands are fighting them. They will attack the places where the planes come from. We will not give up our land – it belongs to our children... come you must eat with us."

"What? Oh no. I can't eat your food. You don't have enough."

"You have come to us. You care. You do not have *arabia* – car – you have walked many miles. You are our guest. You eat."

The girls reappeared with the jars now full of water. They helped each other lift them onto their heads. Kakko could see, despite their smiles, that they were in pain. They were doing permanent damage to themselves she thought. She could imagine her gym mistress gasping in horror. Nevertheless the girls carried the jars back the mile they had walked.

Kakko couldn't explain successfully that she hadn't been dropped off by a car somewhere over the hill. How could she eat these people's food? The water she was given to drink was not bad. But when she thought about the pain it took to bring it, she appreciated every drop. It was more valuable to these people than the most expensive bottle of special drink that Joh had ever produced. This was indeed the elixir of life. Without water in this hot place they would all be dead within hours.

She soon learned that if she didn't eat or drink neither would they, as long as she was there, so she did her best. The children showed her how to eat and laughed when she struggled to put the rough diet into her mouth. She couldn't imagine how long she could possibly survive eating so little of what she sensed had very little nutritional value. She could see that the children, for all their childish glee, were malnourished. The food tasted a bit like she imagined sawdust might.

Kakko got out her camera and panned the children eating and giggling and then she gave the camera to Miriam to take a shot of her as she tried to eat. It was a relaxed time. The food, no matter how coarse, gave them all hope.

Just then, a child stiffened. His keen ears had detected the sound of a plane. Then he spotted a dark dot coming low from the north-west. "Antonov!" he screamed. In an instant the children took to their heels and ran towards the rocks. Kakko pointed the camera in the direction of the plane. "Kakko come, come quick!" She ran to the rocks trying to keep filming. When they reached the rocks the children squeezed themselves into the narrowest of crannies, fully aware that they were also favoured by snakes and scorpions, but these represented far less a danger than the plane that was even now screaming overhead searching out its targets. It circled and re-approached. Kakko kept filming.

"Anna! Anna!" a young mother began sobbing beside Kakko. "Her baby, she is in the hut," explained Miriam. The plane flew low and Kakko spotted a little black blob fall from it. It was a bomb and it fell very near the tukl. Boom! Dirt and vegetation shot into the air. The mother sobbed – her home was being targeted.

What Kakko instinctively wanted to do next was rush out and rescue the baby. She lunged forward but then stopped herself. *Think, Kakko, think!* she shouted to herself inside her head. *Don't be impetuous!* The sound of the plane was increasing; it was coming back. "Oh, damn it!" said Kakko out loud. "Sorry, Mum, I can't!" As the plane passed overhead and began to circle for another run, she leapt from her hiding place and dashed for the hut.

The baby was not hard to find, she was standing by the door, frightened, yelling for her mother. Kakko caught her up in her arms and checked the sky. The plane was coming around. She headed for the trees hoping the plane had not seen her. She rolled on her back keeping one arm around the child and pointing the camera at the plane as it approached. She kept filming. Then she saw a black object fall from the plane. It was coming straight at them! She swore to herself, *You've done it this time, Kakko. You've not only got yourself killed but this baby, too!* She dropped the camera and rolled on her side and, cradling the child the best she could, and her anger at all her idiotic, impetuous arrogance rushed through her adrenalin-fuelled brain in the seconds it took the bomb to land…

The shock-wave tore through Kakko's eardrums as the bomb landed right next to the tukl utterly demolishing it. Then, it seemed the whole world came at her. Fortunately she had her back to the blast, her body between it and the child. She felt the pressure of the air increase and then earth, wood and metal thumped into her. A hot, searing pain shot down one leg and her brain exploded with an anguished redness. Kakko was just conscious of more debris falling from somewhere before her world went black; the bright sunlight no longer penetrated through her closed eyelids.

33

Although she could hear and see nothing, Kakko was aware through her pain that she wasn't dead. The child squirmed in her arms and she held her tight. She, too, had survived. Kakko felt a huge surge of relief that she hadn't killed the child through her actions. At that moment she wasn't aware that she had saved its life.

Kakko's instinct was to continue to lie low and still. Gradually her hearing returned. All she could hear was the scream of the Antonov. Was it readying for another pass? Kakko prayed. She prayed that the little girl sobbing in her arms would survive this. At last the roar of the plane diminished into a whine, then a hum – it was going away. Apart from the sound of the sand settling around her, there was an eerie silence – not a bird, not a cicada stirred.

Kakko tried to extricate herself from the rubbish on top of her, but her leg wouldn't go.

Suddenly the world was no longer silent. The children and the women were all around them throwing off the rubbish. Anna was crying for her mother. Arms reached in for her, and her mother soothed her. Then Kakko became aware of an intense pain in her right upper leg. When one of the children touched her foot it was so painful she cried out involuntarily.

The women tried to lift Kakko away from the edge of the bomb crater. She winced and called out indicating her upper thigh. Her whole leg throbbed. One of the older women lifted her skirts. There was a spreading issue of blood. It was leaking from a wound high up her thigh and lower buttock.

"Ayee," exclaimed Mary. Kakko was buzzing with shock. "Anna?" she whispered.

"She is not hurt," replied Miriam. "She is fine. You saved her!"

The child had survived completely unscathed. Kakko looked over her shoulder to where the tukl had been. There was now just a huge hole in the ground! She reached out to pick up the camera. It was still humming. It was not damaged; it had been running throughout! Kakko pointed it in the direction of the tukls. Oddly the thing that struck her most about the scene was the water jars – they were all shattered with their contents soaking into the soil. All that effort from the children wasted. She tried to sit up to keep filming – and then the pain really hit her! "We must get her out of the sun," cried Miriam.

Somehow they lifted Kakko to the cleft from which she had emerged. Then they were anxious for the children; already some of the women were packing what they could salvage to climb over the mountain to find safety.

"Leave me here. You go. My people will come for me," said Kakko. But they would not leave her. She dragged herself painfully further between the rocks, and then, with huge relief, she saw the white gate.

"Water," demanded Mary, "we must wash the wound." The children rushed to find something with which to get water. While they were distracted, Kakko, clutching her camera, pulled herself through the gate.

She collapsed onto the road outside White Gates Cottage just as a car turned into it. The driver stopped the car and came over to her. He thought she must have been hit by another vehicle that had not stopped.

"My leg," winced Kakko. Her skirts were horribly blood-soaked.

***

Within half-an-hour Kakko was in the hospital operating theatre having a lump of shrapnel removed under a local anaesthetic.

"A flesh wound," pronounced the doctor, "you are a lucky young lady!" But Kakko could only think of those women and children she had left behind who were going to have to leave without any food or water, to walk, who knows where, or for how long. Where was the luck for them? *At least,* she recalled, *this time what I did was right. If I had waited that child would have definitely died. But then, I did think about it – for five seconds!* She knew what people were going to say, but this time she was absolutely sure she had done the wise thing. God had sent *her* precisely *because* she wasn't the sort to hesitate.

***

Amazingly, Kakko did not come in for the lectures she expected. She explained that she had thought first, and then acted, and, as it turned out, it had been the right decision. Her parents were in a state of shock, but not surprise. She overheard her father outside the door to the ward telling her mother that they had to accept that they did not have a daughter with the instinct to play it safe. According to Bandi and Shaun, they were secretly proud of her. Shaun explained that Matilda had said how it was impossible to wash the spots off a leopard.

"A leopard?" queried Kakko.

"A big, wild cat," said Shaun. "Apparently it has a spotted coat of fur. I guess that if you tried to wash off the spots the leopard would scratch and bite you. It's wild and ferocious."

"And she thinks I am wild and ferocious like this cat? They are frightened of me? I don't believe it. Nan is not phased by anyone – least of all by me."

"No, I don't think it's like that," said Bandi pensively, "Nan actually said, 'a leopard can't change her spots'. I think she means that, even if she *herself* wanted to, the leopard cannot alter what she is like. Spots and leopards go together. Kakko and 'rushing to people's rescue' also go together – no-one, not even you, yourself, can change that."

"Then she is very wise," murmured Kakko. "I am *trying* not to act impetuously."

"I think they know that," said Bandi. "I believe they think you have grown up some."

"Do they? Well, perhaps I have."

Apparently, the way she had told the history of events betrayed a certain, mature reasonableness that she had gained from somewhere.

Tam was very attentive, of course; he showered her with gifts of flowers and sweets and was wholly supportive.

Pastor Ruk said some nice things, too. *And he*, mused Kakko, *is a very wise person!*

34

It was two days after she got out of hospital that Kakko spotted the white gate again. This time it was right opposite the gate to the cottage garden and she couldn't miss it. She swung across on her crutches and looked through. She saw a bustle of people and vehicles and what looked like very tall buildings. This was a city. The contrast with the red-soiled bush land emptied of people of her last trip was stark. This place was vibrant, busy and crowded. Immediately she knew what she must do. She had not been given the opportunity to take those video shots for nothing – these people were probably in ignorance of the plight of the black people she had met and who had welcomed her so warmly. This was the place to share what she had seen and known.

Kakko headed home and quickly found the video camera. She took the piece of shrapnel too. "Mum," she shouted. "I have to go. I must go now. There is another white gate." Matilda appeared from her room.

"Kakko. Please don't go! You must rest. You could open up your wound! We haven't got over last time yet. You are so young, so headstrong. You are not really safe."

"Nan. I am almost nineteen. Mum and Dad were having adventures when Mum was seventeen!"

"I know – but I wasn't really aware of what they were up to."

"Do you want me to keep my adventures a secret?"

"No. No," sighed Matilda.

"If I had not gone last time a little baby girl called Anna would be dead. You know that if the white gates are there I am being called. The Creator will care for me. Whatever happens I am always in Her care. These people from Planet Earth taught me that. Under those bombs they had so much faith, God was so real to them – and at that moment to me too. But, Nan, I *promise* I will be careful."

"You're right. I must learn to trust you. But such dramatic things happen around you Kakko."

"Maybe... maybe that is why it's me that has to go."

"Perhaps. But you mustn't blame your nan for being protective... your mother and father are both in town all day, so I will tell them where you are," sighed Matilda. "But you may even be back before them. What about Tam?"

"He has lectures all day. If I am not back before him, get him to check for a gate. Thanks Nan." Kakko gave her a big hug, then gathered up her video camera, put it in a shoulder-bag, grabbed her crutches and swung through the gate.

A minute later Kakko found herself in a crowded street in a big city. In front of her was a round stone building atop a flight of steps. Looking up she glimpsed a stone spire behind which was an imposing glass-fronted building with a deep-set courtyard at the end of which were the letters "BBC". She stood for a moment trying to come to terms with everything. A large man pushed by and nearly took her off her crutches – he seemed quite oblivious to it. "Thank you!" she called after him but he did not hear, or did not want to hear!

"You OK?" said a young women in a tight skirt, matching jacket and high heels.

"Yeah," smiled Kakko.

"Some people are dead ignorant," said the woman.

"Yeah," said Kakko again. "Tell me, what is this place?"

"All Soul's, Langham Place, and the building behind it is the BBC."

"BBC? What's the BBC?"

"The BBC! You must be from another planet! Sorry, I mean, most people have come across the BBC somewhere. You don't sound foreign."

"Thanks. But I don't live here. I haven't been here before."

"You mean London, or here in Portland Place?"

"London. This is London?"

"Yes, right in the middle of it. The BBC is the British Broadcasting Corporation. It's been around since, I don't know, beginning of the twentieth century. 1922 or something? Behind us is Regent Street leading down to Oxford Circus. You've heard of Oxford Street?" Kakko shook her head.

"All Soul's Church?" said Kakko looking up at the imposing spire.

"Yes. Are you going in there?"

"No. I guess it's the BBC I want. I have a video report."

"News?"

"Yes. Bad news. Bombing... of children!"

"You have videoed children being killed?"

"They did not die. Not this time. The people say it happens all the time and nobody seems to know what is happening to them. I have filmed it."

"So you want the world to know! Lady you have come to the right place."

"Thanks. I'm Kakko."

"Karen. Nice to meet you. You OK on those crutches? What happened?"

"Bomb."

"OMG. Tell me about it."

Kakko began her tale. She wanted to tell everyone on Earth about Miriam, Anna and her mother and the others. She had promised them. This was her first opportunity. But Karen realised she was uncomfortable standing up on her crutches with people coming at them from both directions.

"Come on. Do you want to go for a coffee? Have you got time? I want to hear all about this."

"Sure. I've got time," replied Kakko. "I am *here* to tell people about what I saw… and felt and smelt!"

They went into Starbuck's and found a couple of chairs inside the door. Karen ordered two coffees.

"Thanks," said Kakko. "It's so easy to get a drink here. Miriam and the children have to walk a mile to get water. They've probably never tasted coffee," she said. And she began her story. She finished by fishing out the lump of shrapnel she still had shoved in her pocket.

"Yuk! That was in your leg? It could have killed you."

"I know. I'm lucky."

"What annoys me is that most of these weapons come from Europe, America or China somewhere, or the machines that make them do. We're always saying that countries like yours – the one you visited – should stop their fighting. We urge them to come to peace agreements and so on, and even help set up negotiations. But we're hypocrites because it's *us* that are giving them the weapons."

"Why? Why do that?"

"Because people make money out of it. The weapons manufacturers need overseas sales to make a profit. It's all about commercial investment."

"Making money out of weapons for killing innocent children! That's criminal. It's corporate murder!"

"I agree. I wish more people would recognise that. But we have all these rich rulers of poor countries coming to arms fairs to buy the latest killing machines. And there is an enormous illegal international trade in arms."

"But why doesn't your government stop them – these fairs and these traders?"

"Well they want the taxes don't they. And the votes. There are a lot of people employed in making arms. The planes, the tanks, the guns, the bullets – they are made by people who might vote them out. That's democracy."

"Democracy gone mad."

"Quite mad. But if more people understood what is happening then the people would make an issue of it and the politicians would come into line. They would stand out against the arms manufacturers and back other things that would benefit people. After all, we could make money building them hospitals and sending state of the art medical equipment, couldn't we?"

"So, how can I get my story to as many people on Earth as possible in a short time?"

"The BBC. They broadcast right across the world. People will be watching their tellies and using their news apps. You'll be famous."

"I *wish*."

"You have the videos. Go in there and tell them!"

"Right!"

They went out onto the busy street and Kakko looked up at the BBC behind the church.

"Come on," said Karen, "I'll see you there."

As they reached the far side of the church Karen led Kakko down through to the main entrance. She took her hand and wished her luck.

"I'll be watching the BBC news. I hope you make a splash," she said.

"Thanks," said Kakko. "And thanks for the coffee."

"My pleasure. Go well."

Inside the building Kakko approached a reception desk and explained that she wanted to see someone from 'news'.

"Have you got an appointment?" the woman asked.

"N -no."

"ID?"

"Idea? I am here about a bomb." The woman's face drained of all colour.

"W-what do you want?"

"I want to tell someone about the bombs I saw dropped on children. I have a video."

"You mean… you *don't* have a bomb… in that bag?"

"No! This is a video camera. Why should I bring a bomb in here?"

"You tell me?" the receptionist sighed. "But I need your ID."

"ID? What is that?"

"Something to identify you – with a photo. Driving licence, passport…"

"Oh, no. Sorry."

"Well I can't just let you see someone without ID or without an appointment."

"But this is important."

"It's *always* important."

Kakko had had enough. "Last week I was in this place where there were only mud huts with grass roofs," her voice was raised, "and an aeroplane deliberately bombed them. There were no men, just a few women and lots of children. The pilot knew what he was doing. I have pictures. I have a video of the plane and the bombs falling, and the people. *I want the world to know!*" By this time she was almost shouting.

A man in a snazzy suit and striped shirt, no tie, came over. "It's OK, Natalie, leave this one to me. What is your name young lady?"

"Kakko Smith."

"And what were you doing in, where was it?"

"I don't know what the place was called. It was very hot and dusty. They call their houses tukls. I just got taken there, so to speak. That's how it happens with us. I was given a video camera." Kakko pulled it from her shoulder-bag.

"I met these children. They were badly dressed and starving. I was talking to them and they were telling me about the attacks when this plane came – they called it an Antonov – and it dropped bombs on their little compound. Most of them hid among the rocks but a little child was still in the hut. I got her but a bomb landed before we got right away."

"I think I know where you are talking about. Come to my office Miss Smith. Thank you Natalie," he said to the receptionist.

"You're welcome Mr Perch."

Kakko was led to a lift. How many floors they went up she couldn't tell. He took her to an office with a view across one of the streets below. She didn't know which one. He offered her coffee, or something stronger. Then looked at her again and suggested a coke which Kakko accepted. Mr Perch put his head round a door and said, "Patty you couldn't find a coke could you? And coffee for me. Thanks. So Miss Smith," he breathed as he turned back into the room and offered Kakko a seat, "we know what is going on but our problem is we cannot get reporters in there safely and we have no hard evidence. Without it the perpetrators just deny it and accuse us of deceit. Then the government – our government – urges us to back off because they don't want to upset their finely balanced diplomacy."

"What if you did have hard evidence? Evidence that they are deliberately bombing children? I have video pictures and a bit of one of the bombs they dropped when I was there."

"Can I see?"

Kakko pulled out the piece of shrapnel that had been embedded in her leg. "Is that hard enough for you? That entered my body while I was shielding a small child!"

Perch picked up the metal.

"It certainly looks like a piece of a bomb," he observed. "And I am sure you can produce an X-ray to prove it was inside you."

"I think the doctor would give me that. But I don't have one with me."

"No matter. But what really counts is the evidence to prove how it got there."

Kakko handed him the video disc.

"How much footage?"

"Footage?"

"How long is the video?"

"I am talking with the women and children for one hour. Then the attacks – another twenty minutes. Then afterwards I took pictures of the bomb crater and the destroyed tukl from where I was lying but I could not move around. A child took more of me being patched up and stuff laying about but I'm afraid it's very wobbly. And then I had to get out to get attention."

Patty came in with a glass of cold coke and the coffee her boss had ordered.

"Patty, get this to news-desk for me will you." Turning to Kakko, "You say this happened only a few days ago?"

"Yes. The doctors say I should be resting."

"Quite. It's urgent, Patty. Tell them it's still hot." Patty left briskly.

"So how did you get out?"

"It's something that happens to us."

"Us?"

"I will tell you but you must not report it because it might distract. *I* don't want to become the celebrity in this; it's important none of the attention it taken away from these kids. My family... we are led through portals – in our case white gates. We can see them only when we are meant to go through them. No-one else ever sees them... and it can be anywhere in the universe." Perch began to wonder what he had let himself in for. But this young woman didn't seem to be mad.

"You asked me?" she smiled. "You will have to trust me. I

am telling you this privately. My father is from Britain. He was born in Persham."

"I suppose that makes it a bit easier," stammered Perch. "and I don't suppose you have any evidence for all of this?"

"I didn't have to tell you. But I want you to trust me because this is so important. My last white gate led me across the street from your office."

"Led you. Who is behind this?"

"God."

A look of real suspicion spread across Perch's features.

"But now I suppose you think I am delusional. Look, I don't care if you do think I'm mad, what I want you to know is that what is happening in this place is true, and too many people are letting it happen."

Perch's phone rang.

"Yes. Right. The footage is *that* great…? Wonderful. Give us five."

"OK, Miss Smith. Your portals and God are not good breaking news. This department doesn't go in for UFOs. However, you don't *appear* mad to me, and I like you. You've got spunk, and feisty females are irresistible on television. And the footage you have is certainly genuine. So, however you got in there is beside the point. I might not be interested in your god, but I *am* interested in broadcasting evidence of violence against defenceless women and kids – especially if the footage is as compelling as yours seems to be."

"Thanks."

Perch reached for his phone.

"I want this stuff on air. I'm sending Miss Kakko Smith down right now… yes, a bit – not much. Don't spoil the wild look," he looked up and smiled at Kakko mouthing, "make up", "…and you've already got the prime minister lined up for *PM*! Fantastic… just a sec. Miss Smith would you speak to the Prime Minister for us – live on Radio Four?" Kakko nodded vigorously. "It's a yes Charlie. I'll bring her right down."

35

Kakko was whisked across the building to a studio. A woman appeared and asked if she would allow her to do 'a bit of something' with her hair. Then they applied make up. An interviewer arrived. She did not know her, but it seemed that she was one of the well known ones the way everyone treated her a bit special, and they were both miked-up. The interviewer asked about the video and Kakko just told her story, then the interrogation got more difficult – it seemed that she was being cross-examined. After a few more minutes the producer called a break.

"Miss Smith please forgive the way we have to manage this. Do remember we believe you; we have seen the footage. Speak with confidence."

The piece of shrapnel was placed on the table and a camera zoomed in on it and Kakko said a silent prayer. She explained how she felt – even about the broken water-pots. The producer seemed pleased.

"So that is in the can. We can run it on the news channels in the next half hour." His ear-piece drew his attention. "We have the Prime Minster for you Miss Smith."

Kakko heard the PM in some other studio talking about some policy launch his party were engaged on. Then suddenly the interviewer changed the subject.

"Mr Prime Minister, we have just got news of a bomb

attack on children in Africa. An Antonov plane deliberately targeting unarmed women and children. Would you like to comment?"

"I am not aware of this," he replied, "but we have often heard of such things. Our problem is that we don't have enough solid evidence."

"But if we did have solid evidence, Prime Minister, what would your government do about it?"

"That would depend on the evidence."

"I have in our London studio a young woman who has recently returned from Africa with evidence of such an attack a few days ago. She sustained a shrapnel wound and has video footage of the whole thing. The attack appears totally unprovoked, according to the people its purpose was to drive them out. Ethnic cleansing. We are running the footage on our television news channels… Kakko Smith, will you tell the Prime Minister what happened."

Kakko went over the story of the attack again. The PM was apparently listening.

"Kakko what would you like the Prime Minister and the British government to do about – "

The PM broke in, "Jeremy, you know these situations are never straight forward. I do believe you… er Miss Smith, but what you say is just a small incident. This could have been an ill-disciplined pilot, and we have to remember there are two sides to this. War is not a simple business."

"But this is not a war like that," interrupted Kakko, "the whole thing is repeated. I saw where they bombed the last place – and the graves. Do you want me to be present every time there is an attack on unarmed children? Why don't you listen to the people in the refugee camps? Why don't those people allow international agencies in to help with the situation? It's because they don't want you to see what is happening. These children were starving. They knew what was going to happen the moment they spotted the plane – they ran straight for cover. I know what I saw; I know what I heard. Mr Prime Minister they are deceiving you if you think this is an isolated incident."

"As I was saying there are always two sides…"

"Yes, one side has planes and bombs and one side is women and children with nothing to defend themselves with. Yes, Mr Prime Minister there *are* two sides, one of them evil." Kakko was becoming impatient and heard her inner self tell her to slow down, but then she looked up at the interviewer in the television studio and remembered what she had told her, 'Speak with confidence'. She seemed pleased with the way Kakko was going for the prime minister. Kakko became emboldened and said firmly, "Mr Prime Minister, this is not about politics, this is about attacks on defenceless children!"

"Miss Smith, Kakko – if I may call you that," said the PM in a measured tone, "if the British government intervened militarily every time there was an injustice in the world we would be in great trouble. We have done it in the past, and we will do it again when necessary as a last resort, but I do not believe this is the appropriate action to take over this situation –"

"Mr Prime Minster you didn't let me finish telling you what I want the British Government to do. I do *not* want you to send troops or planes to get more people killed. What I want is for you to come out and expose these people for the evil things they are doing – to get all your politician friends from around the world to stop looking at their own interests and begin to act justly. We need to acknowledge that this is *wrong*, that it is *totally unacceptable*. You and all the nations in the world. That is the first thing. And the second is to *stop making weapons*. I say that to everybody on Earth. Cease production of weapons – especially those that are made to sell to others. I am told that the bit of bomb in my leg was probably made in China and the plane that dropped it, I understand, came from Eastern Europe. But there are bullets and land mines there in large numbers. Mr Prime Minister, can you be sure that no British weapons are being used in these attacks? How much ethnic cleansing is done under your nose because you have an economic interest in selling stuff to kill? If you really cared about peace you would act to stop people sending arms to people who use them against unarmed children that – "

"Miss Smith – "

"I haven't finished yet!" continued Kakko. But the interviewer in the TV studio held up her hand. She was listening to her producer. Kakko stopped.

The radio interviewer said, "Thank you Kakko. Mr Prime Minister…"

"Thank you. We have sponsored full peace negotiations in this area and stand alongside the UN and African Union in full support of all their initiatives."

"But," continued the interviewer, "the United Nations appears to have been largely ineffective in this area. The negotiations have not brought a cessation in hostilities. Each time a solution is agreed upon the killing still goes on. What have you say about Kakko's point about the flow of arms?"

"This is not a straightforward question. It is not easy to control arms."

"*Are* British-made arms being used against children, Mr Prime Minister?"

"Miss Smith mentioned China and Eastern Europe…"

"Yes. But what about Britain? What about the EU?"

"Jeremy I have not come prepared to answer questions on this subject."

"No. But you must have some idea about something as important as this."

"We have strict rules about who can sell weapons to whom. But we cannot be responsible for everything once it has left this country."

"So you cannot say categorically that nothing that is made here is being used against children."

Kakko burst in, "Why don't you just stop making them in this country? Just stop anyone making *anything* that can be used to hurt children – anyone: bombs, planes, guns, bullets, mines. This is what is wrong with your world. My father told me about a man called Dietrich Bonhoeffer from your planet. He wrote that you can judge the worth of a society by the way it treats its children. When will this planet learn – "

"Miss Smith, I don't know where you come from. Are you British?" intervened the PM. The interviewer tensed.

"My father is British, Mr Prime Minister, but we live a long way from here in a world where we know how to look after our children, a world where love and justice are normal and that evil like this has been driven out generations ago. It is now *your* turn and it can and should begin with you…"

"Jeremy, I came on the programme to talk about our

policies on economic development, not to be berated by a delusional young woman who thinks she's some kind of alien! Miss Smith, I think our conversation has come to an end. "

"Mr Prime Minister," said the interviewer, "we acknowledge that Miss Smith may appear unusual in some ways but there is nothing delusional in the evidence she has put before us. I suggest you watch the footage we have running. Kakko Smith, we are grateful to you for coming in."

"I am not delusional," stated Kakko defiantly, but she had been disconnected and was no longer 'on air'.

"You are a challenging young woman," smiled the woman presenter, "I admire your spunk."

"I'm sorry, but I can only speak the truth."

"Oh, I don't doubt you do. It's hard to believe though, isn't it? The bit about coming from another planet."

"I know. But it's true. I must be going back now. Just promise me one thing: You won't loose my video disc. But I will take my bit of shrapnel as my souvenir. Now my leg is really hurting so I am going home to do what the doctor tells me."

"Can we get a taxi for you? It will be our pleasure …"

"No thanks, my gate is outside by the church. Thank you for listening to me. And I'm sorry if I got cross with your Prime Minister but it just needed to be said."

"You have definitely asked a lot of pertinent questions, Kakko. Are you sure you're alright? We can see you get a ride."

"No, that's OK. The important thing is that people have the courage to stop supplying the weapons right away. And then get more reporters in. Thank you for having me… and thanks for the coke." And with that Kakko swung herself to her feet.

TREVOR STUBBS

"I'll see you back down to the reception," said the presenter. She saw Kakko to the door and shook her hand. Then watched as she rounded All Souls. She hesitated only for a moment and went off in pursuit – but Kakko had already gone. Just vanished into thin air. She hadn't had time to mount the steps of the church. Perhaps she was telling the truth – after all, all the rest of it was.

After she got back to her studio the presenter asked, "Wow, did you get that Pete?"

"Powerful stuff! Jeremy says the PM isn't chuffed. Where'd she go? Have you got her number?"

"No. She says she's from somewhere out of reach of any phone signal. Wouldn't tell us any more. Reckons she lives on another planet. I thought at first she was batty, but the more I listen, the less I think so. She just disappeared somewhere in the middle of Portland Place."

★★★

Kakko almost collapsed in the lane outside her gate. Matilda was there to help her in and she lay down on the garden bench and began to cry. Matilda put her arms around her.

"My leg's hurting," she sobbed.

"Well, that's a surprise!" announced her nan.

"Where's Mum and Dad?"

"Gone through a white gate," exhaled Matilda. "It's like Clapham Junction here with all this coming and going."

"Clapham Junction?"

"Busy railway station in London."

"Anywhere near the BBC?"

439

"No. What do you know about the BBC?"

"I've just been there. Broadcasting House... I totally mucked it up," sighed Kakko. "I got cross and made a fool of myself. That Prime Minister man really got to me. He didn't care that children were being bombed and I got angry. I flunked it!"

"Prime Minister? Where. In London?"

"In London. I didn't see him, he was in a radio studio but they were asking him questions and brought me into the interview. He wouldn't listen about the bombing. He didn't *want* to listen. He kept interrupting and I got cross and just went on and on and let on I wasn't from Planet Earth One and he told me I was delusional..."

★★★

Jack and Jalli returned two days later. Kakko told her story.

"Flunked it! That's not what we heard," said her dad. Her mum sat beside her and cuddled her.

"What did you hear? Where?" asked a tearful Kakko.

"On the BBC radio. We've been to Earth too. You really said it exactly right. We heard the whole interview on the radio. The BBC is stating categorically that you just turned up. The video clips are going viral. They are conclusive and politicians around the world are all being held to account. Most of the people they are interviewing on the street, most of the vox pops, are in favour of stopping all trading in arms. It is a major issue that has been ignored for so long. The church leaders are saying this is something many people have been campaigning about for years but people did not want to take them seriously. Now they are, at least for the moment, taking it very seriously. The American administration is talking about cancelling the arms fair due to take place in Atlanta next month. The Georgia State Governor is furious, but someone asked him if he wanted the blood of children on his hands. He said something about needing arms to defend themselves, but he couldn't deny the fair was about selling arms to foreign nations. The Eastern Europeans are feeling the heat because you videoed one of the planes made there.

"You have stirred them up, Kakko. Bishops in Africa are applauding you for telling the truth. One said that every time someone like you speaks out, people rejoice. It is so good to know people care, even if it doesn't make any difference on the ground."

"Kakko. We are so proud of you," said her mother. "You've done exactly what was asked of you. If nothing else comes of this, you have saved one child's life, and God loves every single one."

"But where have you been on Earth?"

"Persham. We saw Dave and his family. Abby is telling her father to write to the Prime Minister to tell them Kakko is not delusional, and that they, too, have had experience of such visitations. I expect the news of our visits will be all over the world news soon."

"But if they tell them about our white gates that will distract them from the killing of children."

"Quite the opposite, I would say," said Jack. "It's highlighting the whole thing. It's given impetus to your story.

It could run and run. The arms manufacturers are getting extremely jittery. A lot more of what they do is coming out. The social media is apparently very active and world-wide petitions are being issued on their Internet."

"You've been to Persham?" said Bandi rushing into the room. "You didn't tell me you were going!"

"We didn't know, did we?" said Jalli. "You were at school and the white gate was there, so we went."

"How's Abby?"

"She's very pretty," said his mother.

"She was rather delighted to see us," smiled Jack, "and was full of questions about you. Wanted to know what chapter of *Sophie's World* you were on."

"What did you tell her about me?"

"Oh. Just how you were moping about the house mentioning her every five minutes…"

"Dad. Don't tease!"

"We just said you were well and working hard at school. What else should we have said?"

"Nothing. But what else did you do?"

"We were only there for a few days. We spent most of that time listening to Kakko's interview on the radio and watching the news coverage with her videotape."

"Kakko, you didn't say you'd been to Persham too?"

"No," put in Kakko, "London. I didn't go to Persham. I was only there for three hours, remember!" Kakko's leg was hurting and she was jiggered.

"Now, it is time to go to bed and let that leg heal," said her mother.

"I'm always 'healing'!"

"You're always having adventures! Just remember it has been worth it. We're proud of you. Now, sleep."

"I don't think I'll sleep."

But she did, soundly.

36

"Ooh," groaned Jalli. She was in the kitchen getting her breakfast and suddenly felt woozy. Kakko was still fast asleep but even though Jalli, too, had been on an 'adventure' to Earth, she just had to get into work that day.

"Too much excitement," Matilda declared. "Come on, I'll do that."

But no sooner had Jalli's bottom touched the chair than she bounced up again and retched into the sink. Matilda was alarmed.

"Jack! Jack! Can you come?"

Jack, who was in the bathroom, registered the anxiety in her tone and rushed in.

"It's Jalli, she's just been sick."

"I'm alright," said Jalli. "I feel better now."

"I'm going to call the doctor!"

"No. I'll be alright. I've only been a bit sick. That's all. It's OK. But I *will* make an appointment at the surgery. I've been ignoring it, but I think I know what's the matter… I've missed – I'm well overdue."

"You mean, you think you're *pregnant*!" exclaimed her mother-in-law. "But how? You're forty-four!"

"Forty-four maybe, but that doesn't mean it can't happen! Everyone tells me how young I look and how lively I am… can't say I feel that lively today, though."

Jack stood silent for several seconds, and then said, "So what are we going to do?"

"Wait till I've seen the doctor, and then, if it's as I think it is, find the baby stuff in the loft!"

★★★

The doctor confirmed what Jalli already knew. He said she was about eight weeks.

"Wanulka," said Jack, "you knew this might happen. You even wanted it."

"Yes. I asked for it didn't I?"

"Jalli, I'm…"

"Why the long face? I'm going to have this baby, and I'm going to be alright. This is no time to be gloomy. Come on. I want to celebrate. We're having a baby! And he or she is going to be gorgeous. Come on let's tell the kids…" And she stood and yelled, "Kakko, Shaun, Bandi – family conference! Nan."

"But Muu-um!" said Shaun engrossed in the games console.

"Shaun!"

"OK, I'm coming…"

"Just ten minutes and you can all go back to your toys."

"It's *not* a toy, it's a *game*," protested Shaun.

When they were all sat around the sitting room. Kakko said impatiently, "Well? What is it, then?" and then she looked at her mother and it all added up, "Nooo! You aren't are you? Yesterday you were sick. Now you've got that glow they tell you about – you're pregnant aren't you?"

"No keeping secrets from your daughter! Yes. I'm eight weeks."

"Wow!" said Bandi. Shaun said nothing, just sat stunned. The world in which his game was set didn't have babies in it.

"So? What do you say?" asked Jack nervously.

"I say we have a party to celebrate!" said Kakko with excitement.

"When can we tell people? Can I text my friends?" asked Bandi.

"Already have," said Kakko whose right hand was permanently glued to her phone. "Er… just to Tam," she said in defence when everyone stared at her.

"Go for it," said Jack. "The more the merrier. Text your friends. Post it on your social networks. I reckon this baby will get a lot of attention on Joh!"

★★★

Two months later Kakko's white gate appeared again. After ascertaining it was only for her, she stepped through without hesitation. It led straight to a refugee camp with people like those she had met in Africa. Kakko found the little family she knew. Anna was alive and well.

"Hello Kakko. Your wound… it has healed?"

"It's fine. You made it here to safety, then."

"We made it," said Miriam. "Anna is going to be baptised on Sunday. We all are. We have all become Christians because we know God loves us and never leaves us. He sent you to help us – and others help us too. We are giving Anna a new baptismal name; we are going to call her Kakko."

Little Anna Kakko's mother's face split into a broad smile that revealed her broken teeth. Kakko shed a little tear.

"Will you be her sponsor, her godmother?" asked Miriam.

"Of course," said Kakko. "I'd be honoured. But I live a long way away."

"But in God you will always be near. You pray for her?"

And they all held hands right there and then, and prayed to the Creator who was so close – in every part of the universe and beyond. They gave thanks and prayed for the many little ones and their parents who had not made it to safety. Kakko thought of Momori surrounded by them in her heavenly home. *That is, after all, the place where we ultimately belong,* she thought.

Kakko told them of the new baby they were expecting in their family. It was highly unlikely that he or she would ever have to suffer bombs or have to run away. They were happy for her.

"A new baby is always a blessing if you have food to feed him," said Miriam.

Kakko didn't stay long in the refugee camp. They were tightly packed. They had just enough food to stay alive and a limited recourse to medical care. Kakko discovered they didn't know much about what was happening in the rest of Planet Earth, but she told them about her interview with the British prime minister and the way the world was apparently talking about their situation. She was reassured that at least this mother and child, if not free, were reasonably safe.

37

The family were just about to sit down for their evening meal. They were all quiet waiting for Jalli to say a prayer when they heard a knock at the door.

"Who can that be?" asked Jack. "Bandi you're nearest. Will you go and see who that is?"

Bandi got up and went out to the front hall and opened the door.

"Abby!" he cried.

"Bandi! It's you! This is your house?"

"Sure is, how did you get here?"

"Just walked through a new white gate in the hedge in the bottom of the vicarage garden... and here I am!" she cried with excitement and leapt into Bandi's arms. So life wasn't quite so unfair as she had once believed!

"You'll never guess who it is!" rejoiced Bandi shouting to his family in the kitchen behind him. "It's Abby!"

"And there was I thinking we might have a period of peace and quiet," sighed Matilda, tongue in cheek.

★★★

The gate persisted for Abby and Bandi. It stood between their two worlds without fading. Abby would often just come over after school and sit with Bandi in the dining room with her homework while Bandi did his. At other times Bandi would go to Persham, particularly if Abby and her friends were doing something special. On a couple of occasions he went and shared a picnic with Abby's family armed with all sorts of questions he had from *Sophie's World*. Abby's dad enjoyed these visits almost as much as Bandi and Abby did.

As the year sped on, the challenge of exams forced them apart somewhat. Perhaps the coming holidays they both shared would allow them more time to explore each other's planets.

Tam and Kakko became inseparable. Jack and Jalli wondered how long it would be before Kakko suggested they share a flat or something. Her parents hoped they would wait until at least Tam finished his studies. They need not have worried. Tam was a wise and thoughtful young man and was probably telling his girlfriend, as usual, that they shouldn't rush into things. So long as she was at the agricultural college it made no sense moving near the university.

Shaun passed his exams at the end of term with credits. Whilst retaining some general studies, he specialised further in language and communication.

Matilda spent most of her days with Ada, but she would always be back for the evening meal when the family ate together. "A family that eats together," she declared, "stays together!"

Jack and Jalli busied themselves in their daily lives. Jack brought 'light' into the dark world of the students of the blind school.

As her new baby grew in her womb, Jalli immersed herself in the activities of the insects so important to the balance of nature. Even at that level she occasionally came across something that made her question the fairness of everything. *But,* she told herself, *the very realisation that not everything was just in the universe, was the evidence that an ultimate justice existed beyond it – a true justice by which all human attempts at justice could be measured.*

As for Kakko, she had already had glimpses of that ultimate justice. Now she wanted to know it in all its fullness. But for that she would have to be patient. Very patient. But not so patient that she was going to hold back if she thought she could make a difference. And, she vowed, she would *never* have patience with anyone who tolerated injustice – not ever!

Trevor Stubbs was born in Northampton, England in 1948 and studied theology in London, Canterbury and Exeter. He has lived and worked in West Yorkshire and Dorset in the United Kingdom, and Australia, Papua New Guinea and South Sudan. He currently lives in Keynsham, nr. Bristol.

Trevor Stubbs is married with three adult children and two grandchildren.

For more information about Trevor Stubbs
or to contact him visit:
www.whitegatesadventures.com
and follow him at
www.whitegatesadventures.wordpress.com
or on Twitter
@TrevorNStubbs